# Boudicca's Vengeance
## A Queen's Fight for Her Realm

Richard Scholefield

authorHOUSE

AuthorHouse™ UK
1663 Liberty Drive
Bloomington, IN 47403 USA
www.authorhouse.co.uk
Phone: UK TFN: 0800 0148641 (Toll Free inside the UK)
UK Local: 02036 956322 (+44 20 3695 6322 from outside the UK)

© 2021 Richard Scholefield. All rights reserved.

No part of this book may be reproduced, stored in a retrieval system, or transmitted by any means without the written permission of the author.

Published by AuthorHouse 05/26/2021

ISBN: 978-1-6655-8908-6 (sc)
ISBN: 978-1-6655-8909-3 (e)

Print information available on the last page.

Any people depicted in stock imagery provided by Getty Images are models, and such images are being used for illustrative purposes only.
Certain stock imagery © Getty Images.

This book is printed on acid-free paper.

Because of the dynamic nature of the Internet, any web addresses or links contained in this book may have changed since publication and may no longer be valid. The views expressed in this work are solely those of the author and do not necessarily reflect the views of the publisher, and the publisher hereby disclaims any responsibility for them.

For Davina

# ABOUT THE AUTHOR

Richard Scholefield has lived in Milton Keynes for the last 50 years and has played wargames with historical figurines for the last 47. With a great interest in the ancient Britons, it has been his mission to try to prove where Queen Boudicca, probably this country's most famous warrior queen, was finally defeated by the occupying Roman forces.

Using possibly the only historical record of the final battle, written by the Roman Tacitus as his guide, Richard has spent a number of years looking more closely at the details of his account. Looking at maps of the ancient Briton's roads, the topography of the A5 Watling Street, OS maps of the area and his experience as a wargamer, he concludes she was finally defeated at Little Brickhill, just outside Milton Keynes.

The result of this research is not an academic paper, but a novel, written to describe how, from the author's perspective, the ancient Britons lived under Roman rule and how Boudicca came to lead one of the largest revolts of the era. The character, likes and dislikes of the author shine through in the story, reflecting his tendency to worry about many things, but take great enjoyment from drinking a large variety of beers.

Richard is the holder of a Queen's Scout Award and attributes his scouting days to his happiness and success in life. He worked for Milton Keynes Development Corporation in the civil engineering field, designing and arranging the construction of many roads, sewers and cycleways in the City.

His hobbies include: Chess; Cycling; Wargaming; Beer; Go; and DIY.

Diagnosed with RSI, in 2001 (Repetitive Strain Injury), he has only been able to write this book with the aid of modern computers and voice recognition software, for which he is extremely thankful.

He lives in Milton Keynes, with his wife, Davina, and has three children and two espoused sons.

# ACKNOWLEDGEMENTS

| | |
|---|---|
| Davina Scholefield | My wife, who gave me the encouragement to write the book and who helped to check it all through thoroughly, including my wordy sentences. |
| Mike Winstanley | Our Best Man, who spent many hours going through the document and correcting my poor English and grammar and discussing the corrections over a few glasses of beer. |
| Daughter, Anna Scholefield | Who, after some persuasion kindly agreed to design and paint the front cover. She had little guidance from me on what I really wanted, except the hairstyle I envisaged and that I wanted a face with some character. |

| | |
|---|---|
| Jim Coggins | For his artistic input and painting of Boudicca. My initial brief was for a representation of Boudicca as she is known to the world now, which he has achieved with his representation of the statue of her which is located on the banks of the Thames in Westminster, London. |
| Shirley and David Willis | For happily agreeing, to read my narrative and comment from an historical perspective on the accuracy of my representation of how the Romans behaved. David from a military history perspective and Shirley for her expertise on horses. |
| Robert and Ruth Meardon | Their support, encouragement and friendship and loan of a crucial book on Roman roads in England is much appreciated. |
| Billy Davies | A good neighbour for his guidance and humour. |
| Mike Wardlow | The first person I took on a tour of the battlefield and who was happy to discuss my views on the location of the final battle. |
| Dik Sweeting | A wargaming friend of 45 years, for his input into the accuracy of my historical representation of life and military history of ancient times. |

| | |
|---|---|
| Cathy White | Another good neighbour, who provided a different perspective on my story and gave me the inspiration to add more information about my characters and their lives. |
| Corona Virus | Lockdown gave me the time to write this book, without these restrictions, perhaps I would not have made the commitment. |
| Modern Technology | Thank you! |

Painting of Boudicca on the banks of the Thames outside Westminster.

By Jim Coggins, 2020

# FOREWORD

There have been many books written, and much research carried out, about this Queen, who is so well revered by this country, and held up as a figure to be admired and remembered for all time, that she has a statue in her honour in Westminster, London.

Boudicca had her kingdom cruelly taken from her by the occupying Roman forces, when her husband died. We have a few paragraphs, written by a Roman, named 'Tacitus,' that tells us how Boudicca was invited to a meeting with the Romans, the purpose of which she thought, was to welcome her as the Queen of the Iceni. She did not receive the hospitality she expected, and the treatment that she, and her daughters received, are believed to be the trigger for what happened next.

The Romans under-estimated the strength and grit of Boudicca and the fanatical support of her people, and came to regret their actions.

The book tells the story of Boudicca's campaign to reclaim her kingdom. Written to inform the reader about the way of life of the ancient Britons, it tells how the occupying Roman forces ruled them. How Boudicca inspired her tribesmen and led them in a campaign that saw the destruction of Colchester, London and St Albans.

With the lack of any concrete evidence, many people have put forward well researched theories about where Boudicca and the Romans had their battle. This book outlines another possible location, but in the form of an historical novel.

It is the characters and their stories which represent the life and times of the ancient Britons of the day that, it is hoped, you will find interesting and educational.

There is a challenging word in this book; 'Catuvellauni,' which is the name of a British tribe located around St. Albans. There are many spellings of this word - see if you can spot them all?

The book starts in AD 60, not that the characters in the book knew that was the date. The storyline has been written from the perspective of two main characters in the book - Dan an ancient Briton, a close relation to Queen Boudicca, and Justus, a Roman cavalryman.

Davina Scholefield
April 2021

## CHAPTER I

# INTRODUCING DAN

The birds were singing, and it was a wonderful day. To celebrate his 53$^{rd}$ birthday, Dan had made an attractive decorative roof finial to go on top of his round house. He had turned it on his pole lathe the previous day.

He had borrowed an old ladder from his friend Esico next door and with the finial in one hand and some twine in his belt pocket, he was cautiously climbing the ladder to the top of his sloping thatched roundhouse roof. He was pleased with the belt pocket that had been made especially for him by the leather expert in the village.

Down below his family were watching nervously, while others in the village stood around shouting encouragement.

"You be careful up there Dan, please," his wife called up to him, "you know you're not as young as you were. You should have let Talos do that job." Talos was their middle son - most capable and dexterous, but Dan did not want to admit his frailty, just yet.

"Don't listen to her. You're doing fine Dan, but mind you don't fall off," Esico shouted to him in reply, expecting a clout round the back of the head from Dan's wife, who was standing behind him. He was not disappointed.

Dan went back to concentrating on the job in hand. He reached the top and found a good sound support to tie the roof finial to. With his left hand holding a structural part of the roof and his right hand reaching for his belt pocket, he was put off by the cheering from below and became disorientated. Dan felt the ladder move to his left very slowly. He held more tightly to a section of the roof which he thought was immoveable, but it turned out not to be so solid after all. Everything then began to happen much faster. He found himself sliding down the roof of his roundhouse backwards on his stomach. Wanting to see where he was going, he turned onto his back only to see the ground coming up quickly, as gravity increased his speed.

He landed on the ground with a huge bump, jarring his back most uncomfortably! Neighbours laughed as his family came to his aid.

Dan was not his real name, it was a shortened version of Aeden, a name his Celtic parents had given him. He had lost both his parents some time ago. His mother died giving birth to his third sister, and his dad had died from complications related to a tooth infection. There was nothing special about Dan's appearance, he was of average height and build with brown hair. He did, however, have a lovely smile behind a greying beard, which revealed a mouth full of white teeth. His one defining feature was a deep scar on the right side of his forehead.

The scar had been caused by a Roman soldier 16 years previously. It had been Dan's first experience of the Romans and their brutality. They had arrived on the south coast of

Britain the year before and there had been a number of battles with local tribes. The invaders had won every time! They were slowly working their way North, exerting their authority on the population, and had reached East Anglia, the land of the Iceni. They had come into Dan's village and being brave, he had stood alongside the elders against the invaders. He had misjudged the strength of Roman legionaries and had received a nasty head wound for his stubborn bravery. The wound had given him a troublesome scar for the rest of his life.

Three weeks later, Dan turned in his bed, his new very prickly bed, filled with fresh straw which had been made by two of his five grandchildren. It was not as comfortable as his old bed where the straw had become flattened, but it had become infested and crumbly so needed replacing.

He wondered why his old bed of straw had become so infested. Was it that they were burning the wrong wood on the fire and the wrong smoke to kill bugs was filling the room? Or perhaps it might well have been that the bed was too close to the ground. That would be yet another job for him to do - raising the bed to get away from the critters and lift it into the smoke of the upper room. It was well known that smoke definitely reduces the numbers of creepy crawlies in the thatch of the roof.

It was the middle of the afternoon and Dan was trying to have his afternoon nap. He didn't always have an afternoon nap, but this day had been a little tiring, mending the stockade for the oxen and planting out the early cabbages.

It had not gone well; the ground was unusually hard for this time of year, and he should have rested more. He was not as young as he once was - it's amazing how maturity creeps on and you can't do the things you used to be able to do.

He could not get off to sleep as he was thinking about the next day. He was to accompany his cousin Boudicca, Queen of the Iceni Kingdom, on her trip to meet a significant leader in the Roman administration who had come all the way from Rome. Boudicca's husband, King Prasutagus had died recently, and the Romans wanted to renegotiate the ownership of the Iceni kingdom. King Prasutagus had been a client King of the Romans who looked after the Iceni Kingdom, and the Romans took a proportion of the taxes – a high proportion.

Boudicca had heard that this Roman leader was a really nasty individual, consequently she wanted some support at the meeting. She was taking along some of her close companions and warriors. Her concerns had also made Dan worried about what might happen.

Another reason he could not sleep that afternoon was that he had a wheel to mend on his waggon. It was an old-fashioned solid wheel, not the lighter spoked sort which was far more up to date and modern. Getting the wheel off the waggon, mending it and replacing it was always a chore, as he liked to create new things and not mend old ones. He had always worked in wood and was the local man to go to if you wanted a new waggon built or an old one fixed.

His mind then went back to the finial for the roof of his round house. It was still waiting to be fixed, yet another job he had to do. There was always something to do, so many things to mend or something to create, but now it was Spring, the days were getting longer and there was more time to do them.

He then heard a little noise, a tapping noise coming from outside. He knew what it was but had to look anyway - there was a thrush smashing the living daylights out of a snail, smashing it against a paving stone. Dan had often trodden on the broken snail shells. Thrushes were such lovely birds, they helped enormously by reducing the snail population that ate the cabbages and they always sung so beautifully too. His daughter Anna had trained one of their little white dogs to kill the snails too. The dog never ate the snails, he just hunted them out from the undergrowth and gave them a scrunch. The poor things would then die slowly with their shells cracked.

Dan gave up trying to sleep, his mind was now too active.

His cousin Boudicca was missing her husband greatly. He had been a very charismatic and wonderful man. The whole tribe had missed him, even in the short time since his death, and it would be difficult to fill his shoes. At the moment though, Boudicca was doing quite a good job.

He wondered what transport they were going to use tomorrow to go and see this important Roman over in Ixworth. Although if the truth be known, he was really concerned about how nasty this Roman, emissary of the Emperor Nero, really was. He loved to refer to the Romans as 'nasty' because it helped vent some of his anger towards them. Thinking of the Romans, he rubbed the deep scar on his forehead, a constant reminder of his first encounter with them. They could travel in one of his waggons, although one of Boudicca's main followers, Nomass, had a lovely chariot with good suspension and room enough for three.

Chariots were always something Dan wanted to start making, but waggons were the vehicles he always made. He never really had the time to learn about chariot making. The skills required to build a chariot were far more complicated, the suspension platform that carries the rider being just one element that is difficult to create.

He would discuss transport arrangements with her in the morning and also determine the approach Boudicca wanted to take at the meeting.

Having given up trying to sleep, Dan thought he had better give his pony, Spike, a good clean and brush down before the journey to meet with the Romans. He went down to the field to fetch his pony and bring him back to the yard to clean him up.

He had just started brushing down his pony when he was interrupted by 9-year-old Thomas, one of his grandchildren. He appeared from the direction of Dan's workshop, very alarmed.

"Grandad, grandad there is a wasp nest in the workshop!" Dan thought he should investigate and see what all the fuss was about, so off they both went to his workshop not far away. Sure enough, when they arrived there, up in the rafters of the roof there was a wasp nest!

It was a beautiful creation as most wasp nests are.

Wasps are nasty creatures, a bit like Romans, but how on earth had they managed to create a nest up there without anyone noticing? How to get it down that was the big question. The last wasp nest Dan had dealt with a couple of years ago, he had attacked with a stick and then ran away quickly, but this had resulted in being stung twice!

Then he thought to himself – this nest is looking too big for this time of the year. It was Spring when wasps are only just beginning to be active. Panic over, it was an old unused nest which he had certainly not been looking forward to getting rid of. Why had they not realised it was there before – quite extraordinary. He turned to his grandson Thomas who was coming to the same conclusion, but probably for different reasons. Even at his age he knew there were very few wasps around at this time of year.

Dan then realised that there were three generations in the workshop looking at the wasp nest. There was himself, his son Morcant and his grandson Thomas. Dan was very proud of his grandson who was growing up to be a very intelligent young man, taking after his father Morcant.

"How's it going Morcant, are you okay?" Dan asked.

"Yes, fine thanks Dad, just a bit worried about your visit to meet with the Romans tomorrow. I am not sure how it will go." Morcant paused, looking down at a chair he was making, then continued. "They have come a long way from Rome, from their Emperor Nero, and although they are speaking to others while they are here it seems to me that this is an important meeting. I am most concerned about their motives. The Romans are a very wicked nation. I'm very suspicious Dad."

"Not to worry son, I'm sure it will be fine. You'll be alright looking after this place while we're gone?"

"Yes Dad, we'll be fine."

As Dan made his way back over to his roundhouse, he heard a pony and rider arriving behind him. It was

Scavo who had ridden over with a message from Boudicca about the journey tomorrow. He told Dan that all the men from this village would be going by pony, which would be quicker, although Boudicca and her daughters would go in her chariot. He said that they would depart after breakfast from her house so it would be an early start for them. Dan thought for a moment then said, "why don't you stay over with me for the night, and we can go off together in the morning. It will be getting dark soon and we may even have wild boar for tea tonight?"

Later that evening, Dan's daughter Anna cooked the family and Scavo a meal of bran, peas and wild boar stew with cabbage on the side, which went down very nicely as they had not had it for some time. His neighbour and good friend Esico had hunted and butchered a wild boar two days ago, and the whole village was benefitting. Esico had a number of hunting dogs and regularly went hunting for wild boar in the local woods. Dan's son Morcant had accompanied him on trips a number of times, but Dan always declined the offer, as it did not appeal.

It was 9 miles over to Boudicca's house, so the next morning Dan and Scavo left as the sun was rising. They set out, each on their own large pony – it was a lovely day, no rain, no wind, rather pleasant really. Scavo was very proud of his pony, he had decorated it with tassels and fine leather. It was a fine specimen. Three other men from the village tagged along behind on their ponies.

When they reached Boudicca's township of some 40 homes or more, they were watched inquisitively by the inhabitants, as they made their way to Boudicca's new house. Most of the houses in this area were roundhouses, like the majority of those in the Iceni lands. They went past her old home, a large oval house that was now occupied by a local leader, and on to her new house that Prasutagus, her husband, had had built to impress the Roman governors.

Boudicca's new house was a rectangular building of two stories. It was larger than a normal house of its type, and together with other buildings on her acreage, formed a courtyard which had two entrances. The roof had a decorative thatch, which Dan thought was rather splendid. The other buildings in the courtyard were single story and were used to house some animals and store food stuff. He noticed that the blacksmith's forge had been moved out of the courtyard, possibly because of the noise.

Dan and Scavo took a short break, here in the courtyard, and exchanged pleasantries and chatted about the weather and the previous night's wild boar stew. Ponies had already been saddled up and others harnessed to their chariots, ready to go.

Boudicca emerged from her house, dressed in her finest garments for her meeting with the Roman leader. She wore a long green dress which had been woven in the design of the Iceni tribe's tartan. It had a green background, with a yellow vertical stripe and a blue weft stripe. Over her dress, she wore a heavy, cloak, clasped at the neck with a gold broach, encrusted with three rubies. Around her neck, she wore her gold torque – a sort of heavy necklace, that her husband had given her when they married. Since her marriage to Prasutagus, Dan had not seen her without it. On her fingers, she had three rings, all representing specific icons that were important to the Iceni tribe. Her long red hair was swept up and back, and a strong Mohican braided plait lay down the back of her head and was pulled into a long tail which swept across her shoulders and down the front of her cloak.

On her face, she had painted war-like stripes in red, white and blue to emphasise how important she was and that she meant business in her discussions with the Romans.

"Wow, you look amazing!" said Dan. He was proud to be her cousin when she looked as impressive as this.

She came straight over to Dan, saying quietly,

"Come with me Dan, I need to show you something." She led him through the second entrance of the courtyard out to a newly planted vegetable patch. She then walked down a grass strip, over to a large, special looking stone, in amongst some young pea plants. She kicked the stone and spoke quietly to Dan,

"Beneath this stone is where I have buried my husband's gold, the gold he borrowed from the Romans. Or should I say, the gold they forced upon him as a loan, as part of the deal he made with them for his client kingship of the Iceni Tribe. He became a Roman citizen as part of that deal. I did not fully understand the arrangements – my husband did. I know that normally with other tribes, the Romans keep the gold safe for them, but Prasutagus insisted that he kept it and when it came to paying his taxes, he would take it to them. Damn cheek if you ask me, lending us gold so that we can pay our taxes. They don't want us to pay our taxes in peas and cabbages. Why do we pay the bastards taxes anyway?"

Dan nodded in sympathy, saying,

"Calm down Boo, people will hear you and wonder what's buried there."

"I should have taken more notice of what Prasutagus

said to me about the gold, but he was dealing with it, and I left it at that," she said. "Anyway, that's where I buried the gold, no one else knows about it except you and my daughters. I've told everyone it is where we have buried our dog, so no one should dig him up."

"Your dog, Caesar?" Dan asked a little shocked. "Caesar died? He wasn't that old."

"He didn't die of natural causes Dan, I poisoned him!" Boudicca declared.

"But you loved that dog Boo," Dan replied.

"You can't just bury some gold and expect no one to take any notice," Boudicca said. "You have to have a reason to dig a hole and put something in it. Sad and mercenary, I know, but there's something odd going to happen when we go and see this Roman official. I have a feeling about it, a woman's premonition. Its best that we bury the gold anyway, it's difficult keeping it in the house, someone could go looking for it while we are away."

"We're going away?" Dan asked.

"I have a feeling we are," Boudicca said, "a funny feeling."

They returned to the courtyard. Boudicca mounted her chariot, took the reins and with her daughters by her side, lead the entourage of at least 12 mounted men and women out of the village, south towards Ixworth some miles away. Three other late starting chariots and outriders joined them shortly after leaving, and followed on behind. Dan felt quite proud and important escorting his cousin.

"You won't mention to the Romans that you called your dog Caesar, will you?" Dan asked Boudicca, "they might take offence."

"No Dan – I won't if you won't."

Soon, after they had set out on their journey, Dan, who had not ventured out much in the last few years, realised how the roads had improved and mentioned this to his friend Nomass on his chariot.

"Yes," Nomass said, "It is the Iceni slaves who have improved the roads under the yoke of the Romans. They are good engineers, look at this bridge we are crossing, I find it very impressive, and we are benefiting from it in some ways."

"But the taxes the Romans inflict upon us are cruel", he continued, "I remember before they came 17 years ago, how we were so much better off. Will they ever go home back to Rome? Will it ever get back to where we were before – free!"

"We will be rid of the Romans," Boudicca interjected for she was in ear shot. "I know it, there is anger in my people, the Iceni people. We will fight them one day – we will be free again!" She shouted it with conviction and feeling. Her entourage and Dan cheered with encouragement for her.

It was at this point that Dan glanced down at the slaves working away on a pile of rocks next to the bridge. It was heavy work, and they were tired and a bit lifeless. One of the slaves looked up with wide enquiring eyes and Dan recognised him as being one of his old neighbours who had gone away some 5 or 6 years ago. He could not remember the reason for the man's disappearance. It was a bit of a mystery at the time, but it was believed he had gone on off on some adventure. "A very odd 'adventure,'" Dan thought to himself, "if he ended up being on a Roman slave gang!"

This was a very extraordinary and embarrassing moment for Dan – there below him, working as a slave, was an old neighbour, once a free man, once a very happy free man. A broad shouldered overseer watched over the slave gang with a big stick, black teeth and a missing eye. Dan remembered enjoying a few beers with his old neighbour - what was his name? He could not remember. Now the man was a grubby slave in very poor physical condition. His life expectancy was probably very low, and Dan felt very sorry for him, but they rode on.

They approached Ixworth from the North, arriving by mid-afternoon and after passing a few roundhouses the road widened out as it approached a T junction with a bridge beyond. There were definite signs that the Romans were here and there was a lot of activity and building work going on. There were some unusual rectangular buildings and slaves were working with stone to improve the wooden ramparts surrounding the village. Dan surmised that this was where all their taxes were being spent.

They were just looking around, wondering where they had to go to meet this Roman dignitary, when out of a pitched roof stone building on their right came a Roman legionary in full regalia, followed by a number of others all dressed very smartly in their Roman uniforms. One very significant observation Dan made was that they were all well-armed and looked like real brutes! It was difficult to see their faces beneath the well-made, gleaming, decorated helmets. They looked very foreign and carried some very nasty-looking weapons called pilum. These were heavy spears with a sharp point on the end of a long shaft!

Seeing these Romans, took him back to his first experience of them, 16 years ago, when they first came to Norfolk. That's when he had gotten the scar on his forehead.

It constantly reminded him of their brutality, every time he got a headache or felt the indentation in his skull.

With a few words of incomprehensible Latin, the Roman soldier in charge pointed to a large building over to their left and obediently Boudicca moved off followed by her warrior tribesmen. As Dan followed behind, he concluded in that moment, it was the first time he had seen his cousin lacking an authoritative demeanour. Just a few foreign words were said by the legionary and the whole relationship between the Romans and Britain became evident.

It started raining - not heavy rain, just the type that made you wet.

They were kept waiting for some time in the rain before they went into the building. There was a little shelter for Boudicca's two daughters under a porch, but most of them became very wet. They thought they would be provided with hospitality and shelter prior to the meeting, but they were treated very rudely. Eventually they saw the Roman dignitary. His name was Catus Decianus and he appeared, walking slowly with a menacing attitude and sat at the end of this rectangular room on a substantial chair flanked by his entourage and a number of legionaries. He evoked a sense of authority and it was clear to see he was enjoying it.

The building they were in appeared to have been completed recently. There was an idea from someone that it had been built for a retired centurion, but he had died before its completion. It had stone plastered walls with a tiled roof - quite large, rectangular and very impressive. On the floor in the centre of the room was a mosaic that Boudicca and her tribespeople had never seen the like of before. Dan was also most impressed but was careful not to show any appreciation of it.

They talked through an interpreter and the Roman, Catus went straight to the point, stating,

"Your husband King Prasutagus has died. He was a client King under our Emperor Nero and jointly ruled the Iceni lands with him. He is now dead! So, our Emperor inherits the Iceni lands and property – is that clear?"

Catus went on to clarify, that Boudicca, being a woman, had no claim to property in Roman law and consequently, could not inherit her husband's land and property. This also applied to Boudicca's daughters, Epona and Bonvica, who it had been proposed, should be joint owners with Boudicca. This was an unexpected shock to everyone. Boudicca protested forcefully, shouting and making a scene,

"This is our land. We have been here for generations, long before you Romans came here! You have taken our lands and enslaved many of our people. I will not allow you to take my land and my title. The arrangement we had with Rome was made with my husband before he died, and as far as I am concerned, that arrangement still stands. I am Queen of the Iceni." She paused for a while, catching her breath. Glaring at Catus and thinking what to say next – she continued,

"Go back to Rome and tell your Emperor Nero that the answer is no! I and my daughters inherited these lands and property and will never allow you Romans to take them from us. I will not allow you to steal my land. I will keep my kingdom - it is rightfully mine and my daughters'! You are tyrannical bastards! Take my land from me and there will be reprisals!"

It was a shame that the rain had smudged her face paint and ruined her hair - she was quite a picture! It was extraordinary that no one sniggered with regard to her appearance.

For a while she was allowed to continue gesticulating and speaking angrily, using her eyes and body language to communicate her views very effectively. Catus, in response, looked temporarily frightened, even though he was well protected by his soldiers. But then, having let her rant and rave, he authoritatively ordered Boudicca to be seized by the Roman guards and her followers to be restrained.

Dan, being the eldest person there and looking a little frail for his age, was left alone by the soldiers and he cried out,

"This is outrageous!" and he strongly protested, but he was beaten by three big Roman legionaries. It certainly hurt, especially after the beating had aggravated his old injury gained from falling off the roof. Outnumbered by the Roman soldiers, their protesting subsided.

While this was happening, he hadn't noticed that his cousin Boudicca had been tied to a pillar in the middle of the room, her back had been exposed and she was being beaten. He watched as five lashes bit into Boudicca's back. She was grimacing and bleeding.

"Stop," Catus cried out "I have a better punishment – bring forth her daughters! Let us see if we can match Messalina, Emperor Claudius' wife."

There was more protesting by Boudicca's people, but they too were beaten and Nomass was savagely wounded in his leg. The use of a sword by one of the Roman soldiers was a heart stopping moment that ceased any resistance from Boudicca's comrades.

"Rape those two girls" was the instruction from Catus Decianus.

Each Roman soldier took his turn reluctantly at first, for it was not clear what was envisaged. However, when it was understood by the Romans what was expected, they carried out their role with frenzy and authority. No one in the room had ever seen anything like it before, it was awful to watch! The Britons were forced to look on at the terrible scene.

When it was all over, and while the Romans were off guard, either gloating or feeling guilty, three slaves, who had once been free Iceni citizens, helped Boudicca and her daughters to be untied. Bonvica was really shook-up and distressed – her clothes had been torn and there was blood. With the help of Boudicca's people and some of the slaves of Ixworth, they were assisted outside, where it had now stopped raining. They mounted their ponies and chariots and left hastily towards home, progressing northwards in the gathering darkness.

It was a total humiliation. Everyone was deep in their own thoughts - Dan thought he should have done more, Nomass sat on his chariot nursing his wounded and bleeding leg, the daughters were whimpering, while Boudicca, wounded by the lashes, was seething with rage!

## CHAPTER II

# INTRODUCING JUSTUS

Justus Julius Rufus was his full name, he was 32 and he came from the Po Valley in northern Italy. He was a muscular man, above average height with sharp facial features and thick jet black hair. He was just a small cog in a very big wheel within the Roman Empire.

The Romans dominated the known world from Spain to Persia. It was a massive empire and needed many troops to control it. In 43 AD Britain was invaded by the Romans under Emperor Claudius and Britain became just a small province of the Roman Empire. It was also known as Britannia. It was common knowledge to the Britons that Julius Caesar had attempted to invade Britain 70 years earlier but had failed - mainly due to rough weather that had affected the seaworthiness of his ships. His invading force had been seriously weakened when a large number of his ships sank in a storm. This disaster was kept secret from many Romans as they did not wish to think of themselves as failures.

In 43 AD the Romans tried again when Claudius was

Emperor and this time succeeded. Thus, Britain become one of Rome's provinces and four legions of troops were stationed in Britain on a full-time basis to keep the Britons under control. Each Legion was made up of around 5,500 men, divided into 10 cohorts consisting of 480 professional soldiers called legionaries. These were stationed throughout Britain depending on where they were needed. Each Legion also had approximately 120 horsemen attached to it, and Justus was one of these.

Each Legion was known by a number e.g., Legio 4, but in Roman times it was written as IV.

Justus was a cavalryman and had transferred within Legio XX some 8 years before when he had been an ordinary foot soldier, otherwise known as a legionary. He enjoyed being with the horses and got out and about much more than when he was just a foot soldier within the Legion. He had seen significantly more of this new Roman province Britannia than he would have done as a foot soldier, and he found the work a little easier, especially less marching!

Only two weeks before he had been given the job of escorting Catus Decianus, Emperor Nero's Procurator, on his arrival in the country. The role of Procurator was to execute Nero's wishes. Catus's instructions were to seize Boudicca's and her daughters' inheritance - the total wealth of the Iceni tribe. This was a task that he certainly enjoyed, and he did it with ruthlessness. Boudicca, however, had been unaware of the intentions to strip her of her inheritance and her status as Queen of the Iceni kingdom.

Justus had the rank of Duplicarius, and was second in command of 30 Roman cavalrymen. They were assigned to escort Catus, travelling from Colchester to Ixworth where he, Catus, was to hold an audience with Boudicca. On the journey, Justus and his colleagues soon realised what a really nasty character Catus was. He was discourteous, arrogant and rude to everyone. They had arrived with him three days before and were given rooms in the local legion's barracks. A few cohorts of Legio XX who were stationed here were away on a campaign with other legionaries in Lincolnshire and beyond.

They were given six small bunk rooms, normally with beds for eight men each, so they had plenty of space for their equipment. There was a definite smell of male sweaty bodies in the barrack room, but it wasn't long before they added their own aroma! The locally grown Iceni cabbage certainly fermented nicely in the Roman gut.

There was a newly constructed rectangular hall in the centre of Ixworth, where the meeting with Boudicca was going to take place. Catus, with his secretaries, had been given accommodation in the only other significant building in Ixworth. It was a lovely villa owned by a retired Roman centurion. Having served 25 years in the Roman army in charge of 80 men this centurion had been given a large farm as a retirement present and had built a villa there as part of his pension. It had actually been stolen from the local Britons 15 years earlier and naturally the locals held a grudge.

Justus was instructed to be present at the meeting with six other cavalrymen when Boudicca was invited to talks in the hall at Ixworth. He did not know who Boudicca was and was totally un-informed about his role in the whole business.

Justus arrived at the hall with his six cavalrymen

colleagues. They were all extremely nervous at having been asked to be present at something they knew nothing about.

The talks, through a translator, began in quite a civilised manner. Boudicca (they were to learn her name afterwards) was soon furiously shouting at Catus when he suddenly instructed his legionaries to tie her to the column in the middle of the room. A brute of a legionnaire then lashed Boudicca a number of times.

Then it suddenly stopped; there was some confusion and they brought forward Boudicca's two daughters and tied them to one of the tables in front of Catus. The legionaries were then told to rape the daughters in front of him. Initially there were some reluctance among the troops, but the mood then became excited and a queue developed.

Justus was reluctantly present at the raping of Boudicca's two daughters. He was horrified by the whole thing; he didn't see women quite like other Romans did and was not willing to take part, but at the same time wanted to save face. He was a virgin and kept the fact a secret from others, as men with bravado do. Initially he had busied himself with keeping order amongst the Britons, who were protesting vehemently about the whole situation. However, they were quickly silenced by the legionaries. As the scene progressed Justus managed to brag his way through the situation without committing any violation of the two young ladies. The whole scene was disgusting.

When it was over Catus and his secretaries left, satisfied that Boudicca had suffered enough humiliation. They went off to dine on rabbit and red wine with the retired Roman centurion who had laid on some interesting exotic dancing by slave girls after the meal.

Back in the hall, there was a certain amount of celebration amongst the remaining Romans who revelled and drank over their triumph and ignored their victims. With the guidance of Justus, three slaves untied Boudicca and her daughters. Dan showed his thanks to Justus with nods and appreciative noises in his own language which was acknowledge by Justus. They were taken out to their ponies and chariots and were sent on their way. Justus looked around at his comrades with a feeling of disgust towards the whole event but was pleased with helping Boudicca to her chariot.

Of the Roman soldiers left in the hall, some were jubilant with what they had just taken part in, others not so, but there were questions. Should they have let them go? Was the punishment enough? What would result from this atrocity?

The next morning Justus was up early and felt the need to pack up his belongings, which he did. Over breakfast with his comrades, there was talk of yesterday's events and many were suffering the consequences of yesterday's celebrations. The feeling amongst his men was that there was going to be retribution from the Britons for what had happened and that perhaps something should be done, but what?

The man in charge of the province of Britannia was called Gaius Suetonius Paulinus. He was a competent general and was well liked by his troops. Catus Decionus was a visiting dignitary sent by Nero the Roman Emperor to collect taxes and alter the wills of deceased British Client Kings like Boudicca's husband.

At the time of the injustice to Boudicca and her daughters, there were very few Roman troops in the East of Britain. Paulinus was in North Wales with most of the troops from Legions XX and XIV, attempting to subdue the Druids again. The Romans considered the religion to be dangerous and wanted to extinguish it. The Druids were an elite class of ancient Britons and had spiritual strengths that made many people look up to them. They were in a way the politicians of the day, but from a spiritual sense. A small detachment of Roman Legionaries from Legio XX were in Lincolnshire while the other main body of troops from Legio II were down in Exeter keeping control in the South West.

However, although these troop locations were known to the Roman officers, they were not known to Boudicca. She knew there was a large detachment in North Wales and possibly another somewhere in the West country but had no precise figures. She also knew of another small detachment in Lincolnshire.

Justus knew there were very few legionaries here in East Anglia. The Britons were always rebelling against the Roman occupation, that was why there were four legions here in the province of Britannia. The Emperor Claudius always stated that four legions would be needed in Britain. Britons were antagonistic towards the Roman way of life – the majority certainly did not enjoy being governed by the Romans, while others did and perhaps you could call these Romanised British.

"What was it about the Britons that was so uncouth?" Justus mused to himself. They lived in their smoky roundhouses, they had a mundane diet, they gave status to women in their society and had an odd way of doing things. They had many skills, but one which particularly impressed Justus was their skills was in metal work. He had been very impressed by some very intricate jewellery.

The Romans had been in Britain for 17 years yet very few Britons spoke Latin. This also applied in Gaul and in Spain, where Justus had once served.

In the morning Catus was ordering the packing up of his things and the assembly of troops to accompany his entourage. He did not want to stay in this small town a moment longer and ordered everyone with him to 'get the hell out of here' and back to Colchester, the capital of the Britannia province. After the previous night's atrocities, Catus decided he would have to abandon his task of taking Boudicca's land and title. He needed to leave Britain, get himself across the channel and back to Rome, before the Iceni came back in greater numbers to exercise their revenge.

Within a short time Catus, with his 30 cavalrymen as escort, were on the road to Colchester. The look of indignation on the faces of the few Roman legionnaires left in Ixworth was palpable. They realised they were being abandoned and left to deal with any reaction to the awful treatment of Boudicca and her daughters whilst Catus, the man from Rome, the man in charge, was leaving them to their fate.

The local Romanised Britons in the town also felt the same. There were insufficient numbers of fighting men to cope with any riot that was in the air. Justus felt a sense of relief as he rode behind Catus - he certainly did not want to stay in Ixworth after the events of last night. There was a thought that Boudicca, being a strong lady, and although only a woman, was very capable of revenge.

Women had a different standing here in Britain, surprisingly they were equal to the men, unlike Roman culture where women were of a lower class. Justus was unable to get his head around the idea that women were equal to men.

What form this revolt or revenge for this recent assault on the queen and her daughters would take was unknown. Attacks on the Romans had been discussed by Boudicca's husband and his tribesmen often when he was alive, but nothing had been resolved. Many had spoken about some form of action, but leaders had always only talked about the subject rather than actually doing anything about it.

The Romans had always instilled fear in the inhabitants of Britain and few wanted openly to go against them. There were many Britons who would 'grass up' their fellows in order to score some points with the Romans in return for favourable treatment. To be occupied by the Roman forces was a very uncomfortable, oppressive situation to be in. Roman rules and taxes made life very difficult, but any protests brought swift retribution; every Briton had witnessed crucifixions and saw how dreadful they were!

Crucifixions were abhorrent, and final, but hard labour as a slave on the treadmills of tin mines for a lifetime until death was worse. Treadmills in the mines pumped the water out and obviously had to be manned all day! No tea breaks. It was much better, in every-day life, to keep your head down and hope any labour disputes would be resolved.

## CHAPTER III

# REVENGEFUL ACTIVITY

Dan's journey home with Boudicca was short lived. Boudicca did not want to travel far as she was feeling really uncomfortable and her daughters were still distraught, so they stopped at a hamlet of roundhouses in a clearing in the woods. They were received as friends as the inhabitants knew Boudicca well.

Boudicca and her daughters were taken into one of the larger homes where the queen's wounds were tended to and her daughters comforted by the womenfolk in the village. The others, still suffering from shock were offered food and drink and their story was listened to intently with increasing rage. The villagers were astonished to hear how Boudicca had been beaten, but the raping of her daughters with a public audience was treatment that could not be left unchallenged.

After all the visitors had been made comfortable and their ponies tended to and turned out into a field, Dan and his friends were given beds for the night. The men of the village stayed up late into the night discussing what should be done about this terrible deed.

In the morning everyone woke, still enraged by the events of the evening before. Weapons were found from their hiding places and repaired if necessary, helmets polished, and breakfasts hurried for those men riding off to tell others the story of the atrocity.

The Romans had confiscated many weapons as part of their occupation, but no one in this age ventured out and about to other villages unarmed. Many new weapons and armour were either made or found from their hiding places to prepare for some action of revenge. The Romans did not have enough men to search everywhere and many a Briton had intriguing places to hide their tools of war!

Dan was intrigued by all this activity and he was a little laid back and indifferent to it all. It could be something to do with his long years in this troubled island of Britannia or perhaps his experience of the Romans. He knew awful things had happened and something should be done about it, but the Romans were a strong force and were very difficult to defeat or influence. There was something authoritative in their demeanour and attitude to life, it was somehow built into them, their control of their slaves and their dominating attitude towards people who were not of their race or standing.

He was given breakfast by the womenfolk of the village. Breakfast consisted of lovely hot porridge made from oats and creamy milk. They sat on bench seats either side of an old oak wooden table. The table looked old. He was told it was at least 300 years old which made it much older than the building it was in. "It must have seen quite a number of celebrations and activities over the years," Dan thought. There was the thought that much beer had been spilt on the table and perhaps this was why it had been preserved in this wonderful glossy, smooth state.

The women of the village had been comforting Boudicca and her two daughters after their terrible experience yesterday and for once perhaps, they were speechless and shocked by the whole situation. There was a great feeling of vengeance and 'something must be done attitude' amongst them. Although, nothing much was said, Dan felt the vibes from them as he ate his breakfast.

He suddenly thought he should go and see the two daughters. He was after all the eldest male relative they had and should show the care that a loving second cousin should. He should give them some comfort and love; however difficult he found the situation. He felt that being a man he should have been able to protect them, and felt guilty that he did not do more, yesterday.

But how could he help, he asked himself? The two girls were surrounded by womenfolk comforting them and giving them the love, they needed. He wondered whether it was it a place for a man? Could he hold their hands? Could he understand what they had been through? No, he thought, he could not. Perhaps in a few days, when they had recovered a little, but everything was very raw at the moment. He continued to eat his breakfast and finished with some soft cheese.

After breakfast he went off to find his cousin Boudicca. She was being nursed by another cousin – her wounds were being bathed in saltwater. She was wearing her gold torque around her neck. Perhaps it was something she never took off, he thought.

"Those Bastards" she cried out, as Dan entered the roundhouse. She was lying on her stomach cursing and swearing – "vengeance, vengeance" she cried. There was a young man kneeling by her bedside dressed ready to mount and go on a mission for Boudicca. She, as the Queen of Iceni, was mobilising her troops.

What troops? Dan thought to himself. Every village had a few keen warriors and that was the Iceni way to protect their loved ones, but the Romans were resilient, and it would take organization and deliberation before a successful attempt could be made to wreak the revenge Boudicca had in her eyes! Good gracious, what anger she had! The salt was certainly adding to her venom!

The young man left, keen to go on his mission to raise awareness of what had happened to Boudicca and her daughters, with the elders in all the local villages. Dan approached Boudicca at her bedside just as the young man mounted his pony and quickly kicked it into a trot and then a canter.

"Hello Boo, how's it going?" he asked. He had always called her Boo ever since they were kids together. He was 11 years older but was still young at heart. They had been in the same childhood gang when playing in the woods and the fields around and about their village.

"Bastards! Bastards! those bloody bastards! I'll get them for doing this to me and my daughters. They made one mistake - letting us go!" She adjusted herself on the bed to make herself a little more comfortable but at the same time was testing her wounds. She wanted to get out of bed and get things done.

"How are the girls Dan? I heard Epona is distraught. Have you seen them"? "No Boo, sorry I haven't, they're being looked after by some girls. I didn't quite think it my place, being a man, to go and see them after what they've been through." He paused, "they are so young – it must have been a terrible shock for them."

Boudicca wiped a tear from her eye, there was a soft side to her even though most of the time she outwardly portrayed this hard leader-like attitude to life and her role as Queen of the Iceni.

"I'll get those Roman bastards for doing this," she whispered. "Do you know Dan, I've never seen anyone crucified but after yesterday, I believe they do it, hang someone up with nails through their hands on a wooden cross, for days . . . . . . until they die – they're such bastards! So uncivilised."

Boudicca continued, "They are so hypocritical - they say one thing about us being the barbarians and then they do that to fellow human beings. It's disgusting. Do you remember Dan, about 7 or 8 years ago they crucified this man who murdered his brother, well they thought he murdered his brother. But they found out afterwards that it wasn't him, so he'd done nothing wrong. They just nailed him up on a cross and left him to die. Bloody Bastards!"

One of the womenfolk put another log on the fire in the centre of the room and caused some sparks to float up into the space in the centre of the room. It was always dark in the roundhouses with just the one small doorway, but eyes would soon get adjusted to the dark and there was a certain homeliness about all roundhouses.

Logs were dried before being burnt and this kept smoke to a minimum and people living in the roundhouses were used to it. However, this smoke was useful as it reduced the numbers of mosquitoes, flies and other critters that might live in the warmth of a roundhouse.

Dan turned back do Boudicca and asked if there was anything he could do.

"Yes" she said "I'm organising an attack on that place where we were humiliated. The attack will happen in three mornings from now. I have plans to attack Colchester after that if we have gathered enough forces to do so".

"Woah!" Dan said, "Are you sure you're not taking steps too far and too fast - the Romans are very strong and although your cause is good, I have my worries."

"I agree Dan, but our cause is good, and we have the Romans at a disadvantage. They have split their forces at least three ways. Their main force is in North Wales fighting the druids, another is down in the South West subduing the Dvmnonii and Durotriges tribes in that area and a third is in Lincolnshire. They are divided and we have surprise on our side."

Dan was still doubtful and shook his head, but Boudicca replied,

"We, the Iceni, have been trying secretly to formulate a plan to rid ourselves of the Romans, they have been here 17 years and are still fighting us, trying to subdue us. This recent atrocity on me and my daughters, Bonvica and poor Epona is the last straw. It will provide the incentive to drum up the support we need to mount a realistic attack." She winced at the pain of her wounds and continued,

"We will not be defeated this time, there are many pockets of resistance in the tribes of Britannia who will support us, we just need to combine our forces. We have, in the past, been South and talked to the Trinovantes and they are keen to join us should the need arise."

"What would you have me do Boo," asked Dan. Boudicca's reply was keen and responsive.

"You have 2 waggons with oxen and there is a great need for supplies if we are to mount a successful campaign against the Romans. Load your waggons with food, supplies and sheltering materials as we may well have to camp out on our journey to destroy what the Romans have built in London and elsewhere. Take Nomass with you, he is very good at persuading people to join our cause. He can persuade others to bring their waggons and will help you find the supplies for the campaign. I believe we have a long journey ahead of us but the end result, when we rid ourselves of these oppressive Romans, it will be well worth it."

"I will do my best for you Boo," he paused, got up off his knee, gave her a wink and said, "get better soon - let's meet up in Ixworth."

"Do your best for our people Dan, not for me but for our people." She gasped as she moved again and gave Dan a wave from her bed as he left the roundhouse.

Dan went off to find Nomass, which was not difficult, as he was harnessing his two chestnut ponies up to his chariot - his cherished chariot. He loved that vehicle probably more than he loved his wife. He would ride on the platform supported by the hoops, his reigns in his left hand and his whip in his right. Not that he used the whip on the ponies, he just loved to crack it and make that wonderful sound.

"Good morning Nomass," he said as he approached. "How are you this fine spring morning."

"I am very well thanks Dan." He turned to face Dan as he struggled with the harness for one of the ponies. "I see you've just come from Boudicca; she is one fiery lady and I see she's got you organised helping us smash the Romans."

"Yeah" said Dan, "I'm slowly being convinced it's our way forward, but I do wonder if we're doing the right thing. I'm long in the tooth and perhaps a little too old to be a fighting man. People can get hurt. I see around me the enthusiasm for our cause - just look around us at the activity in this place - it's buzzing. I am slowly becoming a willing helper!

"Have faith Dan, we will defeat them," said Nomass as he winced and hobbled round to the other side of the pony. "How's the leg," Dan asked. "Surprisingly it's not that bad, I have had it bound up and it looked a lot worse at the time with all the blood - thanks for asking."

"Will we be ready to go soon?" asked Dan. "Yes, we will be ready for the off as soon as I've loaded my things on the chariot," replied Nomass.

Once the chariot was loaded up with all the provisions, it no longer looked like the agile fighting machine it was designed to be. When it just had warriors riding on it, in their full war time regalia, it looked impressive. Now, loaded up to the hilt with food and other supplies, it looked a little heavy and cumbersome, but it served the purpose to get back home. Dan mounted his pony and off they set for home.

On the road back home, they noticed there was a lot more traffic than normal, and it was all coming the other way, going south. Mainly, it was men dressed in their 'combats' - ready for war! Most were excited and enthusiastic about supporting Boudicca, but Dan saw the look in their eyes of enthusiasm tinged with anxiety for their task ahead.

Some asked why Dan and his friends were going the other way when Boudicca had asked them to join her. Nomass said they were going home to prepare their waggons to support Boudicca with supplies and tents. Dan explained that Boudicca had plans to go on to London after Colchester and this was going to be a greater campaign than just destroying Colchester!

They then asked if Dan had been there when the Princesses were raped. Dan nodded and described the scene in all its abhorrent detail. He found it most distressing to describe the scene again and realised how barbaric the Romans had been. Princess Epona, the people's favourite, had been particularly badly hurt. This made the crowd of men travelling to see Boudicca very angry for this was not the way anyone should be treated, even by an occupying force.

They were stopped a number of times on the way back home and Dan repeated his story. This had the effect of escalating the excitement and inciting the crowds further to support their queen in her revenge on the Romans. Some people they met on the way were prepared with supplies, having had the forethought that this will be a longer campaign then just an initial riotous mob.

"This is becoming quite an event, Nomass," remarked Dan. "What started out as a little tete-a-tete between

Boudicca and this Catus Roman dignitary is not exactly getting out of hand but turning into a proper rebellion and it's difficult to see where it's going."

"Everyone we speak to seems to be riled up," Nomass replied.

Dan became pensive - "This is going to take some organising if it's not going to end in humiliation," he thought, "I believe we have a strong leader in Boudicca, but has she the skills to organise such a campaign?" He knew Boudicca's character as a loving mother and as a caring cousin to Dan's family, but who could take on the role of organiser and administrator if they were to use this riotous mob successfully against the Romans? Would it fall to him as a senior member of the Iceni? When he considered who else there was, he realised he was one of the elders of the Iceni tribe now.

"Where is this going, Nomass," Dan mused "I do hope it doesn't get out of control, it's got to be done properly. What do you think, Nomass?"

Nomass was away in his own thoughts and eventually responded. "All I know Dan is that these Romans need to be sorted! really sorted, - and I'm going to enjoy doing it!"

"There's another thing," said Dan, "this rebellion has to be started quickly before those in our community who 'suck up' to the Romans let this out of the bag. We cannot afford for the Romans to organise themselves before we attack – we will lose the element of surprise and probably the battle! We need to move quickly, Nomass."

They reached home late in the afternoon just as it was getting dark, and Dan was especially pleased to see his wife and family. His young grandsons Thomas and Damos came to greet him. There was much to talk about, and their story had to be told a number of times as different people from the village came in to listen to Dan and Nomass. Everyone was horrified to hear of the rape of the princesses and the beating of their queen. After his journey and all the excitement, Dan was very tired and although there were many pressing things to do, he quietly retired to bed and to sleep.

The next day was bright and sunny with little wind and the whole village was busy as they prepared waggons and supplies for their journey to Ixworth and on to Colchester. Dan was very surprised at how everyone was donating some of their most treasured food supplies and sheltering equipment. It was all loaded onto the waggons and the best oxen were chosen and well fed before their journey.

Drustan the local blacksmith, together with his two apprentices, were busy all day repairing weapons and modifying agricultural tools into weapons. Hurriedly prepared shields and implements were assembled. Travelling bags, hats and scarves were found. Precious nails were banged into cudgels, made from heavy sticks, which looked particularly nasty with additional sharp pieces of flint protruding!

It was amazing to see what an ingenious Iceni craftsman could come up with in the way of weapons! Dan was worried, as was his nature, that there might be accidents with them. Even the children were sent out and about to collect suitably sized stones to use in slings and to throw at the Roman legionaries. This caused another worry for Dan, as he was concerned about the weight of the stones on the axles of his two waggons. He was always worrying.

Sledges were made from two poles and animal skins to

be dragged behind pack ponies and mules. A small army was beginning to be formed and Dan's thoughts were directed towards items they might have missed and situations they would be unprepared for. It was the things you forgot, that would cause problems later on. His experienced mind was wary that the Romans were strong. When they were miles away, they were out of one's mind, but he had seen them close up and they were formidable opponents. They were well organised, clad in armour head to foot. They were also fearsome warriors and he had heard they practised with double the weight and equipment on, so in battle their usual armour seemed very light to them.

They were trained soldiers and the Iceni were generally just farmers. In the past the Iceni had had minor skirmishes with their neighbours to the south, the Trinovantes and Catvvellavni. There had also been some cattle raids and the usual minor battles regarding women and sometimes slaves between the tribes. When engaging in these minor skirmishes the locals wore helmets, shields and light armour, but not the heavy professional armour that the Romans had.

That afternoon the womenfolk made themselves busy preparing a great feast before the majority of the menfolk went off to battle. There was great excitement, and the stored wine and beer was brought out. Two boars were slaughtered and butchered and the smell of them being turned and slowly roasted on the fires was an encouragement to get everything finished so the feast could begin.

Dan had the foresight not to eat or drink too much that evening as he knew he and his wife might be spending their last night together for some time. They both knew he was off on an adventure that might well take him many miles away from his home into unknown territory and situations. They settled down in their bed and using the warmth of each other's bodies, quickly fell asleep. They slept well that night.

The next day they got up late - the alcohol and excitement had worn off. There were minor preparations to be made but those who were off to fight assembled themselves and away they went to find Boudicca, who they expected to find in Ixworth.

## CHAPTER IV

# Ixworth Burns

On the road to Ixworth, Dan joined up on route with people from other villages, who were just as excited as he was and keen to get to grips with the Romans. As they came closer to Ixworth, the air was filled with smoke and they began to wonder just what had been going on.

When they reached Ixworth, it was all over. The hall where Boudicca had met Catus had been burned to the ground and all the nearby Roman buildings had been destroyed. In some ways, Dan was disappointed. After the expected battle for the village, he had been looking forward to a good night's sleep in some cosy bed or even under the shelter of a roof and walls. That would no longer be a possibility given the chaos and destruction that was all around.

It was unclear what had happened. All Dan could glean from others was that the first Iceni to arrive had not experienced much opposition at all. All the legionaries, Romans and Roman sympathisers had fled, except for a few grandparents too old to be bothered or able to leave.

Ixworth now served as an assembly point for the Iceni, as they had had no clear instructions on what their strategy was going to be.

Dan wondered how to describe the rioters - perhaps they were rebels. They were certainly a mob who had gathered together quickly, but with little or no organisation. He went off to find Boudicca amongst the crowds in the gathering twilight. There were also great numbers of people who were either bedding themselves down for the night in whatever shelter they could find or were trying to sleep amongst the surrounding woods and ruined buildings. Others had met up with old friends and were chatting round campfires.

It was an assembly of Iceni never quite seen in this way before. There had always been regular meetings of the Iceni tribe every two years, held at locations within the tribe's regional domain, but they were more organised and disciplined.

Dan did not have to look for long to find his cousin Boudicca. She had pitched her husband's Royal tent in a small valley, just outside the ruins of Ixworth. She was sat round a fire, outside the tent, talking with a number of minor tribal leaders who had come from the locality and must have been part of the first rebels to arrive two days before. It seems Dan had missed out, like many others, on the initial action - a skirmish that was over quickly, which met with little resistance.

The meeting Dan had stumbled upon was being held by Boudicca to plan the next phase of the revolt. Boudicca looked up, and seeing Dan, invited him over, introducing him to those around the fire. He knew quite a number of them and was greeted with affection and respect. After the initial pleasantries of 'how are you?' and 'how was your journey?' – Dan realised that he might well be the oldest person present. They then got down to business.

*Richard Scholefield*

Map of England - AD 60

"What plans do you have cousin," Dan asked. "We have gathered intelligence today," replied Boudicca. She was revelling in her military authority that she seemed to have acquired in the last two days. "We have found out that Catus left in a hurry and is probably in Colchester by now, seeking a boat to take him back to Gaul, across the channel."

"I think Catus realised what a big mistake he made in the way he treated you and the princesses," said one of the leaders. "He didn't realise he was messing with the Iceni - but he does now, and the coward has left his fellow Romans to sort out the mess," he continued.

"From the moment I met the man, I thought he was a despicable coward, and like something you would find under a heap of dung!" Dan said.

"When we arrived in Ixworth two days ago, there was not a fighting Roman here, apart from some old cronies. I think that when we get to Colchester they may well have left there as well," another leader said.

"Colchester!" Boudicca announced. "That's our next target and we leave tomorrow morning. We will leave word here that Colchester is our next expected confrontation with the Romans. We will be going via Long Melford, and others from our tribe can follow us there."

"Let us hope that Catus is still there and some bad weather has stopped him crossing the channel," said Dan. " I remember hearing, three generations ago, the last Roman that tried to invade Britain was grossly hampered by the weather. He lost many ships, wrecked on the beach," Dan continued with glee. "He didn't have much luck when he reached home either, as I heard he was killed by his own people back in Rome - killed by his own people! They are savages those Romans - they knifed him to death when he was unarmed."

"I think you are talking about Caesar," interjected Boudicca. "Those on ponies and chariots will leave first, as soon as breakfast is over," Boudicca announced. "They will be followed by our foot Warriors, while the waggons will leave last, having packed up our tents and things. We can't have the waggons hold us up on the road to Colchester," she continued. "We must strike fast and hard because, as we all know, there are those amongst us who will turn traitor and inform the Romans of our whereabouts and our intentions. It is better that we get to Colchester before they have time to prepare defences. Is there anything else anyone wishes to say or suggest?" Boudicca asked.

"Yes," said Garos. He was a leader from Swaffham. "I have heard from the Coritani Tribe that there are 300 Roman soldiers up in Lincolnshire - they may well be on the way down here, if they have heard of what has happened."

"Please stay behind after the meeting," Boudicca replied, "and we will discuss plans to deal with them - is there anything else, my followers?" No-one answered her.

After the meeting had dispersed, Boudicca sat down with Garos. He was a large man, 6 foot 3 inches tall and broad shouldered. His hands were especially large, Boudicca noticed, and there was also a strong odour coming from him. They sat on two logs, next to a quietly glowing fire. Speaking quietly, Boudicca whispered, "Right Garos, I have heard rumours of a detachment of legionaries up North, but I'm not quite sure where they are. My guess is that they will come down here to Ixworth to investigate the rumpus we have caused. How many men have you got?"

"I have around about 180," replied Garos quietly. " Some have ponies and chariots, and there are quite a number of slingers. You know the Romans don't like slingers, and I am expecting more. I have sent word to friends in Lynn and Holme who have promised more men, so perhaps I might have as many as 600," he continued.

Boudicca looked up in thought for a moment. "I am minded we should ambush these Romans. So, if there are 300 of them, it would be good to have at least 1000 good men, hidden in the undergrowth on each side of the road to take them out. Perhaps they could be concealed somewhere in the woods northwest from here at Milden. What do you think, Garos? Could you do this?" Boudicca paused, then went on to say, "But the most important thing is to keep this a secret. Very secret, as there are informants in our midst, - I am sure of it." Garos nodded.

"I think the best thing to do," Boudicca continued, "is to send a handful of your best men out on the Milden Road. I am sure they know it well and they can find a suitable place to ambush the oncoming Romans. Then send others further afield to warn of the enemy's advance. Send out other scouts, perhaps to Ely, just in case they take a different route. Can you do this for the Iceni, for Britannia?"

"Yes, I can," uttered Garos, quietly. "I will formulate a plan in more detail over the next few days while I wait for the rest of my followers to join me here in Ixworth."

"Good man," continued Boudicca. "I will leave you Roan of Haver, he has at least 300 men. He has very keen warriors and they will bolster your forces to make sure of success. But remember, keep it secret, don't even let your men know exactly what we're doing, only those you really trust."

"Trust me Boudicca, my men have been working up to this fight for the last 17 years. We will do a good job!"

It rained in the night and everyone woke early to sort themselves out, dry out and have a cold breakfast, as most of the fires had gone out and everything was wet. There were some lucky ones who had paid attention to keeping their fires going and not involved themselves in too much beer drinking. Before long the rain stopped, they packed their things, harnessed their ponies and mules and were ready to get going.

Boudicca then boarded her two-horse chariot and addressed her band of rebels from the top of a small grassy knoll. "Fellow Iceni, I am your Queen and your leader. There is a great will amongst you to right the wrongs that have been done to me and my daughters by the Roman tyrants, and I thank you for your being here today, keen and prepared to teach these Romans a lesson." Her ponies, having sensed the mood, were agitated and eager to get going. Boudicca took a moment to subdue them and then continued, "I have already sent scouts ahead and those of you who have chariots and ponies will follow them. We will cross the River Stour at Long Melford and there we will rest for the night and consider our next move. The Romans are professionals, and we must also be professional to outwit them, and so defeat them! I will see you all in Long Melford. Good Luck."

Boudicca moved off. There must have been a good 50 Chariots and 300 men on ponies, all armed and looking as if they meant business. As they rode past Dan, standing by his wagon, he realised how young they were, some of them almost boys. They were keen, you could see it in their eyes and their attitude as they tried to hurry their mounts on the road South.

Looking at the road ahead Dan could see there was a bottleneck as it filed through a narrow bridge. There would be delays, unavoidable delays. It was 14 miles to Long Melford, and it was going to be difficult to organise the army on its journey. Had anyone given this subject any thought - how do you organise a band of enthusiastic young Iceni?

Dan wondered how the Romans coped in a similar situation, but he had never studied the way they organise themselves. He had seen Romans on the move before, but never more than 30 or 40 at any one time. He had heard they come in their thousands. No matter how many Romans there were going to be, Boudicca's army would take some stopping!

Dan then watched the men on foot file past him. They had put a great deal of effort into polishing their helmets and making themselves smart. They were more numerous than those who were mounted, and each small tribe was led off by their leader, who was riding on his own smart chariot. It was difficult to count them, but Dan estimated there were at least 1,000 men, maybe 1,300. They were marching together proudly and were looking very smart - well as smart as you can be if you have been drinking with your mates all evening and then out all night trying to shelter from the rain. However, by the morning, the influence of alcohol did not seem to dampen their ardour.

As Dan watched the last of them filing past, he realised that he must catch up with the others. However, in his fascination with watching everyone march off, he had forgotten that his own two waggons and their oxen needed to be made ready to go. He need not have worried; they were already harnessed up by his two sons and their friend Scarr. They had been busy in his absence and completed all that was necessary to prepare them for the journey ahead.

Their friend Scarr was just the sort of young man you would want along with you when you are about to go into battle. He was very keen to get stuck in, hence the big scar he had down the right side of his face, caused by an accident, jousting with a friend. When the brains were dished out Scarr certainly did not get his fair share, but he was a keen worker and definitely good to have around in any fight!

His two eldest sons were nearly grown men now and he was proud of them. They were in better spirits than many of the others as they had slept under the waggons, keeping dry, and had better prepared themselves with blankets and animal hides to protect themselves from the damp ground.

As usual, it was slow going with the oxen. The larger of the waggons was pulled by 6 oxen, the smaller, by 4. On a journey, pulling the waggons, the oxen were difficult to handle. They are not intelligent animals and work better in the fields, pulling a plough. When an ox gets to the end of a furrow and turns around with the plough, they set off with renewed energy, but when on the road they seem to realise or believe that there is no end in sight, and they go much slower.

It was late in the morning when Dan joined the end of the queue with his two waggons. Dan drove the larger waggon in front with his younger son Talos coaxing the oxen alongside. Scarr was a strong character and drove the waggon behind. His waggon was accompanied by Dan's son, Morcant, who walked beside the oxen with a large stick. Morcant didn't mind walking; he was just keen to participate in this fantastic adventure with his Aunt Boudicca. Boudicca had once told him that he was her 'favourite half nephew' and it is amazing what this did to a young man's enthusiasm. She had a wonderful relationship with everyone she met, making them all feel very special.

The journey was slow. The oxen had not eaten much fodder the previous night due to the chatting and drinking and the complete lack of good grass in and around Ixworth. It would soon be midday and they had barely completed 3 miles. Travelling at the back of the train of waggons was frustrating and the oxen would soon need to stop and have their midday rest. The animals would also be expecting to eat some good fodder to help them on their way.

Dan estimated that there must be at least 30 waggons in front of him and perhaps another 10 behind. This journey was going to be quite arduous and Colchester was a little over 30 miles away. If they were lucky, they might get there in three days' time, but that would be pushing it.

Dan was suddenly made aware of some imminent action. Talos, having been walking normally on the right of the oxen, was moving with urgency and stealth. He had seen something and was hastily taking out his sling from his belt. Dan looked up to see what had caught his attention. A roe deer was crossing the road in front of the leading oxen. Dan's gaze then went back to Talos who was showing good dexterity in loading his sling. Twirling it around his head it began to whirr in the air, but the deer had gone. However, Talos had foresight, and sure enough two more roe deer came out of the woods on the left following the first. Concentrating on the second of the two he released the slingshot with accuracy towards the creature. The stone whizzed through the air at the trotting deer, and Dan was excited by the thought they would have venison for their evening meal. It was not going to be so, the stone missed the animal's head by a whisker, the creature not realizing her close shave with death. A fourth deer came across the road as Talos hastily loaded his sling again. He was not quick enough, the deer skedaddled into the undergrowth on the right of the track and both Dan and Talos shook their heads in disappointment.

Dan considered trying to overtake the waggon in front, as it was slower than his, but this would mean leaving the road. It was a poor road, but it did have some structure to support his two waggons. However, leaving the road would mean travelling over some rough ground. Looking to the side of the road where he was now, he could see that others had tried this in the past and got stuck and made large grooves in some wet ground. It was springtime and although the ground was becoming firmer, last night's rain had made the ground a little boggy.

They should not have left Ixworth so late in the morning. Perhaps letting the mounted boys go off first was a mistake, but then if there was any confrontation to be had at the front of the column, it would be best to have the fighting men there. This was not a situation that Boudicca was familiar with, nor did she have the experience of how to organise a military campaign.

Dan thought to himself, "Boudicca must have another meeting tonight and they would have to discuss their tactics when they reached Long Melford, possibly followed by some consumption of beer! But wait a tick," Dan suddenly realised, "where was the beer? The beer was in the waggons with him, and he was now some miles behind Boudicca and her advanced guard. They would arrive at Melford with no beer, supplies, tents and no food! Oh dear, this needed some organising!"

In the late afternoon, Dan saw that the leading waggon had stopped next to a large meadow on the right of the road and others had pulled up behind him. Wisely, the driver of this waggon had only pulled a little way off the road, as the ground was wet, and the waggons were very heavy. There would be no way of getting all them back on the road should they get bogged down in the soggy ground.

They had also made a wise decision to stop here, as the grass in the meadow had grown just enough to be able to feed the hungry oxen. There was also a small stream on the left of the road and the leading waggoners were taking their oxen for a drink. They were making sure their animals were well fed and watered before lighting fires and making shelters for the night.

Dan helped his sons and Scarr unharness the oxen. He estimated that they had travelled around 8 miles today, which was good going, as they had not started until late morning. He left his boys tending to the oxen and went to see the man in charge of the leading waggon.

As Dan approached, the man turned and recognised him as Boudicca's cousin. "Hello Dan, how are you doing?" he said. Dan was a little embarrassed as he didn't know the gentleman and had to say, "Sorry I don't know you, do I?"

"No, I don't suppose you do," he replied, "but I know you, as you are related to Boudicca."

"Oh right," said Dan, I must be famous, he thought. He continued, "You have found a good spot to stop for the night I see - I wonder where the others got to today - have you heard anything?"

"No, I've not seen nor heard anything all day. They must have got carried away with themselves riding on ahead so far. They are way too keen, if you ask me. What about you Dan, have you heard anything?"

"Nothing, not a thing, I haven't heard a thing all day. As you say, I think they've gone ahead like mad men, but then I suppose it is best we catch the Romans by surprise. I suspect that is their intention," Dan replied. "Sorry, I didn't catch your name."

"Luke, from Diss."

"Pleased to meet you Luke," Dan said, "Once we get set up, please come and join us. I am in the two white waggons over there. We have plenty of beer, although it's shaken up a bit, and my wife has packed some wonderful salted wild boar for us to have with some cabbage."

"Thank you, yes please, I'll be over as soon as I've set up myself. It will save me lighting a fire and cooking."

Scarr started a good fire with some dry wood he had taken from of the back of the waggon, and went off to find some more, in a nearby copse. It was not long before they were all sitting down with their new-found friend Luke, sitting and chatting around the campfire, with a plate full of wild boar stew. Luke asked a question,

"So, what do you think is going to happen when we get to Colchester?"

"I should think, with all those tribesmen I saw earlier, they will trash the place. I'm only hoping no one gets hurt, but I don't see that happening," Dan replied. The evening went on chatting about the adventure before them.

The next morning everyone was up early, and the oxen were yoked up, ready to leave, very soon after breakfast. Fires were put out and all the temporary camping stuff was packed away in the waggons. Dan's two waggons started out on the road before most of the others and he found himself behind Luke's waggon very close to the front of the column.

They were lucky to have two warriors on ponies, who went on ahead to scout and help to ensure the road was clear. Passing waggons who were coming in the opposite direction was not always easy, especially when they were a long column of 40 waggons. Single waggons could pass relatively easily by just slightly pulling off the road while the other waggon passed, but with the long column, tempers could be frayed. The single waggon would have to wait for the whole column to pass, unless some good manoeuvring could be done. This journey was not going to be easy.

It was not a bad road and it was a lovely spring day. The grass should be growing quite quickly now, so fodder for the oxen should not be of too much concern and they were making good progress. This was going to be quite an adventure, even if they were just plodding along at a lovely slow pace.

They went through a small hamlet of roundhouses. Hunting dogs barked, and children ran alongside the waggons asking questions and showing a lot of excitement. They might never in their lifetimes have seen so many waggons on the road at one time.

When they had travelled about four miles, the wagonmaster on the leading waggon shouted back down the line that this would be a good place to stop and rest the oxen. He pulled off the road on to some firm grassy ground next to an early flowering meadow. There was a wood opposite for those who needed a little privacy for a comfort break. Dan noticed, growing just along the outside of the wood, that there were some lovely large dock leaves. This was his favourite plant that made this time of year a better time for such visits into the woods. The oxen were unhitched and allowed to graze under the watchful eyes of a couple of dogs and the younger members of the column.

Dan thought that they might well reach Long Melford by the middle of the afternoon and shared this thought with Luke. Luke agreed. As they were chatting, eating a light lunch of mashed peas and oats, three men rode up on their ponies and one of them recognised Dan. He rode over and dismounted from his pony, by hooking his leg over the horse's head. It was Scavo, one of Boudicca's right-hand men - he was becoming a regular messenger for Boudicca.

Dan spoke first, as Scavo was catching his breath.

"How's it going, Scavo? I see you are still riding that fine pony of yours. I guess Boudicca sent you to find out how we're doing?"

"Something like that," Scavo replied, as he tied up his pony to the brake handle of Dan's waggon.

"Well," said Dan, "we haven't got very far, as you can see. We are doing our best with these oxen, but as you know very well, they can only manage 8 to 10 miles a day. If we push them any harder, we won't progress any faster as they will tire more quickly. At the moment we're giving them their daily lunchtime break."

"Will you get through Long Melford and on towards Colchester by this evening?" Scavo said.

"If all goes well," Dan replied, as he tried to swallow his food. "And then perhaps some of our supplies will be thankfully received by those boys up ahead. They must be getting quite hungry if they can't find much food around on this journey of ours."

"I don't know about them, but I'm certainly getting hungry. I'm running out of the food I packed in my bag when we left," Scavo said. "I thought our boys might have stolen from the villages we've been through, but it looks as if they have respected the villagers we've seen," he continued. "They could have ravaged the villagers' stores of food supplies, but they seem to have been very well behaved," Dan said, scraping what little food there was left on his plate onto the grass.

Dan stood up and surveyed the scene of the oxen eating the grass and his fellow travellers resting by their waggons enjoying the sunshine. It was very peaceful, and he wondered what was going on go ahead, where the main body of Boudicca's followers might well be eagerly marching on towards Colchester. "They may well have already got there," Dan mused, and then said to Scavo.

"So, where do you think Cousin Boudicca is now, Scavo?"

"I should think, by now, she's got to Colchester, Dan. She is probably considering what her next move is," he replied.

"Her next move may well be out of her control, knowing how angry our boys are and how strong their desire is to get to grips with the Romans," said Dan. "Word has it, that there aren't many Romans in Colchester," replied Scavo.

" It is rumoured that they have left the place undefended, as you know, so our boys may well have just gone in and ravaged the place."

"I didn't know it was undefended - haven't they built any ramparts or any defences around the place then?" Dan asked.

"No, surprisingly they haven't, but they have built this fantastic, beautiful building in the middle of the town that I have never seen the likes of, ever before. It is a lovely, massive building! But when it comes to building any defences for the town, they seem to have prepared very little. There was just a small wooden rampart and ditch, and that has fallen into disrepair. Most odd! They are not as efficient and prepared as we thought the Romans would be."

"Perhaps they have been putting all their work into that huge building of theirs and forgotten the fundamentals of defence," Dan said. "Yes, that's a big mistake!" declared Scavo nodding.

Thinking out loud, Dan responded. "They are leaving themselves wide open to Boudicca's temper. I can't see her hanging around if she knows the place is defended by just a handful of soldiers, and she won't be able to hold back her men, if I know the Iceni! A band of headstrong nutters!" Dan gesticulated with his arms, as he shouted the words.

He realised he was getting in a temper, and perhaps ought to calm himself before his enthusiasm rubbed off on the wagon-masters around him. It would do no good to encourage them to increase speed and tire out the oxen in an attempt to get to Colchester sooner. They had to plod along at their two to three mile an hour speed and be patient - they would get there soon enough.

*Boudicca's Vengeance*

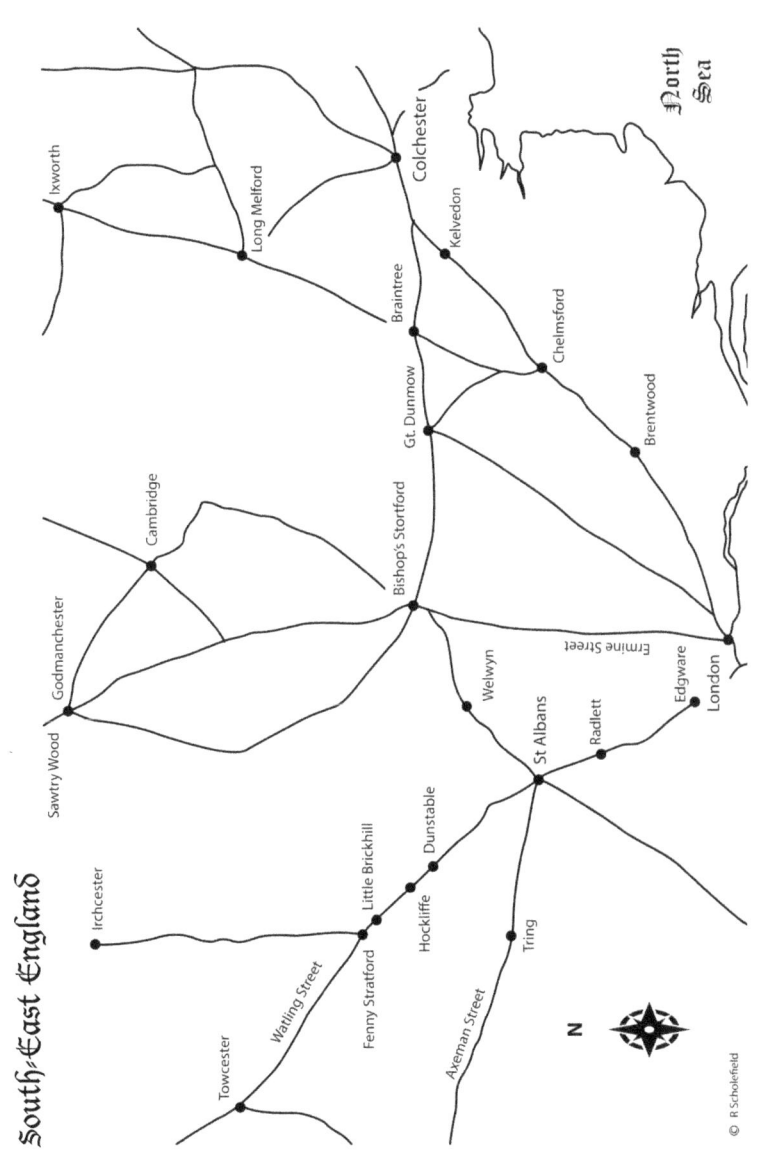

This plan shows the principal towns and roads of South-East England in AD 60.

## CHAPTER V

# CATUS LEAVES FOR ROME

Catus Decianus, having made a real mess of his negotiations with Boudicca at Ixworth, realised his mistake and was travelling back to Colchester as soon as he could. He was being escorted by Justus's turma of 30 Roman cavalrymen. They made good progress towards Colchester and arrived at the crossroads in Long Melford by the evening, where they stopped for the night.

The staging post here was a rough affair. It was very uncomfortable and was managed by Romanised Britons, whose hospitality was poor. This made Catus really ill-tempered, so everyone kept out of his way. However, it provided a roof over their heads and warm food in their bellies, which was welcomed in this recently acquired Roman province of Britannia.

The roads and buildings in occupied Britannia were beginning to improve - roads were being paved and the system of staging posts in this area was slowly improving. Considering it had only been 17 years since Claudius had initiated the invasion of Britannia, overall living standards had improved for some, despite the aggression of a few of the local inhabitants.

Justus was worried about the consequences of the events that had taken place in the village of Ixworth, particularly the treatment of the daughters. He kept turning them over in his mind. They should not have treated Queen Boudicca so badly and then raped her daughters as well. She was the leader of the Iceni, a great tribe, covering a large area of this part of Britain. He had never seen that behaviour by his fellow Romans before. He had seen the normal Roman punishments; floggings, torture and crucifixions, but not rape, that was something abhorrent to him. He saw how the Iceni were angry as they left Ixworth and wondered again, what the aftermath would be.

There was no holding Catus back with his desire to return to Colchester quickly. After a hurried breakfast of hot oats and milk, they prepared the horses, packed their mules, checked they had not left anything behind, mounted up, and were on the road as the sun rose on a splendid orange horizon.

Catus and his accompanying cavalrymen rode south towards Colchester, the Roman capital of Britannia. It was quite a beautiful day, considering the recent bad weather, and they soon warmed up. They had become quite cold overnight in their damp and rough accommodation. Justus felt that their hosts did not look after them very well and someone in authority should intervene or perhaps have the hosts replaced. He had spent the night in far better accommodation in many other staging posts across the Roman Empire.

It was about 15 miles to Colchester and the horse Justus

was riding was behaving much better than others he had ridden. On long journeys, where they had to cover a lot of ground in one day, they had to change horses at staging posts, which he found most inconvenient but necessary. Many a horse would get really tired as they approached the next staging post. As most horses had been ridden along the same route many times between staging posts, often for many months, they knew the route well and sometimes slowed knowing they were reaching their destination. Sometimes a replacement horse could be quite challenging to ride. They seemed to delight in being difficult, bucking at times and spinning round at the slightest provocation.

However, he always had the same four-pommelled saddle that had been perfectly worn in, and it had also saved his bacon a number of times. What a tremendous invention this saddle was. The two pommels at the front allowed him to bend right forward over the horse's neck. It helped him with the agility of his horsemanship and was snug around his backside. It gave him tremendous confidence in tight spots and was so much better than riding bareback.

They reached Colchester by mid-afternoon and Catus, wasting no time in going straight down to the docks to enquire when the next boat was available to take him across the channel. He was very keen to leave Britannia and to his delight he found that a boat would be leaving on the evening tide. He dismissed Justus and his cavalry companions without a by-your-leave or thank you. He collected his chests, belongings, and paperwork, and boarded a transport vessel with just two of his close colleagues. The transport boat was very basic with limited shelter from the elements, unlike some of the other larger boats.

Justus, with his colleagues and the remains of Catus's entourage, stood on the dock totally bewildered. What a rude and nasty man Catus was. Perhaps it was best that he was on his way, they were free of him and that was quite a pleasing feeling.

They slowly turned their backs and proceeded towards the town centre. On reaching their destination, they went to the central square of the town, known as the Forum. They said goodbye to the remaining members of Catus's party who he had been left behind in Colchester. They then went to find the usual stabling for their horses, and the barracks where they would be staying the night.

Justus and his colleagues had been to Colchester many times. After settling their horses and checking in to their barracks, they decided to visit the Roman baths for a refreshing soak and a chat.

Walking through the town centre, they looked up at the first grand building that the Romans had built in the province of Britannia. It had been named 'The Temple of Claudius'. It was a splendid sight, with its eight polished erect columns and steps up to the front, it was a truly wonderful piece of architecture. It reminded Justus of the fantastic buildings of Rome that he had seen, when he had visited during his teenage years.

The Roman baths were good, and Justus was pleased with the recently delivered wood ash that they cleaned themselves with. They left feeling fully recovered from the long journey, and went onto one of the many good inns in the town. There they had some good imported Roman wine, some food and relaxed for the rest of the evening.

Having spent an uncomfortable week or two with

the extremely rude Catus, this evening on their own, demonstrated the benefits of being in the Roman army. It afforded them the freedom to spend an evening enjoying a drink with colleagues. All too soon though, they would be brought back to reality, as in the morning they would have to go and see their senior officer to be given their next assignment.

It was lunchtime the following day when 10 of Justus's colleagues were assigned to other duties. Cavalrymen were always in short supply, so were often deployed all around this province of Britannia. Justus and the remaining colleagues were told to rest a few days in Colchester before being allocated to their next task.

On the second morning, they were told to proceed to the town of London on the Thames. Here, they were to seek orders from Tiberius Claudius Maximus, one of the commanding officers based in that Town. They thought that he would send them northwards, escorting supply waggons to the staging posts on Watling Street. This would be a mundane and tedious task for Justus but would be a vast improvement on the assignments given to the poor, foot slogging infantry.

That morning Decurion Gnaeus, Justus's commanding officer, had terrible stomach upset and could not ride. A Decurion was in charge of 30 cavalrymen called a Turma. Justus was a Duplicarius and second in command of a Turma.

So, the remaining 19 men, with Justus in command, set off bright and early, leaving poor sick Gnaeus behind with his tummy troubles. Gnaeus, one of Justus's good friends, was always having tummy troubles, blaming the local climate and bland food. Justus teased him as they left.

"Perhaps it was the congealed Iceni gruel at that seedy staging post we stayed at in Long Melford a few days ago?" Gnaeus did not think that was funny but thought Justus might be right.

They took the road to Chelmsford on a cloudy day, a little warmer than yesterday. Justus could not tell the difference between the two tribes who lived in this area. Perhaps you could just hear a different accent in their incomprehensible barbaric language, and they smelt different too. He had managed to learn a few words of the local language, but they were urged not to do so. Instead, they were encouraged to try to and impose their Latin language onto the barbarians. Many however, thought this was a lost cause.

The Catuvellavni tribe seemed keener to learn Latin than the Iceni or the Trinovante. This led Justus to think that these people were more friendly to the Romans and that helped him to sleep better at night, when in their region. He had nightmares about Iceni warriors coming to garrot him in the night, an awful nightmare!

He was suddenly woken from his thoughts, when his horse slipped on a stone next to the road. He realised all was well, the men were behaving themselves, keeping alert and attentive to their job.

Justus was now in charge and he felt both proud and nervous. This was the first time, on his own and in command. What responsibility! Would he make the right decisions when called on to do so? What would his men think of him now that he was in charge? They had been more like his mates before, and now he was their commanding officer.

They stayed overnight in Chelmsford, using the communal bath houses of the town and the hospitality of the inns. Drinking into the night once more, with his long time colleagues Clodius and Morinus. He had been an ordinary trooper like them, less than a year ago, and now he was a Duplicarius and their senior. However, since they were no longer under the watchful eye of Gnaeus, it was a different atmosphere. The complexity of senior and junior ranks were soon less significant after the second drink.

As they walked back to their barracks in the dark, Justus wondered how his old mate and boss Gnaeus was getting on with his bad stomach. It was especially dark, with no moon to guide them, but they had stayed in the small Chelmsford barrack block before and knew their way. It was not a place that you would want to walk around on your own, at night, even if you were a large soldier and armed. There had been a few attacks here recently, and the local legionaries had been attempting to catch the culprits. A crucifix cross had been erected at the entrance to the Northgate but was empty at the moment. Its purpose was to nail culprits there until dead to discourage attacks, and was ready, should a felon be caught.

---

They set off the next morning on the road to London and on reaching Brentwood, three of their horses, showing signs of fatigue, were changed for fresh ones at the staging post. It also gave them the opportunity to eat and rest before continuing their journey.

After lunch they set off again, and as they were passing the small Catuvellavni village of Barking, a Roman messenger came galloping up behind them with news that Ixworth had been attacked by the Iceni and everyone had been killed! This was all the news he gave them as he quickly galloped on to the next staging post where he, the messenger, would change his horse and ride on again to London.

What should we do? Justus thought to himself. Here we are, on our way to London, with a military emergency 50 miles in the opposite direction. What was he to do, now that he was in command? There was not much information to go on, but a decision had to be made. So, Justus, exercising his authority for the first time, ordered his men,

"We continue to London to seek clarification on the situation and request further orders. Let us make haste."

They encouraged their horses to quicken their pace as their hearts beat faster. London was less than 10 miles away and the going was good. They would be there in no time and would seek out their commanding officer to find out what they must do. Justus believed he had made the right decision and wondered what action they would see. His first real action!

## CHAPTER VI

# Fantastic Architecture

Dan had been looking at the traces of smoke they could see on the horizon for some time now as they approached Colchester. What had his cousin Boudicca done? Perhaps as Dan suspected, the Iceni had lost control, rioted and burned the place to the ground. What a shame, Dan thought to himself. If this was true, he would never get to see this wonderful building he had recently learned about, The Temple to Emperor Claudius.

They would arrive there before dusk which would enable him to take in the full extent of what had happened. Perhaps he could find some of his friends from his village and offer them food from his waggon. They must be getting hungry, especially if they had had an active day - burning and looting.

"Burning and looting!" Dan thought to himself. "Was this going on in Colchester? What had they got themselves into?"

As they came closer to the outskirts of Colchester, they could smell the smoke, and the screams of women soon became audible in the distance. There was certainly a great deal going on and he tried to hurry the oxen pulling his waggon. A pointless task, oxen were oxen!

As they came closer Scarr, who had been leading the oxen at the front, shouted out to Dan

"I've got to go and see what's happening, don't worry I'll come back soon." Before Dan could call him back, he had gone off to join in the commotion that Dan could hear up ahead. This was totally irresponsible of Scarr, as the oxen needed leading and they would not go on too far without him.

The oxen were not very good without guidance, even from someone as senseless as Scarr. As Dan tried to move the oxen and the waggon off the road, other men ran past him, following Scarr's example. This left the whole waggon train stationary and without much control. With reluctance Dan came down from his waggon, and although wishing to investigate what was happening up ahead in Colchester centre, he felt obliged to unyoke the oxen himself and see to their needs. He gave them some fodder from the back of the waggon and wondered where he might find some water for them, as they had not had any since that morning.

All this time he could hear screams and shouting. Women and children were obviously being attacked in a very brutal way; Dan felt guilty that he was not there to try control his fellow Iceni. What could he do? Could he abandon his oxen and go and get involved?

Dan decided that he could wait no longer and just had to go and see what was happening. He tied the 6 oxen to the waggon and began walking fast, half trotting, towards the shouting and screaming. He had not gone very far, when 3 horsemen, accompanied by a chariot with two passengers, rode past him hurriedly. He could not tell, were these men from his own Iceni tribe or were they from the Trinovante tribe who lived in this area?

The Trinovante were the locals here and it looked as if they were coming to join in with the Iceni against the Romans. There were normally feuds between the two tribes, but it looked as if these had been cast aside to join together against the common enemy - the Romans.

Dan nearly shouted out to them as they passed, but he knew they spoke with a different accent to him, and it would be difficult to understand them. There were also some Belgae amongst the Trinovantes, and they were sometimes incomprehensible when they spoke.

The Belgae were a race who had arrived from across the channel many years ago and had been taken in by the Trinovantes in this area but had also integrated into the Cantiaci tribe, who lived in the Kent region of Britannia. The Belgae were an odd, but interesting race, with some strange customs. They were slightly taller and uglier than the local people and they had sharp features and big hands. It was also rumoured that their children were badly behaved. However, they had brought with them new breeds of sheep as well as new building and cooking methods. They were largely friendly and were bringing new ideas to the area. Some were beneficial, some not so.

Dan was brought back to his senses, when he saw a house up ahead that had just been set on fire by a group of men. It was one of these new Roman houses, square, with a tiled roof. It was not going to be a house for much longer, because the fire had taken hold and the men stood back as it blazed away.

Dan stood with the men watching the house burn, but they then took a few steps back as the heat increased. Dan then turned to the man nearest to him who seemed to be their leader and spoke.

"That would have been a nice place to sleep tonight wouldn't it?"

"Oh yes, it was an accident," replied the man. "There was an old chap who had become friendly with the Romans. I think he was originally from your tribe, the Iceni, but he had become Romanised. He was wearing a toga and he was hiding in the store-room in the back of his house. When we dragged him from his hiding position, he put up quite a fight for an old man, but in the struggle, he knocked over a lamp, and that's what started the fire.'

"Oh, I see," said Dan.

"Silly old fool," he went on, "he could have got changed into some old clothes and run away when he heard us coming. Perhaps 'run' was not quite the right word as he must have been at least 70. I reckon he was 'losing his marbles', you know what I mean?" They watched as the fire destroyed his home.

"I know what you mean," replied Dan. "My own father became very confused before he died. That and his toothache, we did not know what he died of. I am sure he didn't know what was happening at the time. It was very upsetting for the family".

"Anyway," continued the stranger, "We had to leave him in there, unconscious - he was bleeding from his head - silly old fool. I'm sure he swore at us in that Latin language the Romans use."

"It's getting quite warm here," Dan said, rubbing his scar on his head. "It's nice to feel a bit of heat, though it's a shame about the old boy's house and the poor old boy himself."

Dan realised he was being side-tracked and he took his leave from the small crowd who were watching the fire and continued on his way towards the centre of town. As he walked down the main road, he witnessed a great deal of undisciplined looting with men going in and out of houses to see what they could find. The screaming of the women was distant now and he felt a little nervous with all the unruly drunks around. He did not want to get mistaken for the enemy, as it was getting dark now, and he was a little uncomfortable walking on his own. He walked on, hoping to find Cousin Boudicca or perhaps someone he might know in amongst the disorderly crowds.

He need not have worried, as the road turned a corner into the town square, there in front of him was The Temple to Claudius.

"Wow! What a magnificent sight it is, in all its glory," he thought. It was lit up by a burning building off to the right of the square. In the square was Boudicca, standing on her chariot, addressing the crowd, who stood there listening to her attentively. Dan stood there utterly amazed. "Wow! Wow what a picture," he thought. This would be something he would remember for the rest of his life. He had never seen such a splendid building. The Romans were certainly very clever to have built such a wonderful temple with its 8 impressive columns and steps at the front.

He stood there in complete awe for a while, slowly shuffling forward into the crowd that were listening to his cousin. He was oblivious to everything around him as he examined the building with his eyes, taking it all in. Those columns lining the front of the building, those steps leading up to the front of the building, the roof! It was truly impressive!

Eventually he gathered his thoughts together and made his way over to Boudicca. He listened to the last words of her speech.

"Let me repeat again, this is what we are going to do," she said. "I have spoken with the Trinovantes and have been asked by them, to go straight to St. Albans. I understand their reasons, so we are going to take St. Albans." There was a roar of approval from the crowd. She continued,

"However, I want to make sure that any Romans that may come across the channel in support of their countrymen, are prevented from attacking us from the south and over the bridge at London. So, a number of us will also go to London to burn the bridge over the Thames. Let us go forth my brothers, we are strong together!"

Boudicca stepped down from her chariot looking a little tired. As the crowd dispersed, Dan went over to her, greeted her with a smile and said

"Hello Boo, I see you've had an eventful few days. I think you've started something don't you?"

"We have so much support - people have come from everywhere including the Trinovantes. There must be at least 30,000 of us. It's so good to see everybody. The leaders and I have made plans to attack St. Albans as you may have heard just now.

Where have . . . . ."

Boudicca was interrupted by a shrill scream coming from within the temple - a long agonising scream.

They both looked up at the temple and Dan realised that it had been surrounded by Iceni warriors who had given up trying to get into the building, and were just quietly chanting outside the temple, considering their next move. Dan realised that there were some Romans inside, who had barricaded themselves in.

"They won't open the doors to us," Boudicca said, "mind you, I don't blame them. Some of our warriors are extremely angry and agitated, especially since I told them about how my daughters, and I were raped and beaten at Ixworth. They were in a frenzy earlier. You should have seen them Dan, I don't understand how I have this effect on people."

"Goodness me, it seems so cruel!" said Dan. "They've locked themselves in the temple and if they come out, they could be lynched, whipped and definitely tortured! And what's worse is, they know what's going to happen to them! What a terrible predicament to be in - it's so cruel. These people were not responsible for the way you were treated. I'm not sure how it can be resolved Boo. Surely you can do something?"

"I will sleep on it and perhaps we'll have an answer in the morning," Boudicca replied. "We might be able to coax them out with an offer of some sort of clemency or something. I'll have a word with the leaders in the morning. Tell me Dan, what sort of day have you had?"

## CHAPTER VII

# The Temple Burns

They would not have to wait until morning for the temple issue to be resolved.

Dan returned to his waggons and set up camp for the night, as he could not find anywhere in the town to sleep and he felt better with his sons and Scarr together, sleeping under the waggons. The whole area around Colchester was crowded with Iceni warriors, their chariots, ponies, oxen, horses, waggons and belongings. People were everywhere. The only thing missing was children.

However, he was content with where they had left the waggons. They had pulled them off the road, placed chocks under the wheels, lit a fire and laid the bedding under the waggons. It was quite cosy, all that was missing was their womenfolk.

They were just settling down for the night under their waggon when there were some louder excruciating screams coming from the town centre. Although they were a long way off, there were definitely some women in distress. Dan realised it needed to be investigated. He crawled out from under his waggon and stood up. He guessed the screams were coming from the temple. So, with his two sons, and Scarr, they got up quickly and put-on extra clothes and ran to the town centre. Others around them were doing the same.

On reaching the town square, in front of the temple, Dan saw three figures up on the roof. They had removed a number of tiles and had started a small fire in the upper rafters of the temple. They were shouting down through the hole in the roof at the Romans in the temple below, something like.

"That will get you out of there!"

The people in the temple were obviously aware of what was happening, and the women were screaming. There was a realisation by both those within the temple and those outside, that the building would soon be ablaze, and the occupants would have to come out or burn!

Dan looked around him and there were increasing numbers of people around the building who, like him, had been woken by the noise and were waiting to see the fire take hold. Some were glorifying in the awful situation, others like Dan, showed sympathy towards those in the temple, but there was nothing they could do but watch.

It was not long before Dan saw the front doors of the temple were slowly opening and the occupants were trying to get out. Obstacles had been placed behind the doors to stop anyone entering, but now these obstacles were causing the occupants problems in getting out of the building. One man, the first to come out, was in full armour with helmet, sword and shield. He stood there hesitating, seemingly too confused to understand the situation he was in. A number of warriors came forward and threw their javelins at him. He ducked and moved quickly to avoid being hit by the first few missiles, but the light was bad, and in the darkness, he did not see the javelin being delivered with force from his left-hand side. It hit him in the hip! He went down on his knees in agony as the Iceni warriors looked on, not wanting to close in on him as they saw other Romans coming out of the temple.

Although there were not many steps in front of the temple, Boudicca's men were reluctant to charge, but instead continued to throw their missiles. Some of the missiles were rocks or stones and, together with the occasional javelin or arrow, were quite effective at keeping the Romans close to the temple. Some of the younger men were armed with slings and Dan observed they were remarkably accurate. However, they had to advance beyond the line of their comrades in order to swing their slings and deliver their stinging missiles. Dan suddenly recognised one of these young slingers was Scarr and he called to him to come back. With all the noise going on Scarr did not hear him, but continued to launch his well-aimed stones at the Romans emerging from the temple.

While all this was going on, Dan saw that the temple was billowing smoke and those emerging from the building were now women and children, the men having emerged first. The women were no threat to the Iceni warriors, but they were shown no mercy and the tribesmen now advanced up the steps to attack these women, as they came out of the burning building. Many more people came out of the building, coughing and in distress.

The soldier who first emerged from the temple and had

been hit in the hip, had now been struck a number of times by slinging stones, and was in no way able to defend himself. He was slain by a large warrior, that Dan recognised had come from Ixworth.

No-one could possibly come out of the building now. It was filled with smoke and behind the smoke, flames could be seen further inside. The heat increased and Boudicca's people slowly moved back into the square as the flames took hold. It was a tremendous spectacle to witness and quite a tragedy for the magnificent building.

There had been many people in the building, perhaps as many as 600, but only a few women were left alive, and these were mothers holding babies. Dan realised that the warriors had shown them some mercy, but how badly injured were they? Bad burns or the effects of smoke do not always appear until later, which was something Dan had learned from his own experiences.

Dan looked around him as the building was totally engulfed in flames. There seemed to be many thousands of Iceni and Trinovantes in the square, all looking up at the flames. Cheering had long since died down as everyone looked on, each with a different thought in their mind. As they watched, the roof of the temple collapsed, and a great cloud of sparks and cinders rose in the air to fill the night sky.

Dan and his sons spent a melancholy night attempting to sleep under his waggon. It had been a significant event when the Temple to Claudius burned down and every member of the population of Colchester, Roman or Briton, had either fled, been killed by warriors, or had died in the burning ruins of the temple.

The attack on the Temple had really started something! This was it - a revolt had begun against the Roman Empire and Dan was most concerned about the future, particularly for his cousin Boudicca who he loved and admired. She appeared to be the leader of the revolt and everything depended on her and how she would handle the next few weeks. It was not going to be easy trying to manage a massive assembly of warriors who had never fought together in such numbers before.

They had come from miles around, from many different villages and hamlets, with many different dialects, leaders and ideas. How, would they be controlled? Would they stick together? How would you feed them all? Each one of them was an 'individual'. However, most of them had a common goal and that was to defeat the Romans, and all of them had great faith in their leader, Boudicca!

## CHAPTER VIII

# Boudicca's Meeting

In the morning, Boudicca held a meeting with all the leaders of the Iceni and Trinovantes. Dan sat quietly next to his cousin to show her his support.

"Good morning Boo, how are you?" Dan asked.

"I am well thank you cousin, a little tired and anxious, although I can't let anyone know my worries, can I?" Boudicca whispered in reply.

"No, I don't think you can Boo, but you have many strong followers and many good leaders to ask for guidance and advice," Dan whispered back. "There must be a number with experience in campaigns like this, fighting the Romans. Have you asked them?"

"I've put out a few feelers and I am hopeful . . . . ."

As Dan sat there, he realised he was one of the eldest, and thought perhaps that others looked to him for direction and wisdom. He might be old and even wise with it, but he had very little experience in any form of leadership or fighting, though he was there giving his cousin any advice she asked for. Sadly, his main skills were in woodwork, with a little blacksmithing on the side, which meant he couldn't help much on warfare tactics.

Dan and Boudicca sat in the square on chairs they found in the surrounding buildings, as the dying embers of the temple were still smouldering. Those who were interested in the proceedings stood around listening eagerly to the discussions, in anticipation that there would be further action against the Romans. Boudicca had a great presence, she stood up to address the meeting standing over 6-foot-tall, broad shouldered and with powerful dark eyes.

Those who were not involved in the meeting set about to burying the dead. They were loading the bodies of the Romans who had perished the night before onto waggons, as the meeting went on. Their clothing and possessions had been removed during the night by those who wanted better, especially the footwear.

Boudicca stood on a stone plinth in the centre of the forum and addressed the tribesmen before her.

"So here we are - we have recaptured our city from the Romans and won a wonderful victory! Let's confirm what we are going to do next." Boudicca was nervous and took a breath,

"At a meeting last night, my trusty leaders and I decided that we will go to St. Albans, but must also go to London to protect ourselves from any Roman reinforcements who may come across the channel in support. I know I may be repeating myself, but I wish to make it clear to all of you who are with me – we are going to divide our army. Some of you will go direct to St. Albans, and a smaller army will come with me, to London."

"We must go to St. Albans, the capital of the Catuvellavni

tribe and large Roman town. I have heard much talk from the Trinovantes amongst us, that we must go to St. Albans. They have old scores to settle with the Catuvellavni. Yes, I know there has been a feud between those two tribes for decades." There were a few cheers from the Trinovantes attending the meeting in support of going to St. Albans and some raised their hands wishing to speak in support, but Boudicca was on a roll."

"We will also go to London, as it is of great value to the Romans as a crossing point on the River Thames to the lands of The Cantiaci Tribe in Kent. It is also a significant port, for trade with the lands across the water."

"To re-cap therefore, I suggest that we go to both places. The Trinovantes, with half the Iceni, will go directly to St. Albans, via Great Dunmow and Bishop's Stortford. That is a good road. They will go cautiously, for the Romans will soon know our intentions, and we do not know precisely where they are. As you know, they have spies and informers amongst us, but we are strong in numbers and know the country. I have sent scouts out towards Lincolnshire, others north on the Watling Street and a small party to Andover, so we will be aware of their movements."

Boudicca paused, as she knew all good speakers did. The audience could then digest what she had just said. She continued,

"Meanwhile, I will go on the poor coastal road with a small fast-moving force of Iceni to London, kill the Romans there, burn the bridge over the Thames, and then march north up Watling Street to St. Albans. We can keep in regular contact with each other by messenger every day and coordinate our attack on St. Albans from different directions. That is my plan. Are there any questions?"

"Yes," said Boudicca, pointing to the leader from Diss, who said "It is 60 miles to St. Albans from here. Some of us could get there on our chariots in two days. Our warriors could take four days to walk, but our supply waggons will take 6 or 7. How will we manage our travelling arrangements?"

There were a few grunts and nods from the tribesmen, and Boudicca replied.

"It is good to keep an army fed and watered, so we will move at the speed of the waggons, and send out advance parties on chariots and ponies, to scout ahead near St. Albans. They will soon know we are coming. You cannot keep a large army like ours secret and expect to surprise them in St. Albans. That would be impossible."

"When we reach that destination, we will plan our attack carefully, attempting to keep our casualties to a minimum. I do not want to see our blood spilt in St. Albans. Does that answer your question?"

The leader from Diss nodded and said,

"Thank you, that sounds like a good plan."

A question then came from the other side of the meeting, the woman leader from Bungay. She stood up and tossed her hair back. She was almost as tall as Boudicca, but had a few more bad teeth and a nasty scar on her cheek. She spoke at the same time as someone was raking among the ashes of the temple behind her, causing smouldering embers to flare up.

"Boudicca, do you know how many of us there are?"

"I have asked that question myself and concluded, with the help of friends, that we are between 12,000 and

15,000. However, one reason for moving slowly towards St. Albans is that I am expecting more people to come from the Iceni tribe, and still more Trinovantes warriors, to join our numbers. I have sent out word to many Britons asking for help! We will become one tribe, a tribe of Britons!" (Boudicca thought to herself, "Now there's an inspiring thought!")

Dan stood admiring his cousin addressing the gathering crowd. Her gold torque around her neck, her decorative, elaborately carved spear and the red cloak she wore, set her off fantastically. He was very proud of his cousin. She had come a long way since marrying King Prasutagus.

The crowd had become quiet for a moment, so Boudicca continued,

"The Coritani tribe from Lincolnshire, and the Cantiaci tribe from Kent, will also hear of our revolt against the Romans, and will come to our aid. They have many fine warriors and many of chariots. Our rallying point will be St. Albans. I would not want to be a Roman in St. Albans right now."

The leader from Bungay followed up with a second question.

"How many of us do you think there will be when we get to St. Albans?"

"I am hoping that there will be around 40,000 of us but would like more!" Boudicca announced, "and knowing how large our army is going to be, I hope that will encourage many more to come and swell our numbers!" She paused, and pointing her spear at the sky, shouted,

"Let us go to St. Albans with confidence and enthusiasm!"

"Hooray!" There was a great roar from those attending the meeting and those looking on from the periphery.

## CHAPTER IX

# More Escort Duty

Justus and his 19 cavalrymen colleagues had spent the night in the London barracks. Talking to the locals, Justus discovered that Catus Decianus had ordered 200 legionaries, based here in London, to go to Ixworth to quell any uprising that may result, following the rape of Boudicca's daughters.

Justus and his colleagues concluded, that the boat Catus had taken from Colchester, must have docked here in London, en route to the continent. No one had heard from the legionaries. It was a mystery as to what route they took nor what had happened to them.

The evening of their arrival, they had been drinking wine and water in the inns of London talking about the incident in Ixworth. As with all news, there is often speculation and fear and the desire to find out more of what happened. One poor man, an elderly Roman, originally from Augusta Tieverorum in the Rhineland of Germany, was most worried. He had drunk a little too much and in broken sentences he said,

"I have a daughter. She married a legionary, a retired

legionary. They were granted some land on his retirement in that region and they both live in the Ixworth area. I have four grandchildren out there too. I don't know what to do."

"I would not worry too much; it is early days, and we haven't had much news. They may well have got back to their farmstead and found some protection," replied Justus, comforting the man. He then thought he should continue to talk to the man to take his mind off his worries, so Justus asked for some more wine, then asked,

"What do you do for a living?"

"Thank you for asking, I am a wine trader. I found that London was a good place to work from. It has good links to the continent, where my wine comes from, and I can distribute my goods across the country quite easily from here," the old gentleman said quietly.

"Ah right," said Justus, "and where do you send your wines to, how far away?"

"A lot goes to St. Albans and a fair amount is transported to other towns using the river," the wine trader replied.

They continued the conversation into the early evening. Justus found wine a good subject to talk about. The evening was much less worrying for the old gentleman after they had all had a few more drinks!

Meeting this elderly gentleman brought home to Justus the emergency of the situation and he and his colleagues spent the rest of the evening discussing their worries with those drinking in the inn. One of the subjects they talked about was London. Although it was a small place it was expanding noticeably, especially now that the bridge had been built over the Thames.

The next morning Justus received his orders to escort

17 waggons northwards to St. Albans along Watling Street. It was a mundane task, ensuring supplies were not attacked, but under the circumstances, with the minor revolt in Ixworth potentially escalating, he might see some excitement. If other tribes in the area found out what was happening, they might want to join in as well, increasing the likelihood of the whole Roman army having to quell the uprising. Roman soldiers often escorted supply waggons, as they were frequently subjected to attacks and raids on the goods they were carrying.

He went off to look for the waggons that he had to escort. While he was looking for them his mind wandered. He reflected that he might just be escorting some of the wine belonging to the elderly gentleman he had spoken to the previous night.

It took Justus a little while to find the waggons he was to escort and the man in charge of them. He recognised him as someone he had accompanied on journeys before – his name was Plod.

"How is it going?" Justus asked Plod. He always found the name Plod amusing, but he didn't have to think for very long, why he was called Plod.

"Hello Justus, it's going very well. I was told that it would be you escorting us," Plod replied. "We should be on the road as soon as the legionaries join us. I'm expecting them very soon."

"That's good," Justus said. "I'll get back to my boys and we will catch you up on the road ahead. That won't be too difficult at the speed you go. We are going north, up Watling Street, are we?"

"Oh yes, we are this time," Plod said. "I remember last

time you escorted us, we took a different road, and you spent a day trying to find us!"

Justus left Plod to his preparations for the journey - harnessing up his oxen and loading the waggons and walked off to find his colleagues. On rounding a corner, Justus met 20 marching legionaries, obviously coming to escort the waggons on their journey. They made a wonderful scrunching sound with their hobnail boots on the gravelled ground. Justus found it immensely exhilarating hearing the scrunch of boots, as they marched, all in time with each other. The authority that exuded from 20 marching men was something he always found exciting.

Justus caught the eye of the commanding officer who promptly ordered his troops to stop.

"Company halt!"

"Good morning," Justus said. "It looks like you and I have got the job of escorting the waggons up Watling Street."

"Oh yes, so you're the cavalryman assisting me on our journey, " the officer said.

Justus was taken aback by the use of the words 'assisting me'. He suddenly realised that the officer was senior to him and so he saluted, saying,

"I will assemble my men and meet you, er . . . . soon along Watling Street, Sir"

"Very good," the officer said curtly, "don't be late."

Justus walked off quickly to find his men. Was this going to be an easy assignment, or did it already have the makings of a difficult adventure?

He found his men and was surprised that they had already harnessed up their horses and were nearly ready to move off. They had even prepared his horse and after checking the girth, he mounted and took note that three of his colleagues had new mounts. Every new mount came with potential problems. No-one knew how they would react in response to unusual circumstances, and Justus preferred that his men rode horses they were familiar with.

There was a modern way of protecting horses' hooves and that was to use a hipposandal, a leather shoe that went over the horses' hoof. It was known to give better grip for the horse. However, Justus had not seen many of those in Britain yet. It was a new invention and those in charge in the Roman army had not yet fully endorsed the use of them.

"Right men. Mount up and let's get out of here and onto Watling Street. I have introduced myself to our commanding officer for our journey escorting these waggons, he is a Centurion of the XX Legion. So, be on your best behaviour and pay attention to his orders."

Justus acknowledged, now that he held the rank of Duplicarius, he had to command his men and be assertive with his orders. He could no longer be on friendly terms with them. He was their commanding officer, exerting authority and he believed his men understood that too.

During the journey, there was very little communication between the centurion and Justus. There was no need really, as the centurion soon realised that Justus, with the 19 cavalrymen under his command, was proficient.

Justus had put three men on each wing, some 50 yards to the side of the waggon column on the road. He placed eight men at the head of the column, two rode out at point, almost half a mile ahead, and two rode 200 yards behind the whole waggon train. Therefore, in the event of an ambush, they would be well warned, even if the men out on the extremities were ambushed themselves and were wounded or lost their lives. This was standard Roman military practice when escorting travelling groups.

The centurion in charge of the infantry, dispersed his 20 legionaries in amongst the waggons on the road. It was very easy going for them as the roads were well paved, and the speed was 'oh so slow' with those oxen pulling the ladened waggons.

## CHAPTER X

# Justus meets Paulinus

It was another lovely day in late spring. Speaking to Plod, who was at the head of the column of waggons, Justus asked him,

"We seem to be making good time, are we going to make the usual staging posts at Edgeware for our first night's stop?"

"Eh yes," Plod answered. "I shouldn't think there will be any problems on route, and I do like the Edgware staging post as a place to stop for the night. The old landlord there has some lovely beer. He says he puts a secret ingredient in it, and that's what makes it so tasty."

"The secret ingredient comes from the pond that he uses to make his beer, I have seen it," Justus declared. "I don't think there is anything special about it - he's just lucky with his source – mucky water!"

"I am going to ride on ahead and catch up with my riders in front, at point," Justus said. He liked the idea of keeping in touch with everyone in his command, his new command. He felt he generated more co-operation from them, if he built up a respectable relationship with them.

As he caught up with them, he saw some cavalrymen coming the other way on the road ahead. He immediately tensed up and went on his guard, but he soon realised that they were friendly troops and so encouraged his horse to quicken his pace towards them. On reaching them and talking with them, he understood that they were riding at point for Paulinus and his men. They were all on horseback and coming into view, some 500 yards further up the road. Justus's heart suddenly jumped a few beats and he realised he would soon be speaking with the top Roman in Britain – Legate, Suetonius Paulinus!

Paulinus spoke first as he approached.

"Greetings Duplicarius, where are you from? What are your orders?"

Justus responded, "Duplicarius, Justus Julius Rufus, at your service sir." A Duplicarius was second in command of 30 cavalrymen called a Turma.

Paulinus looked a little startled. He was distracted for a moment, as the name Rufus jogged memories, long forgotten, and he took a few seconds to reply,

"I did not ask who you were, although I am pleased to meet you, Duplicarius Rufus. I asked, where are you from and what are your orders?"

"We are from London, Sir, escorting supply waggons to staging posts at Edgware, St. Albans, Flamstead and Dunstable, Sir. My commanding officer, Centurion . . . . . eh - sorry Sir, I don't know his name - he is with the waggons."

Clearly and precisely Paulinus said, "Gather your men

Duplicarius Rufus and return with me to London. I will inform your centurion of my orders," and he was gone.

Justus did as he was told. With his point riders, he turned and followed Paulinus. As they reached their waggon train, Justus spoke with his cavalrymen and told them to follow him as they were to go back to London with Paulinus. Reaching the Centurion in charge, Justus was about to explain his orders from Paulinus, when the officer said, "Its fine, Duplicarius Rufus, take your men and go with The Legate."

Once altogether, Justus and his men caught up with Paulinus and his accompanying six officers on horseback. He was wondering why Paulinus had only six men with him when one of them came back to join him. Slipping his horse in beside Justus, he said,

"Legate Suetonius Paulinus would like you to join him – now."

Justus's heart was in his mouth again as he prodded his horse and rode forward to join Paulinus.

"Sir, you asked for me?"

"Ah, Duplicarius Rufus, what news from London, and what news have you had of this Iceni revolt?"

Justus looked at Paulinus with enquiring eyes and a frown. He wondered how Paulinus had found out about the Iceni revolt, when he was 250 miles away in North Wales.

Paulinus, sensing Justus' thoughts said, "Have you not heard of pigeon post? I knew of the revolt some four days ago and have been in the saddle since we left Anglesey. I have picked up more news from messages on the way South. However, what do you know of the revolt? Tell me!"

"Were you aware Sir, that King Prasutagus died recently

and Catus Decianus came to negotiate his will, on behalf of Emperor Nero?"

"Yes, I was," Paulinus said.

"Sir, Catus met with Boudicca, The Queen of Iceni."

"Yes, I know Queen Boudicca, I have met her," Paulinus said, "a very strong lady, so what happened next?"

"He, Catus, made demands on her and her daughter's inheritance, from her husband's estate, that she thought were unreasonable and totally unacceptable to her. Catus said that Emperor Nero wanted all of the Iceni lands. When she refused, he ordered her flogged, and demanded that her daughters were raped, Sir."

"Good God man, raped! Sons of Zeus! That can't be so?"

"It was Sir, I was there."

"Why did you not stop it?" Paulinus asked.

"There were senior officers there, Sir," Justus replied quietly.

"That is the reason we have a revolt on our hands. What happened to Catus? I've only met the man once. Did not like him. Nero sent him to collect taxes, inheritance taxes. So, what happened to Catus?"

"We escorted Catus back to Colchester, where he boarded a boat, Sir."

"Sons of Zeus!" so he's gone then?" Paulinus said angrily.

"Yes Sir, he's gone."

"Anything else to report, Duplicarius?"

"Well Sir, the Iceni have joined forces with the Trinovantes, and I've heard a rumour Sir, although I haven't seen it for myself . . . . . . they burned down The Temple to Claudius."

"Burned down the Temple!" Paulinus replied, "Sons of Zeus! Sons of Zeus!"

Paulinus kicked his horse into a canter, saying,

"We must get to London, there are things to do."

On his arrival in London, Paulinus went straight to the military commander.

"Come with me Duplicarius Rufus, you're a big man, I want you behind me. Bring four of your good men."

Going into the office of the local military commander, Justus realised that both men knew each other.

"Welcome Paulinus, Sir, what can I do for you?" the centurion said.

"Centurion Facilis, what preparations have you made for an attack by barbarians, these Iceni barbarians?"

"Yes Sir, I heard of the revolt, and I am strengthening the ramparts, but I only have an understrength half century of men, sir, and four of those are sick. I did have more Sir, but Catus Decianus came, he arrived by boat Sir, and ordered 200 of my men to Colchester, to defend the town and quell the rebellion."

"Ah! Holy Zeus," Paulinus cried out aloud. "Only 200, a valuable 200! What chances have they got against such numbers."

"That's what I thought Sir, but you know the man, he has great authority, you can't argue with the man, there was nothing I could do."

"What a terrible waste of 200 good legionaries, Paulinus ranted. What do you know of our irresponsible friend?"

"Oh, you mean Catus, he got back on the boat, after they picked up some tin and a dozen hunting dogs to take back across the channel, and off they went."

"Well, he's gone. He can't cause us anymore trouble, at least he's in good company with those dogs. Scum of the earth, that man! Right, were we?" Paulinus cursed and then, staring into space thinking, asked,

"When did the 200 men leave?"

"They went yesterday afternoon Sir, early in the afternoon."

"So, if we send an officer with some cavalrymen after them, we might be able to stop them? What, road would they have taken?" Paulinus asked.

"Yes Sir, that would be the road though Brentwood and Chelmsford, Sir," Centurion Facilis said.

Paulinus turned to an officer on his left and said,

"Valerius Caput, take three of the Duplicarius's troopers, go after the 200 legionaries and stop them reaching Colchester. Give them orders to march to Towcester, and take care Valerius . . . . . . . Right, where were we?"

"Are you talking to me Sir? I have commandeered 15 slaves and put them to work on the ramparts with my men." Centurion Facilis was nervous and was expecting a reprimand as a result of all the recent events.

However, Paulinus began thinking about London again and replied,

"We have no way of holding London against these rampaging Iceni, as I understand they have been joined by the Trinovantes. Is that your intelligence too, Centurion Facilis?"

"Yes Sir. I'd heard the day before yesterday, that they'd taken Colchester, and were surrounding the Temple to Claudius. Most of the inhabitants found shelter in the Temple but I fear Sir . . . . . . "

"Yes, man what is it?"

"I fear Sir, I heard yesterday, that the rebels had burnt the temple to the ground and all those inside had been killed. I am afraid Sir, that my wife and daughters, who went to visit relatives in Colchester, were quite likely to have been in the building at the time."

"I am sorry for your possible loss Centurion Facilis. You have my sympathies," Paulinus said quietly.

"But I have no confirmation, Sir."

"We may never know what happened to them. They might still be alive," Justus said, sympathising. He stepped back quickly, realising that it was not his place to talk to officers more senior than him.

Paulinus disregarded the interruption and then gave an order to the centurion.

"Stop work, recall your men from the ramparts, have them pack their kit and march them North, to St. Albans, and await further orders from me there. If I'm not there, at St. Albans, I will leave orders for you on your arrival. Understood Centurion Facilis?"

"Yes Sir," there was some hesitation in his reply.

"Centurion Facilis, you will leave within the hour! I know it will be dark soon, but you will march into the night to our Edgware staging post. There is no time to be lost. Continue your march, first thing in the morning."

"I will stay here tonight and will leave as the sun comes up tomorrow. You will accompany me Duplicarius Rufus. Is everyone clear with their orders? "

Yes, Sir," everyone said in unison.

Before stepping outside, Paulinus hesitated at the door, he looked up to the clouds outside with slightly watery eyes.

Unknown to everyone present, Paulinus had two loved ones in Colchester, and had hidden it from everyone. Like the old wine merchant and Centurion Facilis, he had enormous worries about his relatives, but did not mention it to anyone. That was the sort of man he was.

Paulinus stepped outside Centurion Facilis's office to be confronted by a number of local romanised people, who had become friendly with, and used to, the protection of the Romans. They had been listening at the open door to what had been said.

An elderly gentleman stepped forward and begged,

"Sir, you don't mean to leave us, do you?"

"Unfortunately, I have to. I have less than 60 legionaries here and we are expecting a few thousand rebels coming here from Colchester. I can't possibly hold London."

"But Sir what do you expect us to do?"

"I'm very sorry, very sorry indeed, but I strongly suggest you make your way to friends and family, possibly to the south of here. The Iceni are coming from the North. Good Luck!"

"But Sir . . . . . ."

Paulinus Suetonius did not hear, he was away, off to find the Roman administrators of London, warning them to be ready in the morning to depart. London was being abandoned. Paulinus was followed by Justus and Centurion Facilis, all of them were in a hurry.

The next morning, Justus got his men up and out of their beds early. They ate breakfast, packed their belongings. His men fed extra oats to their horses and were ready to go before the sun came up. Justus also had the foresight to order his men to rope up and bring the remaining horses with them from the London staging post. There would be none left for Boudicca's Iceni.

Paulinus did not disappoint with his punctuality. He was ready to depart London, as the skies brightened. He, and his now larger entourage of 15 officers and administrators, mounted up on their horses. Justus and his men were readying themselves to tag on behind.

As they were about to leave, they were surrounded by a number of the London inhabitants pleading with them to stay and protect them. Paulinus kicked his horse saying,

"I'm sorry everyone, but I must go, can I suggest you do the same."

## CHAPTER XI

# Dan's Road to London

After the meeting held in the square, outside the remains of the burning Temple to Claudius in Colchester, Boudicca asked her cousin Dan for a quiet word.

"Dan," she said, "You, as my eldest cousin, have over the years, given me plenty of good advice and guidance. The best piece of advice you ever gave me was to marry Prasutagus, bless him."

"Wow! . . . . I can't remember giving you that piece of advice Boo, thank you, I hadn't realised. Wow . . . . . "

"I would like you to come to London with me. You have a wise head on your shoulders, and I think we would all benefit from you being by my side."

"But what about my waggons and my sons?" Dan said, with concern.

"Don't you worry about your waggons Dan; I've already seen to those. Do you remember our cousin Cartimandua, Cart as you call her? Have you not seen her here, on the march?" Boudicca said.

"Oh Cart, yeah I know Cart very well, I have not seen her for maybe three or four years," replied Dan.

"Well, she is going to take your waggons to St. Albans for you - I've arranged it," answered Boudicca.

"Well thank you Boo; I would like to see London. I have not been there since the magnificent bridge was built. There was not much going on there before the bridge, and now I hear it's a good trading port with many warehouses," Dan said.

"I've heard similar things, but it's still only a small place. However, the town is more important now that the Romans have built the bridge over the Thames there," Boudicca replied.

"And that's why I need you there with me, as some have advised me to destroy the bridge and I would like your views on that please Dan."

Dan thought for a while and then said, "If we destroy the bridge, the Romans will have to go a long way up the Thames to the next crossing point. On the flipside, if we destroy the bridge, we can't go and see our friends the Cantiaci in Kent very easily. We would have to go by boat."

"I only did the boat journey once," Dan continued. "I went to my brother's wedding 20 or 22 years ago, to a lovely lady - somewhere in North Kent. That's before the Romans came. I have not seen him since."

"Getting back to the job in hand, let's set off in the morning with chariots and horsemen. We need to get to London quickly before it is defended, I don't want them to be ready for us," said Boudicca.

"You can ride with me in my chariot."

Dan quickly replied, "but what about your daughters, they have been riding with you up to now have they not?"

"I have sent them back home, they are too young. Had they been three or four years older, I would have welcomed them along, for they are feisty young girls and are keen to have vengeance for what the Romans did to them. But we are at war now and their place is at home. So, there is room on the chariot for you. What do you say Dan?"

"Thank you Boo, that would be an honour. I do hope my knees can cope with the rough roads."

"You'll be fine Dan. My chariot has very good suspension, and if you're really suffering, you can sit on the floor, or we might even find a pony for you."

"Thanks Boo, where will I find you, and what time are we leaving?"

The next morning, Boudicca set off for London with half the army. They left behind, in Colchester, the tribesmen and waggons, who moved much more slowly. They would have to make their own way to St. Albans via Great Dunmow and Bishop's Stortford, but they would first wait for more Trinovantes to join them. It was agreed that they would rendezvous with Boudicca on the outskirts of the town, just south of St. Albans, prior to attacking it.

Boudicca led the way in her chariot. She wanted to get to London for the morning of the third day. She realised that time was important, because the Romans would now be aware of what had happened in Colchester and would be on their guard.

They had been on the road just a short time and all was going well. Dan, riding on Boudicca's chariot, looked back at the column behind, to estimate the number of chariots and horsemen she had brought along with her. Dan counted at least 50 Chariots, possibly 65, but could not count the tribesmen on horseback. There were quite possibly over 2,000.

"I see you are feasting your eyes on the people we have with us," said Boudicca.

"Yes, it is amazing Boo, where they have all come from. They all seem very keen, but they will all need to be fed and so will the horses."

"I think most of them arrived while we were at Colchester. We were there for two or three days and word must have got around," Boudicca replied. Before continuing, she paused as she negotiated her chariot over some difficult ground. "We are making a mess of the ground here. I hope everyone gets through alright. It's going to be badly poached by the time everyone gets through."

"Have you taken a head count, Boo?" asked Dan.

"I asked one of the girls, who is very good with numbers, to estimate how many we had here with us. She reckoned about 2,300 on horseback and had counted our chariots at 63."

"That's fantastic," Dan said. "I've never seen so many. Oh, and while I remember, did you bring along any one from the Trinovante tribe? We are in their territory and they may not be pleased to see us if they are not aware of our common objective against the Romans."

"Yes, I had already thought about that Dan, thanks. They're over there look, those 10 to 12 horsemen there, mostly dressed in a mucky tartan orange colour."

They continued chatting as they rode towards London, and the subject of the Roman army came up again.

"Dan, do you know how many legionaries Rome has in Britannia? Those who have witnessed legionnaires marching on the roads of Britain have been astounded by the numbers."

Dan then told Boudicca a story.

"There was this family making an ox tail stew for their evening meal. It took a Roman army longer to march past their roundhouse than it took them to make, cook and eat the stew."

"Goodness me," Boudicca said, "that's a lot of Romans."

Dan continued, "and what's more, there were no waggons in this long procession, they were just men. They had mules that carried the heavy stuff like the tents. The soldiers carried their own kit and I understand it can be quite heavy. It is said they can travel 18 to 20 miles a day, but I'm not sure of the true facts. I don't know of anyone in the Iceni tribe who has studied it."

It was lunchtime when they got to Kelvedon, where they had to cross a river. Here the Romans had been building a bridge, but knowing the Iceni were coming, they were now nowhere to be seen. They had abandoned the bridge building and gone.

The crossing was a little difficult, as they had to use the ford and part of the old bridge. It was particularly challenging for the chariots. They had to step down from the chariot and do a little heaving and carrying, but they managed to cross. It did, however, take them some time. No one in the chariots escaped with dry feet and most remarked about how cold the water was. Dan was distressed to have cold, wet feet as he continued in the chariot with Boudicca.

He should have brought with him a change of footwear as some of the others had done.

There was another river crossing at Hatfield Peverel that the horsemen of Boudicca's party used. This was not as difficult to cross as the one at Kelvedon. However, even this alternative crossing caused some delay to horsemen. The whole route was not easy to travel along. It was not a good Roman road like the one the other half of the army were taking, through Bishop Stortford and onto the village of Welwyn.

The whole party spent the night a few miles the other side of Brentwood, in the middle of the countryside, where they could graze their ponies. It was a lovely meadow next to a wood and a babbling brook, where they could make shelters and have their campfires.

That evening, a number of local tribesmen joined them around Boudicca's campfire. She asked them how far it was to go to London and if the Romans were there. The tribesmen had heard that the Romans had deserted the place and the town was empty.

It was a dry, cool night and Boudicca allowed Dan to snuggle up to her to sleep and keep warm.

## CHAPTER XII

# Boudicca Arrives in London

The next morning, they advanced on London on a war footing, with everyone either on a horse or in a chariot. The men had spiked their hair and painted their faces blue and yellow. It made them feel good and collective in their purpose. They had swelled in numbers, as a few more had joined them en route the previous evening. Word of the revolt must have been getting around to many people and if this was the case, the Romans would also know about it. There must be at least 2,600 on horseback and maybe as many as 70 chariots now.

Boudicca had sent out scouts ahead. Most military tacticians understand that this is good practice. It is a good idea not to have your whole army ambushed, but instead, just sacrifice a few scouts sent out ahead, to warn the main body coming on behind. As they approached London, Dan and Boudicca could see the smoke coming from the domestic buildings. Shortly, half a dozen scouts returned, saying that London was deserted save for escaped slaves and a few old folks who weren't really too keen on leaving.

There was not much substance to London. It was a small port, strung out alongside the Thames. There were a number of buildings used for storage, stables, enclosures for oxen, a few commercial buildings, a number of roundhouses and small rectangular Roman buildings.

The one striking feature of London was the bridge over the Thames. Dan had never seen such a magnificent construction. He had seen the Temple to Claudius at Colchester and was absolutely impressed with that, but the bridge was different. It had architecture but it also had defiance against a great river. He had seen the river Thames before, further upstream, but here it was tidal and had a great width to it. The Romans were certainly very skilful and impressive engineers. Being a man who worked in wood himself, Dan looked in awe at the great supporting tree trunks descending into the soft riverbed.

There were not many people about, just the odd slave or two, looking a bit lost and perhaps wanting some attention, but not really knowing what to do.

"This is what I need your advice about Dan," Boudicca said, as they crossed the bridge. "Do I burn it?"

"What, this lovely construction! But it's fantastic and it gets us across the river," Dan remarked, as the wheels of Boudicca's three horse chariot made a wonderful rumbling noise across the bridge. The river was in full flow below them, and Dan was truly impressed by the construction skills of those who had built the bridge.

"We are at war, Dan. At war with the Roman war machine. If we head inland up to St. Albans and beyond, this bridge will help any Roman reinforcements coming from the continent. Reinforcements will come through Kent, the Kingdom of the Cantiaci, and will want to cross here, and will advance on our rear-guard as we travel North."

"I understand Boo," Dan said. "I was in total agreement with you before I saw the bridge. You may well want to destroy the bridge to stop any reinforcements coming up behind us, but if we win against the Romans, this bridge will serve us greatly and would help us get reinforcements from the other tribes in this area, or to travel south to attack any Roman landings on the south coast."

"Wow! I hadn't thought of that Dan, you're thinking a long way ahead, and perhaps beyond normal thinking." Dan took the compliment quietly and replied,

"There are always two or more sides to any proposal, it's always worth thinking of all the possibilities."

They reached the far side of the Thames, turned the chariot around and look back across the river to London, watching the rest of the chariots cross. They stopped in a lovely grassy meadow by the river. The birds were singing, and it was a wonderful day. As the remaining chariots joined them, they both descended to the ground, tied the horses up to a small sapling of an oak tree, and sat on the grass overlooking the Thames.

Dan noticed how his cousin sat down gently to protect her back. It must still be sore from the thrashing she got in Ixworth recently, he thought. The grass was just dry enough to sit on, without getting a wet bottom. They both sat quietly, not speaking, as they both knew the other wished to think. Dan ran his finger over the deep scar on his forehead, musing. What was the best thing to do? What had they let themselves in for? Was it the right time to revolt? Could they just go home? What was the best way forward? Did they really want the responsibility of all these decisions?

"Perhaps the best thing to do, Boo, is to go and find some beer, some good, tasty beer, and discuss it at length with the leaders of the tribes," Dan suggested.

"Good idea Dan - let's do that!" Boudicca said aloud. They both climbed back onto the chariot and Boudicca cracked her whip encouraging her horses over the bridge back into London.

## CHAPTER XIII

# News of the Massacre Arrives

There was plenty of shelter from the overnight rain for Boudicca's small army of horsemen and charioteers to spend the night in the small trading port of London, on the banks of the Thames. The place had been nearly deserted, because the inhabitants had fled before she arrived. Only a few slaves and the old and infirm remained and they made Boudicca's army most welcome.

Most woke the next morning with thick heads from a night of drinking. They realised they did not have to hurry to leave to get to St. Albans because the other, more significant part of the army, with all the waggons and infantry, would be slow moving through Bishop's Stortford and Welwyn. The rendezvous at St. Albans with the waggons, pack horses and supplies was planned for at least four days' time hence.

Boudicca held a meeting with her tribes' leaders in one of the large warehouses of London at midday, which was quickly over, because many of the participants wanted to continue with their pillaging and the collecting of valuables from the warehouses. It was agreed that they should burn the bridge over the Thames, so that any Romans coming from Kent would have to go the long way around and cross the Thames, much further upstream. However, this would have to be delayed, because a number of tribesmen had crossed the river to see Cantiaci friends and relatives they had to the south side of London.

Scouts were sent to find them and tell them about what was going to happen to the bridge. They would have to hurry back so they could cross with their horses and chariots before the bridge was burned. Since the arrival of the Romans, 17 years before, and the building of the bridge soon after their arrival, many intermarriages had occurred between the Trinovantes and the Cantiaci tribes. Many of the Cantiaci were Belgae who had come to Kent from Belgium and Dan felt it was interesting to see the mixing of language and cultures in the children of these intermarriages.

The other reason for not burning the bridge too soon was that many tribesmen from the Cantiaci wished to join Boudicca and the revolt against the Romans. They began streaming across the bridge during the afternoon, after the meeting which had agreed the way forward. The word from those crossing the bridge was that many more supporters were to follow, and please could Boudicca wait for them? It had occurred to Dan, that many of the Cantiaci had been joining them on their route from Colchester.

After the main meeting, Boudicca took Dan aside with three other leaders for a good chat about the plan ahead. She started by saying,

"There is a lot of booty here in London and we would

be foolish to leave it here when we need it ourselves to feed this growing army of ours. I have begun to realise how complex the organisation of this whole adventure is, and I would like you four to take command of the logistics. Is that okay with you?"

There was nodding and agreement amongst them, and Dan noted that Boudicca had, knowing their skills, chosen an old friend of his and two women leaders for this task. She was one smart cookie was Boo! Dan then said,

"What we should do then, is assemble another waggon train here in London, if we can find the oxen and carts, and send them ahead towards St. Albans. That way it won't hold up the rest of the chariots and those who are on horseback. Alternatively, the new waggon train can stay behind, waiting for the Cantiaci to come over the bridge, before we burn it."

"Good idea Dan," Boudicca said. Dan felt chuffed with himself, as he became aware that he was enjoying the role of advisor to his cousin.

It was then that a messenger arrived. He had been sent by Garos of Swaffham. As the messenger was readying himself with his report at the entrance to the warehouse, Boudicca briefed those around her.

"I sent Garos to ambush the Romans coming down from Lincolnshire, I do hope he has good news."

The man approached. He had arrived hot and sweaty and a little worn out, as all messengers normally do. Boudicca spoke first and asked a question.

"What news do you have, from Garos?"

"My Queen, I have great news," the messenger said, as if he'd been practising it for half his journey. "We have massacred the Romans in the woods of Sawtry, north of

Godmanchester." There was a great roar from the assembled people in the warehouse.

"Yes," Boudicca asked eagerly, "what happened?"

"We sent out scouts, who were undetected by the Romans. We knew the route they were taking and Garos, knowing the area very well, prepared a site in the woods of Sawtry, for the ambush. He made sure no one trod on or disturbed the ground in and around the area of the ambush, for he knew Romans looked for trodden down foliage when on the march through woods. Garos was very clever. We all took up our positions, some way away from the road through the woods. We chopped away at two trees on opposite sides of the track. This was done so that we could fell them quickly onto the road at the front of the column of Roman soldiers. On the word of Garos, the trees were felled, and they crashed across the road, to stop the column of men in their tracks."

"Yes! Yes, I know that" Boudicca said. "Hurry, tell us what happened."

"Garos ordered us to use missiles against the Romans before we closed in on them from both sides. We had a number of slingers who were told to hit the mules and horses on the rump, and this caused great confusion and disorder amongst the Romans. Slingers can be very accurate as you know, Mam."

"Yes, yes I know. Carry on, what happened next?" Boudicca shouted, frustrated by the messenger's unnecessary elaborations.

The messenger continued,

"Ah yes, those of us who had no slings threw stones, quite big stones they were, and they caused a lot of casualties.

The Romans were in a bit of a mess, officers were trying to shout orders above the screaming, the soldiers were dropping their equipment, you know all that stuff they carry. There must have been 2,200 of them. Their pack mules were uncontrollable and were running off. They were trying to get the leather covers off their shields, I don't know why, as they work perfectly well with the covers on."

Boudicca glared at the man and spoke.

"Yes, please continue."

"When they were in total disorder, nursing their wounds and trying to form up, we descended upon them. Well, that was as I saw it on my section of the fighting. Others may have different stories, as it was a long column of Romans. They didn't stand a chance and we suffered only 18 casualties dead. That was tragic though, some of them were my friends and one of them was a good drinking mate." He was quiet for a moment, reflecting on his mate, and then he continued,

"We killed all but a few officers. Garos told us to save them for his interrogation work."

Some of those listening, squirmed.

"What information did Garos extract from them? Wish I had been there," an Iceni woman said with interest.

"I do not know, I left soon after to bring the news to you," he replied.

There were many more questions everyone wanted to ask the messenger and he stayed talking to all the interested parties. Afterwards, there were great celebrations, which obviously involved more beer and the resultant sleep.

Later that afternoon, many Cantiaci tribesmen came hurriedly into London from the south, over the condemned bridge. They were fearful that it was going to be destroyed very soon, as this was now common knowledge. As they crossed the bridge, they joined the throng of tribesmen on the banks of the Thames.

Everyone was seeking more information on the battle that had occurred in the woods of Sawtry. As more and more riders, who had been at the battle, came to join those already there, many more aspects of the same story were told, each one embellished in different ways.

## CHAPTER XIV

# JUSTUS LEAVES LONDON FOR ST. ALBANS

Paulinus was in a hurry to get to St. Albans, and this caused Justus to worry. He was concerned that there would not be enough horses at the Edgware staging post for everyone in the party. They would all need fresh horses, and there might only be a dozen at Edgware. He had taken seven extra horses from the London staging post, but this would not be enough for everyone.

Was this really his concern, Justus asked himself. There was a revolt happening at this very moment and it wasn't clear where the rioters were. Perhaps the Iceni mob might well have become an army by now. A formidable army! This was all an unknown and the unknown can be frightening, more frightening than knowing what you are up against. Where might this army be right now? If it was in Colchester four to five days ago, where could it be now? Might it be coming west, towards St. Albans, because logically that is the next big Roman town. Perhaps they were in luck, and having razed Colchester to the ground, the Iceni rebels might have dispersed and gone back home and Paulinus was worrying about nothing.

Justus knew that there are many things for a military commander to think about and Paulinus, riding out in front of this column of 31 riders, was considering all the possible scenarios in his mind. Best thing to do, Justus thought, was to keep quiet and not give Paulinus any unnecessary worries, just be there to support him. After all he, Justus, was one of the more senior Romans in the column.

If you are the worrying kind, there is always something to worry about, and the next concern for Justus was happening now. He had noted that two of the administrators from London, were not the most competent of riders. They had spent much of their lives sitting at a desk. It appeared that it had been some time since they had ridden. This was obvious looking at their style of riding. The pace was certainly not at the gallop, but there was the occasional canter, and Justus had concerns for these two administrators. They were also the rotund version of the human race and this was adding to their difficulties. It wasn't something that should really concern Justus, so he changed his pattern of thought.

They would arrive at Edgware soon, where they could change their horses and have a light meal of herbs and oats, washed down with a jug of ale - that wonderful ale they served in The Boot Inn at Edgware. Here the water to make the beer was taken from the pond out the back. It was always good to have something to look forward to, even if it was only a jug or two of ale in The Boot.

On reaching The Boot Inn, Paulinus was greeted by the Inn Keeper.

"Good morning Sir, it's good to see you again."

"Yes, greetings. We need new replacement horses quickly. How many have you got?" Paulinus demanded.

"Eh, a dozen maybe 14 . . . . . . I think, I will have to check with the Hostler." The manager responded.

"We'll take them, get people to change the saddles. Now!"

"Yes Sir."

"Duplicarius Rufus," called Paulinus.

"Yes, Sir," answered Justus. He still couldn't get used to being called 'Duplicarius.'

"As there are not enough fresh horses for all of us, some of us will have to continue on our tired horses. Do some maths for me please. I'm going to leave four of my men behind, so work out how many of your men will have to follow-on later. Tell them sorry, but they will have to use the tired horses to continue onto St. Albans. We will need to use these fresh ones to get there sooner. Wish them good luck from me."

Justus quickly replied,

"That's eight troopers and me to come with you, Sir."

"Very good Duplicarius," Paulinus said, noting Justus' quick response. "Get your men fed quickly and we'll be on our way."

Paulinus went off to find the manager of the Inn, and between mouthfuls of food, told him about the situation and advised him to pack up his things and get the hell out of the area. The manager had already heard the rumours himself, from passing travellers, and also wanted to leave as soon as possible. Justus, who had been listening to the conversation wondered what would happen to all that lovely beer the manager had in the cellar.

Justus instructed a competent colleague to take

command of those left behind, telling him to take it easy on the tired horses, and then continued,

"It might be an idea to block the road and hold up the rebels that may be coming from London." The trooper nodded, saying,

"Leave it with me, Sir."

Justus smiled and said,

"Hopefully I'll see you in St. Albans."

The Boot Inn's hosteller led out a fresh mount for Justus, a lovely black horse. Most of the horses used by the Roman forces were brought over to Britain from Tuscany. They proved very hardy in the dismal climate, being squat and strong but sometimes skittish. Justus

checked the saddle rug and girth then jumped onto his new horse, ready to begin the rest of the day's trek.

The first part of their journey took them up a steeper road than they were used to, through great wooded areas, and although the road builders had chopped the trees back for a good 50 paces on each side of the road, new foliage had already begun to grow. The usual ditch had been dug alongside the road to help protect travellers on the road from ambush, but this was of little comfort. Justus still felt vulnerable from attack and wondered where those Iceni barbarians might be? Had they made it over here from Colchester already? They were probably 60 miles away, but could they be here already lying in wait for Justus and his men?

His mind then started to wander again and he began to ask why they called these people barbarians. He was told that it was a derivative of the sound they made when they spoke, something like – bar ba babar - bar, hence 'Barbarians.' He supposed that their babbling made perfect sense to them, but to Romans, it sounded gibberish, barbarian like!

The woods they were travelling through were certainly spooky, and as all the new growth was now in full foliage, it could potentially, conceal half an army. He should not feel frightened and apprehensive like this. He was clothed in armour, he had a good strong helmet on his head, a large oval shield, a fantastic four horned saddle and he hoped, a good horse! He was also well trained, something the Roman army prided itself on.

He remembered his training as a foot soldier. They would wear double the weight of armour and carry a much heavier shield whilst exercising, something he found quite hellish. This brought huge benefits in battle though, as their normal armour felt as light as a feather and they were much more agile in combat, when it really counted.

He spoke sternly to himself – I should not feel vulnerable and anxious, he was a Roman soldier. But actually, he did feel frightened, there was no getting away from it.

The next village they went through was Radlett, a place full of clay pits and pottery kilns. His fellow Romans had certainly made good use of the local resources here. Thinking about his favourite subject, he wondered whether they made good beer drinking jugs in these kilns.

Another reason that Justus remembered Radlett so fondly, was down to the very attractive young lady he saw here about a year ago now. She had beautiful dark eyes and had looked up at him as he rode past. They had gazed at each other for what seemed ages, although it was probably only about 3 seconds. She had such lovely eyes, and he noticed the way she carried herself too. So very attractive - there was something about her - something special. Justus wondered if he might see her again as they rode through. He found it strange how these moments remained in his memory.

His thoughts went back to the Iceni revolt. How he cursed that man, Catus Decianus, who had initiated the whole thing in the first place. He had treated Boudicca and her daughters so badly, and then had just left the country. He had gone, leaving his fellow countrymen here in Britain to resolve the mess, and was probably halfway home by now. Justus hoped the hunting dogs on the boat had escaped and torn him to pieces. How he cursed Catus Decianus.

His thoughts were interrupted by the riders in front, encouraging their horses to trot for a while. Paulinus was in a hurry to get to St. Albans.

## CHAPTER XV
# Boudicca Leaves London

Boudicca was not in a hurry to leave London. The reasons were many. There was plenty of good grazing here for the horses, food (and wine) for her army and shelter in the warehouses from any unpleasant spring weather. There was also a constant stream of Cantiaci tribesmen and women arriving from Kent, reinforcing her army. They were coming over the lovely Roman bridge that her cousin Dan appreciated so much. She would have to burn the bridge soon and take her army north to St. Albans.

It was mid-morning. Dan and Boudicca were having a chat about things when she said,

"I've learned from a couple of locals that the senior Roman in Britain, the big man himself, was here, only the other day. He had come down from North Wales to see for himself what we've been up to! I didn't realise, how important we were," she laughed.

"I wonder how much he knows, and what he's going to do about it," Dan mused.

"I heard he didn't have many men with him. I wonder if

he's bumped into anybody we know and got himself killed! Boudicca grinned, showing all her white teeth.

"That would be a bit of luck if he had," Dan said.

※

It was lunchtime, and Dan was thinking about food and discussing the weather with his good mate Nomass. More importantly, they were considering Boudicca's quandary as to when to move on to St. Albans. Dan was also thinking about his sons and Scarr. He wondered how they were getting on with his two waggons, and whether Cartimandua was looking after them. They were taking the shorter route westward from Colchester, through Great Dunmow and Bishop's Stortford.

Dan was looking forward to meeting up with his sons again in St. Albans. When they were altogether again, as one army, they would attack and take the town back from the Romans. That was Boudicca's plan. He envisaged the city would be destroyed by the enthusiastic followers in her army, as it was not easy to control their exuberance.

Everyone knew how keen the Trinovantes were to settle an age-old feud and, to put it bluntly, 'go and smash the Catuvellavni' whose Capital was St. Albans. The Trinovantes felt that the Catuvellavni were co-operating far too much with the Romans, and they wanted to teach them a lesson.

Just then, as Dan and Nomass were considering lunch, a messenger arrived from the other half of the army, the infantrymen who were travelling with the waggons straight to St. Albans.

He dismounted from his horse and without tying it up, caught Dan's eye saying,

"Where will I find Boudicca?"

Dan pointed to the entrance of the warehouse to his right, and the messenger went straight inside quickly followed by Dan and Nomass. Dan was a little worried about the horse that had been left outside, untied, but he was in a hurry to find out what the messenger had to say to his cousin.

Boudicca was immediately aware of the messenger's entrance. She stopped her conversation with a couple of the women leaders and turned to face the new arrival. The messenger was a stout, red faced, redheaded man. He spoke to Boudicca through his thick ginger beard and moustache.

"Mam, Garos has sent me with a message."

'Ah Garos, the man who thrashed the Romans in Sawtry Woods," Boudicca said. She noted with some disgust, the messenger's very bad teeth.

"Yes Mam," the messenger said respectfully.

Boudicca wanted to tell the man that he need not be so courteous by using the word 'mam', but she was half enjoying it. She also wanted him to get to the nitty gritty of what he had to say, so ignored it. She spoke firmly to the messenger,

"I thought Garos was still in Sawtry Woods. How did he get down from Sawtry Woods to you with the infantry and wagons, so quickly?"

"Oh Mam. After the battle, he left his troops to make their own way south, while he rode on ahead with a small party of warriors. He found us quite easily. It's amazing how much attention you attract when you're moving 30,000 people across the countryside."

"Now I understand," Boudicca said, "what is your message."

"Mam, Garos sent me with the message that they, the Trinovantes, are going to attack St. Albans tomorrow." He looked up into the roof of the warehouse thinking. Yes tomorrow, I was not sure what day I meant.

"Are you sure?"

"Yes, I left Garos with the advanced army closing in on Bishop's Stortford," the messenger said.

"The advanced army," Boudicca asked inquisitively, "what do you mean."

"Yes, the leaders thought it best to press on with the warriors, leaving the waggons to move at their own pace. Those on foot might walk 12 to 15 miles a day. They'll be ready to . . . . ."

"What the hell do they think they're doing!" Interrupted Boudicca, "I left instructions to walk with the waggons. That way the waggons will be protected. The warriors will be not be tired and they will have supplies on route, carried in the waggons."

Boudicca was getting very cross and everyone shuffled back a little. It was not good to be around Boudicca when she was angry.

"Sorry Mam, I'm just the messenger, I just . . . . . ."

Three men came into the warehouse in a hurry. The messenger looked round and everyone could see that he knew them, as his eyes lit up.

"Ah you found me then," the messenger said. "These are my friends who helped me carry the message. Garos thought that it would be better if four of us came, just in case we ran into some trouble on route. As it happened, we did run into a little trouble."

"Oh, what was that?" Boudicca asked.

"We were going through Edmonton and my friend said there may be some Romans garrisoned here. So, after having a think about how to proceed, we decided to draw straws. The loser would go in unarmed and investigate. Being unarmed, we hoped he would not be suspected as being part of the Iceni army. I drew the short straw Mam, so I went into the village to investigate. Striking up a conversation with some locals, I found out that the Romans had only just left, coming towards London – here."

"How many Romans," asked one of the women leaders to the left of Boudicca.

"Eight," the messenger replied, "and they left with two mules carrying their equipment."

"One extra mule then, they normally only have one mule for 8 legionaries," Nomass interrupted.

"What did you do after that?" Boudicca asked.

"We knew we had to get to London to give you the message, so we followed on behind the Romans, as we knew they were on the road ahead of us. We asked people along the way, to confirm they were in front of us. However, as we progressed along the route, eventually, when we asked, nobody had seen them. We reckoned they had turned off somewhere perhaps, into the woods. We are not really sure as we never actually saw them." His three friends who had just arrived, nodded in agreement, as he told the story.

Boudicca calmed down a little after her rant. She was resigned to Garos attacking St. Albans tomorrow, as she could not do anything to stop it, but asked,

"Why did they not wait for us? That was what I told him to do," Boudicca asked.

The messenger replied,

"Many of the people in Garos' army who will be attacking St. Albans tomorrow, are Trinovantes. They are very keen, almost in a frenzy you could say, to attack the Catuvelavni of St. Albans. This tribe consists largely of people from Belgae, and as you know, they are hated by the Trinovantes."

Dan whispered in Nomass' ear,

"You must have heard how the Belgae arrived from Belgium 150 years ago and took lands in the Chilterns and settled around St. Albans. They call themselves 'Catuvellavni' and they have never been liked as a people. There is a constant feud between the Catuvellavni and the Trinovantes, and the Trinovantes come off worse, most of the time. They are only getting their own back in attacking St. Albans." Nomass nodded.

"We leave for St. Albans in the morning, bright and early," Boudicca announced. "Find some olive oil in these warehouses somewhere, I have seen some. Pour it on the bridge tonight so it can soak into the timbers. We burn it before we leave!"

※

Someone young and irresponsible, who was far too keen to see the bridge burn, set fire to it in the early hours. Nearly everyone in Boudicca's army who were still sleeping, were woken by the sound of the blaze and came out of the warehouses to watch. The olive oil was certainly helping the bridge burn, Dan thought, as he looked upon the scene with mixed feelings. It had been a wonderful bridge and would have lasted hundreds of years but alas, he understood the reasons for burning it.

They were having breakfast and preparing to leave, as the last of the structural members of the bridge dropped into the Thames with hissing sounds and smoke, as the embers were extinguished. They left shortly afterwards with a much larger army, now that new people had joined with Boudicca's army from the Cantiaci (Kent) tribe and more Trinovantes (Essex). Many of them might have just come on this adventure for the experience and excitement. There was no getting away from it, it was exciting!

Dan noticed that there were a number of families who had come along, and although the man of the family was possibly the warrior, he had brought his family with him. In two instances, he saw someone who must be the old grandma, sitting up on her wagon. He then reflected on himself at his age of 53. He was no longer of a fighting age and would be unable to help, should there be any action on the road ahead.

The army was now loaded up with the booty they had taken from the warehouses. Wine, flour, dried peas, timber, salt, wool, hides and leather were just a few things Dan had seen piled into the waggons. Some of the stolen goods were not properly protected from the weather, and although it was not raining at the moment, it would be a waste to see it get wet and consequently lost, but there were too many waggons to warn everyone of potential disasters.

Wine, in those days, was usually stored in something called an amphora. It was a vase shaped vessel with a pointed bottom, two handles and a stopper. Dan and every other lover of wine, were concerned about the way some of the amphora, carrying the wine, were loaded on to the waggons. The road would be bumpy, and it would be a shame to see good wine go to waste through a cracked vessel.

❧

Dan rode on Boudicca's chariot, having helped harness up the two ponies. The early morning sun on their backs was very welcoming. Boudicca led the stream of chariots up the Edgware Road and on towards St. Albans, 20 miles away.

"We should be there by this evening," Dan said.

"Yes. I reckon we will," replied Boudicca. "I'm not waiting for our supply waggons though, I want to get to St. Albans sooner, rather than later. Garos is probably attacking St. Albans right now."

"They must have marched across from Colchester pretty quickly to attack the place this morning?" Dan suggested.

"I do hope Garos has been successful. He should have waited for us to come up and to help him as we planned. I don't want to see good Iceni lives lost needlessly," Boudicca said.

"He made a good job of wiping out those Romans in Sawtry Woods, didn't he? Mind you," Dan continued, "at Sawtry Woods he had his own men, and his own followers. Here in St. Albans, there may be some confusion with tribesmen who are not familiar with the way he works."

It was early afternoon when Boudicca and Dan were approaching Edgware. The scouts Boudicca had sent ahead were coming back towards them. Something appeared to be wrong, so Boudicca stopped her chariot to speak to them.

"What is it?" Boudicca asked.

"The road is blocked, just before the Edgware staging post. There's a couple of fallen trees and some rubble in the road. We didn't want to go any closer in case we were ambushed, but we didn't see anybody."

"What do you suggest we do, Dan," Boudicca asked, minded that this was the first tactical military decision she would be making.

"We need to get through Boo," Dan said. "We have no idea how many possible attackers there might be – there could be quite a number?"

"What do you think we should do then?" Boudicca asked.

"Could I suggest that you send a dozen men forward to investigate?" Dan then added, "it might be best to assemble some more men to be held in reserve, just in case they are needed, and pass the word down the column for everyone to keep their eyes peeled for anyone hiding in the woods."

A dozen men and three women dismounted and cautiously went forward. A couple of extra men went down each side of the road close to the edge of the woods.

Dan stood on a fallen tree trunk at the side of the road to give him an elevated look at what was happening. There appeared to be much nervous discussion amongst those who had gone ahead, they were crouched low and moved slowly. They were obviously aware that there could be some Romans close by.

When Dan thought that the advanced party were confident that they was no danger, he asked for help to remove the blockage. In no time it was cleared, and they waved Boudicca through. By the time everyone had remounted their horses and got on their chariots at least 2 hours had passed, and it was late afternoon.

"I don't believe it Dan," Boudicca grumbled. "There was just a pile of rocks and a tree trunk in the road and it held us up for all that time. I don't think, that after all this delay, there is much point in trying to reach St. Albans today, we may get there at an awkward time. I am tired and hungry, let's stop here at Edgware, where there is some shelter from this rain that looks to be coming."

"Sounds like a good idea," Dan said.

"We can get an early start in the morning," Boudicca continued. "Also, those ladened wagons can catch us up before nightfall and they'll be carrying something to eat. There must be over 2,500 of us to feed."

The abandoned Edgware staging post was just up the road, and the first thing Dan did was to go in and find out if there was any of the good beer he had heard about. Although the place was quite crowded, there was some beer. He was in luck.

He then asked an Iceni woman with a jug of ale in her hand,

"What's the name of this Inn?"

"I think it's called The Boot," she said, slurring her words.

# CHAPTER XVI

# PAULINUS GETS TO ST. ALBANS

Mounted on fresh horses, Paulinus, now with only 13 of his original party from London, pushed on at a good pace towards St. Albans. Radlett was now behind them - St. Albans to their front, only four miles away.

Justus was pleased with his new horse; he had been lucky. Two of his troopers were having difficulties with theirs, but they still managed to press on at pace.

Paulinus went on ahead of the group, accompanied by two of his officers. Justus, with the remaining 9 mounted men, slowed their pace a little and dropped back as Paulinus slowly drew ahead. With St. Albans getting closer, Justus was not too worried about Paulinus' safety, and very soon his leader vanished from view.

As they arrived in St. Albans, Justus noticed that some of the legionaries stationed in the town, together with some slaves, were hurriedly strengthening the town's defences. He also noticed that more building work had taken place since he was last here.

Justus led them up to the garrison's headquarters, where they found the three horses Paulinus had ridden hard to get to the town. They were steaming hot from their fast ride and a couple of women slaves were attending to them. As Justus dismounted, he was approached by two middle aged men who asked him,

"Where are the rebels, have you seen any? How far away are they?"

Justus said, "We have come from London and there . . . . . . ." He stopped himself as he did not want to lie or say anything that might frighten the residents. He had experienced how panic could spread quickly by just dropping the wrong word into an answer, whether or not the information was true. He finished his sentence off by saying,

"We haven't seen any rebels on our way here, so I think you're alright for the moment. They may well have disbanded and gone home. I don't really know what's happening."

Justus knew Paulinus would be in the main garrison office and thought he should at least venture to the front door to see what was happening. As he reached the front door, he was recognised by Paulinus,

"Duplicarius Rufus, come in," Paulinus beckoned. "You may as well come in and hear the news." Justus went in as he was ordered, interested to know what had happened.

"So, tell me again Centurion Tiberius," Paulinus asked the garrison's officer.

"We heard that there had been a rumpus at Ixworth," Tiberius replied, "and knew that the rebelling barbarians, had moved on to Colchester and destroyed the Temple to Claudius."

Paulinus shook his head in disgust and took a moment to think.

"At that point Sir, I sent a message by pigeon to you in North Wales, via our fort in Chester.

Then we started to strengthen the ramparts around the town here in St. Albans. Then, two days ago, we had word that Boudicca's army was coming directly for us here in St. Albans, on the road via Great Dunmow, Bishop Stortford and Welwyn."

Justus nodded in agreement without saying anything.

"Is there any idea of the size of her army?" Paulinus asked.

"My reports say that they are in excess of 4,000. The first scouts I sent out found it difficult to get close enough to get any numbers. I'm sure you are aware of the difficulty, Sir. We lost two scouts, sir," Centurion Tiberius said with emotion. "I am awaiting reports from my second detachment of scouts that I sent out."

"If your scouts estimated 4,000 barbarians, there may well be 6,000 or more," Paulinus stated. "Where do you estimate them to be now?"

"I believe they came through Bishop Stortford yesterday evening, Sir."

"Sons of Zeus, at a push they could be here . . . . . now!" Paulinus exclaimed. He then looked with alarmed eyes, directly at Justus who jumped to attention.

"Sir."

"We must go! Saddle new horses for us and be ready to leave very soon." Justus immediately stepped outside to organise the horses and was met by one of his troopers, an intelligent trusted colleague, Clodius Felix, who said,

"We are taking care of everything Sir; I suggest you go back inside and learn what's going on."

As Justus went back in, he saw Paulinus turn to Centurion Tiberius, and speak.

"I'm sorry, Centurion, but I must get back to my Legion, Legio XIV, and other auxiliaries. They are coming down from North Wales to join me en route, somewhere on Watling Street. I came down in advance to find out what was happening. Now that I have seen the situation for myself, we have to crush this rebellion, and I need my Legions to do it."

"Sir," Centurion Tiberius said. He was beginning to understand the situation. He was going to be abandoned to hold St. Albans with the few troops he had.

Paulinus continued,

"You know of Poenius Postumus, commander of Legio II down in Exeter. I have sent him a message – ordering him to join me at Towcester, with a minimum of 8 cohorts. I am telling you this to keep you in the picture. That should bring our strength up to 14,000. One last thing Centurion Tiberius, if you find it necessary to abandon St. Albans, please do not hesitate. I will not hold it against you. Understand?"

"Yes, Sir. I understand. Thank you, Sir." The centurion said, glancing at his second in command, to confirm he had heard the same important statement.

"14,000 men should be enough troops to quell the rebellion sir," replied Tiberius. "Oh, if I need to send a message to you Sir, to where should I send it?"

"I will be somewhere between here and Towcester, or maybe a little further north if things get difficult," Paulinus answered. "We must be off Centurion. There is much to do. Is there anything else?"

"No, Sir! Thank you, Sir."

Paulinus came out of the garrison office and went straight to Justus and said,

"Is everything ready to leave, Duplicarius Rufus?" With those words Paulinus approached his new horse, a baye gelding, gave him a pat and a little 'man to horse attention,' checked the girth and mounted. He then led the way out to Watling Street.

As they trotted through the northern timber gatehouse of St. Albans, Justus noticed that the people weren't going to hang around trying to defend their city. Word had circulated about the atrocities in Colchester and also the number of Iceni and Trinovante tribesmen on their way to St. Albans. The rebels might be just a few miles away and would arrive very soon! Centurion Tiberius could not possibly hold the city with just a small number of legionaries.

As they travelled along Watling street towards Redbourn, their next staging post, they had the River Ver on their right and woods on their left. They were passing a number of people, who had obviously left St. Albans before them. They were carrying their possessions as if they were refugees. Some had waggons pulled by oxen, others had pack mules, but many were ladened and walking. It certainly was a desperate situation. Paulinus was full of energy, inspired to resolve the issue with these Iceni and encouraged everyone with him to move on at pace.

Justus knew that there were at least nine roads out of St. Albans. He guessed, judging by the amount of refugee traffic on this road, that most people had taken the option of going north towards Towcester and away from barbarian activity to the south and east.

The road was busy, and it was very sad to see so many people leaving their homes. All these people, now homeless, wouldn't really appreciate the seriousness of their plight until a few days later, when they would be tired and hungry, and the Iceni had attacked their rightful homes.

They were still some miles away from the Redbourn staging post, when Paulinus waved Justus forward for a chat.

"With all this activity on the road, I have my doubts that there will be fresh horses at Redbourn. What do you think Duplicarius Rufus?"

"I agree. There is a great deal of disarray amongst our fellow travellers that we are overtaking. I'm not sure that there will be effective management to change horses at Redbourn. What did you see on your way down here, Sir?

"It was like any other staging post. It had a good dozen horses for exchange and the usual three auxiliary troops, a number of grooms, catering staff and facilities," replied Paulinus.

When they arrived at the staging post all was well, as many of the refugees had not travelled this far yet.

"Let us change the horses here quickly and push on to Markyate," Paulinus said, and they did so. They pushed on again, up a long steady climb with hills on both sides and were in Dunstable for lunch, where they had a rest, and a much appreciated sit down. A few locals wondered what a powerful Roman general was doing at their staging post and gleaned a little information from Justus' troopers. They were soon on the road again, hoping to make Little Brickhill by nightfall.

It was quite a climb out of Dunstable, up the slippery chalk slope, and down the other side, but there were some locals on hand to assist. It cost them a little loose change in recompense for their help.

The next length of road was flat and uninteresting. They had left the chalk escarpment near Dunstable behind them. The road here was a lot easier for the horses and Paulinus made them trot occasionally. He was in rather a hurry and the system of changing horses definitely enabled him to travel 50 miles a day.

Justus, being the ever observant Roman, saw some waggons up ahead, way in the distance. He wondered whether they could perhaps be Plod with his waggons. Justus remembered that they had left London together, two days ago. Being ever wary, he kicked his horse to draw level with Paulinus and said,

"Shall I go ahead and check those waggons out, Sir?"

"Yes, Duplicarius Rufus, that seems a good idea. Take a man with you," Paulinus replied, cautiously.

Coming up behind the waggons, he could see four Roman legionaries, at the back of the column acting as escort. One of the four turned around. Hearing the sound of horse's hooves approaching, he wanted to check who was coming up behind the column. He saw Justus and the other trooper, and gave the alarm to his colleagues. It didn't take him long to recognise Justus and shouted to his colleagues.

"It's alright they are friends."

The remaining 16 legionaries, together with their centurion, were spaced out, in amongst the waggons, as they trudged along. Justus kicked his horse again and overtaking a number of waggons came up level with the centurion saying,

"Sir, I am with the Legate Suetonius Paulinus, coming up behind, I'm sure he will want a word with you."

"Oh right," the centurion said, stiffening up and adjusting his uniform. "I've only met the gentleman once, when he first arrived here in Britannia. What news from St. Albans?"

"The people are beginning to panic and there are many refugees on the road behind us," Justus answered, "I guess you might have seen a few coming past you."

"Only those on horses, and some of those were in a hurry," the centurion said. "When we left St. Albans, the rebels were close to Welwyn and we heard there were several thousands of them. I think they could attack tomorrow, and I don't reckon much to our chances of holding the place. I hope my mate Tiberius is alright, he's a good drinking mate of mine, I've known him for years."

Justus was a little taken aback by the friendly manner of the centurion. In their last encounter, he had come across as being quite a gruff and curtly man. Perhaps he had changed his attitude, now that there was an emergency. He replied to the centurion,

"I should think he will be fine, Sir. The Legate gave him permission to abandon St. Albans if he felt the position was untenable. He might well be on the road behind you now, and catch you up."

Paulinus then came up behind them and Justus thought he should move back to his men, who were following on behind.

The next place of interest to Paulinus was Hockliffe,

where he stopped, just on the far side of the village at a small wooden bridge over a brook.

"If this bridge was not here, this brook would cause quite an obstacle to any army wishing to cross. Would you agree?" Paulinus said, looking at Justus.

"Yes, Sir, I do agree. It would be very difficult to slither down the slope one side of the brook and try to climb up the slope the other side, particularly with waggons. It looks very sticky clay, and the bottom is at least 5 foot beneath the road surface. They may even have to rig up a rope to assist people climbing in and out of the brook," Justus said.

"And they would come out the other side with wet muddy feet and I'm not sure how the animals would manage?" Paulinus said.

Justus was wondering what the legate had in mind. He also realised, that he had been talking in a very informal manner to the senior commander of the Roman army in the province of Britannia. His next comment was a little more official,

"Yes, Sir, they would have very wet feet."

Paulinus thought for a while. He was looking around him at the long drag of a hill in front of them and the soft boggy ground all around Hockliffe. A short time passed while he moved around on his horse. He was obviously thinking to himself and his military mind was thinking things through. No one dared to speak to him, as they knew something was afoot.

"Duplicarius Rufus, I have a task for you and your men."

"Yes, Sir." Justus said smartly.

Suetonius Paulinus announced,

"Gather round troopers. I want you all to hear this

as I don't want any mistakes. I want you to go back into Dunstable and wait the arrival of these barbarians, for I am sure they will come this way after finishing with St. Albans. I feel it in my water. There are a few hills in the vicinity that are good vantage points - for you troopers to stake a 'look out' from. You may be there a few days. When you see the barbarians coming, Duplicarius Justus, I want you to estimate how many there are, and send three of your troopers to give me your answer. Do you understand?"

"Yes, Sir."

"Then, before you leave Dunstable, go and fetch the horses from the staging post and take them and the small garrison we have there and make for Fenny Stratford. Once there, report to me. If I am not there, go North on Watling Street until you reach Towcester. Look for me there."

"Yes, Sir."

"On your journey to Fenny, I want you to come to this bridge and burn it. I want every timber destroyed, so they cannot rebuild the bridge without a great deal of effort."

"Yes, Sir."

"You will wait here while it is destroyed, watch it burn troopers. Do you understand that order? Make sure you're on the right side of the bridge beforehand, yes?"

"Yes, Sir," they all responded. There were nods amongst the troopers, as no one dare interrupt when Paulinus was in full flow.

"This is my plan. I am sending word for Legio XIV; some of Legio XX and Legio II together with auxiliaries to rendezvous at Towcester. If you see any lost legionaries or auxiliaries send them north on Watling Street to Towcester.

As you know we have a fort there. Do you understand troopers?"

"Yes, Sir."

"Most importantly, do not tell any others of this plan unless it is imperative that they know. Understand?"

"Yes, Sir."

They all knew that if they did not carry out their orders precisely, the consequences would be dire. Roman officers were known to fall on their own swords, rather than be disciplined after disobeying orders.

Justus gathered up his 9 troopers, and when they were ready to depart back to Dunstable, he saluted Paulinus and led his men south on Watling Street towards Dunstable. They were all glad to be on their own again and not under the scrutiny and command of Paulinus, who was a very strict but fair leader.

Paulinus rode off in the opposite direction, with four officers to accompany him. After trotting for a while, Paulinus slowed the pace to a walk to rest the horses. He then spoke to his men and said,

"If it has not already occurred to Boudicca, then it will do soon. She has to bring my legions to battle because if she does not, she knows we will enter the Iceni territory and wreak havoc there and her people will suffer greatly. She has to force a battle between us in the hope that she can defeat us and save the Iceni from any humiliation. If she returns home, her army will melt back into their roundhouses and will no longer be a fighting force."

"Yes, Sir, I follow your thinking," said one of the officers.

"The hope is that Boudicca will find the destroyed bridge, realise that it was a deliberate act by my forces, and she will realise she has to travel in this direction to make battle with me," continued Paulinus.

"You are rather clever, Sir."

"Yes, I know!" said Suetonius Paulinus. He always made a note of officers who flattered him in this way and knew what they were trying to achieve. Paulinus rarely promoted anyone who took this approach with him. He recognised that those with excellent leadership skills would be with their men, and not with him.

## CHAPTER XVII

# A Night in Edgware

Dan loved the beer he was drinking in The Boot Inn at the Edgware staging post. It was exceptional. He could not remember when or where he was when he heard the story about this good beer, but he was very pleased that he had found it. He was halfway down his second jugful, and joyfully talking to a number of others who had joined him, when Boudicca came in. The chatter in the bar subsided on her entrance, as most people in the inn knew who she was.

"There you are Cousin," she announced, in a way that let everyone in the room know they were related.

"Yes, you have found me," Dan said with a smile, and asked, "are you alright, you look a bit hassled and jaded. What's it like out there, Boo?"

"Mud, muck and puddles, it's chaotic. Congestion! There are loads of waggons and horses on the road," Boudicca said, standing in the middle of the room. "Some people want to go on to St. Albans, others are content to stay here for the night. They definitely need a bigger waggon park. There are horses, oxen, ponies, pack animals, and children running around. Someone has even laid their hands on a lovely looking bull. There are a couple of cows being milked out the back, and no one can get to the pond to water their animals. It's a total jumble!"

"Oh dear," Dan said, emptying his jug of beer through his beard and wiping it clean with the back of his hand. "Is there anything I can do?"

"I can't see that there is anything you can do - for the moment, but thanks for asking. Half the lads have gone on - they are keen to get to St. Albans. I think they want to meet up with their mates who have been travelling on foot via Bishop's Stortford, but it's very difficult for them to get past the confusion outside."

"Someone needs to sort out all those waggons and horses parked outside," came a loud voice, descending the steps into The Boot. The Inn was below the level of the road outside and there were three steps to enter the bar. "I've been on the road all morning and I have barely moved more than 3 miles!" shouted a short man, from the doorway. A second man responded,

"We can't let this happen again; we have to find out what went wrong!" He was on his third jug of beer.

At that moment, someone standing over the trap door to the cellar shouted out,

"All the beers gone!"

On hearing that, Boudicca approached the man who had said it. He had a full jug of beer in his hand, she grabbed it and downed it in one, saying as she banged the jug down on the table,

"I needed that! This job is getting to me!"

Dan had not seen this side of his cousin before. "She

must be under a great deal of stress, trying to control and influence all the warriors who had joined her," he thought to himself. They must all be seeking guidance from her, and she was dealing with a situation she had never experienced before. She may own a spectacular chariot and had experienced a few rough and tumble conflicts before, but nothing on the scale of this revolution. His heart went out to her. Was there anyone closer to her than him? Should it fall on his shoulders to give her all the support she needed?

She then came over to Dan and manoeuvred herself to sit down between him and his new drinking companion. Although a tall woman, Boudicca was agile with her body, squeezing herself into the small space on the bench seat, snug between them.

"Ah, I see, you don't recognise him either Boo," Dan said, "this is our cousin Neil who lives in Rushmere now." Boudicca then cranked her head to have a closer look at the gentleman she had squeezed up alongside.

"Holy druids, so it is, Neil!" Boudicca uttered in astonishment, "when did I last see you?"

"Many years ago, long before I got married," Neil said, with a big smile, "it's good to see you too Boo." He was the only other person, apart from Dan, who had ever called her Boo.

They exchanged a few more pleasantries and stories of each other's experiences over the last decade or more. Cousin Neil explained how he lived just down the road now, and then Boudicca returned back to the business in hand saying,

"We are a long way from home Dan, and I don't think I'm in control anymore - control of this whole thing. Have you any ideas?"

Dan thought for a moment, realising from her demeanour that perhaps the drink his cousin had just had might not have been her first this evening. There could well be a second source of alcohol nearby, Roman wine perhaps? He decided he should answer her as best he could, even though she was a bit light-headed with drink. He chose his words carefully.

"It is not going to be easy cousin," he said, "would you agree Neil?" Neil nodded without saying anything. He had only just joined the adventure and had not experienced the long journey from Ixworth. He was also beyond light-headedness, closer to drunk, and not at all talkative.

Dan began to feel guilty that he had been sitting in a crowded hostelry drinking beer, while she had been trying to control the mess outside. She was now trying to attract attention to her leadership dilemma and was not getting much response, from either cousin.

"Yes, I know it's not easy," Boudicca said. "Everyone is very keen, exuberant might be the word, but how do you control them?"

The alcohol that Boudicca had drunk was now properly kicking in! She spoke a little louder this time, as she wanted others around her to hear,

"I didn't really want to be Queen of the Iceni, to be their leader like this. I am Queen of the Iceni because I fell in love with my husband, King Prasutagus. He was a great man and I loved him. This role of Queen of the Iceni was thrust upon me, something I have had no training for, but nonetheless I have to carry it out. I will have this responsibility, until my dying day. Being seen as the leader comes with the title but I wish I knew how to do it."

Dan looked around at the people in the room. Some had heard Boudicca make her plea for help, but most slowly resumed their chatting, laughing and generally enjoying themselves. They were having a great time on this adventure away from the mundane routine of normal life.

Dan had difficulty processing what she had just said, but responded anyway,

"It can't be easy controlling a great crowd of people." He paused while thinking of his next words. "I'm sure they want instructions, but it's how you go about getting their attention. You can't just go out there and try to talk to them. There must be at least two thousand or maybe even five thousand people, and they're scattered up and down the road."

"I understand that, but how do I achieve it?" Boudicca asked. "I can't get on my chariot, overtake them all on the road, telling them I've got a meeting planned for . . . . ."

Just at that moment, a man burst into the room,

"Someone has stolen my bull!" he exclaimed. "I left it tied up on the corner of the building for a moment and now it's gone. Did anyone see anything?"

The man was looking at Boudicca in the hope that she, being the person in charge, could resolve the situation. There were bigger things on Boudicca's mind than a stolen bull, but reluctantly, as she was the leader, she felt she should attempt to find a solution, so she asked,

"Did you not think to ask a friend of yours to mind the bull for you?"

"No, my two mates have gone off up the road, off to St. Albans where all the action is," the man replied.

"Why did you bring the bull all this way with you?" Boudicca asked.

"I didn't bring it with me, I saw it looking lonely in a field and . . . ."

"Well, there you have it," said Boudicca. "Perhaps someone thought it looked lonely tied up outside here."

Later that afternoon, Boudicca, having sobered up, held a small meeting with the few leaders she had managed to round up. She stated a few facts to them.

"We have our other army, mainly from the Trinovante tribe, which took the quick route to St. Albans from Colchester. Most travelled on foot and are accompanied by many of our waggons. They appear to be near St. Albans, and maybe they'll be attacking the city in the morning. I think our good friend Garos has taken command there, but that's not a bad thing - we do need leaders."

One of the leaders said,

"Those Trinovantes are very keen, headstrong in fact. They have old scores to settle with the Catuvellavni of St. Albans."

"There's not much to talk about then. I just thought I would let you know what was happening," Boudicca replied, "it would be good to get to St. Albans by about mid-day and see what's going on there."

Boudicca's mobile army, which once consisted of chariots and those on horses, was now encumbered with waggons and followers on foot. The waggons, brought by the tribesmen of the Trinovantes and Cantiaci of Kent, were full of booty and food from the warehouses of London. The numbers had also been swelled by others who had travelled on foot.

Many were experienced warriors with all the gear for fighting a battle, but others were just there for the adventure. That afternoon, the enthusiastic ones left to go on to St. Albans, where they knew that is where the action would be. Others stayed put in Edgware.

Staying put for the night at least meant there was some shelter, but most had to spend the night under waggons, in leather tents as the Romans did, or even just out in the open. Dan noticed that many had been fortunate in finding leather tents the Romans had stored in the warehouses of London. On examining one of the tents, he detected it was made of calves' skin. Looking at all the seams, it appeared that quite a number of calves went into making just one tent. It was heavy, especially when wet.

People sat around campfires eating the food and drinking the wine they had plundered from the London warehouses. Many chatted with friends and relatives they had not seen for some time and a good time was had by most.

In the morning, most of the tribesmen woke stiff and cold, for it had been a chilly night. It was a foggy damp morning, not really spring like, but after a quick breakfast, most were on the road to Radlett. Boudicca's chariot was not leading this time, but was in amongst the long train of waggons and those on foot, who had joined the army recently. They were making very slow progress. Dan, standing by Boudicca's side on her chariot, was wishing they could get on a little faster. The heavy waggons in front were holding them up, and there were limited places to overtake without going into the soft mud, each side of the road.

Some waggons had got away early after breakfast, keen

to get going, but were now holding up the column. The few who left on horseback could easily overtake, and were doing so, much to Dan's annoyance. Boudicca then asked Dan,

"How far is it to St. Albans?"

"Oh, it must be at least 9 miles, possibly 11," Dan said.

"Good gracious!" Boudicca said loudly, "I hadn't realised. It's going to be all over by the time we get there – quick!" She cracked her whip and steered the horses onto the mud at the side of the road, trotting past the slow moving waggons.

Boudicca and Dan were discussing what was happening up ahead in St. Albans. Had Garos attacked the city without any cavalry support? Not that he needed it to attack ramparts. It would have been nice to be there, to see the momentous event. There was another question. Was Garos in charge at St. Albans? Was he a self-proclaimed leader because he had done so well at Sawtry Woods? Perhaps everyone now wanted to follow him. Either way it was good for their cause, provided he won battles.

St. Albans was still a long way off. They would not get there before mid-day.

Boudicca and Dan arrived in St. Albans in the early afternoon, too late for any action. The city had been successfully overrun by Garos and the Trinovantes.

There was great excitement, especially among the Trinovantes, who had spiked their hair and painted their faces prior to the assault on St. Albans. Most were celebrating with alcohol and there was a great sense of relief. A small minority of the younger tribesmen were behaving badly and had ransacked homes for booty. Some had even beheaded a few elderly inhabitants, who were unable to escape before the attack. However, the majority behaved well and were calm and peaceful now.

Boudicca went off to find Garos to congratulate him on his achievement, while Dan went off to have a look around St. Albans. He wanted to be on his own, even though he was surrounded by fellow tribesmen.

There were conflicting stories amongst those who had witnessed the attack. Some said that there had been quite a battle, and others said everyone had run away and there was little or no resistance at all. The end result was that the city had been taken with very little loss of life on either side. It was alleged, by the Iceni, that a number of the Trinovantes, in their thirst for vengeance against the Catvvelavni, set alight some buildings. The strong winds that developed later that morning fanned the flames, resulting in many buildings being burned.

Dan knew that the Trinovantes had been defeated in battle a number of decades ago by the Catuvellauni, and they still held a grudge. He understood their anger and their actions in destroying vast areas of St. Albans. They had certainly wreaked their vengeance on the City. The Catuvellauni tribe were renowned for their expertise in the slavery trade and Dan saw a number of happy souls who had been freed by the taking of St. Albans. He felt they may well join Boudicca's army.

In one row of shops, many samian pots had been upturned and had spilled their contents of valuable goods across the veranda of a shop front and on to the road. It was a shame to see such destruction of property and possessions that must have taken so much effort to produce.

Dan had never been to St. Albans before and he was

very impressed with the architecture and the sheer size of the town. It must be an influential town, but less so now it has been destroyed. It was similar to Colchester but somehow more established, with more commercial activity, which included a local iron works. There was also a great deal of building work underway and the Romans had been making a huge impact, until the arrival of the Trinovantes who had, just hours ago, begun to take the place apart!

# CHAPTER XVIII

# Celebration

The day after the destruction of St. Albans, there were great celebrations, especially amongst the Trinovantes. It was a shame that those people bringing the waggons from Colchester, and the others coming from London, missed out on the celebrations, as they did not arrive until the following day.

Some waggons coming from Colchester slowly arrived during that afternoon. Many tribesmen were tired after their journey of some 60 miles. Dan waited anxiously on the outskirts of St. Albans for the arrival of Cartimandua and his sons, Morcant and Talos, who were bringing his two waggons. The vehicles came in single file trains, as the slower waggons held up those behind and then there would be a gap before the next slow train of waggons.

A few of the oxen that had already arrived were showing signs of sore feet because their shoes had worn out. Those with good shoes appeared to have fared better. Dan reassured himself that his oxen had been recently shod and, therefore, he knew that his own animals would be fine and that his waggons would be arriving soon.

While waiting for his sons to arrive, he wondered how they would re-shoe their oxen, should the need arise, it could become a problem. An ox could not stand on 3 legs like a horse without a frame to hold them up. Back home the village blacksmith had the right facilities which included a strong frame, to hold up an ox while it was re shod. It would not be that easy, as there were so many oxen in Boudicca's army. Even if they did find a shoeing facility, it would be impossible to get them all done.

Dan realised they had not given too much thought to shoeing their beasts before they left Colchester. There were two other ways to shoe an ox if it was imperative to do so. They could be laid down on their side with their legs tied together. This, however, was not a pleasant experience for the ox or the blacksmith trying to fix on shoes. The other way was to dig a pit and lay the animal in the pit upside down to get to its hooves, but that was dangerous for both the animal and the blacksmith and involved a great deal of hard work.

Dan's thoughts were interrupted by a man approaching him from his right.

"You're Boudicca's cousin, aren't you?" he asked.

"Yes," Dan said, "I have that relationship to endure." He was not sure he quite knew what he meant by that statement, but he had said it now anyway.

"You wouldn't by any chance know whether she was after a new husband, would you?" the man asked. Strange question, Dan thought to himself, not knowing quite how to answer it.

"I've got no idea mate," Dan said assertively. "Her husband has only recently died, and she's got other things on her plate at the moment, like trying to look after this lot."

The man shuffled away. He was a very odd man, Dan thought, then carried on anxiously looking out for his sons and his waggons.

Dan was trying to envisage how many waggons might be coming from Colchester. There could be 200 or maybe perhaps as many as 450, it was difficult to tell, but counting waggons was not his prime objective. He was waiting for his sons together with their friends Cart and Scarr.

There were many others waiting for the arrival of their particular 'family waggon' or collection of waggons associated with their own village. Many were waiting to see their loved ones again, while others were hungry – these vehicles carried their food and supplies. As the waggons continued arriving, Dan glanced back into St. Albans to look at that those that had already arrived and were clogging up the streets. Interesting thought, traffic jams and traffic, perhaps someone should take up the study one day. He continued to look out for his family and friends.

There they were, he could see them in the distance. Not many waggons were painted white, like his, and there were two together, away in the distance, and approaching slowly. As they came closer, Dan walked towards them and met them halfway, greeting them with a big smile.

It was wonderful to see his two sons again. He thanked Scarr and cousin Cartimandua for looking after them. He jumped on board the leading waggon and directed them away from the congestion, to a place outside the city, to park up for the night.

"Did you have a good journey?" Dan asked Talos, his younger son.

"Yes, Dad, it was good, the road was kind to us and there were not too many hold-ups. We were lucky with the weather and generally we kept dry. Oh, and Cart is a good cook too." Dan was quite impressed with the amount of information Talos had given him. He was becoming a grown up.

Dan helped them park up the waggons, unhitch the oxen and see to their needs. They set up a campfire from their own supplies, then asked their neighbour for a light from theirs which was already burning. They erected a bivouac shelter between their two waggons, and Dan fetched out the chair he had bought from home to sit on. The younger members of the party sat on the ground, but he found that was too uncomfortable these days.

Talos then went to collect some more firewood from a nearby spinney and Cartimandua made a hot drink. It is always good to make somewhere feel like home, even though it is temporary. Dan then suggested to Cartimandua, they should go into the city centre to find their cousin Boudicca and find out what plans she might be conjuring up.

"Good idea Dan," she said, "let's see if we can loot anything on the way, shall we? Are you coming Scarr?"

"But that is stealing," Dan replied.

"Isn't that what the Romans have been doing to us for ages?" Cartimandua said.

When most of the waggons from both armies had arrived, Boudicca, having made a number of attempts to get some form of order amongst her warriors and leaders, succeeded in arranging a meeting to discuss their next course of action.

Boudicca stood in the ruins of a building, adjacent to the main square, in the centre of St. Albans to address the meeting. She had elevated herself and stood on some red brickwork. Before she spoke, she nervously adjusted her gold torque around her neck.

"Fellow Britons, I stand before you as your Queen, an unelected leader, but will do my best to carry out your wishes against our common enemy, the Romans. We have together destroyed the two main Roman cities in Britain, Colchester and St. Albans. In doing this we will have made them pretty angry, but not as angry as we are. We have pent up anger, from their uninvited presence in our country!" Boudicca paused for a moment, took in another breath and continued.

"The Romans have been here for 17 long years; enslaving us, taxing us, and in some cases crucifying us. It is our turn now to fight back and we have done that. But we have more to do, and I seek your guidance on to how to achieve it."

Boudicca then got down from the wall she had been standing on and continued to chair the meeting from the floor. She was less imposing from that point, but she felt it was easier to allow everyone have their turn to speak.

Many of the Trinovantes, having destroyed the capital of their enemies the Catuvelavni tribe, just wanted to go home. Although they had joined together with the Iceni people to defeat the Roman army, having achieved their objective of routing the city of St. Albans, they were losing their taste for battle.

The leader of the Trinovantes spoke well. He stressed

to Boudicca that they had come along with the Iceni to exact a great vengeance against the Catuvelavni and the Romans. They had successfully achieved this and were not so interested in being involved in any further action. Dan could half sympathise with this leader; he was older than Dan and looked quite tired. He had just had enough.

Boudicca argued that they should all be committed to this revolution against the Romans. If they went home, there would be retribution by the Romans when they were back in their villages. She argued that this was the Britons' chance to rid themselves of the yoke of the Romans forever.

Boudicca realised however, that to finish this forever, they must bring the Romans to battle. Hopefully, this could be achieved by fighting smaller armies, rather than having to take on all of the Romans occupying Britain in one big battle. They knew that some of the Romans were up north somewhere, at the end of the Watling Street. So, by marching up Watling Street they would hopefully they would meet them. With any luck, they would just be a third of the Romans in Britain, and the Britons could move on to take on other smaller Roman units later.

A wise man from the Cantiaci Tribe of Kent, similar in age to Dan, then made a very important point.

"We must recognise the fact," he said, standing up on the same piece of red brickwork Boudicca had used, "that the Romans, in North Wales, have been cut off from their homeland. Their way back to Rome is through St. Albans. We have taken their two most important cities, Colchester, and this one. We have barred their way home. Also, the Romans may well have many loved ones in these two cities, loved ones they should have protected and did not. They will, I feel, be worried for them and will return here with some urgency to crush us."

There was silence after he spoke, as everyone took in what he had stated so profoundly.

The subject of the meeting then changed to the order in which the troops should move off up Watling Street. There were many ideas put forward. Should the waggons go in front, followed by the warriors on foot, with mounted troops front and back of the column; or should those on foot go ahead with a few cavalrymen, and the waggons come up behind. This was discussed at length, and not for the first time. Dan remembered it been discussed on the way to Colchester.

A major problem was that those who were mounted, moved the fastest. Those on foot came next. On arrival at their destination, the supplies - tents, food, and cooking utensils - were all in the waggons, that could only manage 8 to 10 miles a day. This was a real problem, as it meant those mounted and those on foot had to sit around waiting at the end of the day's journey, tired and hungry without shelter, while the waggons caught up.

However, the ironic thing was, it wouldn't really matter what was agreed then, because in the morning, people would pack up their things in the waggons, and if there was the opportunity to get on the road, they would do so. It's part of human nature to be keen to get on the road and on to the next destination.

In the end, they agreed that some horsemen should go ahead to scout the road. This would be followed by some good warriors, followed by the waggons and finally the remaining tribesmen on foot, with a rear guard formed up of horsemen. The leaders, having agreed what to do, would have great problems in disseminating this information to everyone. There were now thousands of people, making up Boudicca's whole army.

After the meeting everyone went back to their own restful campfires, sang a few songs, chatted over the day's events, and bedded down for the night. They didn't know it, but there were over 75,000 people there that night.

In the morning Dan had a wonderful breakfast of bacon, eggs and oat cakes - his favourite! The oat cakes were flat pancakes made of oats, egg and milk and they soaked up the bacon fat from the pan and tasted divine! However, this maybe the last of the eggs, and milk was hard to come by.

It was now four days after the sacking of St. Albans. The first enthusiastic warriors left St. Albans for Dunstable, and as they did so, there were a few slow-moving waggons arriving in the city from the south. The army was still growing.

"Our prayers to the Good God Dagda have been answered Dan," Boudicca said, "look how our numbers are still increasing." The Celts had a number of gods, perhaps 15, one of them was Dagda and he was the Good God - Boudicca's favourite.

"Yes, I think our prayers have been answered," Dan said in response, "we have a large army."

As Boudicca was readying herself to set off towards Dunstable, she called out to Scavo and beckoned him to her side. She said,

"Scavo, I am most interested to know, and I think others

are too, how many followers we have here. Please take up a position, just outside the City with two of your good mates, mates who can count. Use stones if you have to, and count how many there are of us. Yes?"

Scavo nodded saying,

"I've wondered that too, Mom, we were talking about numbers last night, as we were sitting round the campfire." Boudicca then continued,

"I want to know numbers of horsemen, waggons, warriors and we will call anyone else 'the rest.' When the last one leaves St. Albans, I want you to come and find me somewhere at the front of this 'Magnificent Army.' I, and many others, will be interested to know the result. I think it will help tremendously the morale of everyone here, to know how many there are of us. Yes? I will then let everyone know at the next leaders' meeting and they can cascade the information down to all of their followers."

"Yes, Mom," Scavo said, "your idea of using stones is a good one and when I get to 100, I will use a big one."

"Good idea, Scavo."

That morning, all of Boudicca's followers showed respect for her and allowed her to lead the great column of tribesmen, out of St. Albans. As she did so, her fellow countrymen and women stood each side of the road and cheered her as she went past. She felt very proud and honoured that they had organised this for her. Very proud indeed, she smiled and waved to the vast crowds from her chariot with her cousin Dan by her side.

She turned to Dan and said,

"It's good to see all these tribes coming together, coming together to fight the Romans. All of us, people of Briton!"

Dan acknowledged this statement with a meaningful nod, saying,

"Yes, I agree Boo," Dan mused, "normally we're fighting each other, raiding each other's stock and taking the occasional slave. I wonder if they will return to the old ways, when we rid ourselves of these Romans?"

It was lunchtime when the last of the great column moved off from St. Albans, alongside the river Ver. Many had been standing around, waiting to tag onto the end of the column. Others had elected to walk on the verges, rather than wait. These verges soon became muddy and slippery, especially as the ground was wet near the river. Waggon crews, walking alongside their charges, were experiencing difficulties when their waggon moved to the edge of the road.

When the last of the waggons had left St. Albans, Scavo and his three mates, having counted everyone in the army, mounted their ponies and went in pursuit of their Queen. However, they had also seen many of their army, particularly members of the Trinovante Tribe, heading east and going back home. In effect they were deserting.

The first place the army went through was Redbourn, where Boudicca thought it best to break their journey and stop for a while. They had travelled 5 miles and whilst the road had been generally good, some lengths had been paved, but others where rough.

The Romans had not yet paved every section of road, but had managed to repair and improve the old road with loose broken stone. Stone, which had been broken up by slaves.

On stopping, Boudicca passed word back down the

column that this would be where they could rest and graze the oxen. They had been on the road for a number of hours and although most of the army were fit and young, they had not travelled this sort of distance very often in their lives. Some of them were carrying quite heavy loads which were made up of necessities like weapons, blankets and food. Others were weighed down with booty they had acquired in London, St. Albans and other places.

Boudicca, Dan, and Nomass, sat on a tree trunk next to the road in Redbourn, watching their army walk past. They were not moving fast - it was more of a methodical trudge, as slower people in front held up others behind. The faster ones overtook the slower ones whenever there was the possibility of getting past. However, this was difficult, for the road was less than five metres wide in places. There were bottlenecks too. Boudicca herself was the cause of one. As people walked past, they stopped or slowed to see their Queen having a break. Two warriors actually approached Boudicca sitting on her tree trunk and kneeling before her said words like 'it is a pleasure to serve you, Mam'.

Some waggons had started off earlier than perhaps they should have, and were now holding up the procession.

"Perhaps we could re-organise the order of the procession, Dan," Boudicca suggested, but Dan was too busy people watching.

Boudicca's army was a tremendous collection of tribesmen, from all over the south-east of England, and their large numbers made progress along Watling Street very slow. People were stopping for many reasons, which held up the traffic behind. There were broken vehicles and the occasional lame animal. Some tried to pull off the road, but it was not always easy to do so. It was all very frustrating.

They managed to reach Markyate before nightfall, after leaving St. Albans. On her arrival, a tent and campfire had already been set up for Boudicca and her close friends and they all sat down on a couple of substantial logs someone had found for them.

She was interested to know Scavo's findings, and she asked assertively,

"I wonder where Scavo has got to. He is late. He was counting our people, wasn't he?"

Just then, Scavo turned up, and got off his horse. He walked warily over to where Boudicca was sitting on the log and she asked,

"Where did you get to then?"

"We've been counting all morning, and then it's taken us all afternoon to catch up with you, Mom." Boudicca was very keen to know how many they had counted and said loudly,

"How many of us are there then?"

Scavo read from the Roman clay tablet he had found,

"We counted 42,460 tribesmen on foot, although a number of them were youths.

660 Chariots.

2,230 horsemen and women.

716 waggons.

1,880 mules – but I smudged that so I'm not sure?

12,800 wives, children and others.

"Goodness gracious, there can't be that many," Boudicca said totally shocked. "But that's thousands!"

"59,500," Scavo said, "plus a few more, because there were sometimes two or three people on a chariot. Perhaps, by the time you got here at Redbourn, Mom, the last people were still leaving St. Albans. Well almost."

By lunchtime on the second day from St. Albans, they were going up the steady slope towards Dunstable.

It was here that Boudicca's leading scouts saw what they thought were Roman cavalrymen, high on the chalk ridge, to the right side of the road. There were three of them moving hurriedly along the ridge, being chased by Boudicca's scouts. They moved along the ridge for a short distance and then disappeared beyond it, out of sight.

Garos was riding alongside Boudicca's chariot when they heard the news of the Roman cavalry. Both rode along quietly, for a moment, thinking about what this meant.

## CHAPTER XIX

# First Contact

A few days earlier in Hockliffe, Justus, having received his orders from Paulinus, formed up his 8 cavalrymen in pairs ready to depart back to Dunstable. He thought he should do it smartly and efficiently in front of the Roman Governor of Britannia. When they were assembled, Justus saluted Paulinus and led his mounted men south on Watling Street towards Dunstable. They were all glad to be on their own again and able to relax, especially tonight in the staging post in Dunstable, which was one of the larger ones along Watling Street. It was adjacent to the Roman fort in Dunstable and was renowned for being quite lively in the evenings.

On the way back to Dunstable, on what was normally a busy road, they had to climb up the chalk escarpment into town. The traffic had caused the well-trodden chalk to be a little slippery here and there, at the steepest parts of the escarpment. This section of the road was in need of attention by Roman engineers.

The refugee traffic leaving St. Albans going north, had not helped. These were people who had heard of the impending attack from Boudicca and her supporters and were leaving before the trouble started. The more people who passed over this chalk slope, the more slippery it became, especially in wet weather. Most travellers on Watling Street found this a difficult section of the road and waggons needed some special assistance. However, Justus and his colleagues managed to get up the slope, although they did have to dismount and take care.

They reported to the garrison commander who was an Immunis. An Immunis was a rank above a normal foot soldier who had a trade such as clerk or blacksmith. This took him off normally duties, but did not give him any more pay.

The Immunis stood with his hands on his hips outside his office, waiting for Justus and his troops. He obviously wanted to know the latest news of the rebellion, which was causing great anxiety in Dunstable. The refugees travelling north, gave conflicting stories. Although the Immunis wanted to know Justus's latest information, Justus also wanted to know his.

"What news from St. Albans?" Justus asked.

"I understand that the rebels are approaching St. Albans from the East. The last we heard, they were nearly at Wheathampstead, that is 10 miles east of St. Albans," was the reply.

"Yes, I know where Wheathampstead is," snapped Justus, "and I know the staging post manager there too. I wonder if he's all right? He has probably got away, as there's no way these rebels can take anyone by surprise, they seem to advertise their presence long before they arrive."

"So, what of you?" Justus continued, "are you ready to

leave if they come this way?" Justus suddenly realised he may have let some information slip out, which was very easy to do when questioned. Silly me he thought, what did Paulinus tell him?

"They're not likely to come this way, are they Justus?" the Immunis asked.

"It's very difficult to know," Justus replied, "they may well be content after trashing St. Albans. Especially the Trinovantes. Once they have settled the score with the Catvvelavni they may well be on their way back home."

"I don't fully understand these Barbarians, one tribe attacking the other. However, I'm very glad they do; it saves them fighting us so often," the Immunis said. Justus dismounted and his troopers followed his lead. He handed his horse to a young slave girl, who took the horse into the stables.

"What is your news from that Legate I saw you with first thing this morning?" the Immunis asked.

"Ah, now there is a question. I think it best to say nothing for the moment, there's much at stake. People are listening and people talk, but I don't think there's too much to worry about at the moment," Justus said.

"Who was that Legate? I seem to recall, he came through here a couple of days ago, going south, and he was in quite a hurry, he didn't even stop for something to eat."

"Well, let's hope he's got things under control, shall we? As we said, the rebels will probably go back home or go somewhere else and won't come up this way," Justus said. Again, he noted that he had said too much, perhaps he should go and find his bunk.

It is quite amazing how some people can get you to

say something when you've got to keep your mouth shut. It certainly would not be a good idea to tell the people of Dunstable the rebels were coming this way. There would be more panic and more refugees clogging up the roads. Paulinus needed the roads clear and open for his legions to come down from North Wales.

Justus found his bunk and was very pleased with it. It was full of fresh straw with a lovely thick leather cover to it, stopping the prickles sticking through. He was soon asleep.

He was woken some-time later by one of his troopers, and together they went off on foot, to find the others for their evening meal. They began by enjoying a drink and a chat to think through their plans for tomorrow.

Later, during their meal Justus told them of his plan.

"I think the place to look out for the rebels coming up Watling Street, is those hills on the left, as you go out of here towards St. Albans. We can hide up there with our horses behind the crest. There are no woods in the way to block our view of the road, and as soon as we see the rebels coming, we can mount up and find a route back here to Dunstable, grab our things and our two pack mules and get back through Hockliffe to burn that bridge."

"We need to tell the Immunis and bring the Garrison legionaries along as well," Morinus said. Morinus was one of Justus's troopers.

He did some more thinking and then said,

"Tomorrow, I want three of you to take some lamp oil out to that bridge, collect some kindling and hide it near the bridge somewhere where it will keep dry. When we arrive there, which might be in a few days, depending on when the Iceni arrive, we can quickly make a fire and burn the bridge. Understand?" He was speaking a little like Paulinus and everyone, including himself, seemed to notice.

"The rest of you will come with me to find a suitable look-out place on those 'Downs' as the locals call them. We will take the road eastwards from the town centre here and then go up the hill on our right. There is a good vantage point there."

"We can get up to the hills from that road. I have been there before and know it well," Justus whispered, as there were others on a nearby table, who may have overheard.

That evening, they had a good meal and enjoyed the ales of Dunstable. The next morning, they were up late. They thought the enemy would be slow leaving St. Albans to travel in their direction, so it was mid-morning when the two parties set off in different directions to carry out their plans. Three of them went off to the little bridge in Hockliffe, and Justus guided the other five troopers, out of Dunstable and up to the hill, where they could find a good vantage point, looking down on Watling Street.

Justus found a lovely spot on the dry grass of the chalk Downs, looking down on Dunstable to their right. To the south, on their left, they could see the sad, heavily laden refugees, coming towards Dunstable up the long drag of a slope from St. Albans. The troopers' horses munched on the short grass behind them, while the troopers themselves laid down and enjoyed the spring sunshine. The birds were singing, and it was a wonderful day.

A gang of six young boys came by, and Justus guessed they had finished their lessons and chores for the day and were allowed out to play. He was not sure their parents were fully aware of the situation; the rebels could be here very soon, and it's not good to have your children out playing when you may want to leave in a hurry. These children were Romanised Britons and the approaching Trinovantes might take violent action against them.

However, these six boys had a minder, who was following on behind them. He was a slave, but obviously a responsible and trusted slave, who must have accompanied them wherever they went. The slave could protect them against a minor threat, perhaps a gang of older youths, but they really should return home, especially if Boudicca's rebels came. They might then become refugees, like the people of St. Albans.

Justus was surprised when he next looked round behind him, the boys were gone. There was no need to worry about them anymore, he had enough worries of his own.

It was then that Morinus, one of the troopers with good eyes, saw in the distance some waggons coming up the road.

"That can't be the rebels surely," Morinus whispered, "the rebels would have outriders and look different."

"I think you are right but I'm not sure who they might be," Justus replied. The waggons came closer. It could be Plod again, Justus thought, and sure enough as they came nearer still, it was easier to recognise them as Plod's waggons. The 20 legionary escort was still with them.

Justus could not stay here all day, he had things to do and people to see and check on. He got up off the ground to go. He was leaving his troopers with orders to keep a good look out. The moment they saw any sign of the rebels, they were to return to the barracks in Dunstable. Trooper Morinus would accompany him back down to Dunstable.

Justus tightened the girth on his horse, as he had loosened

it when they arrived, to let the horse eat. He then mounted and the two of them proceeded back into Dunstable.

At the fort in Dunstable, Justus met up with the three troopers who had prepared the bridge for burning and after having a short lunch with them, he told them to go with Morinus and relieve the troopers on look-out duty at the top of the hill.

While Justus and his troopers were barracked at the fort in Dunstable, the Immunis was constantly quizzing them on why they were in Dunstable and what were they doing when they went off on daily rides. Justus found it increasingly easy to answer his questions as he appeared naive regarding military movements and Justus did not have to be that honest. The Immunis pressed him again.

He finally decided to tell the Immunis what was going on, and to be ready to leave at a moment's notice when the rebels were coming, but not to tell the rest of those in Dunstable before they left.

Plod's 20 legionary escort had gone north towards Stony Stratford. The fort there was large and would normally have a minimum of two centuries (a century was 80 men) to hold all the walls, against a strong attack. The fort in Dunstable would be abandoned.

It was three days later when Justus had a feeling that this might well be the day when they would see the Iceni rebels approach Dunstable, from the direction of St. Albans. He went with three of his troopers to the usual location for watching for the Iceni. They were sitting down on the chalk hill, in the late morning sun, overlooking the road from St. Albans, when Morinus, pointed out horsemen coming along the road. It was difficult to make them out at first, for they were a long way off, but they slowly became clearer and there were some chariots amongst the horsemen.

Morinus was only 19 and had good eyesight. From their hiding position, low down on the ground, he told Justus exactly what he could see. Justus did not want to leave too early before he had established that this was the main army of the rebels. However, leaving it too late might mean that they would get caught by the enemy's scouts, who they now spotted coming along the ridge. They would be with them quite soon. It was time to go before they were seen.

Justus ordered his three men to mount up, and taking one last look at the approaching rebels, to get some idea of their numbers, kicked his horse into action. Unfortunately, in their hurry, they forgot to ride away from the ridge but rode along it, and were seen by the rebel scouts who chased after them. The rebels were some distance off when Justus looked back and shouted to his troops.

"There is no need to gallop boys, they're a long way off."

They were cantering along when Morinus the third trooper, suddenly went over the top of his horse. The horse had fallen, tumbling over itself as if one of his front legs had given way. It was whinnying in pain and most distressed. Justus following behind, had seen the young man's accident. He had fallen hard and appeared to be in significant pain lying on the ground. Justus reigned up alongside him, trying to work out how serious Morinus's injuries were and quickly assess the hazardous situation they were in.

"Oh bother!" the young man cried out. He tried to pick himself up off the ground. He got to his knees but was in considerable pain. He cried out,

"I can't - my shoulder! my shoulder!"

Justus was very anxious for him, especially as the three enemy tribesmen, having seen the incident, were galloping up fast. They were now only about 200 yards away. The other two troopers had not seen what had happened and were totally out of Justus's thoughts. He realised the only thing to do was to attack the three Iceni tribesmen galloping towards him, and leave Morinus on the ground. He kicked his horse hard, and it responded quickly. Before Justus had time to think, he was closing on the two leading horsemen. They were not expecting to be charged and pulled up in shock! This lone Roman, clad in armour with shield and spear was coming at them fast.

Justus's thoughts were racing, his training had told him to go for the larger of two opponents. The theory being, that the smaller of the two will not support his colleague when he sees the big man go down. Both of his opponents were now stationary, when Justus delivered his spear into the chest of the elder and larger of the two men. Justus's horse took him past the point of impact and in his racing mind, he saw the third enemy horsemen had pulled his horse up too, probably in shock. But Justus was also in shock, as this horsemen was a young woman. There was no time to think, how do I fight a woman. He then noticed there were three more riders coming up the hill towards him.

There was still shock and anxiety showing in his two opponents. Both were very young and were looking at the incident in disbelief and bewilderment. Justus was stationary and saw the concern on their faces. He decided that the two knew the wounded man on the ground, and would have looked to him for guidance. They were transfixed, confronted with a confident armoured Roman drawing his sword from its sheath. All three adversaries remained immobile while they considered this life and death situation. The young tribesman was the first to move, after hesitating for a moment, he encouraged his horse to leave the scene. The young woman, obviously the braver of the two, followed having considered her chances on her own against what appeared to be a skilled Roman cavalryman.

Justus then turned to see his kneeling wounded opponent collapse forward on the ground with a deep moan. Returning his eyes and concentration on the three mounted tribesmen coming up the hill, he realised he had not much time to return and help his colleague Morinus. If he could get him to his feet, they might be able to double mount on his steed.

It was no good - Morinus could not get to his feet. He was in a bad way and was whimpering,

"I've hurt my shoulder and this arm is broken; I can't do anything. Please go, save yourselves, Sir." Justus hesitated, summing up the odds, but the three enemy horsemen were closing fast, and had been joined by the younger pair who had ridden off before. Justus reluctantly nodded to Morinus on the ground, and rode off to join his other two troopers. He did not look back.

Justus and his remaining troopers came hurriedly into the fort at Dunstable. They quickly dismounted and raised the alarm with the garrison's legionaries and his troopers, who had been resting in the fort. They shut the large double gate and manned the ramparts. Knowing something was wrong the Immunis, in command of the fort, came running out of his office and urgently asked Justus,

"Are they coming this way - the rebels?"

"Yes, I am afraid they are, we had a skirmish with them up on the Downs there," Justus said, pointing to the left of where the sun was in the Sky.

"Holy Zeus, what shall we do?" The Immunis shouted at Justus. "How many of them are there?" The poor Immunis was a complete mess, not capable of reacting sensibly in this situation and it came through in the panic of his voice.

Justus replied,

"I suggest you come with us, as I advised the other day. Or you could stay here and protect the local people, here in the Fort."

"But I only have eight men."

"Then I suggest you make a tactical retreat, as we are doing, or put it another way, you run for it," Justus said assertively. Turning to his troopers he said, "let's change horses and pack our stuff on our two mules." The troopers who had been left behind in the fort had made the necessary preparations and all that was left to do, was to change the saddles on Justus's horse and those of his two companions returning from the downs. They then asked where Morinus was. Hesitating, not quite sure how to break the bad news to the others, he said,

"I'll tell you on the way."

There were a few moments of despondency amongst the troopers as they realised what had happened. They shook their heads and exchanged sad glances. Regardless of that, they had a job to do and being professional they got on with it.

"So how many of them are there?" the Immunis asked again. Justus was tightening the girth on his new horse, his new black horse. He realised it was the same one he had had before. He stopped for a moment, staring into space, calculating how many Britons he and Morinus had seen on the road.

"There were at least 3,000 maybe 5,000.

"Zeus, Holy Zeus!" the Immunis uttered.

"That is what we saw," Justus went on, "but there may have been many more following on behind. It's not easy to tell and it's not one of my skills."

Justus went over to help one of his troopers who was checking the load on one of the mules. He was tempted to remove a small leather tent and a heavy cooking pan but thought better of it. You never know when they might come in handy. Justus returned to the panicking Immunis, saying,

"There are some spare mounts in the stables. You and your men could tag along behind us, if they organise themselves quickly. But we are going now, up Watling Street towards Fenny Stratford and on to Towcester."

"That means leaving the people of Dunstable to fend for themselves," the Immunis said.

"That's a decision you will have to make for yourself, you are the man in charge." Justus told him, mounting his black horse.

As he led his troopers out through the gate, opened by two anxious looking legionnaires, the Immunis shouted to the others,

"Get those horses out of the stables." It was the first proper military decision he had made in his life; he was deserting his post and it may well have had serious consequences when he reported to a senior officer at a later date.

※

They left Dunstable, but not quickly, as they did not want to cause alarm to the Dunstable residents. Doing so might well bring panic, and where would they go? Any extra refugee traffic on the road would not be a good thing. When the rebels arrive, they might not be violent towards them, especially as they were Britons. There were many pros and cons to any decision, and Justus hoped he had made the right one.

They climbed up and over the chalk escarpment and hoped the novice legionaries following on could bring their horses down the slippery chalk slope. Two miles further on there was a high point on the road before Hockliffe and Justus stopped and turned to see who might be following them.

Away in the distance Justus could make out riders and guessed they might be the legionaries because of the glinting armour they were wearing. More importantly it appeared there were only around eight of them this also suggested that they were the legionaries and not rebels. Pointing at the mounted legionaries, he gave an order to two of his troopers,

"Wait here for them to arrive and tell them we're burning the bridge at the north end of Hockliffe and to get a move on. Also keep your eyes peeled on the far distance and let me know if you see any rebels coming. Understand?"

On arrival at the little bridge Justus found that his other troopers had found the oil and combustible materials to light the fire. It had been placed on and under the bridge ready to light.

## CHAPTER XX

# Boudicca meets the Young Roman

Garos was riding alongside Boudicca's chariot, when they heard the news of the Roman cavalry up on the chalk ridge up ahead. Both Boudicca and Garos rode along quietly, for a moment, thinking what this meant. They were puzzling about to what to do. In the end Boudicca said,

"Come on Garos, let's go up there and see for ourselves, we may also get a better picture of the situation." Garos led the way, waving to a number of his fellow tribesmen to follow him.

It was a steeper climb than they had envisaged and, on reaching the top, both the horses and the riders were short of breath. They rode along the ridge to find their fellow warriors standing over a wounded Roman cavalryman, next to his dead horse. One or two of them were kicking the Roman as he lay on the ground and Boudicca told them to stop, as she dismounted from her chariot.

She approached the young man; he was no more than 20 years old and looked very frightened and in pain.

"What are you doing here, in my land? This is my country! Why are you Romans here?" she shouted at him. There was a blank, puzzled look on his face, as both of them realised they did not speak each other's language.

"Does anyone speak their stupid language?" Boudicca asked.

One of the older warriors, with an odd limp, stepped forward saying,

"I understand a little."

"Ask him where his mates are, and why they left him," Boudicca said. The warrior was a little more respectful of the Roman cavalryman and knelt down next to him. In a very slow pronunciation of some latin words, he spoke to the Roman. It seemed that the young man was more cooperative now, and a number of words were exchanged. The warrior stood up, and said to Boudicca,

"His colleagues did not want to leave him, but he could not get on a horse. He says he doesn't want to say where his mates are."

"Kick him!" Boudicca demanded. They did not need to be asked again, the same warriors kicked the poor young man, and he yelled.

At this point, Garos seeing everything was under control, jerked his horse to join his fellow riders further along the ridge.

Meanwhile, the old warrior knelt again beside the injured Roman and spoke quietly and gently to him. While he was doing this, another warrior pointed to the dead horse and said,

"There is a rabbit hole here, that's what the horse trod in and it broke its leg."

"Bloody Romans bringing rabbits over here - we didn't have this problem before they arrived. Damn animals, they're always escaping." By this time the Latin-speaking warrior had an answer for Boudicca, saying,

"Mam, he says his colleagues have gone north, to join up with the army that is coming southwards, down Watling Street."

After a few more questions, Boudicca had understood the gist of the story. She calculated that there would be a Roman army here, in Dunstable, in maybe 7 to 12 days. Boudicca wandered away from the others staring into space, thinking to herself and worrying.

"What do we do with him?" one of the warriors asked, kicking the Roman again.

"Put him on my chariot and I will give it some thought," Boudicca replied. Two burley Iceni warriors picked the Roman up, who was screaming in pain and placed him on the chariot. One of them took his helmet and put it on, the other took his boots. He had already lost his chain link corselette and his sword. Others were taking his four pommelled saddle and the bridle off his dead horse, while others were discussing whether they should butcher the animal. An opportunity for fresh meat should not be passed over lightly.

Boudicca respectfully led her horses down the steep chalk slope, and while doing so, she looked up to see two rabbits running away down their hole. The young Roman on the chariot moaned.

On reaching the road, Boudicca asked everyone why they had stopped. They would never get to Dunstable at this slow pace. Dan remounted the chariot, awkwardly standing next to the young wounded Roman cavalryman. This morning the cavalryman had been a fine figure of a man. He was now reduced by dislocation and broken bones to a near naked mess.

Boudicca's army moved on up the long drag towards Dunstable. She hoped all the waggons and slow-moving foot soldiers could keep up, so that they could all spend the night in Dunstable. There would be some shelter for those vulnerable to the elements, but the majority would have to sleep under the waggons, in tents, or on the open ground. However, here the ground should be dry, as the chalk underfoot drained easily.

The young Roman cavalryman was lying uncomfortably on his side on her chariot. He was restrained beside her feet, and moaned when they went over a rough bit of road. He was only the same age as her daughters, she thought. This made her think about them and wonder how they were. Had they got back home safely? Did she do the right thing in sending them back home and would she have felt better having them by her side?

The young Roman moaned again, bringing her thoughts back to the present. She would have to get rid of him somehow, but at the same time she was weighing up what additional information she could glean from him. She looked down at him and said,

"Where is your mother? Why aren't you with her, looking after her and providing for her? Why are you out here in my land? This is my land!" She kicked him again for good measure.

For the rest of the afternoon Boudicca turned over in

her mind the question, the big question! How far away was the Roman army and where would they meet in battle?

On reaching Dunstable, they found the place void of Romans and only a few Roman-friendly Britons remained. At the crossroads, in the centre of town, was an abandoned fort, a number of recently built whitewashed Roman buildings, and some old pre-roman buildings. Boudicca was not the first to get to Dunstable that afternoon. There were many of her followers already there. They were keen to get to grips with some Romans and acquire any booty that might be around. One of the problems with stealing other people's possessions was having to find a way to carry them. It would be very useful back home, but carrying it was difficult. It was made easier if you had a pack mule or waggon but, on the whole, if you were on foot, it was difficult to carry anything that could not be eaten or drunk at some point in the near future. On balance, it was perhaps the wine that was the favourite.

Before putting down roots for the evening, Boudicca thought it would be a good chance to organise a meeting for the morning, to give some direction to her leaders and to hear their ideas. She posted a messenger on the road to inform every leader about the meeting that would be held the next day, as they came past the Roman fort.

Boudicca settled down for the evening in the fort that the Romans had abandoned. It was a logical place, as most of her people arriving in Dunstable could see the fort, close to the crossroads, and everyone seemed to know that was where she was. Boudicca began to realise that perhaps there were nearly 60,000 people in her army, as there were many campfires, tents, bivouacs, horses and mules all around the whole area. There were many, many people, and still more were arriving. All were trying to find a resting place somewhere on firm ground. Luckily, the chalky ground here in Dunstable provided this.

Tribesmen stood around the crossroads in the centre of Dunstable, waiting for their waggons to arrive. As it began to get dark, many of them were strung out on the Watling Street, and people began to set up their campsites by the side of the road. There was a great deal of congestion and confusion with so many waggons, people, oxen, and tents.

The official and the self-appointed leaders had lit their campfire in the interior of the fort, as the buildings were too small for the large gathering of tribesmen that Boudicca had attracted. Dan, being one of the eldest there, was privileged to sit on one of the chairs brought out from the office, while most of the assembled tribesmen sat on the floor, around their blazing campfires.

He was considering whether to go and find his sons and spend the evening with them, or to stay with Boudicca. It was difficult to know where his allegiances lay. Then he considered how he might find his two waggons, in amongst all the others out there. He had painted his waggons white and that would make the task easier, but his legs were tired from standing on Boudicca's chariot for most of the day.

Although the chariot had suspension, the toll on his legs had made them feel quite wobbly. He was very pleased to be able to sit down on a comfy chair and enjoy the warm fire, rest his bones and enjoy good company. He would think about searching for his sons later on. The other advantage of being here with Boudicca, and some of the leaders, was that he could listen to the conversations about how the campaign was going. He could then pass this information onto his sons later on. Yes, that would be a good plan, Dan told himself.

Dan was beginning to get warm by the fire and everyone was chatting amongst themselves. A messenger came into the fort to see Boudicca. He recognised her immediately and came trotting over, shouting across the fire to Boudicca,

"They have burned the bridge at Hockliffe!"

Boudicca beckoned the man across towards her saying,

"Come a little closer, so I can hear what you're saying." The Messenger spoke again as he walked around the fire to get closer to Boudicca. He was a tall, gangly, dark haired man with a strong black beard, and Dan noticed, like most messengers he had a face full of bad teeth. He repeated his message.

"They have burned the bridge at Hockliffe. It only goes over a small brook, but that will hold us up in the morning."

"Was there any suggestion from the man that sent you, about what we could do to cross the brook?" Boudicca asked.

"Yes, that was Garos, he sent me," he said. "We could fill the ditch in, Garos told me to say, and if we put some big stones in the bottom that could keep the water flowing, so we wouldn't cause a dam and make a lake."

"That sounds like a plan," said one of the leaders sitting close to Boudicca."

"Yes," said Boudicca, "we can get some boys down there first thing in the morning when it gets light, it's too late to do anything tonight."

"That sounds like a plan!" shouted the same leader." It was obvious he had started drinking early and it was not a lot of help to the situation. There were people like that, Dan thought.

## CHAPTER XXI

# Hockliffe

Justus had arrived back in Hockliffe on the same afternoon that Boudicca had arrived in Dunstable. When they rode past the staging post in Hockliffe, The Copperwheat Inn, he gave them warning that the bridge was going to be burned very shortly and if they wanted to be on the right side of the brook, they needed to pack up their things quickly. They needed to bring the horses they had there and anything else they had of value. They could bury any valuables somewhere in the garden if they wished, so that they could retrieve them later, on their return. Justus and his troopers then went on to just outside Hockliffe to where the bridge was over a brook.

At the bridge Justus found his fellow cavalrymen had used their initiative to start a fire some distance away from the bridge.

"Ah good man, well done! So, you have some tinder fungus," Justus said with relief as he arrived. "I was worried, we may have run out of tinder fungus. Thanks for not eating it. I made the mistake of eating it when I first came across it, not realising it was used to light our fires!"

One of the troopers then said to Justus,

"This fire can be transferred quickly to the kindling and that great pile of wood, ready to burn on the bridge."

"Well done boys," Justus said. "We just have to wait for your mates to come through Hockliffe and on to this bridge, we also have the people from the staging post and the legionaries from the fort coming. They should not be long, I saw them way away in the distance, coming up the road."

The people came rushing out of the staging post as the troopers and the legionaries came past and they all grasped the urgency of the situation, to get across the bridge before it was burned. They all helped each other with the spare horses and possessions.

When they all arrived at the bridge, a trooper shouted to Justus,

"There's no one behind us sir, we saw no one."

"That's good, that means we've got plenty of time to prepare the fire, and burn this bridge."

Everyone loves a very good bonfire, and this was no exception. The legionaries and the troopers, stood with their backs to the horses, watching the fire take hold. There were a few sparks, lots of flames and crackles as the fire enveloped the bridge. They had to stand back to avoid getting smoke in their eyes.

Both the legionaries and the people from the staging post understood the situation. It was just a very hurried decision. They had left their lives behind, in what had been their homes. They were not fully aware of what was about to happen in Dunstable and Hockliffe when the rebels arrived, but they thought they had a good idea.

Soon after the fire took hold of the bridge, Justus gave some thought to organising the allocation of horses, that had been taken from the staging post. As it turned out, everyone had a horse and there were two spare, to carry the possessions of those from the staging post. Two of the younger children had to double up and ride with a parent, and they, being children, were enjoying the experience, unlike their parents who were wondering where they were going to sleep that night.

There were some minor difficulties with the lack of saddles and bridles but three of the troopers volunteered to go back carefully across the brook, and bring more of these items back from the staging post. They would catch up with the others later on.

Justus now had around 25 people he felt responsible for - his own troopers, the legionaries and the two families from the staging post. They rode off in pairs, up the hill out of Hockliffe, towards Fenny Stratford and possibly beyond to Towcester, where one of the families had relatives.

༄

It was less than 5 miles to Little Brickhill, where Justus and his charges had left the bridge that must still be smouldering. Watling Street had been quite a trudge, with a few undulating hills to climb, but there was a welcoming staging post at Little Brickhill, where they stopped to assess their situation. The Inn here was called the Green Man. The families from the Hockliffe staging post had a very good natter with those based in Little Brickhill. They all knew each other, without ever meeting – they handled the same horses, listened to similar news, both up and down

Watling Street, but had never met each other. They talked at length, almost ignoring the plight they could soon be in. The hostlers at Little Brickhill staging post would probably have to abandon their post very soon. They had all seen the refugees filing past their homes, but hadn't considered whether they might have to consider this action eventually.

Meanwhile, Justus was chewing over his thoughts with his Cavalrymen and the Legionnaires from Dunstable.

He started by asking,

"I wonder how far Paulinus has managed to travel up Watling Street, to rendezvous with Legio XX and Legio XIV. They are coming down from North Wales, as we speak."

Clodius Felix, one of the more experienced cavalrymen, was quick to answer,

"Sir, I spoke to one of Paulinus's aides when we were travelling together, a few days ago, and he said that Paulinus had given strict orders for his Legion to march down to Towcester, where they were to wait for his return from London. They had heard of the Iceni rebellion via pigeon post. The message had first gone to Chester and then was relayed on to Paulinus in North Wales by messenger on horseback."

Justus then replied,

"Yes, I understood the same thing from Paulinus myself, but he was very careful not to say too much in case it . . . . . . Oh, Holy Zeus! I wonder if Morinus knew of Paulinus's orders?

Poor Morinus, I left him on the downs near Dunstable. I wonder if the rebels have interrogated him. Oh, Poor Morinus! I should not have left him."

"You had no choice Sir, there were at least five rebels, you could not have protected him and kept them all away," Clodius said.

"I suppose, I did my best," Justus answered. "But the big question is, do I tell Paulinus about Morinus, when I see him?"

"I think you have to Sir," Clodius stated. "It is the right thing to do." Justus had known Clodius for a number of years, they had ridden in the same unit, experiencing many difficulties together and had relied on each other many times. They had also bonded well together in many drinking establishments and had similar views and beliefs. It was a good friendship.

"I understand," Justus said, "I will tell him as soon as we meet up. We must go, gentlemen, Fenny Stratford awaits. It's not far away."

The two families from the Hockliffe staging post were engrossed in their chat with the family of The Green Man Inn. Their children were playing together outside and everyone was having a good time, despite the imminent danger! Justus came across to them and, interrupting them at their table, said,

"It's time for us to be off. You are in good hands here, but you may well need to move on if there is any danger of the rebels coming up this way. From the information we have, I believe they will do so soon.

"Thank you for bringing us this far," said the man from Hockliffe. "I think you could well be right, and we'll probably see you in Fenny."

"It is sad to say this, but I suggest you pack your things ready to leave at a moment's notice. And yes, perhaps we will see you at Fenny Stratford - I'm not sure how far we will be going ourselves," was Justus' parting reply.

Justus and his colleagues mounted up on fresh horses, as they were not sure how far they were going. They still had the rest of the afternoon and evening left in the day. As they left Little Brickhill, they stopped to have a look at the view, which was quite amazing. Justus always found it interesting to see how much better the view was sitting up on a horse. Although only three feet higher up than the standing man, it definitely gave those on horseback an improved outlook on their surroundings, as all good generals knew.

The view was similar to the one they had seen from the escarpment at Dunstable, in that they could see at least 8 to 10 miles into the distance. They could see almost to Stony Stratford, which was the next staging post after Fenny, where they would be stopping for the night. They were riding into the unknown.

## CHAPTER XXII

# THAT IS A STEEP HILL!

Dan and Boudicca were both up early. Boudicca had spent a good night's sleep in the abandoned Roman fort in Dunstable, but Dan's night was not so comfortable. He had spent a long part of the night tossing and turning worrying about his two boys and Cartimandua. In the middle of yesterday evening, he thought it would be a good idea to go and find them, to see if they were alright. He could not find them, even though he had painted his waggons white. He did find some white waggons, but they weren't his. He was sure they were somewhere in the camp, but it covered such a large area. He just wanted to know where they were and whether they were safe.

Going without their breakfast and leaving their possessions in the fort, Dan and Boudicca, together with a few leaders and hangers-on, went out to Hockliffe to see the burnt bridge.

They were keen to investigate and plan how to get the army across the brook. Both of them were old and wise enough to know that the best way to solve a problem was to go and have a look-see.

Before they left, Boudicca was reminded that the Roman cavalryman needed to be interrogated a little more to see what else he knew. He was looking pretty unwell, and he certainly was not getting any care and attention that might keep him alive - more like the opposite.

A mile out of Dunstable, they slowly climbed up the side of the chalk escarpment which was quite steep towards the top. This they reached without much trouble, but then the horses were fresh. It was much steeper down the other side and Boudicca had reservations about taking her horses down there. The gradient appeared to be steeper than 1 in 10 and neither Dan nor Boudicca had ever seen such a steep slope before. They lived in East Anglia, where the ground was generally flat. They halted at the top, hesitant about the descent. Also, being chalk, the road was a little slippery, even though stone had been put on top of the chalk to aid grip.

"I don't like the look of this Boo," Dan said. "I think we should get off the chariot and lead the horses down the slope, what do you think?"

It was then that a young hot-head, who believed his chariot could take the slope without any problem, recklessly over-took Boudicca, descending the hill much faster than he should have. His horses were trying to hold the chariot back, as was normal when descending a slope, but the chariot was heavy, and the whole thing, with the two passengers on board, accelerated and soon the horses lost control. One of the horses slipped and fell. The other went down with it, in quite a catastrophic way. There were screams from both horses and the young men until they reached the bottom of the slope, in a tangled mess. One man was whimpering and cursing, and the horses were screaming and in a terrible state. The other man was quiet and still.

"Oh God," Dan cried, "I have only heard a horse cry out like that once before."

"I have never heard anything like it – ever, it's horrid!" Boudicca exclaimed.

The audience at the top of the hill wanted to rush down and help, but they had second thoughts after seeing what had happened to their foolish comrades. It was a steep slope indeed. They picked their way down slowly, having dismounted from their horses and chariots. On arrival at the bottom some minutes later, it was difficult to know how to help the two injured men, but a plucky warrior realised the horses were beyond help and he finished them off with his sword. The charioteers were comforted by their friends who examine their injuries with care.

"We need to get on," Boudicca said heartlessly, and getting on her chariot she moved off with the remainder of her followers.

"I'm sure they will be okay; their friends have stayed with them," Dan said.

Once moving, Boudicca asked Dan,

"That is a nasty steep hill we've just come down; how do you think we can bring the waggons down there?"

"I'm not sure," Dan said, thinking it over in his head. "The brakes on our waggons are not good enough to stop gravity taking effect. The waggons would plummet to the bottom. I will give it some thought, perhaps we could ask the locals. They must witness what is normally done to get waggons down the hill. After all, this is a major transport route for supplies."

It was further from Dunstable to the burnt bridge than Boudicca had realised, perhaps a good 3 miles. As they arrived, they saw that there was quite a congestion of tribesmen, horses and chariots, even though it was still early in the morning. They must have got up early and be keen to get on with the march.

However, when they got though the throng of people to the burnt bridge, they found that efforts to make the brook passable by the army, had already started. There appeared though to be little organisation of who should be doing what. Many had no tools and were working with their bare hands, in their hurry to get the job done. Some had thrown timber and branches into the bottom of the ditch so that water could flow through them and not cause the brook to block up and flood the area. Some other tribesmen had made fascines, which were large bundles of twigs, tied together. These too, had been thrown into the bottom of the brook. The water flow was low at the moment, and it flowed through the fascines and other deposits in the bottom, quite well. Dan though, was concerned that should it rain and the flow increase, there might be a great flood across the road which would be very muddy for everyone.

Dan thought about trying to take charge and be the 'engineering officer' for the project of filling the brook, but he realised it would be very difficult to take command of the hundred or so dismounted horsemen all trying to help. The work was proceeding quickly, and he thought the moment to take charge had passed. It can be very difficult to control others without the authority to do so and without some personal charisma. Boudicca had the authority and charisma but did not realise the work was poorly organised.

"We may be making it difficult for ourselves if we get some heavy rain Boo," Dan said.

"We will be through here soon," Boudicca replied, "you worry too much Dan."

He thought to himself, some women are really good at organising, but, to convince them to do something differently and properly, when their mind is set, is not worth trying.

"Everything here seems to be under control Dan. I've told Garos he is in charge here, in the vanguard of my army," she said proudly. "Let's get back to this steep chalk hill, and see how we can get the waggons down it."

Boudicca and Dan rode back south on Watling Street towards Dunstable, a short journey that would take them back up the steep escarpment that caused so much trouble earlier that morning. En route they passed very many warriors and tribesmen who had already left Dunstable. Boudicca's chariot was certainly going against the traffic and there were masses of them, some recognised her, and waves were exchanged. She found it most heartening and she gave everyone a big smile.

The young men's chariot was still at the bottom of the hill with the two dead ponies, but the young men had gone. Two hungry looking dogs had just arrived on the scene and were having a sniff around the carcasses.

"I wonder how badly the boys were hurt?" Dan asked, concern in his voice. There was a rider to Dan's left, on a lovely grey pony, who, having over-heard Dan said,

"I think they are okay, although the passenger was a

lot worse than the driver and was unconscious for quite a while."

"That's good to know," Dan said. At that moment he saw a shepherd off to the right, and called out to him.

"Hey!" he shouted and jumped off the back of Boudicca's chariot as it was going slowly as it approached the steep slope. Dan walked over to the shepherd.

Boudicca shouted over to Dan, as he was walking away to talk to the shepherd,

"I'll see you at the top Dan!" She too climbed off the back of the chariot to help ease the climb for the horses.

When the 53 year old Dan came huffing and puffing up the hill to meet up with Boudicca and her chariot at the top, she asked him,

"What did you go and talk to him about?"

"If ever you need to know something about a place, you ask someone you think might live in the locality. He was a shepherd and lives here in the large hillfort over the back there. I asked him if he knew how they got heavy waggons down this hill."

"That's clever," Boudicca said,

"When you get to my age Boo, you get to know these things."

"Well then, what did he say?"

"Oh yes, he said they wrap a rope around the stake at the top of the hill here - look there's a post there," Dan explained, pointing to a large diameter post sticking out of the ground next to the road.

"They then tie it to the back of a waggon, having first unharnessed the oxen. They then let it down the slope nice and easy. There is a lot of friction between rope and post."

But then he laughed and said, "they've had a few accidents as you can see from the debris at the bottom of the hill."

"Oh yes, I think I see what you're saying," Boudicca said, still trying to understand the mechanisms involved and what Dan was laughing about.

Dan saw that Boudicca had not taken note of the broken waggons at the bottom of the hill and, pointing at them, said,

"Look hidden in the undergrowth, next to those young lad's chariot! Loads of busted waggons!" Dan giggled again to himself, it was something that appealed to his sense of humour.

"We just need to get some rope then," Boudicca said, "as it looks like someone has taken it. Or perhaps we have to bring our own. I'll ask someone back at the fort to look for some. Someone must have a length somewhere."

"In case you are wondering Boo, the shepherd boy's father has an extra team or two of horses to bring the waggons up the slope."

"Sounds like it could be a full time job for someone, getting people up and down this steep hill," Boudicca responded, " I wonder where the man is now. We could go and look for him."

Dan and Boudicca then went back to the fort in Dunstable, to find out how the interrogation of the young Roman cavalryman was going, and to tell all the waggon-masters the arrangements to help their vehicles down the slope. When they were told about the steepness of the slope, some expressed worries that they would not be able to get their waggons back up the hill to go home. However, when it was explained to them that there would be local people who people help pull the waggons back up the hill, their worries seemed to go away.

On visiting the young Roman, Boudicca found him in a sorry state. Not that she was concerned for his well-being, as she gave him a good kick before turning to the two women interrogators. One of them was her cousin Cartimandua. Both women seemed to have enjoyed the task given to them. Boudicca asked them,

"So, what have we learnt. What information have you extracted from him?"

"His name is Morinus and he had been with his Roman legionary colleagues in Dunstable two days prior to us arriving. They had been ordered to look out for our arrival from the top of the hill. The big Roman boss man himself was here. He left them in Dunstable and went north to find his legions, and hopes to return soon," Cartimandua said. She was feeling very pleased with herself. Then Boudicca asked,

"Anything else?"

"He said there is a legion down in the West Country, and word has been sent to them to meet the Roman Governor, Paulinus at High Cross on Watling Street."

"Where is that?" Boudicca asked.

It's 50 miles north of here, up Watling Street," Cartimandua answered.

"Did you enjoy your work, girls?" Boudicca asked, looking at the young Roman with a big smile on her face. A smile that inferred he was going to receive more torment. It is amazing how one human can communicate with another from a foreign land, by just using their eyes and body language. The restrained Morinus squirmed on the floor, with distress in his face.

"Oh yes we did, it was delightful work," Cartimandua said, also looking at the Roman, with a similar smile.

"Perhaps I should have questioned him myself," Boudicca said, "do not hurt him anymore, he might die and may well be of use to us later."

"That's a shame," Cartimandua said. "A number of our colleagues have been in to see our prisoner and taken out their frustrations on him."

"I can see that! He's quite a mess. No, that will have to stop. Feed him and see that he is looked after." Boudicca had spoken.

"Oh, there you are Cart," Dan said with relief, "I was looking for you and the boys last night and was worried about you. Where did you park the waggons?"

"Oh, hello Dan, we had a mishap with a yoke. John and Talos had to spend some time mending it yesterday, but it's all sorted now. We arrived a little late last night - and parked down the road a bit.

"It's good to see you anyway Cart, I am please you are all safe. Perhaps I'll have a look at the yoke later," Dan said.

※

It took them nearly two days to get all the waggons, chariots, items of booty and stolen animals down the escarpment and along to Hockliffe. The waggon masters were good at organising lowering the waggons down the slope, by the rope method Dan had discovered. As each waggon had to wait its turn to be lowered down the 1 in

8 gradient, a long queue developed going back nearly to Dunstable.

Boudicca and Dan stayed at the steep slope for the first day, helping the waggon masters to supervise the hazardous incline. However, being keen to scout ahead, they left on the morning of the second day.

Once Boudicca and Dan left, a number of conscientious tribesmen stayed behind to oversee and help with the difficult task of getting the waggons down the slope. One thing these tribesmen did notice, was that fewer people were coming along the road out of Dunstable. Perhaps some had decided to go home with their booty, and shirk the responsibility of fighting alongside Boudicca. The steep slope might also have influenced their decision.

It was quite easy to drop off the back of the train of slow-moving waggons and tribesmen. Just sneak into the woods at the side of the road making the excuse they were going for a squat and wait for the army to pass by. Others could make out that their waggon had a broken wheel or that their oxen had gone lame, and they would catch up later. The end result, although not apparent to the leaders up ahead, was that the army was shrinking!

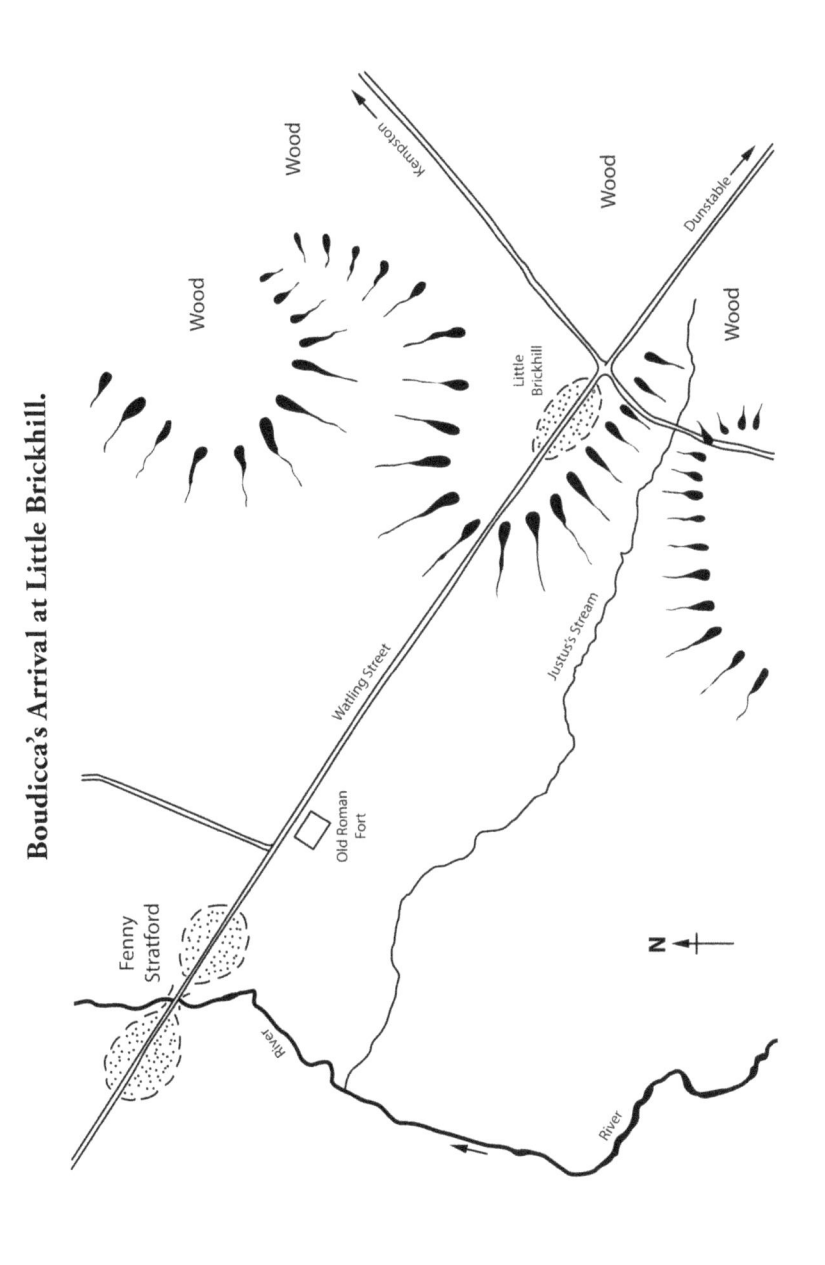

*Boudicca's Vengeance*

**Boudicca's Arrival at Little Brickhill.**

Boudicca and many of the leaders, together with the vast majority of enthusiastic tribesmen, went on ahead to Little Brickhill some 10 miles further on from Dunstable. It took them most of the day and they reached the small village as the sun was setting.

Boudicca pulled up at the top of a long descent. She and Dan got off the chariot to stretch their legs and let the horses rest.

"Look at that view Dan, you can see for miles," Boudicca said.

"That's a lovely sunset, "Dan said in awe, "look at the colours."

"This would be a good place for a battle," Boudicca announced, as two Iceni leaders dismounted their horses alongside her. One of them was an adviser and the other her good friend Garos.

"Yes, you can see a long way," Garos replied. "What a commanding view we have here! We could wait here for the Romans to come and make their fatal attack up this hill. Is that a good idea?"

"I do believe it could be," Boudica replied. "I think it best we take a look around first though." There were a few moments of silence while the four of them took in the view. Coming from Norfolk, they seldom saw such distant views.

"Any Roman attacking up this hill would be puffed out when he got to the top. Well maybe, if they were close to my age," Dan said. There was more silence as they were totally absorbed with the view. The sunset was slowly turning a wonderful orange.

"I wish I could see all the detail out there in that view, but my eyes are not that good these days," Dan mentioned.

"You're not that old," Boudicca replied. "Shall we stop here for the night and see how things look in the morning. This could be a good place for our battle with the Romans, we will have to see what others think. I wish I knew how far away they were. When will they get here? I think we need to scout around a bit, get a feel for the location, chat to others. I do like to get everyone's ideas before making any decisions."

They went down the hill a short distance to the staging post and stopped outside the Green Man Inn on the left, to see where they could sleep for the night. Well, they thought this must be The Green Man, because it had a Green Man on the inn sign outside.

"Looks like everyone left in a hurry," Garos said, coming out of one of the buildings. "There's no one here but two old crones and some chickens."

"This will do us nicely," said Boudicca. "Let's unhitch the horses and get a fire going."

"I'll hunt around for something to eat," Dan announced.

They were joined that evening, by a number of others, who had marched on ahead of the waggons, keen to see what was up ahead. One of them was Nomass on his chariot. Dan and Boudicca were very pleased to see him. They all sat down by the fireplace, exchanging stories of their adventure, a long way from home. It was a momentous adventure for many, as they had never been this far from home before.

Little Brickhill had never seen such a diverse collection of Britons before. There were tribesmen from the Iceni, Trinovantes, Cantiaci and Catuvelavni. All were getting on well with each other on this campaign, despite their feuds in the past. They were together now against the common foe, the Romans. Many thought that this would be a good hill to stand and hold against the Romans. Also, most of them instinctively knew the Romans were on their way south and not far away.

They were very fortunate that The Green Man had got a good stock of beer and wine. They settled down for the evening in good company, chatting, feeling safe and warm and comfortable. Each tribe had its own accent, which was very distinctive from others, and this sometimes made communication difficult and words had to be repeated. However, jokes about bodily functions, the difference between men and women, misunderstandings, food, and alcohol remained the same despite people's differences, and gave them a common bond. All these subjects, human contact and the alcohol made for a wonderful evening.

## CHAPTER XXIII

# The Heron Inn

Justus, with his troopers, and the Immunis' legionaries from Dunstable, approached the old Roman fort. It was on the left of Watling Street, at the bottom of the hill from Little Brickhill. It had been abandoned some years previously, but its ramparts and partial wooden fortifications were still intact beneath a decade's growth of vegetation. It had served a good purpose, when it was first constructed at the junction of the road to Irchester, but it had been built on boggy, flat ground that did not drain well.

The fort had been constructed by a Legion, passing through at the time of the early conquest of Britannia 17 years earlier. A Legion would build a temporary camp/fort every night when in enemy territory. Therefore, this must have been enemy territory, at one time in the past. Perhaps they chose this site as it was easy ground to dig, and therefore the fort could be constructed quickly, because they might be threatened by a local tribe. A legion of 6,000 men would have constructed a protected camp, such as this, in less than a day. However, this had been more than a camp and had perhaps been upgraded to a temporary fort, and had operated for a few years. Now, as it was no longer required, it had been abandoned like many others in this province. The earthworks had become overgrown with bushes and young trees.

"That's the road to Irchester on the right," Justus said, pointing to the road off to the right. He was attempting to educate some of the younger troopers under his command, something he was always trying to do. A few yards further on, he spoke again,

"I lost a silver denarius here a couple of years back, when I went for a squat over there. It's mine if you find it."

They went on another 400 yards and clattered over the wooden bridge over the Ouzel at Fenny Stratford. The horses' hooves produced an impressive sound as they trotted across the bridge and into the northern part of Fenny Stratford.

Fenny Stratford consisted of two small villages, one each side of the River Ouzel. The lower, southside of the river, was inhabited by semi-Romanised Britons, some of them still in their roundhouses. The higher, north side was most definitely Roman inhabitants, many of them retired legionaries. Here many of the buildings were rectangular and two stories, some with thatched roofs some with tiled roofs. Justus, having travelled Watling Street a number of times, had always wondered how the two communities lived so close together in apparent harmony.

Arriving over the bridge, The Heron Inn and staging post of Fenny Stratford was the third building on the right. It was a modern Roman style building with whitewashed walls and tiled roof. Justus was greeted by the Inn Keeper coming out of the front door, wiping his hands on his apron, saying,

"Hello Justus, how the Zeus are you?"

"I am very well, thank you Flavius. How are you?" Justus replied.

"I am very well," Flavius said, with a big smile and grasping Justus by the arm shook hands warmly in the Roman fashion. "All the better for seeing you."

The Hostler took Justus's horse from him, saying,

"Thank you, Sir," and led it away to the stables, behind the inn.

Flavius and Justus were old friends from the Po Valley. They had joined the army together, and had served in the same cohort, mainly in northern Germany. Their mothers were also good friends, working together in the pot factory of their village, in northern Italy. Justus was not sure he had ever mentioned to Flavius that he had been adopted, but this was not the time or place. Flavius had retired from the cavalry two years ago and had married Anatolia and set himself up as the Inn Keeper of the Heron Inn. Like Justus, he had been a legionary and had transferred to the cavalry.

"There is something happening down south, have you any idea what it is Justus?" Flavius asked inquiringly, even though he must know half the story from passing refugees.

"Someone upset the Queen of the Iceni. It was the last straw for her, and she has organised a revolt, which is now getting out of hand. In fact, it's way out of control! They have destroyed Colchester, including our Temple to Claudius, and sacked St. Albans and London," Justus said.

"Wow! Holy Zeus! That's a revolt. It's true then," Flavius said, "that means we've been cut off from the continent and

Rome. Our legions are miles away. Some of our soldiers came through here a few weeks back. The last we heard; they were in North Wales."

"I don't blame her for throwing a wobbly. I was there when they flogged her and then raped her daughters. It was shocking! It was disgusting!" Justus explained. Deep down inside, Justus wanted someone to talk to, and Flavius was just the man. He was a good listener; an old mate and they both viewed the world in the same way. Both ducked their heads, under the door-way as they went into the inn,

"I need a drink, have you any good wine on the go?" Justus whispered, and then he shouted out to his troopers,

"See to the horses' boys, I'm busy in here."

"Pull up a chair and make yourself at home. I'll be with you in a moment," Flavius said, pointing towards his right. Justus went over to the fire-place in the corner of the room, and sat down. He was pleased to see Anatolia, Flavius's wife, come into the room sooner than he thought, with a jug of wine and water.

Justus had not paid too much attention to Anatolia last time they had met, but this time she seemed voluptuously attractive. Perhaps it was the spring warmth that changed a woman's appearance. Anatolia was a very attractive woman. His thoughts were broken by his old mate Flavius, who came into the room and sat down opposite him, as Anatolia moved away.

"Now Justus, you tell me all about it . . . . . ."

After a long heart to heart chat about the stressful things that had happened in the last 15 days, Flavius asked Justus,

"So, when will these rebellious Iceni be here?" Justus responded slowly as the wine had taken effect.

"Well, they've got two places where they will be held up. The first is the steep slope after Dunstable and the second is the bridge I burnt. They could be here tomorrow, at the earliest maybe, but more likely, in three days."

"Holy Zeus! They will trash this place when they get here! Holy Zeus! What do we do? Anatolia! Anatolia!" Flavius cried out to his wife, as he went off to find her.

Anatolia came storming into the room, her eyes ablaze with anger!

"Justus, you've been here, drinking with my husband for ages, and it's only just now that you've seen fit to tell him that there's a band of rebels coming up the road. Why didn't you tell us before?"

"I did not want to scare you." Justus was racking his brain for a good excuse and trying to clear the alcohol away from his brain. "I thought you knew. They might be here the day after tomorrow," Justus muttered, not daring to look Anatolia in the eye.

"Tonight, we will pack our things together and go first thing in the morning. I am sorry love, I'm so sorry," Flavius apologised.

Justus left the scene, as it seemed fitting to do so, before Anatolia became really angry. His troopers would be ready to leave for Stony Stratford in the morning. It was less than 10 miles away; they should easily get there for lunchtime.

The Immunis's legionaries seemed happy to stay in Fenny for the night, at the small barracks behind The Heron Inn.

It was nearing the middle of the night when Anatolia very quietly awoke and turned over to face her husband's sleeping body. Anatolia nestled up against his head, first breathing and then whispering in his ear.

"If we destroy the bridge, Honeypuff," for that was what she called him, "those nasty rebels won't be able to get across the river." Flavius was not paying too much attention to what Anatolia was saying as he was very sleepy. Anatolia snuggled closer and mentioned the bridge again.

"So, Flavius Honeypuff, what do you think to my idea? Justus gave me the idea when he told us about the bridge he burned and destroyed at Hockliffe, down the road. Could we burn our bridge, here?" she asked as she moved still closer to him.

"Remind me love, sorry, I was not fully awake when you mentioned it last time," Flavius whispered, as he was in two minds. One mind was trying to go back to sleep. The other mind was trying to wake up and attend to his wife.

"I said, if we destroy the bridge, those nasty rebels won't be able to get across the River."

Suddenly his brain switched on! One moment he was trying to rouse himself, the next he was thinking about how to destroy the bridge. She had got his attention!

"Right!" Flavius spoke softly, as he didn't want to wake anyone else in the household. "If you want the bridge destroyed, we'd better get out there and do it now. You get me some lamp oil, and I'll get some firewood. But first we had better get some clothes on."

They were lucky, as the moon was nearly full, and it was a clear night, making it easy to see quite clearly outside in the road. Flavius knew, from his military experience, that if they crept down to the bridge, sleeping people would suspect something. Therefore, with a big bundle of firewood in a leather bag and his wife beside him, they walked down to the bridge in a normal fashion. She carried the lamp oil and a small iron bucket of embers from the fire. The river was low, which enabled him to climb down the bank, underneath the bridge, where his wife handed him the necessary materials to light the fire. Carefully and strategically, as it was quite dark under the bridge, he placed the embers at the base of his prepared combustible pile of wood.

It did not take the fire long to take hold, especially with the added lamp oil. Then, not wanting to be seen next to the fire, Flavius and his wife went quietly back home. They were getting undressed, ready to get back into bed, when they heard shouting. Obviously, they knew the reason for the shouting, so they put their clothes back on for a second time and theatrically went out to see what all the shouting was about. The whole village was out of bed putting the fire out, with the easily accessible water from the river. Bother! Anatolia thought.

In the morning Flavius went down to the bridge to see what damage they had done. He was disappointed to see that there had not been very much damage to the bridge. But it was damaged enough for a waggon not to be able to go over it.

While Flavius was examining the scene, he heard a familiar voice behind him,

"I wonder who did that?" Justus uttered softly.

"Umm, it could have been anyone," Flavius said, "and I wonder why?"

"Whoever it was, obviously didn't want anyone to cross the bridge," Justus replied.

"We certainly don't want the rebels to cross the river, it's best they keep south of here, and go somewhere else with their violence and destruction," Flavius said.

"They cannot cross with their chariots and waggons without extreme difficulty. Unless they mend the bridge," Justus said.

"But that would take some time," Flavius stated, "by which time, Paulinus might well have his legion's here."

"I am trying to work out where they might be now. They could be here anytime in the next five days, I should think," Justus said.

"Let's try and work it out shall we," Flavius said, as both men turned to slowly walk back to The Heron Inn. "How long ago did that awful incident happen, with Boudicca and Catus?"

Justus went through things in his head, adding up the days since the event, that terrible event that he witnessed. After a short time, he came up with his calculated answer.

"I think it was about 14 or 15 days ago."

"And how far is it to North Wales? Around 250 miles, maybe a bit less," Flavius responded. So, when we were in the Legion, we could manage 18 to 20 miles a day, so that makes it about 13 to 14 days march away."

"Wow, that's good then! We've got to add a few days for messages, packing things up and other delays. Oh, talking of messages, did you know that Paulinus was told of this revolt by pigeon post. He said he received the information within a day of Colchester being attacked," Justus said.

"That means the Legion could have started marching

down here the day after The Temple of Claudius burned," Flavius said. "Pigeon post, I've heard of it," he went on, "we obtained it from the Persians, but I've never rated it as being reliable. There is so much to organise. You've got to know which pigeon homes to which place and how long you can keep them before sending them home. If you keep a pigeon too long in one place, surely it must think it has a new home. No, I've never believed in pigeon post."

"Paulinus seems to think it works," replied Justus. "It's a great communication method, but one that I do not fully understand." Just then they were joined by the Immunis.

"Ah," said Flavius, "you're the man who deserted his post at Dunstable." Flavius felt he could say such risky things, as he had been senior to the Immunis, before he retired from the army. "Yes Sir," said the Immunis. He then continued directing his words to Justus,

"My men and I will remain here, in Fenny Stratford, and assist the locals in holding this bridge against the rebels. I shamefully abandoned my post in Dunstable. I should not abandon two posts."

"Good man," Justus said, "I admire you." He was surprised that the Immunis had actually said that. He didn't think he had it in him, to stand and fight.

"I too admire you," Flavius stated. "I will get my old armour out, well that which I did not sell, and polish it up. I will join you holding the bridge for the sake of my wife Anatolia, and my family."

Justus then announced to both Flavius and the Immunis.

"It's good talking to you Flavius, and I wish we could stay longer, but I have orders to continue up Watling Street and meet up with Paulinus. I am leaving three of my men here, in case there are developments, and there is a need to send messages north, up this road to Paulinus."

"I understand that you've got to go, Justus," Flavius said, "orders are orders."

"I am sorry I have to leave you in this predicament, but I will stress to Paulinus your position, and perhaps he will hurry to bring his Legions here."

"Thank you, Justus. I know you'll do your best," Flavius said, with anxiety.

Justus responded,

"Let's have breakfast and then get my boys mounted up."

## CHAPTER XXIV

# Waiting for the Waggons

Boudicca, Dan and Garos were up early the next day. They were eager to scout around and have a 'look see' after breakfast, at their surroundings in Little Brickhill.

Other mounted warriors also went out to have a look around the area, with a view to this being a good place to hold out against the Romans. It was a good breakfast of bacon and eggs, followed by some pottage that had been left from the night before. They put on their outdoor clothing, soggy moccasins, and their hats and proceeded outside. The clear skies last night left a chilly morning.

"It's good to fill yourself up with a big breakfast, when you don't know when and where your next meal is coming from," Dan declared. They left cross-roads in the small village and walked North-East along a local road. The good view they had experienced from the hilltop at Little Brickhill itself, slowly disappeared over their left shoulders as they walked.

"This road goes towards Kempston and Irchester

beyond," Garos said, holding up the Roman route tablet in his hand. "I found this in the Green Man Inn."

They walked out of the village, down a dip and up the other side and on for some 500 yards. Here they saw that the top of the hill went round to the left and overlooked the Watling Street below. The road itself went right a little, and on towards the North-East into the Woods.

⁂

Boudicca, Dan and Garos arrived back at The Green Man Inn at Little Brickhill, to be greeted by Nomass sitting outside. He looked very pleased with himself, swigging away on a jug of beer.

"Hello Mom," Nomass said, as he was very respectful of his leader. "We've seen some Romans further up the road, in Fenny Stratford. They were on the other side of the bridge. A dozen of us, on chariots and horses, went down past the roundhouses you can see there." Nomass pointed down the hill to the roundhouses, on the other side of the abandoned Roman Fort.

They all looked down to where Nomass was pointing and Boudicca said,

"Oh yes, I see it."

"There were a dozen Romans the other side of the bridge. They must have seen us coming, because they were all dressed up in their finest armour and we could see that they were armed with those nasty throwing weapons. We stayed out of range and tried to see what they were about."

"There is quite a bit of smoke coming from the buildings there," Dan said, "so there must be quite a number of them."

"Oh, we did see quite a number of women and kids

there too," Nomass continued. "There appeared to be some fire damage to the bridge. My mate, silly sod, he went a bit closer than we did, to investigate and got shot at. He told me it looks 'substantially damaged' on one side, so although you can get across in single file, he reckons we could not get any waggons across the bridge. Oh yes, the missiles missed him."

"Substantially, that's a big word for one of your mates to use, Nomass, I didn't know you moved in such educated circles," Boudicca said, in acknowledgement.

"That's his only skill, Mom, using big words, he's not much good at anything else."

"He has a second skill," Boudicca replied, "he is brave."

They all went inside the Green Man Inn to discuss what to do. They were not in a hurry to leave, as they were lucky that the people of the staging post, having left quickly, had left plenty of food behind. There was still plenty of that half-eaten wild boar to finish off with some peas and pottage.

They were halfway through their discussions when a number of Iceni riders came into Little Brickhill. Boudicca went straight outside through the small doorway and asked them,

"How far away are our waggons?"

"Sorry Mom, we can't answer that. We were some way ahead of the waggons yesterday evening, when we decided to rest for the night in a small wood. We slept rough under the stars, most uncomfortable it was, but the ground was sort of dry."

"Very sandy soil round these parts," another rider said.

"I wonder what's keeping them?" Boudicca asked, "perhaps we ought to send a couple of riders back, to see what's happening."

"Those oxen looked tired and they are very slow moving. There are also a few hills after Hockliffe, and you know how oxen struggle up hills. They also have to rest halfway through the day," Nomass said. "The warriors who were walking with them looked pretty tired too. It's not something they are used to. Walking long distances, that is."

Later, some scouts came riding back to The Green Man Inn. Boudicca had sent them out earlier, to have a look around towards the south west - the opposite direction to which Boudicca had taken earlier. They reported to her that in that direction, you go to a place called Stewkley.

"Thank you," Boudicca said, "anything else?"

"The road is a bit twisty, and it goes up and down, but it generally keeps to the ridge and you can see for miles over to the right. That is, over to the west from the ridge, if you know what I mean," one of the scouts reported.

"If the Romans were to attack us over on that side, do you think they could take us by surprise?" Garos asked.

"No, I don't think so, it would be a long way round for them, and we could see them moving across the plain at the bottom of the hill," the scout answered.

"I'll go and take a look this afternoon," Garos said, "there is nothing like going to have a look-see for yourself. There's so much out there to take in and appreciate."

"I would like to go with you Garos," uttered Dan, "but my moccasins need a few stitches and would fall apart if I went very far. Otherwise, I would love to join you."

"Why don't you mend them cousin?" Boudicca asked.

"My mending stuff is in one of my waggons with Cartimandua and my sons. I can stitch them up, when they get here. I have been asking around, but nobody's got their mending equipment with them or they have used all their thread."

Unbeknown to those who had reached Little Brickhill, especially the leaders who had gone off enthusiastically, there was a long column of Britons almost stretching back to Dunstable. There were some breaks in the long column, as those moving faster bunched up behind the slower movers. Getting the waggons down the slope just out of Dunstable was causing great delays that resulted in the whole of Boudicca's army being strung out over many miles.

Crossing the muddy filled-in brook just north of Hockliffe, was causing more delays and distress. The advanced parties of tribesmen, who had arrived at the burnt bridge and had filled the ditch in, had no idea of the chaos and trouble they caused for those that followed. When the brook was initially filled-in with fascines, the water flowed through them easily. Unfortunately, these fascines then became squashed and clogged up with silt and the filled-in brook, became a dam. A small lake had been formed. The water flowed over the top of the dam and across the road, causing a sea of mud. The soft sludge was just a short distance for the tribesmen to cover but not an ideal road. After crossing this short muddy stretch, tribesmen had to walk with sodden, wet moccasins. It was extremely uncomfortable and squidgy around one's feet.

There was still another 10 miles to go in this condition, to catch up with the leaders at Little Brickhill. However, those slowly trudging on behind the leaders felt abandoned. They had no idea how far they had to go to catch up, and were rapidly losing the will to continue. Boudicca and her fellow leaders should have realised those behind needed more encouragement and gone back to inspire them and keep them involved in her plans, but Boudicca was someone who led from the front, expecting those behind to be just as enthusiastic as she was.

Cousin Cartimandua was one of those left behind, and was a little narked at having to look after Dan's two waggons. She did not see the benefit of Dan riding alongside their cousin Boudicca. She was assisted by Dan's sons Morcant and Talos and their friend Scarr, but they had all had a hard time looking after and controlling the oxen. It had been especially difficult getting the two waggons, the 14 oxen and themselves down the 1 in 8 steep, chalky, slippery slope out of Dunstable! To top it all, there had just been some light rain prior to their descent. Their oxen had been lucky, but others had fallen and become lame.

Some animals were too lame to continue, so they had to be slaughtered for their meat. There were two significant results from this. The first was that some heavy waggons had less oxen to pull them, making life even harder for those that remained. The second result was that no one went hungry, they feasted on the meat. However, they were valuable animals, and a critical component of the economy and their loss would be keenly felt. Other waggon drivers stopped, to reconsider their situation, while their lame oxen were nursed.

Then, later in the afternoon at Hockliffe, Cartimandua and the boys found themselves trudging through 6 inches of liquefied, cold mud where the brook had been filled in.

After all this, they had found that they were amongst some of the last of the waggons in the long column of travellers.

Cartimandua had had a bad day! They decided to stop and camp for the night, before attempting the next hill. It was not easy though, to find somewhere to park their two waggons. Many others in front had just pulled off the road, blocking access to the grassed areas at the side. She did not blame them for doing that as it would be difficult to get off the wet soggy grass, back onto the road, if you were some distance from the road. It was easy to tell that the ground here was clay, even in the fading light of the evening.

Oxen and heavy waggons do not move very easily on grass, it makes life much easier to keep to the road. Cartimandua decided to move on up the hill in the dark, past many parked waggons, to find somewhere to stop and camp for the night.

They reached the top of the hill sometime after sunset and looked down into the valley and across to the opposite hilltop about a mile away. They had heard a rumour that there were over 400 waggons in Boudicca's army, and the view in front of them confirmed this. Parked each side of the road were waggons lit up in the dark, by the campfires alongside them. There would be nowhere to park their two waggons in the next mile of Watling Street. They were tired and hungry, as were the oxen. They started to descend the hill carefully, as the waggon was heavy, and the brakes were poor. Then someone called out from a campfire at the side of the road as they were passing.

"Hey Cartimandua, come and park over here. If you unhitch your oxen, we can bring your waggons and leave them between ours, and that way you won't block the road."

It was a great relief. The men round the campfire helped them unhitch their oxen and manhandle both their heavy waggons off the road, manoeuvring them between their own vehicles. When the oxen were grazing and the chocks placed under the wheels, the same man, with unusually white teeth, said,

"Please, come and join us, we have plenty of lamb stew and biscuits."

Cartimandua, Scarr, Morcant and Talos sat down with their new friends, by the campfire. They were very tired from a difficult day of travelling. Cartimandua sat down next to the man who had invited them, as she felt obliged to do so. She was not sure if she knew the gentleman, especially in this light, but he did seem to ring a bell in the back of her mind.

The white toothed man, who had invited them to their campfire, then asked Cartimandua,

"You must have the ear of Boudicca, as you are her cousin?"

"I'm not sure I do, but why do you ask?" Cartimandua said, still trying to remember where she had seen him before.

"Have you any idea, what has she got in mind for the Romans when she meets them?" the man asked.

"I am very sorry, but I don't know. I was given the job, a very responsible job, of bringing our cousin Dan's two waggons, and his sons here," Cartimandua pointed to the three young men with her." By the time we arrived in St. Albans, all the action was over! The city had been taken, the place looted and young men ravaged! I missed out there," she joked. Those around the campfire were listening intently to her story and chuckled, so Cartimandua continued,

"There was hardly any time to rest before we moved on, fairly swiftly, to Dunstable. We could have put more supplies on our waggons if we had arrived earlier, but we just have the normal dried food stuff that we bought from home. That reminds me, how far are we from home, here?"

"Oh, that's not easy to work out, as our route has been the shape of a dog leg. However, I think we have travelled at least 85 miles to get here from Ixworth. We might be 70 miles from home as the crow flies," the white toothed man answered.

"Oh, heavens above, that's a long way back home, and that's only to Ixworth!"

"Yes, I know," the man said, "we've come a long way." Scarr then interrupted the conversation,

"I am not used to walking these sort of distances, the furthest I go is to my girlfriend in the next village, and then sometimes, when I stay over . . . . ."

Cartimandua, cut him short saying,

"We don't want to know about that Scarr."

"But it gets quite interesting . . . .".

"We don't want to know about that Scarr."

Cartimandua, then started to undo the laces on her moccasins, saying,

"I must see to my feet. Morcant, please could you get me a rag from the waggon?" The same man quickly responded, saying,

"I've got a rag here, if you'd like to use it." He offered her a warm rag, that he had been drying on a couple of sticks by the fire.

Cartimandua wondered if the white toothed man was being over-friendly for a reason. Then the moment went, and she attended to her feet, wiping the mud from between her toes. This was the mud that she had picked up when extricating the waggon from the mud in Hockliffe. She was thinking, as she cleaned her feet, was this man worth befriending?

After their evening meal under the stars, Cartimandua noticed a young couple on the opposite side of the fire, snuggling up to each for warmth. They were enjoying each other's company and their adventure up Watling Street. The man got up and brought over a heavy amphora, from his waggon, and went back for some rather nice drinking glasses. Wine was poured and past around. Cartimandua turning the wine around her glass, asked the young man who had poured it,

"These are lovely, I've never seen anything like them before, where did you get them?"

"What, these drinking containers, I found them in a big house in St. Albans, they are rather nice, are they not," the young man answered. "It was one of the advantages of getting to St. Albans first."

"They are fantastic!" Cartimandua complemented, as she continued turning the red wine around in the glass, looking at the fire glinting through the glass. She was in total admiration for the glass in her hand.

Everyone had a good chat and singsong around the campfire and became merry.

At the same time, nine miles away, Boudicca was spending her first evening in Little Brickhill. She and her close friends were having bacon, eggs and pottage. They were with Iceni friends, and had full stomachs. But there were many others, in this rag and tag army, camped out in the open, with no shelter and no food, because their waggons had been left miles behind. Those with the waggons were having a good time singing around campfires with wine the wine having gone to their heads, like Cartimandua and company. However, they were not looking forward to going to bed, lying on the ground under whatever shelter they could provide for themselves.

※

All through that afternoon, leading members of Boudicca's army had been coming into Little Brickhill slowly and continuously. The small village of Little Brickhill was beginning to become crowded with horsemen and women continually arriving. They were some of the faster moving of the long train of tribesmen travelling up the Watling Street. These people were also some of the keener and more excited adventurers of Boudicca's army. The slower less motivated warriors were further back in the column of unsupervised troops. Most of those arriving were hungry. They had eaten the small amount of supplies they had brought with them from St. Albans, on their march north through Dunstable and on to Little Brickhill. St. Albans had been the last opportunity for them to replenish the food they carried on their person.

Boudicca and Dan then overheard one of the scouts ask loudly,

"Is there any food left? There was quite a bit when we left here this morning, but it seems to have all gone."

Dan's thoughts went back to the beginning of the campaign, when he had mentioned to Boudicca that an army needed supplies, and this required organising. He had volunteered to help her with this, but in all the excitement, he had neglected to give it the consideration it needed. However, things had moved on a pace, with little or no organization. Dan acknowledged to himself, that he had played his part in this chaos.

There had been great excitement in advancing quickly and attacking St. Albans, which the Trinovantes had spearheaded. They had left St. Albans with similar eagerness, but here in Green Man Inn, Dan began to see the excitement dwindling. Many were keen to move on to the next location, without great thought about the logistics of the whole adventure. Here they were, some of the leading elements of the grand column of tribesmen, at a place called Little Brickhill. It commanded a great view to their front. Behind them however, supply waggons faltered on a congested road, while the leaders were too busy planning the next move ahead, without consideration for those behind.

Dan looked over at his cousin Boudicca, sitting at a table in the Green Man Inn. She was surrounded by fighting men, all wanting answers to their questions. When will our waggons be arriving? How far away are the Romans? What news from our scouts? Is there any food in this place? Questions she had real difficulty answering. Questions she had never had to even consider before!

This was a whole new experience for her - organising 60,000 tribesmen from four different tribes. Someone had to be in control, but it was not easy for her and probably would not be easy for anybody.

Boudicca stood up and banged the table hard with her empty jug. Everyone slowly stopped talking and there was silence in the room. Raising her voice so all could hear her, she shouted,

"There will be a meeting tomorrow afternoon, here this inn, a little before sunset. By then perhaps, our waggons will have arrived, and everyone will have their campfires lit and be settled in. I will be announcing our plans for the next few days and discussing our tactics. In the mean-time we stay here, getting to know the place and resting. Thank you everyone."

She sat down, tired.

## CHAPTER XXV

# WE MEET AGAIN

Justus, with his remaining 5 troopers, was making good progress on his way up Watling Street, in the hope of meeting Paulinus coming the other way. He had left three of his men at The Heron Inn staging post, in Fenny Stratford, with his old mate and retired colleague Flavius.

The going was good in the morning sunshine, as it had not rained here recently. Although there were only six of them, Justus had sent a man out ahead, in case of ambush. It was amazing how the original group of 30 cavalrymen, usually called a Turma in Roman military terms, had been reduced to 6 in less than 20 days, but there was an emergency. The Iceni revolt - led by Boudicca.

They stopped at the Stony Stratford staging post to change horses and have a bite to eat. Stony was one of the larger resting places on Watling Street, not far from the River Great Ouse. The town had many inns, and Justus especially liked The Bull, where the food was always good. On this occasion he and a fellow trooper had a lunch of eggs and salt bacon. Remarkably, Stony had become Romanised very quickly, and Justus noticed marked differences every time he came through the small township.

It was one of those places that was renowned for flooding, although the staging post itself normally escaped the worst of the damage. Justus enjoyed stopping over here, as the place was always that much friendlier than other towns, they stayed in. Everyone seemed to be happy here.

They set off after lunch, towards Towcester, less than 10 miles away. Towcester was a large place and was the next town on Watling Street north from St. Albans. There was normally a large garrison of legionaries based there. If he was lucky, he might see some of his old friends and colleagues there, as it was quite a busy garrison town. However, with many troops away in North Wales, it might be an empty place.

With Stony Stratford half a mile behind them, their new mounts clattered over the bridge crossing the Great Ouse River. The bridge had not been built long, and Justus remembered when it was a wide, shallow, stony bottomed ford, that could not be crossed in times of flood. The bridge had made a huge difference to the way that travellers, especially those with waggons, crossed the river. The river, although quite small, presented a linear obstacle that stopped the movement of everyone in times of flood, and made it difficult for waggons even in the height of summer.

As they left the river behind them, they passed a number of mausoleums, on the right of the road, and Clodius Felix, one of the troopers, pointed one out saying,

"That is one of those pipe burials I was telling you about. That dead chap must have been a wine lover, he's got a pipe that goes down into his coffin, so his mates can give him some wine, even though he's dead."

"Shush," Justus whispered, "you shouldn't go shouting that around, he may have a loved one nearby."

"Sorry, Sir," Clodius whispered back. "He must have been quite an important bloke, looking at the size of his vault."

"He didn't pour all his wealth down his throat then, like most of us do, he saved some for his mausoleum." Justus had the last word on the matter.

The next 10 miles, along the road to Towcester, was straight and undulating. The passing scenery consisted of the occasional meadow but was mainly woods. Justus aimed to make Towcester for lunch and to change their tired horses for new ones. Travelling at their normal pace, he was attempting to estimate when they might meet Paulinus or it might even be his whole army, Legio XX and Legio XIV. He gave that idea up as his thoughts were broken when he noticed their pack mule in front of him in difficulty. This animal carried all their equipment and had developed a slight limp on is rear right leg that might need attention, should it get any worse.

Justus enjoyed the hustle and bustle of Towcester, for it was always a hectic place. It was situated on a significant crossroad in the middle of Britannia, and he felt it was one of the top six towns in Britain. It was a Roman town through and through, unlike other towns that had been built on existing Celtic sites. In choosing this virgin site to develop a town, they had not upset many local citizens, as they had done elsewhere. The architecture was coming on nicely, and the people seemed to be settled. The town had character and, very important from a Roman point of view, it had strong timber ramparts, that were being reinforced here and there with stonework. He felt proud of what his countrymen had achieved in such a short time.

There was a significant garrison here, well located in the middle of the country, ready to move in any direction depending on where the trouble was. Although Paulinus had taken the majority of the garrison's legionaries with him to North Wales, he would have left enough men here to make a stand against Boudicca's tribesmen, that might be coming up Watling Street.

Towcester's location, in the centre of Britannia, did mean that it was a good place for a rendezvous of legions. It was here that Paulinus had ordered Legio II to march from Exeter, to reinforce part of Paulinus's Legio XX and all of Legio XIV coming down from North Wales. The two legions, with auxiliary troops, might well be in excess of 18,000 men. Justus was looking forward to seeing the two legions in Towcester very soon. It would be a sight that he had not seen in his lifetime. He had not been involved in the initial force of four legions in 43 AD when Emperor Claudius had ordered the invasion of Britannia.

Justus had also felt very lonely and vulnerable since Boudicca's flogging. There had been no significant Roman force anywhere he had been in the last 20 days, and he was certainly looking forward to feeling protected again, by his fellow Romans.

Justus's stomach was telling him that it was close to lunchtime, and knowing the local topography of Watling Street, he concluded that they were perhaps only two miles from Towcester. However, up ahead he saw that Clodius

Felix, his trooper riding out in front, was in contact with riders coming the other way. Could this be Paulinus? It was! This time he had more troops with him, possibly as many as 200 cavalrymen.

"Greetings, Duplicarius Rufus," Paulinus shouted as he approached. "Join me as we ride along and brief me as to what has been happening." Justus told him all that he had experienced since last they met, and having concluded his report, he asked Paulinus,

"And what of your legions, Sir?"

"I have Legio XIV with me and a small number of cohorts from Legio XX together with the usual auxiliary troops. I trust them to be about 20 miles behind us. The total number is probably around 10,000 men. Let us hope that this is enough, because Poenius Postumus from Exeter does not look like he is going to join us." Legate Suetonius Paulinus was on a roll and continued his dialogue with Justus,

"If we wait for him, the initiative may well be lost. If I understand these Britons at all, if they realise, they have the upper hand in numbers, the Eastern tribes may be joined by those in this area, and we will have more than just four tribes against us. There are over 20 tribes in this Zeus forsaken province. I do not want to fight them all, when I only have four legions this side of the channel. Perhaps I should say three and a half legions after the battle of Sawtry Woods, that I have recently heard about."

"Yes Sir, it was terrible to learn of that disaster," Justus replied. Paulinus continued again,

"This revolt is less than 20 days old. What do you suspect, Duplicarius Rufus, will happen when the revolt is 40 days old? What numbers will we be up against then? Will they multiply?"

"That is a difficult question, Sir,' Justus answered, "but I suspect you are right. This revolt started with just the Iceni Tribe, but, I believe from the little information I have been able to pick up on the way, has now been joined by the Trinovantes, Catuvellavni and some Cantiaci."

"Yes, Duplicarius, thank you, therefore we have to act quickly. I do not want to find us fighting the Brigantes from Yorkshire, I could see them being formidable. These Barbarians are very good at guerrilla tactics, and we could lose many of our troops in that way. I want to nip this revolt in the bud, and soon!"

"Yes Sir," Justus replied.

"Enough of this talk," Paulinus said, "have your men fall in behind mine, and wish us God's speed to Fenny Stratford."

Justus and his 5 troopers fell in behind the other 200 men, and he began thinking of his stomach and the possibility of changing horses again soon. What he should have been thinking about, was the coming battle, and his role in it. He found it a relief to be in the company of 200 of his fellow countrymen, and no longer in loan command of just a few troopers.

## CHAPTER XXVI

# GOING HUNGRY

The meeting Boudicca chaired yesterday afternoon had been productive. They had agreed on three things:

**One**; here in Little Brickhill, on top of the hill, they had a very good view of the ground over which the Romans would be coming and thus, would be safer than if they moved further on North, up Watling Street. They would wait here for their whole army to arrive.

**Two**; to send out further scouts to investigate their surroundings, particularly the river and the burnt bridge in the valley between them and Fenny Stratford.

**Three**; to find out what was happening to the rest of the waggons carrying all their supplies.

Boudicca, and all those who had gone ahead of the rest of the army, had spent the night in Little Brickhill. Some had had the benefit of sleeping in buildings, but many others had to bivouac uncomfortably in the nearby woods. Rain had been forecast by those who knew 'weather craft' and many prepared for it. Those who knew the craft of bivouacking quickly taught others how to do it. People stretched twine between adjacent trees, and using copious amounts of twigs and young bracken, provided themselves with some form of shelter. However, not all of them were skilled in this type of construction and many became quite wet during the night. That was very sad!

Those that had been able to sleep, woke wet and cold. Others, unable to sleep at all, were up all night trying to keep themselves warm by their fires. The rain had not been hard enough to put fires out, that had been well looked after. Most went in search of breakfast and generally found none. One lucky person found 5 chicken eggs and secretly kept them to himself and his mate. A second lucky person found the same chicken hen house, and rung their necks, so he and his mates did not go hungry. Most realised the importance of the waggons carrying their food and shelter. To march on enthusiastically ahead of their waggons meant they would be cold and hungry when night-time came.

Slowly, throughout the morning, the long column of tribesmen arrived at Little Brickhill and for once, someone was organising where to park the waggons and graze the oxen. The little village was on a crossroads. Watling Street went down the hill towards Fenny Stratford, just under two miles away, and the road that crossed this ran along a ridge. It was agreed amongst the leaders, that the place to park the waggons when they arrived, would be along the ridge. It would mean that they did not have to pull the waggons too far off the road onto the wet ground, making it easier to get back on the road afterwards. Also, the ground here was not very flat, and manoeuvring the heavy waggons around on the slopes was hazardous. Once a waggon begins to move, there is not much a load of blokes can do to stop it, when on wet sloping ground. If there are no chocks to hand when the waggon starts moving, gravity takes hold!

It was not long before waggons were being parked on both sides of the road in either direction. Boudicca knew that approximately 710 waggons would be arriving at Little Brickhill over the course of the day. She therefore instructed a number of responsible people to direct each waggon, either left or right, down the side roads to a suitable parking place alongside the road.

All these waggons had a great number of oxen to pull them. Fortunately, there was a great sloping meadow down to the river at Fenny Stratford. Here the spring grass had grown well providing much fodder for the oxen.

Those directing the waggons felt they were doing a responsible and worthwhile job, especially as Boudicca, their Queen, had personally asked them. The ridge had an excellent view towards Fenny Stratford in the North. It was strongly believed, this was the direction the Romans would come from, if the Britons were attacked.

Knowing they were going to stay here for a night or two, people began to unpack their tents and make themselves at home. Naturally, as each waggon arrived, there were crowds of people around it, eagerly wanting to get at their food and supplies. Generally, this happened in an orderly fashion, but people were hungry, and tempers went a little awry here and there. The average number of people each waggon could carry supplies for would be around 80. Although there were pack mules and individuals who carried their own food and equipment, when a waggon arrived there would be many people around it attempting to unload it and get at their own supplies.

In amongst all this confusion, the oxen were led away to rest and eat grass on the nearby slopes.

Boudicca was expecting over 700 waggons, but as afternoon became evening, stories of waggons stopping, or being delayed, increased. A few of Boudicca's helpers estimated that around 480 waggons had arrived and parked up, in and around Little Brickhill. She and some of her leaders began to suspect that a number of followers had deserted. Perhaps they were tired of walking, perhaps their waggons had broken or perhaps they just wanted to return home with their booty from London and St. Albans.

Checking on the number of waggons in the growing dusk was not easy and to what end? There was evidence that a few people were joining the army from the surrounding area, who had not been involved in the destruction of St. Albans.

Some of the last people to arrive, like Cartimandua, had not had time to rest since they left Dunstable three days earlier. They had stopped and rested at night, but the days had been long and hard. Sometimes they had been held up in queues, due to break-downs, and with the constant need to rest and graze the oxen it had been most tiring. It was good to eventually find somewhere a little more permanent, where they could rest and take stock.

Boudicca agreed with Garos that they should hold another meeting in the Green Man that evening. She was becoming more confident in her leadership role, and asked the scouts to come forward with their reports of what they had seen. A spokeswoman came forward.

"Yes Mom. There is a river, about 2 miles north of here, that we have to cross if we want to go on. There is a bridge, there are many areas of soft ground and marsh nearby. Consequently, the ground becomes less suitable for chariots and horsemen, the closer you get to the river. We had to pick our way across the better ground. I would not want to have to fight on that ground, although it would be a good area for our slingers to work from. They would have to take their own ammunition with them though, as the only stones down there would be in the river." Everyone chuckled.

The spokeswoman continued nervously; she was not used to public speaking.

"We went down to the bridge, Mom, on horseback. We were accompanied by a number of warriors, perhaps 400, who wanted to get a closer look at the Romans. Some of them went past us to the river to see how deep it was."

"Were they not shot at?" Boudicca asked.

"No, Mom, they went further upstream and downstream, where we could tell that there weren't any Romans on the other side of the river. Two of our party waded all the way across to the other side. I reckon they were on a dare! There were some armed Romans on the other side, but no more than a dozen. They had erected a barricade across the road, and on each side, they had dug a ditch and put stakes on top. It looked quite defensible. There were other people there as well, who were not soldiers. They probably came from the village. If you understand what I mean Mom."

"Anything else," Boudicca asked,

"Three of our foot warriors went forward with shields, to have a closer look at the bridge. They were shot at, though. Two or three Romans had bows and the arrows looked quite threatening, so our boys retreated. The ground near the river was really boggy, there was moss and loads of that bog grass, they said."

"So, they were shot at, then," Boudicca stated.

"Oh yes, Mom, they were, sorry I forgot."

"What were you doing all this time?" Boudicca asked.

"We estimated the range of their bows and remained beyond that distance. They did shoot at us, but the arrows fell short. It was quite easy to go forward with so few arrows falling, you can see them coming through the air at you, and dodge out of the way.

"I have heard that the arrow that gets you, is the one you don't see coming!" shouted a one-eyed man from the back of the room.

"Continue," said Boudicca assertively, "never mind him." Boudicca had not noticed the poor gentleman only had one eye.

"Two of our brave boys went forward and retrieved some arrows. They were easy to see, sticking up in the short grass, and I have two of them here for you Mom. It is the short range arrows you lose in the grass." Those listening nodded.

Boudicca had obviously seen arrows before, but these were Roman arrows and a little different. She looked at the first one that was rather shoddy in its workmanship, and was probably used for sighting. However, the second was rather a splendid missile, with a sharp iron head and lovely goose feathered flights. It was certainly a well-crafted and vicious-looking piece of kit, almost as well made as those crafted by the Iceni.

"Oh, you wouldn't want that sticking in you, would you?" Boudicca said, with a cringe.

The spokeswoman then continued her report,

"Another four of our young men went down closer to the river, and used their slings against the Romans. As you know, they have a longer range than the Roman bows and our boys managed to reach the Romans, and some stones landed behind their defences. It made some of them retreat."

"We thought about attacking them across the bridge, but we did not know what traps they might have laid, nor how many more of them there might be. Also, knowing the bridge had been half burned, it would have been difficult."

There was a short pause.

"That is about it." said the spokeswoman.

## CHAPTER XXVII

# An Evening with Paulinus

As Paulinus was leading his 200 cavalrymen towards the wooden bridge into Stony Stratford, he sent word back down the column for Justus to come forward. Justus hurriedly trotted to the front.

"You sent for me, Sir," Justus said.

"Oh! Duplicarius Rufus, "I aim to stay in this town tonight, but I really need to gather your thoughts on what might lay ahead in Fenny Stratford. Can we dine together this evening? Will you suggest somewhere, as I'm not that familiar with this place?"

"I would recommend The Bull, Sir, it's on the left," Justus replied, a little startled at having been asked to dine with the man himself.

"Jolly good," Paulinus said, "I'll meet you in The Bull later, when I have unloaded, and left these men in their barracks."

Justus, accompanied by two colleagues, Clodius Felix and another, arrived at The Bull Inn early, as they did not know what time Paulinus was going to get there. They drank their first jug of ale slowly, not wishing to get intoxicated before Paulinus arrived. Although Justus had visited Stony Stratford a number of times, he still took the precaution of going to the Inn with two colleagues. There would be safety in numbers he thought. After all, there were many Catuvellavni tribesmen in the area, who might think of joining the revolt by attacking a lone cavalryman.

It was not possible for a Roman, unfamiliar with this area, to fully understand the mood of the local populace. There were insufficient numbers of legionaries here at the moment to police the town. However, the arrival of an extra 180 Roman cavalrymen in the local barracks should be intimidating enough to calm the locals, and not cause them any problems in the Bull Inn.

They were halfway down the first jug of beer, when a brute of a legionary came into The Bull and nodded to Justus before thoroughly inspecting the place. He went through to the side room, the backroom and the kitchens before exiting again out of the front door. Paulinus was the next man through the door, followed by two officious-looking officers. The brutish legionnaire then followed the officers in and stood by the front door, obviously assigned as Paulinus's minder. Justus and his two colleagues sprung to attention as Paulinus entered.

Justus's two colleagues respectfully left - leaving their drinks behind.

Paulinus and his colleagues came over to sit with Justus, and he said,

"It's quite nice in here, I am pleased you recommended it."

"Thank you, Sir. Glad you like it," Justus replied.

Justus was introduced to the two officers. They shook hands in the Roman fashion and exchanged pleasantries, before sitting down at the window table. A young serving wench, with meticulously plaited hair and a faded red tartan top, served them wine and water.

Before the food arrived, Paulinus asked Justus,

"What news from Fenny Stratford, Duplicarius Rufus?"

"Shall we begin with the bad news, Sir?" You have heard of Petilius Cerialis and the loss of his cohorts south of Peterborough, at a place called Sawtry Woods?"

"Yes, I have heard. Bad news indeed, we lost around 2,000 men," Paulinus commented. "I intend to lose no more."

"I thought you must have heard, Sir," Justus said.

"Let's get down to business shall we. What news from Fenny Stratford, Duplicarius?"

"When I left," Justus said, "the rebels seemed to be content to remain at the top of the hill, in Little Brickhill. I think they've experienced delays with their supply waggons that had been following on behind the leading parties."

"Ah yes," Paulinus acknowledged, and Justus continued.

"I had a word with a wagon-master friend of mine, by the name, Plod. He says he always has difficulty on the steep slope out of Dunstable, down the escarpment. He has been delayed many times - if things don't go well."

"I know the hill you mean. I must get our engineers to sort that out, after we have taken care of these Iceni troublemakers. The survivors, if there are any, can help Legion XIV to reduce that slope," Paulinus remarked.

"That will teach them to behave themselves under Roman rule," one of the officers said.

They all then enjoyed a good flavoursome meal of wild boar, with peas and turnip. Wild boar seemed to be on the menu in most places at this time of year. There was no farmed meat left as the locals slaughtered their surplus farmstock in the autumn months, not wanting the expense of feeding them through the winter.

The conversation continued.

Throughout the meal, Paulinus talked about the forthcoming campaign. He began by briefing his two officers on the most recent developments. It seemed, Justus thought, that the two officers had not been fully briefed en route to Stony Stratford and had only just recently joined the main Legion. Justus decided it was not his place to ask about their recent travels.

Bankus Diknus, one of the officers, asked,

"How many troops are you expecting, Sir, and when will they be here?" Paulinus bent down, taking a tablet from his blue leather bag on the floor, and read from it.

"We will have:

4,400 Legionaries.

1,400 Cavalry of mixed ability.

2,900 Auxiliary infantry - there are some good troops there.

550 Archers.

350 Light horsemen.

100 Skirmishers

Nearly 10,000 men, and the leading elements of the army should be arriving here late tomorrow."

"That should be enough to sort these rebels out," one of the officers said, "how many of them are there?"

"We've had word that there may well be in excess of

35,000," the other officer said. There was silence, while all four men took in what had just been said, and Justus took a shy swallow from his jug.

"I thought Poenius Postumus would have sent word to me of when he is expecting to arrive from the West Country, but I have heard nothing," said Paulinus. "If he doesn't get here soon, there will be consequences for him. We need his troops. Half a Legion would be very useful."

"Yes Sir, I'm surprised we haven't heard from him," Bankus Diknus remarked, "but if word about this rebellion has reached the Dvmnonii tribe of Cornwall or the Durotriges, he may well have his hands full with his own revolt. He might have sent word, but the messenger might have got ambushed – you know what these Barbarians are like."

"We do not have many skirmish troops, Sir. They are very useful, especially if we've got some boggy ground," the officer opposite Paulinus mentioned.

"Yes, I know you love your skirmishers, Martinus. Perhaps we could use some of our auxilia troops on the boggy ground, but the ones I have with me are too good for fighting in that terrain," Paulinus said, and then continued, "we also have 30 ballista, but as you know, they are heavy and have been delayed on their way south. However, we did pick up four in Lichfield on the way through, and they should be arriving with the main army, or perhaps a day or two later."

"Those ballista are lovely bits of kit. I don't believe the rebels would have seen them before, as we don't have the opportunity to use them very often," officer Martinus said, with a chuckle.

The evening continued after their meal, much to Justus's surprise. He thought a commanding officer such as Paulinus would have many more duties to perform before bedtime. Perhaps he trusted his junior officers to sort things out. One very important thing to sort out, he continued to muse, was how were they going to feed 10,000 men en route to the battle. The barracks here in Stony were not extensive, but he realised that everything must be under control. Justus continued to dream away in his thoughts, while Paulinus was talking to his officers.

Ever since Justus had first met Paulinus, he had been wondering why this senior officer had treated him so favourably. After all, he was only a lowly Duplicarius, and Paulinus was almost a God. He was soon to find out.

The two officers that accompanied Paulinus, stood up, and making polite excuses, left the Inn. However, they were good enough to pay the bill before they left and made a point of informing Paulinus.

Paulinus then turned to Justus and spoke quietly.

"Before I go into any detail, I need to ask you one question. Does the name 'Todia Claudia Rufus' mean anything to you?"

"Yes Sir, that's my mother, well sort of my mother," Justus answered. "My foster mother – a lovely lady."

"Ah good, that confirms my thoughts. I suppose you're wondering why I am treating you so considerately, especially regarding our relative positions?"

"Yes Sir, I am a bit confused."

"Are you aware of our family relationship?"

"No Sir, I'm not. My parents, Julia and Domitious died when I was young, and I was brought up by a kind, lovely lady called Todia Claudia Rufus in the Po Valley. I always called her my mum."

"Ah! So that's where you went to," Paulinus said, "I was not sure at the time, and I was busy elsewhere. Morocco perhaps."

"Right," uttered Justus, looking a little confused.

"The lady who brought you up was a dear friend of mine, but I lost contact with her when she re-married, and moved to the Po Valley. Is this making sense to you?"

"Right, yes, sort of," uttered Justus again, still looking confused, but nodding this time.

"Todia was the best friend of my sister, Julia, who was charged with caring for you, when your parents died. So, you are my nephew, my sister's son, and only son!"

They both got up from their chairs, Justus still trying to comprehend what Paulinus had said. Paulinus then gave Justus a big hug. Was that the Roman way of doing this sort of thing - a big hug? Well, that's what Paulinus felt was appropriate. When they eventually released each other, there was a tear in Paulinus's eye.

"I have found you, 'Justus Julius Rufus', I have found you." They both sat down again, looking at each other with different eyes – talking and appreciating each other.

They were both different men when they left The Bull Inn.

## CHAPTER XXVIII

# THE DAUGHTERS ARRIVE

It was just beginning to get dark, and Boudicca was talking to her colleagues about battles, and trying to get warm around her campfire. Boudicca, together with her leaders, was trying to envisage what would happen when they confronted the Romans, when Dan appeared from out of the smoke. He sat down to join the conversation, rubbing his eyes and looking to see if there was a better seat, away from the smoke. All the wood was wet and produced an abundance of smoke. There was not the keen wind to blow it away as it had been the day before, even though they were on the top of a hill. Dan started by saying,

"One thing I do know about battles, which I learned from an old uncle of mine, is that you may well have plans for the battle, **But**! On 'first contact' with the enemy, the plan changes. So, you must be ready to change your plan, although I know that is not easy to do. That's as far as my advice goes."

All those around the crackling campfire looked into

the flames. After a few moments thought, Garos, who was sitting next to Boudicca asked Dan,

"But how do you change your plan?"

"Let me give you a recent example," Dan said, staring into the tree branches up above them, thinking hard.

"Your battle Garos, with the Romans in Sawtry Woods, not long ago now. The Romans on first contact with you needed to change their plan. If they had been able to do that, things might have turned out differently. However, your plan prevailed, and they were, 'on first contact with you,' disorganised! They were unable to formulate a plan or even change it, consequently they lost the battle."

"But my plan never changed, and it worked perfectly okay. So where does your theory come into that scenario?" Garos asked.

At that moment, they heard horses arriving. It was Boudicca's two daughters with a number of Iceni friends.

"Hello Mum," one of them said, getting down from her chariot. "You took some finding in amongst this lot. There must be thousands here."

"What the hell are you doing here! I sent you home, where you would be safe!" Boudicca exclaimed.

"We are old enough to be warriors, mother," the other daughter explained. "We are here to boost the morale of the Iceni, in our battle against the Romans." The first daughter spoke again, and shouted so all could hear,

"We were raped by the Romans and we believe we are justified in coming here to support you, and all those fighting back. We were the ones who were violated!" The words they both spoke seemed to be well rehearsed.

Boudicca and the tribesmen around her were all

gobsmacked but proud of the girls, making such a bold commitment and combining it with such good words.

The two daughters joined their mother sitting round the campfire, but away from the smoke. More chairs were fetched and the warriors who had accompanied the daughters joined them. They exchanged experiences, retrieved blankets from a nearby tent and poured some Roman wine from a large amphora.

Questions were asked, such as how did you know where we were? Which route did you take to get here?

"We came via Cambridge and Wimpole and then through a place called Shefford. It was quite a good route, direct, and the roads were not too bad," one of the warriors said. He was a big man and had coloured his face and spiked his hair, as all Celts do when preparing for battle. The elder daughter sat close to him, as if they were good friends.

Someone put more wood on the fire, throwing up sparks into the night sky. Bowls and spoons which had been used earlier were collected up, wiped clean and new hot pottage was poured into them for the newcomers.

One new arrival asked where the local water source was, as they were not too keen to walk down to the river, which they had heard was two miles away.

"There's a stream down the road there," Dan replied, pointing towards the south-west, "it is just down the slope, you'll hear it flowing when you get close. The rule is poo downstream of the road!"

There were lengthy discussions amongst Boudicca and her warriors on what to do next. It would be good to find out if more people and waggons would be arriving to swell their numbers. Dan thought it would also be good to get others to give their feelings as to how to proceed. Should they go on up Watling Street and perhaps meet the Romans at a disadvantage, on ground they hadn't fully scouted out? Or should they stay where they were on their hill, in a commanding position, and perhaps put in some field defences along the ridge?

Another conversation around Dan's campfire was about why their numbers had reduced. Cartimandua, Boudicca's cousin, was one of the last to arrive, and said,

"We saw some cowards on the way here! As we were coming north with Dan's two waggons, there were many others going back home. The cowards were going the other way. Some had stopped because their feet were sore, or they felt poorly. Others claimed their oxen were lame or their waggons had a broken wheel. There were many excuses and perhaps some had good reason, but others were being cowardly or just very tired and hungry."

"So, they made out they were tired?" Garos asked angrily. We need people here to fight these bloody Romans." Well, how far have they walked?" "Let's work it out, shall we."

"I've already worked it out," said one of the leaders, "it's over 110 miles, more like 120 since we left Ixworth, and that is taking the shortcut through Bishop's Stortford."

"Others like me," Dan said, "went further, down to that River Thames, where the warehouses were, you know, London." He had had a little too much wine to drink and was getting carried away in his estimation of distances. "That has got to be close to 140 miles. That is a long way when you're not used to it, and all in about two weeks. And we don't know how much further we've got to walk, if we had a plan and knew where we were going, it might be different."

"I think we should stay here." said Luke from Diss. Dan looked across at the man who had just spoken and remembered him from two weeks ago, when they had first met outside Colchester. A great deal had happened since then, Dan thought to himself, and then Luke continued, "I have come a long way with people from my village, we are tired and so too are our oxen. My waggon has broken twice on the journey here. I would very much like to stay here where we can see the Romans below. Surely, we can make a stand here.

"I don't know about your waggon, but my feet are sore," said a rounded woman with a face like a witch. "I have come from Bungay, which is 30 miles north of Ixworth, so I must have walked 140 miles, and at my age it's been a long walk, I can tell you. I think we should stay here for at least three days to let ourselves recover. Look at the ground we're standing on here - it's a little muddy under foot, but what's it going to be like if we stop somewhere low-lying. At least here on top of this hill the ground is not that wet and as our friend from Diss says, we can see the Romans below."

Another warrior stood up, he had painted his face and spiked his hair for the meeting, as it gave him confidence. He began by saying,

"There are many amongst us who are keen to go on tomorrow, but as we have witnessed, there are many who are losing faith in our cause to smash the Romans. They have turned around and are going home. We all know they are cowards, but we can't afford to lose many more that way, we must be strong to fight the Romans. Can I suggest, my

Queen, that we stay here for two days and then reassess the situation? A lot might happen in two days. The Romans maybe closer than we think. After the rest, we might well be in a better position to decide how we go forward."

He stopped for a moment, taking a sip of his hot drink, and continued,

"I am willing to fight the Romans, but I want to fight them on good, favourable ground. I do not want us to be caught unawares, somewhere on the road ahead, on ground that is disadvantageous to us and more helpful to the Romans. This is good ground. I like the idea of the Romans trudging up this hill to attack us and arriving knackered where we can smash them."

This was evolving into a good debate, and people spoke their minds in a sound logical fashion. Dan, being one of the elders present was taken aback by the good words spoken by his younger tribesmen and women. He was pleased to hear how sensible they were and how well thought-out their arguments were.

A short stout Belgae man stood up to speak. Dan loved the Belgian accent. He found it attractive and amusing.

"My name is Eowen from Maidstone. I had great trouble getting my waggons down the slope out of Dunstable, even though I had some good help – thank you. The slope ahead of us is not as steep, but the brakes on my waggon are poor. My oxen are untrained in holding the weight of the waggon as they descend any hill. It is going to be difficult to get down this hill here, and I have concerns. The second thing is, look at the state of my moccasins. I know you can't see very well in this light, but they are falling apart. I wish I had bought another pair with me," he said with a great laugh, "I had no idea we would be going this far from home. I think it best that we stay here to fight the Romans as our friends have just said."

"Thank you Eowen," said Boudicca, "some good points have been made. Is there anyone else who would like to speak?"

"I am missing my home comforts. I am not enjoying camping out. I have a lovely home back in Mengham near Godmanchester with all the amenities you could ask for," a short middle aged blonde woman said.

"I too have sore feet and am missing my kids. I'm just not used to this type of life, but I do know, we have to rid ourselves of these Romans. Life was far better before they came," said another.

Dan stood up, he believed it was his turn to have his say.

"This is a momentous decision we are making here; we have the future of Britannia in our hands. The Romans are coming, I can feel it in my water," (Dan liked to bring a little comedy into his speech as it made people pay attention). "They are coming in numbers, but we are more. Here on this hill, the ground is in our favour. I agree that we wait here and recover from our journey. We can prepare and make defences against attack. We can defeat the Romans and we will! Our tribes are united and the whole of Britannia will remember the day we stood against the Romans and won!" He was shocked at his own ability as an orator. He sat down, content that he had said and played his part.

Another woman stood up and spoke,

"I too have sore feet. My knees gave out on me a number of miles ago and I had to ride in the waggon. My man and I nearly turned back after Hockliffe, but I didn't want to let my fellow Britons down. I miss my home comforts – in fact I love my home comforts! - I do not like living on the road like this – it is most uncomfortable. I would like to rest here so my body can recover."

The fire had become quite lively, but someone thought it would help to put another log on the fire, and in doing so, he got a face full of smoke that stung his eyes. A second man had a look in the big pot on the fire to see if there was any pottage left, and it was evident from his body language, that there was very little. He took it away from the fire to avoid the remaining contents burning. The grass around the fire had turned a little squelchy, and people's bottoms were getting wet and uncomfortable from the wet logs they were sitting on. Others showed signs of tiredness, possibly from the alcohol they had drunk.

All this time Boudicca and her daughters had been listening to the discussion and realized that their attack in Ixworth was the start of all this. Many around the fire believed the meeting had ended and started to stand up slowly and move away, back to their waggons and tents. Dan also took the opportunity to leave. He exchanged nods with Boudicca and walked off to find Scarr and his sons.

It was a dark, clear night and the moon lit his way between campfires. It would be difficult to see the campfire he was looking for amongst all the waggons and trees. People were indistinguishable in the dim light, huddled round their fires. He did not want to take people by surprise by creeping up on them in the dark. However, he did listen to their conversations as he passed by. Conversations that were very similar to those that he had listened to at Boudicca's campfire.

People were tired, oxen were tired and waggons were breaking down.

Dan was having difficulty finding his own waggons as he was walking down the road away from Little Brickhill. He was sure he would find his family soon, on one side of the road or the other, as he stumbled along. The drink was getting to his head and he was slightly disorientated, but he knew if he followed the road with vehicles parked each side, he would eventually find his own in the moonlight. Sure enough, he did. There on the right were his two white waggons, his temporary home in this mass of transitory homes.

It was comforting to know this was where he had family and friends and a safe bed for the night. His moved towards where his two sons Morcant and Talos plus two other figures were seated around the campfire. He assumed the extra figures were probably people from an adjoining waggon, but no! there was his daughter Anna! What the hell was she doing here?

"What on earth are you doing here Anna!"

## CHAPTER XXIX

# Early Breakfast

Justus was up before sunrise. Getting up earlier than the sun was problematic, as oil lamps had to be lit and the lack of light meant stumbling around trying to find things. It is much better to get up with the sun. However, they skipped breakfast and Paulinus was on the road with his escort and Justus alongside him, just as the sun was rising. They were making their way south towards Fenny Stratford 7 miles away. It was a journey without complications as Paulinus had sent scouts ahead to ensure there was no ambush. When they reached Fenny Stratford, the sun was coming up over the hill, behind the rebel army.

Justus could see the smoke from the fires of the rebel army many miles away, as he approached the town. He thought they must have been putting wood on the fires all through the night, keeping the fires going ready for breakfast. He wondered how long could these people camp out, roughing it like this, before they felt the need to go home. It couldn't be very comfortable living as they were, even though it was late spring, and the summer was coming.

When they reached the Heron Inn of Fenny Stratford, Paulinus ordered his 180 strong cavalry escort to have breakfast in the barracks, behind the staging post. They were used to providing for large numbers on occasions such as this, but it did take some time to heat the water up. Justus's breakfast consisted of cheese and biscuits and a hot drink, which was provided by Flavius and his wife Anatolia.

Paulinus recognised Flavius as being a retired legionary. He approached Flavius asking,

"Tell me, what do you know about the rebel army? Have you seen much of them and how many do you reckon there are?"

Flavius was taken aback by Paulinus's direct approach, but realised all good generals talked to everyone in order to gather information. It is a well-known fact, that talking to the man who does the job, rather than his boss, can be most advantageous. Flavius replied, telling him of the skirmish they had had the day before, when the rebels came down and exchanged a few missiles across the river. They had set fire to byres where the sheep were sheltered and also to the roundhouses and workshops across the river.

Paulinus looked at the burnt buildings in the foreground and then up the hill at the line of waggons on the horizon with woods beyond. It was difficult to make out specific details, as the waggons intermingled with the trees, hedges, dips and bumps. He thought he could see the people moving between and around the waggons but, his eyesight was not as good as it used to be in his younger years. He then asked Flavius,

"What is your name and with what Legion did you serve?

"I served with Legio XX and my name is Flavius Longus Avso, Sir."

"Please to meet you Flavius," Paulinus said gruffly, looking up and gesticulating with his head towards the hill. "How many do you think there are?"

"I'm not at all sure, it is difficult to estimate, Sir," was his reply.

"Have a guess man," Paulinus asked again, assertively.

"I started to count the fires last night, estimating there would be about 20 people around each fire, but lost count very early on. All things considered Sir, I think there must be at least 25,000 up there on Hawk Ridge, but there may well be more in the woods, beyond the horizon. I then tried counting the waggons, Sir. I got to 85 Sir, but there are others behind and I'm sure there must be quite a number hidden and in the woods. Given each waggon supplies around 200 people, that's only 17,000 people in their army. If you want to call it an army, Sir.

"Ah! Hawk Ridge, that's what it is called. I like your maths, Flavius, any more observations?"

"Yes Sir. As you can see, their oxen and horses are grazing on the slopes in front of the waggons and I am sure that there will be more as the morning progresses, as they bring them from the woods. My mate and I have tried counting the oxen yesterday to estimate the number of waggons they might have and concluded that could be as many as 350. It's very difficult, Sir, and my maths is not as good as it was.

"Neither is my maths. Who is this mate of yours?" Paulinus asked, sucking air between his teeth and looking into space. Then his eyes lit up, as he turned to face Flavius.

"His name is Dagao, Sir, he's a Romanised Brit."

"And do you trust him Flavius?" Paulinus asked inquiringly.

"Oh yes Sir, he's one of us, he's been my mate since I took over The Heron Inn some years back. He lives in that house there, Sir, with his wife and family."

"When I've eaten breakfast, bring your mate Dagao to see me," Paulinus requested.

"Yes Sir," Flavius said, a little bewildered.

Paulinus walked over to the Inn. On the way, he saw Justus and beckoned to him to come over. They entered the main room of the Inn together, and in moment, a table was cleared for him by his men, who then moved away. As he sat down, one of his senior officers joined him and all three of them ate together. Anatolia served them as really special people, giving them, bacon, eggs, mashed turnip with herbs and some fresh bread on the side.

They were halfway through their meal when Paulinus made a confession, saying,

"I might have made a military mistake."

"What's that Sir?" Bankus Diknus, his officer asked hesitantly.

"We should have killed all those oxen in London," Paulinus replied, "it would have been a shame to see all those carcasses, but the rebels have made good use of those oxen, bringing their waggons here. They are well supplied, whereas we or not, and it's not a good military situation to be in. On the other-hand, the waggons enabled them to bring the whole army here, in one concentrated group, so we can dispose of them in one battle."

Promptly after their meal, Flavius arrived with his

mate Dagao. They were invited to sit down at Paulinus's table, where they were introduced. Paulinus looked in turn at Justus, Flavius and Dagao, so that they knew he was speaking to them.

"I have got a small task for you three gentlemen, a proposition in fact. I want you to get dressed up in typical Iceni clothes, and as it gets dark tonight, I want you to slip into the rebels' camp up on the hill there, and find out a few things. Understand?"

There was shock and concern on their faces, as they nodded in agreement, not being able to totally take in what was being asked. Paulinus continued,

"I want you to take in the mood of the rebels, any defences they might have, their dispositions, the condition of their army and most importantly, try to get some idea of their numbers. Have you got a dog?" he asked, looking at Dagao.

"Yes Sir, I have," Dagao replied.

"Is it trained and well behaved?"

"Yes Sir, I use it for the sheep."

"I suggest you take the dog with you. It will look less suspicious as you walk through their camp. Come with me," Paulinus said, as he walked out of the Inn to a place where they could see the enemy's hill in the distance. Pointing, he said,

"Do you see that small valley there, that defile? I want you to walk up there, into their camp, and there at the top is a road. I want you to take a left there and proceed over the crossroads, in the centre of the village, and continue on until you exit the camp on the far side. Then come back to the river there," Paulinus pointed again over to his far left this time.

"There will be two fires close together on this side of the river. Cross the river there, where it will not be too deep. You will be expected. Understand?"

"Yes Sir," was the unanimous reply.

"One thing you haven't asked me," Paulinus said, "is, how do I know there's a road at the top, and how do I know the topography of the hill?"

"That had crossed my mind, Sir," Flavius said.

"Right, I will tell you," Paulinus said, pointing at the hill.

"On my way to London, last week, I saw that hill, and thought that would be a good place for a battle. Consequently, I scouted around the whole area and lodged it in my mind. Just in case this eventuality came up, and it has."

Flavius, Justus and Dagao looked at Paulinus a little open mouthed and with a lot of respect, recognising the foresight he had had.

Paulinus, hesitated for a moment then carried on talking,

"Right Flavius, repeat what I've just said, to confirm to me that you understand what I want you to do." Flavius did as he was asked, being a man who was used to taking orders, and then replied,

"You said it was a proposition sir, what's in it for us?"

"Ah, I am glad you asked, I will ensure the safety of your wives and families while you are gone. Is that alright?"

"Yes Sir. We understand."

## CHAPTER XXX

# Observation

In the light of the fire, Dan stood there shocked, looking at his daughter Anna, his mouth opened with body language that said - why the hell are you here.

"Don't look at me like that Dad, I am my own woman and I decide what I do and where I go. Aunt Boudicca wants our support and that's why I'm here."

"But we are at war with the Romans. It is going to get rough, and people will get killed," Dan said angrily.

"I know that Dad, that's why I'm here. Fewer of us will be killed if we have greater numbers," Anna stated strongly. Dan picked up a drinking jug, turned it upside down and emptying the remaining contents. He wiped the bottom with a corner of his tartan cloak, then went over to the back of his waggon, where an amphora was partly tipped up and, tipping it some more, filled his jug with wine. Returning to the fire he took great mouthfuls of red Roman wine they had picked up from St. Albans. It tasted good, but did not solve the problem of having to be responsible for his daughter.

The next day was to be a day of rest and observation.

Watching the Romans in Fenny Stratford would be the only task Boudicca and her leaders thought necessary for now.

However, Garos, being energetic and keen, woke some of his horsemen early that morning, to go and visit the Romans on the other side of Fenny Stratford bridge.

There are always things to do first thing in the morning, and consequently it was not that early when Garos' party actually mounted up and went down the hill, past the old fort, and approached Fenny Stratford. As they went past the old, abandoned fort, three men and a woman from the Trinovante tribe came out from the undergrowth growing in the fort and waved to Garos and his men. They exchange pleasantries and greetings for the day ahead and Garos asked them what they were doing in the old fort.

"Our leader sent us down here as lookouts – to keep an eye on the Romans. We were out here before the sun was up," the big Trinovante tribesmen said, and then asked,

"Have you come down to have a look at those Romans, who arrived a while ago?"

"What Romans?" Garos asked.

"There were about 200 of them," the big Trinovante answered, "they arrived on horseback, earlier this morning. Their horses are tethered behind the buildings. Did you not see them arrive?"

"No sorry, we didn't spot them, and no one told us," Garos said. "You can't see everything from up the top. That could be why you were sent down here, as lookouts."

"Those 200 could be the first of many to follow. There might be lots more on their way," said the big Trinovante.

"Ah, me thinks it's the advance guard of the Legion that will be arriving soon. Very soon!" shouted a second

Trinovante, who gave Garos the impression that he missed out on having his fair share of brains, when they were dished out. Perhaps he had other skills.

Garos did not want to talk to the Trinovantes any longer than was necessary. Their accents were difficult to understand, and he had wasted enough of the day already. He kicked his gelding into a trot and went on towards Fenny Stratford and the bridge. They went past the burned buildings that someone must have set light to, the previous day.

"Why do they do that?" Garos asked his companions, pointing to the burned-out buildings. They didn't answer.

As they approached the river, each side of the road became a little boggy. They saw the tall dark green grass that grew in clumps in wet ground, and the thick layers of soft moss.

Garos only had eight horsemen with him and did not want to attract too much attention, so he halted out of bow range. Remaining mounted, he looked at the bridge with the barricade beyond it. There were two or three Romans poking their heads above the barricade and quite a number of dismounted cavalrymen beyond.

Garos did his best to have a good look at the Romans and the goings-on in Fenny Stratford but saw no more than a few troops looking back at him and others going about their business. There really wasn't a great deal to see, but as there were only a few Roman legionaries here, he deduced they would not be attacking yet.

On the other side of the river in Fenny Stratford, three of the men looking at Garos were Justus, Flavius and Dagao.

## CHAPTER XXXI

## Slingshot!

Justus, Flavius and Dagao were looking across the river at the 9 mounted rebels who were looking back at them. The three men were discussing their forthcoming task with trepidation. They knew if they were spotted and taken prisoner, life expectancy would be painfully short.

Justus had seen much larger rivers than the one that faced them. A man could wade across this river at a number of different places, somewhere up or down stream where the flow was fast but shallow. Here at the bridge, it was deep and slow moving.

It was an obstacle for waggons, and it would certainly get anyone on foot wet.

"Shall we take a walk upstream and see if we can cross the river somewhere without being seen?" Flavius suggested. "We can't use the bridge as the rebels might be watching."

"I suppose that's a start," Dagao said, "I've lived in these parts all my life, but I have never had to cross the river without being seen. There's a ford about half a mile from here, we can have a look there now, in daylight."

It was three quarters of a mile to the ford, but it seemed longer, as the ground was boggy, and the spring grasses were tall. The three of them looked at the ford but decided it might be guarded by some rebels, so they went further upstream and found a possible crossing point where the river was wide and shallow. Fortunately, there were some low bushes on the far side and some reeds on the riverbanks both sides.

"I think we have found our spot, gentlemen," Flavius said, and Justus agreed.

"I remember this part of the river from my boyhood days," whispered Dagao nervously.

"All we have to do now, is find a way to cross the river keeping ourselves dry. We can't walk through their camp in wet trousers and moccasins."

"That is easy," Flavius whispered back, "we just take everything off and carry it above our heads, and the dog can give herself a good shake on the other side."

Having made a mental note of where they were to cross the river that evening, they slowly walked back downstream towards Fenny Stratford chatting about tactics and their chances of success. Suddenly, Flavius let out a great scream and held the back of his thigh. He went down on one knee cursing!

For a moment Justus wondered what had happened to his old friend, but quickly realised that he had been hit by a slingshot in the back of the leg close to his right buttock. He looked across the river to see two young men smiling and loading their slings again. They began to twirl their slings around their heads, looking and concentrating on Justus and his two colleagues. Justus made the mistake of looking down at Flavius to see how he was, taking his eyes off the two slingers about to deliver their stones. He returned his gaze towards the two youths, only to see that one of them had just released his missile. Justus turned his back and ducked in anticipation, as he could not see the stone in the air, but knew it was on its way. The stone whizzed past his right shoulder and made a disturbing sound as it passed through the grass in front of him.

All three men knew there was a second stone on its way. Ducking down low and moving quickly, although Flavius was hobbling, they began to jog away from the river. The arrival of more slingshots adding to their anxiety.

Once out of range, Justus realised that they had been a little cowardly. However, being unarmed as they were, it was a different experience. When dressed in full armour, helmet and shield, it was much easier to be brave. Being subjected to slingshot when near naked and not expecting it was unnerving, even to Justus as a professional soldier.

When they were well out of range, they stopped to have a look at Flavius's leg. Undoing his drawstring and taking down his trousers, Flavius was unable to see the wound for himself, but Justus and Dagao could see a large red mark on the skin. The skin was not broken, but a large bruise would be developing very soon.

On the way back, Justus was conscious that he had not considered just how close the enemy might be. If he had been awake, he might have seen the two slingers on the other bank. The slingers must have seen him and his colleagues before he saw them - it should have been the other way around. He was a professional soldier. He had been relaxed, thinking the enemy were up on the hill, when they were in fact much closer. It looked like they were grazing their oxen and horses on the slopes down from the line of waggons on the horizon. Thinking about it logically, perhaps some of the enemy might be on this side of the river and spying on them in a similar vein as the plans they had to spy on the rebels tonight.

On the way back Flavius was limping badly, but still able to walk. He said to the others,

"My hobbling will help our deception tonight, as they won't think an old git like me could possibly be a spy."

"You said it," Justus replied.

Flavius continued,

"Dagao, if we are challenged tonight going through the rebel camp, you will have to do all the talking. Will you be able to do that?"

"Of course, I can. I have the gift of the gab, as you know Flavius."

## CHAPTER XXXII

# A Quiet Day on the Hill

Garos gently turned his horse away from Fenny Stratford and trotted back up the hill with his 8 companions behind him. It had been strange seeing the Romans as enemies across the bridge. They had been enemies before, but as an occupying force. Obviously, this time they were proper enemies they would soon have to fight face to face.

They passed the old Roman fort again and the big Trinovante with his mates came out of their hiding place to have a chat.

"What news from the Roman occupation of Fenny Stratford?" the big man said jokingly.

"Not a lot to say really, we looked at the Romans and they looked at us," Garos replied, and noted that the big man did not have a fire going and therefore no hot food or drink.

"Are you coming back up the hill for some hot food," Garos continued, "or will you stay down here all day?"

"We have cheese and biscuits while we're down here. We take it in turns to keep watch, so we can go back up the hill to have some hot food. We hope to be relieved by others soon," the big man chuckled.

Garos then realised how much he was in need of the latrines and quickly said his goodbyes to the big man. The sensation had come on quickly, out of nowhere, and he encouraged his horse into a trot, followed by a canter, giving the reason for his urgent departure to his companions.

He was racing up the hill, it was now becoming very urgent indeed. The slope of the hill increased, and he was becoming surrounded by people grazing their animals on the slopes. There was just open terrain, there was nowhere to hide and squat!

It was no good, he was not going to make it. He pulled hard on the reins, stopping his horse, but the action of bringing his leg over to dismount had consequences. He was in a big mess and truly embarrassed, although no one around him knew what had happened. Running water would clean up the problem but that was over 800 yards away. He slowly walked over to where he knew the stream was, passing young girls grazing their oxen, trying hard not to be embarrassed by the warm sensation running down the inside of his trouser leg.

Later that morning, around midday, Boudicca held another meeting with her leaders to discuss tactics and the way forward.

Garos's incident became top of the agenda with giggles, although now he had now found some dry clean clothes. The upshot of the mocking was if they were going to stay here for a few days, they would have to dig more latrines, and better prepare their meals. The whole place was beginning to become quite smelly, and you had to watch where you trod, especially in the dark.

"It must be noted though," Boudicca admitted, "most people were responsible and went further afield to relieve themselves."

The meeting then moved onto more serious matters. In the light of Garos's intelligence from Fenny Stratford, it was agreed there was a strong likelihood that the Romans would be arriving in strength at Fenny Stratford, in the following few days.

There followed a great debate on what they would do when the Romans arrived. Would the Romans attack them, or would they defend the river and make Boudicca's forces feel obliged to attack across the river? Should they wait for the Romans to advance up the hill and charge down at the last moment, or should they make a defensive line at the top of the hill, as they had heard this was what the Romans usually did? They could then hold the attacking forces back from behind this line and perhaps hit them in the flank with their horsemen and chariots while engaging the Romans' front. Discussions became arguments and the end result was inconclusive. However, what they did agree to was to meet again the next morning.

Afterwards, Boudicca had a further discussion with her cousin Dan and Garos. She started by saying she found leadership hard. She had talked about this before and had not found an answer. There were many people with different views, and it was not clear to her which idea was the best course of action.

"Sometimes there is a clear course of action," Garos said,

"like at Sawtry Woods. Everyone fell in with the plan and it was well executed. But here we feel safe on top of this hill, and the situation is different. I don't really have a plan or an answer - not yet anyway - I will think on it."

"I am no military expert, Boo," Dan began saying, "but it is a great feeling to be above your enemy and to see them coming. You can direct our men as you see the enemy advancing."

Garos interrupted, saying,

"but is not easy controlling the thousands of warriors we have. A signalling system might need to be thought about. For the moment, I am content to stay here."

"I have just thought," Boudicca added, "I must ask someone to count how many people we have now, as it has been very difficult to estimate. We were just short of 60,000 people last time I arranged a count, but some have left, the cowards! And others have thankfully joined, like my daughters. My bothersome daughters!"

The worrying conversation went on for some time without any proper resolution.

However, the next day, the discussions had inspired activity. New latrines were dug, and many spent the day improving their temporary sleeping shelters, fetching water, mending waggons, making and repairing weapons, tending to livestock, attending to sore feet, cooking a decent meal for a change, gathering firewood and a host of other activities. Most were busy and those that weren't discussed the military situation, but with little experience to draw on.

Dan repaired his moccasins and chatted to his daughter Anna about her journey.

## CHAPTER XXXIII

# Walk in the Dark

Justus, Flavius and Dagao had received orders to go and see Paulinus, before they went for their walkabout in the enemy camp.

"You wanted to see us, Sir," Justus said, as he tentatively walked into the Heron Inn, which had become Paulinus's headquarters for the time being. Justus noticed Paulinus had a purple cloak over his uniform. It must have come with other supplies that Justus had seen arriving recently. Purple cloaks were very rare and expensive, because purple dye was difficult to make. Other colours were much cheaper to produce, but purple had an air of royalty and importance about it. It surely gave Paulinus a great sense of authority and leadership, which was apparent when he spoke.

"Yes, Duplicarius Justus, I just wanted to wish you good luck, and to go over the details of the assignment." All three were offered a seat at Paulinus's table and they talked quietly with him and the Immunis from Dunstable, and another of his officers. Talking quietly like this ensured as few people as possible knew of this espionage expedition, just in case ears were listening, and word got back to Boudicca.

At the end of the briefing Paulinus said,

"The officer in charge of the two fires this side of the river, to help you locate the crossing point, will be organised by the Immunis here." Justus's heart sank, as he exchanged glances with Flavius. Of all the plonkers in the world Paulinus had to choose the biggest one! Could that man organise a slave market after a war? There was nothing he could do about it, questioning Paulinus' authority was not possible; they would just have to trust in Zeus.

After the chat with Paulinus, Justus went off with Flavius to find some suitable clothes to wear on their spying mission. It was then that a worrying thought crossed his mind. There was something concerning him about his 'new uncle' Paulinus. He was thinking to himself - if he was his nephew, why was he sending him on this dangerous mission into the enemy camp. Surely if he valued him as a nephew, he would look after his wellbeing, and not risk his neck like this. He pondered on this disturbing thought, a little concerned. No, most concerned!

Having found some suitable clothes, Flavius and Justus went off to Dagao's house to discuss tactics and their preparations for their dangerous task, to infiltrate the enemy camp.

It was around midday when there was noise and activity outside Dagao's house, and the three men went outside to see what it was all about. There were a number of legionaries arriving outside the Heron Inn. Paulinus was there to greet them and came out to talk to their senior officer. Justus went over to talk to one of the junior officers, who he recognised as being a member of the London garrison.

"It is very good to see you, how did you get past the rebels?" Justus asked.

"It's a long story," the legionary said, "we took the Watling Street out of London, but we did not have a road tablet to tell us the way. Somehow, we got to Watford, our commanding officer, Centurion Facilis cannot navigate. He has other skills. When we got to Watford, we heard there was trouble at St. Albans and therefore took Akeman Street through Tring and on to Fleet Marston. That's a nice little place, Fleet Marston, on a crossroads."

"Yes, I know it," Justus replied, "lovely Inn there, The Duck."

"Good little Inn that, snug and warm when you can find a seat," the legionary continued. "Then, in the morning, we took a right towards Stewkley and on hearing the rebels were in front of us, at Little Brickhill, we took a detour. It's been a rough few days, but we found some staging posts on the way and the main thing is we got here." Justus looked up the column of legionaries.

"How many of you are there?" Justus asked, looking down the line trying to count.

"127, last time we counted, we picked some more lads up on the way. They'd been the garrison troops at Edmonton," the legionary replied.

Everyone at Fenny Stratford was very pleased to see the new legionaries, especially Paulinus, who had worries that the rebels might attack across the river before his Legion arrived. Justus then caught Paulinus' eye, and this reminded him of the task ahead that evening, so Dagao, Flavius and Justus went back into Dagao's house to finish preparations.

It was a turning into a still, cloudless, chilly night as the three men, accompanied by the Immunis and four of his Legionnaires, picked their way upstream. They were not too close to the river, as they did not want to be seen. They found their chosen crossing point, just as it was getting dark, and there they got undressed from the waist down. Somehow Dagao's dog, a shaggy border collie, sensed the excitement and fear in the three men and nuzzled up to her owner Dagao.

Justus tied his borrowed Iceni clothes together in a bundle and led the way across the river, holding his clothes above his head. The water was not as deep as he had expected, but it was cold and came up above his knees. At one point he half stumbled, and the water suddenly became deeper, immersing his crutch and reaching his belly button. He nearly cried out with the shock of the cold water but managed to resist. It was a little difficult walking through the reeds and deeper water. They reached the far side and struggled up the muddy bank and got to dry land under the cover of a few bushes. They were fortunate that there were no brambles or stinging nettles.

Dagao's dog shook herself a couple of times and the three men were careful not to stand too close as she did so. Drying themselves off with the rags they were carrying, and getting dressed under the cover of the bushes, was difficult in the darkness. They emerged from the bushes and familiarised themselves with their new surroundings.

The moon was 3/4 full and being a clear night, they could see quite well. Justus looked at their route ahead of them up to the horizon, where he remembered the pattern of trees on the skyline from that morning's scouting trip. However, this was where Dagao grazed his sheep, so both he and his dog knew the area well.

The dog was keen to get going, and Dagao thought it best not to put her lead on for the moment. Perhaps the dog was intelligent enough to wonder why they were going out rounding up sheep in the middle of the night, when usually it was done during the daytime.

Justus was beginning to believe that Paulinus's idea of taking the dog with them was good for their morale, as well as being something to take their minds off the dangers of the task ahead. However, it had just occurred to him that people like to talk with dog owners. Therefore, Dagao might have to do more talking than anticipated, because Justus could only speak Latin and Flavius could only speak a few words of the local language. It was good that Dagao owned the dog and knew the local language.

Justus, Dagao and Flavius set off boldly, initially across some boggy ground, towards the rebel camp. Smoke from the fires indicated that the wind was coming from the East. Flavius's limp also gave some authenticity to their spying activity. What spy would limp into the enemy camp, unable to run away if challenged. It was all falling into shape.

Dagao led the way, throwing a stick for his dog as he went. Flavius had suggested occupying the dog, to make it look more like they were part of Boudicca's army.

They had to walk over to the left a fair distance as they went up the hill. Their objective was to find the defile that Paulinus had briefed them about. He had been astute enough to believe this could be a good place to take the battle to the rebels. He had been very clever to have had a good look around when he was here recently. He had noticed that there was a weakness in the defile, on the left flank, for an army holding the hill.

The commander of the army on the hill had a blind spot, being unable to see the defile on the left. Paulinus aimed to send his legionaries up this channel in the hill, in his attack against the rebels. The defile had a stream running in it, which helped the three men to navigate up the channel.

All three men had this knowledge in their heads. The horridness about knowing this information was if they were caught by the rebels, and tortured, they would inevitably spill the beans and Paulinus would have to think of another plan. However, the benefit of knowing this information was they could report to Paulinus with more clarity, knowing his plan.

The ground became less boggy as they went up the slope, away from the river. To their front, the open valley gradually became a narrow valley and then further up the hill became a narrow defile. All was going well, and their prospects improved still further, when they saw in front of them, a man and a youth, herding their four oxen up the hill, returning to the camp. Although it was nearly dark now, the three men exchanged glances and Justus indicated to Dagao to put his dog on her lead.

The slope became steeper as they went into the narrowness of the defile and the number of oxen returning to camp increased. It also became muddy due to the number of animals returning via this route. The little stream continued to be on their left, and they could hear it in the encroaching darkness, burbling away down the slope. They continued to follow the cattle herders alongside this stream. All was going well. Flavius made out his leg was giving him some trouble, and stopped, so they would increase the distance between them and the rear cattle herders.

They now entered the rebels' camp slowly, as the density of bivouacs and campfires increased. They knew they would be coming upon a road soon and were pleased when the cattle herders in front of them turned right up this road. It was here, alongside the stream that many people were filling their water carriers from the stream. On reaching the road themselves, they turned left. Waggons were parked each side of this road, and the density of people and campfires increased as they made their way up the road. The pedestrian traffic, walking in both directions on the road, was considerable. There was a great number of campfires and tents on the right, as they walked up the hill, away from the stream. Some campfires had people singing quite beautifully, others had people chatting. They walked on, Flavius limping with his severely bruised thigh, and Dagao's dog was behaving herself on her lead.

Justus was counting the waggons and Flavius had to count the campfires. Dagao's job was to be aware of where they were and watch out for anyone trying to make conversation, or anyone else who might suspect and challenge them. He had to be ready with some prepared words.

Justus was surprised by the sheer number of people. There were thousands! The road seemed to be the main thoroughfare between campsites and other destinations, like the latrines, and the stream. The stream was their major water source. The road was very busy with people walking in both directions, so they did not feel vulnerable to a challenge. There were just so many people. Justus hoped he would not have to visit the latrines, as he could tell from the smell, they were disgusting. Roman latrines were communal, but hygienic on the whole, these barbarians had different standards.

It was dark now, but the campfires on each side of the road made the place very homely and somehow comforting. There was much chattering going on, but to Justus, it was just a babble of foreign voices.

They walked past a special tent, just before the crossroads at the top of the hill. It might have been Boudicca's tent, for there were many people around the campfire there. Most were tucking into their evening meal. They walked on without hesitation, Justus felt more relaxed than he should have been, walking among so many people, so many friendly people, so much laughter and conversation. He felt strange that he was so relaxed, when he should be biting his fingernails to the bone.

As they went over the crossroads at the apex of the hill, Justus looked to the right along what he believed to be Watling Street. He was attempting to count the waggons each side of the road, but gave up when he reached 200. The moonlight definitely helped them in their job as spies. They could see the muddied footprints at the sides of the road and realised the whole place was becoming very squidgy underfoot away from the roads.

They went down a long dip in the road and up the other side. They had walked in complete silence through much of the camp. All three knew that if they talked to each other in Latin, they might give the game away, should they be overheard by any of the rebels.

They walked on.

## CHAPTER XXXIV

# Alarm!

Later that evening, Dan was tucking into his favourite meal of oat cakes, eggs and bacon with Boudicca, when a young man rushed into their campfire circle shouting with excitement,

"I saw him! I saw him!" the young man cried out. "He was walking through the campsite just now."

Garos, sitting by the side of Boudicca, stood up immediately, taking care not to spill his evening meal, and responded,

"Who did you see? Calm down lad."

"I just saw the man, the Roman, who I hit with a slingshot this morning," the young man shouted, "I hit him in the back of the leg, and I've just seen him now. He went down the road over there. He just walked past our campfire with two other blokes." It took a little while for Dan and the others around the campfire to comprehend what the young man was saying.

Then Dan understood.

"Goodness me, they're spying on us, let's get after him!" Dan cried aloud.

Garos, Nomass and Boudicca jumped into action on the words of the youth, who said he had just seen the Roman he had struck with a sling stone. They grabbed a spear each, and hurried off behind the youth, who was leading them. Others followed in support, although there was some confusion about exactly what was happening. They just understood it was an emergency and wanted to get involved. Dan stayed behind as he believed it to be a young man's game.

After running a fair distance down the dip and up the other side, the young man shouted,

"They came down here, I saw them!"

The young man trotted a bit further, then slowed and stopped, bewildered about where they could have gone. There were so many people walking about, sitting round campfires, and much activity, causing great confusion for the pursuers.

"They could not have come this far, they must have turned off," the youth said, out of breath.

Garos shouted out,

"They could have turned off left, or dived into the trees over there, let's spread out and try and find them." They spread out into the gloom and the expanse of the campsite.

There was a great shout of excitement from the darkness over to the right, and everyone who had been chasing the Romans focused on the shouting and ran towards it. However, it turned out to be a false lead and all agreed that the opportunity had been missed. The Romans had escaped amongst the thousands of warriors and their campfires. The darkness had not helped.

They returned to Boudicca's campfire to find their food had gone cold. They felt despondent and vulnerable.

※

Justus had adopted a scheme to assist him counting the waggons. He moved one small pebble from his right pocket, to his left. The number of pebbles in his right pocket was reducing significantly when Dagao, who was leading their little group, pointed to the left and lead them down a rough, muddy track. The path had been well trodden, and there were many people using it, trying to keep to the grassy sides where it was not so muddy. Flavius was having trouble limping along slowly and trying to move out of people's way.

To their left, they could see the dim lights coming from Fenny Stratford. They walked along the ridge, overlooking the small village, and slowly the campfires thinned out and the path became less muddy. The path then took them down a slope and into a small valley, where they turned left and continued downhill along the valley floor towards Fenny Stratford. They then passed the last campfire, where the people around the fire looked up to acknowledge them. Dagao exchanged a few words while Justus and Flavius had their hearts in their mouths, and then the three of them walked on. They suddenly experienced a feeling of great relief, after the stress of being in the enemy camp, and they walked slowly on, Flavius limping and Dagao's dog still keen for her walk. They were all totally oblivious of the excitement they had caused, when the young lad had spotted Flavius.

There was just the one anxious trial to overcome - getting back across the river. They had been walking for a mile and a half when the ground became softer and Dagao reassured them, in a whisper, that it would not be too boggy as they approached the river.

Justus spoke for the first time since they originally crossed the river.

"Keep your eyes peeled for the two fires the Immunis has lit. I think they will be small ones, in order not to attract too much attention."

There they were. Two small fires in amongst some bushes on the far side of the waterway. This time they were not too keen to take their clothes off, but far keener to get across the river to safety, so they waded in, fully clothed, meeting the Immunis on the other side. There were smiles all round and Justus actually gave the Immunis a hug.

※

"Goodness knows what they found out about us," Boudicca said, "it was a pretty nifty trick, but I don't see how we could have avoided it especially with the great numbers of people we have here."

Nomass responded, "I'll try and think what we can do, maybe we could start by putting some guards down by the river - if that's the direction they came from."

That evening the subjects talked about around the campfires on the hill were: the latrines, firewood, home, food, the oxen, the unknown, the Romans and the rough sleeping conditions, in that order. The latrines were disgusting! You had to walk further to get firewood, their food was sufficient, but the sleeping conditions were rough.

Boudicca and many of her followers began to realise that they had really upset the Romans. They had destroyed their two top and most important cities in Britannia. Colchester was the Roman capital and St. Albans was their second city, both destroyed. Word had come up Watling Street that after they had left St. Albans, fires had been set and many buildings had been destroyed. They had also taken London, a significant trading port linked to the continent. Many of the Romans soldiers must have loved ones in these places and would be anxious for them. Boudicca's army were in a strong position here, occupying high ground between the Roman troops and Rome itself. They also probably had more food than the Romans.

They just needed to hold on and win the coming battle.

# CHAPTER XXXV

# THE BRIEFING

After a briefing from Justus and Flavius on the information they had collected from their evening walkabout in the enemy camp, Legate Suetonius Paulinus held a meeting with his officers.

Gathered together in the Heron Inn, Fenny Stratford, were all the senior officers of Legio XIV & Legio XX, together with officers from the auxilia and cavalry troops. All these senior officers had been asked to march ahead of their legions, to attend this morning's meeting. Justus had also been asked to attend. He was surprised as he was a much lower rank than all the others.

"Thank you for attending, gentlemen," Paulinus began. "Before I outline my plan, I would like to reassure you, gentlemen, that when I choose a battle plan, I always use tactics that have proved to be successful in the past. This battle plan is taken from our old friend Alexander the Great. Our plan involves attacking a small section of a large army, cause casualties, panic and confusion in that small section and consequently, make the rest of their army run away."

Paulinus paused for a moment, taking breath and making eye contact with those present. He continued,

"I will outline my plan to you, using this map that I have drawn on the floor here, but please keep my ideas secret for the moment. As you know, the enemy has spies. This is what we are going to do."

Paulinus fiddled with his pointing stick, while taking another breath.

"As you can see, gentlemen," he said, pointing to his chalk sketch on the floor, "the enemy rebels are on the hill to the front of us. They are just under 2 miles away and it is a steady slope up to their position. It gets a little steeper at the top of the hill. At the crown of the hill is a crossroads – the main road, Watling Street, that goes up the hill and is crossed by another, along the ridge. This other road that crosses Watling Street, has a great number of waggons parked along it. These waggons stretch along the top of the hill for nearly a mile – you can see them from down here. Around these waggons, the rebels are encamped, and we estimate there are 80,000 of them. Do not worry yourself about the numbers, some of them are women, others are old men, and they are a disorganised, motley crowd." Paulinus then pointed to Justus and said,

"I have this information directly from our colleague here, who has privileged knowledge of the rebels. Everyone with me so far?"

"Yes, Sir," was the answer. They all knew that Paulinus was a competent general who had achieved significant victories in North Africa. He had a great air of authority about him. Paulinus continued his speech to his officers.

"Gentlemen, as you know, the Roman Empire has 27

legions, each of 6,000 men. Four of these legions are here in Britain. Claudius, our once esteemed Emperor, had the foresight to appreciate the Britons would be difficult to control, and thus gave us four legions. Nero our present Emperor, gave these Legions a very good commander - me. That is why I am here."

Most of those in the room thought *'what a pompous git this man is'*, but they all knew his reputation and felt confident in his ability as a leader. And perhaps the most important thing is, if you are going to take on 80,000 rebels or more with 10,000 men it does help to be pompous. Paulinus continued,

"This Duplicarius here, by the name of Justus Rufus, served in the Legion a few years back and will do so again, when we attack the enemy. He will accompany the leading cohort, alongside its commanding Centurion, the Primus Pilus. He will lead you to a weakness in the rebels' position, up a narrow valley." Justus was totally shocked, as he was not expecting this. However, he pulled himself together and continued listening. It also took Justus a few moments for the meaning of what had just been said, to sink in.

"The Duplicarius here, bravely visited the camp last night, as a spy, and therefore knows it well. We will give him a special standard and escort, and the legion will follow him."

Paulinus continued, referring back to the map on the floor of the inn. "Half of our auxiliary force will front the main rebel positions, along with cavalry, on our left flank. These men, together with our skirmishers and archers, will be in the centre, creating the impression there are more of you than there are. Many are young with plenty of energy and can carry this task out easily. We understand that our auxiliary troops are not as well trained or equipped as well as our legionaries, but unless the enemy come off the hill and get closer to us, they will not realise this. These men will be ready to retreat into the boggy ground, alongside the river, if necessary. Please tell them this! Their job is not to win the battle but to occupy the majority of the rebel forces. It is most important that they understand this - their job is not to win the battle, but to face the enemy without advancing. Understand! Everyone still with me?"

"Yes, Sir," they all said in unison, listening intently.

Paulinus paused again, then carried on giving his briefing,

"Right. Let's get back to the legionaries and the other half of the auxiliary troops. The auxiliary troops will operate in front of the legionaries, to disguise their numbers. Then the legionaries will, at the right moment, advance, with purpose, up this wide valley, towards the enemy's left flank on the hill."

Paulinus paused again,

"Our legionaries will advance up this valley. They will not make the usual noise to frighten the enemy, they will go quietly. Understand! The channel will get narrower as you advance up the slope. It will become a narrow defile. I have seen this for myself, when I visited the battle site, a number of days ago now."

Everyone in the room was shocked by this statement, it took them a moment to realise just how astute their commanding officer was. Paulinus carried on,

"As the legionaries advance up the valley, between the hills, I'm expecting many rebels to be on the hill on the left and maybe some on the right. The legionaries are not to advance up the hill on either side, but to remain in the valley, and turn to face any attack on their flanks. I'm expecting these attacks to be carried out by ferocious and excited tribesmen.

The legionaries will hold their ground, and face the onslaught of this attack. I repeat, it is most important that they stand and hold their ground. The auxilia advancing behind the legionaries will, in turn, take the tribesmen in the flank as they attack our front line, thus." Paulinus pointed again, to the sketch on the floor. Justus along with many other officers, were impressed.

"I do not expect all the rebels to attack from these two hills, they will be spread around the battle area. Only those on the forward slopes of the valley will see the legionaries. We will not, therefore, face a tremendous number of barbarians.

After we have repulsed this expected attack by the rebels, we will continue up the valley, to the top. Here, there is a road that runs at right angles, with many waggons parked each side and along it. We will drive the rebels back against and through their waggons. When you reach this road, the enemy should be in full retreat. Legionaries will take full advantage of the situation, crushing and pursuing the enemy."

Paulinus took another moment for his officers to absorb what he had said, and went on,

"Our cavalry will be used to pursue the fleeing enemy and will follow them and continue the chase. Are there any questions or suggestions gentlemen?"

"Sir, you have told us when some of our legions are arriving, but when do you expect the rest?"

"As we all know, we are expecting some of the legionaries to arrive tomorrow, but they should all be here by the day after tomorrow," Paulinus said. "This means that some of the last to arrive will have been marching for 16 days to get down here, from Anglesey. I ordered them to take two days rest on their journey down here. I do not want tired troops fighting this battle. It is unclear what is happening with Legio II who are expected from Exeter. They are commanded by Poenius Postumus, and although I ordered them here, I am beginning to believe he is cowardly, and now doubt that he will arrive. If he fails to follow my orders, I am expecting him to fall on his sword."

Another questioner asked,

"Yes Sir, when are we expecting the ballistae to arrive? You know how our enemies fear their long range."

"The ballistae should arrive late tomorrow, four of them. We will assemble them and test them out, first thing the following morning, before the commencement of the battle. I found them particularly useful against elephants in north Africa, so I think they will be equally effective against charioteers. We will disguise them from the enemy, thus taking them by surprise, when they carelessly get within range. Something tells me the barbarians have not seen ballista before, and will be shocked! We will deploy each ballista separately in amongst the auxilia and archers. We will assign a dozen men to each, to help carry them to the battlefield. We all know how heavy and cumbersome they can be."

Paulinus then concluded his briefing,

"Gentlemen, thank you for attending the meeting. I am having a platform built at the rear of this building as we speak, so that I can address the troops before our attack. It is important that our men see me and know our plan. I repeat it is imperative that all our troops understand the detail of our plan before we execute it. However, it is crucial that it is kept from the ears of any enemy spies that may be in this town. So, take care about where and with whom you share this information."

Paulinus looked around at his officers, exchanging eye contact with each and every one of them. He said assertively,

"Thank you for attending gentlemen."

## CHAPTER XXXVI

# A Day in Camp

Boudicca's Britons spent another day in camp. This would be approximately day 21 or 22 after the horrendous incident in Ixworth, but no-one was quite sure.

Having reassessed their situation with her closest advisors, Boudicca and her leaders were satisfied they could face the Romans here at Little Brickhill. Some had walked almost continuously since leaving Ixworth and needed to wait here for the next few days, to recover. Others had joined Boudicca recently, having walked here from nearby local places, but they still needed time to collect themselves together.

They had a significant battle ahead of them and needed to prepare both mentally and physically. This would be the first proper battle they had ever fought against the Romans. Leaders needed to bond with and motivate their men.

The major issue for Boudicca and her leaders, as the days went by, was maintaining the motivation of their followers for the forthcoming fight. When they had attacked Colchester and St. Albans, there was almost a frenzy against the Romans, but as the days went by on this journey, this enthusiasm dwindled, and Boudicca had concerns. Would her fellow tribesmen fight with determination when the time came to it. She had no answer except to give rousing speeches, which she found difficult and challenging. The practicality of speaking to 60,000 followers was not an easy task. She was also concerned that discussing these thoughts with her closest friends and colleagues must, in some way, cascade down to the individual warriors themselves, thereby diluting their commitment to the cause.

Later on, that evening, Boudicca and her cousin Dan had a heart to heart in the corner of the Green Man Inn of Little Brickhill. Someone must have had a word with Boudicca's immediate followers, for they left her and Dan alone to have their chat. Both had drunk wine and felt a little more relaxed about what they said to each other. They treated each other like brother and sister, and she started, as if to confess, by whispering to Dan,

"There have been many times in my life when I could have chosen a different path. Men I have fancied, and made advances to, have turned me down. Men have wanted me, and I turned them down. Why, Dan? Life is very complex; I wish I knew the right direction to take at every junction. Why have I always had to make so many difficult decisions?"

"You are not alone Boo; I too have had similar experiences. Many times in my life a woman has made approaches to me with very attractive propositions, and I have turned them down. What would my life have been, had I accepted any one of them? Does anyone know the answer? So many things might have been different."

"We have a situation now Dan, where the right decision

regarding these Romans will totally influence our lives and the future. We could all go home, leaving our campfires burning, and the Romans with their tardy legionaries, might never catch us if we were to spread out, and go home separately. But we are of a mind to stand and face them not knowing the consequences."

"I am hopeful that we will crush them, Boo," Dan said, "for we probably outnumber them 10 to 1, and we will have Dagda the Good God on our side. We have worshipped him enough these past few days."

"Let us hope so," Boudicca said in reply, "and could I suggest we worship 'Ana' my second favourite, tomorrow, and the coming battle will be ours!"

"You mustn't talk like that Boo, she could well be listening - second favourite indeed," Dan said quietly.

"Well perhaps I could change her to my favourite and demote Dagda," she whispered, and they were both quiet for a while, realizing they should not be talking like this about their gods.

"I have heard that many nations have been here before us, in this situation, and the Roman Empire has prevailed," Dan said pessimistically, "I have heard the Romans are brutal in warfare, and their opponents succumb."

"Yes," Boudicca said. "They are extremely proficient in warfare, organised and deadly. Many people have stood up to them, but the Romans have a relentless attitude and have prevailed. A relentless attitude! I have heard their empire is vast and we are just another crumb on their plate."

"Oh Boo, we must not be defeatist. We have strength, our warriors are determined. When battle comes, I believe we can win," Dan exclaimed. "Some of us have rested here for three days now. We have rekindled our spirits after our journey, and have accustomed ourselves to the ground we will fight on. I believe our Gods like this ground. We have food and supplies for a number of days. I am not sure what food supplies the Romans have. Our people need you to be strong and assertive and we will prevail against these Romans."

"Yes, you are right Dan, and we must follow up Scavo's idea with the latrines."

"Oh, what is his idea then?" Dan asked.

"He suggests that we dig latrines across the front of the hill, in front of our positions. The Romans will have to cross our latrines to get to us. They will be covered in mess and may not even want to cross the ditch where we have been making our deposits. Sorry, cousin, is that too detailed?"

"No not at all. Yes, I like that idea. He's a clever young man, Scavo," Dan said, "although perhaps we are getting a little silly, the wine is talking, perhaps we should think on it."

"There was something else I wanted to . . . . ." Boudicca was interrupted by their cousin Cartimandua coming into the inn saying,

"Do you know what? He's only gone and died on me."

"Who or what has died then?" Dan asked with concern.

"That young Roman. I don't know whether someone killed him, or he just died, we'll have to have a look when its light, in the morning. I wanted to keep him alive a bit longer, he was fun. The things I was thinking of . . . . ." Boudicca interrupted her cousin.

"Stop it Cart, you're disgusting sometimes, we don't want to know."

"I've only got these ideas from the Romans themselves. I have heard they do horrible things to people. I will have his head and give it to Nomass for his chariot," Cartimandua replied.

*N.B. It was custom for the Celts to have trophies of their victims and the head of an enemy was a regular trophy.*

## CHAPTER XXXVII

# THE LEGIONARIES ARRIVE

Boudicca was having yet another lunch time meeting, this time in the cosy, Green Man Inn at Little Brickhill, when Scavo burst in.

"The Romans are here they've just arrived! You can see loads of them at the bottom of the hill - come and have a look."

Boudicca and all the leaders rushed out into the road outside the Inn and, as Scavo had said, there in the distance, their helmets and armour gleaming, Dan could just make out a large number of soldiers. It was difficult to count how many there were but, they were there. One of the leaders, a big man with grey hair from Downham Market, said,

"I can't wait to sort them out, teach them a lesson in combat and send them back home to Rome." There was similar such talk amongst the crowds of tribesmen who had come to vantage points on the hill to get a look at the newly arrived Romans.

Dan's mate Esico gave him a pat on his back and said,

"I'm going down there Dan, to have a closer look. Are you coming?"

"Yes, of course I'll come along with you," Dan replied. At the same time, he was thinking I hope I don't have to get too close. I haven't got the body of a young man anymore. I have no weapon. I can't run like I used to.

I should not be thinking like this, Dan was telling himself, I'm here to support my people against these invaders. I should give my kinsmen all the encouragement they need to defeat the enemy. He was not a coward; he was just getting too old to fight. As Dan was thinking this, many around him started to walk and even jog down the hill to have a closer look from this side of the river. Safety in numbers, Dan thought, and off he went with Esico.

As Dan and Esico got closer to the river, the Roman figures that had seemed quite small in the distance, slowly became clearer. When Dan and Esico were past the old fort and within half a mile of Fenny Stratford, they could see that the Romans were not preparing for battle. They were pitching their tents and making ramparts around the complete camp. They were digging latrines, collecting firewood and doing all the other necessities of camping. The camp was well out of range from this side of the river, but in clear view on the gentle slope beyond.

There were a number of fully equipped soldiers, ready to repulse any sortie the tribesmen might make across the bridge. There were also others stationed further up and down the river in case any attempt was made by warriors at a river crossing. However, most of the Romans were preparing for a night in camp, while the lucky few had been given the small barrack block of Fenny to sleep in.

A few of the tribesmen came closer to the river and waved and gesticulated at the Romans. They were surprised at the Roman's humour who gesticulated and shouted back at them across the river. A few youths attempted slingshots at the closest Romans, but were not visibly successful, but they did make the Romans take note and retreat out of range.

Nomass, always a cheerful soul, seeing Dan and Esico in the crowd came up behind them and made a comment,

"We should have come down here sometime in the last day or two, and pushed those Romans out of the place and trashed it. Then they wouldn't have had those nice comfortable places to sleep tonight."

"We should have thought about that before," Esico replied, "but I don't suppose anyone fancied getting themselves cold and wet crossing that river. I reckon the water is rather cold!"

Nomass had seen enough of the Romans and turned to go back, as he had things to do in camp. He had to feed his horses, and there was a slight issue with one of the wheels of his chariot, that might need attention. It might be difficult to fix here without a workshop, but he needed to know what was wrong, so he could decide whether to use the chariot in the coming battle, or prepare to fight on foot. He would be disappointed if his pride and joy of a chariot could not be seen on the battlefield by his fellow countrymen.

He then saw Dan and realised he had skills, when it came to fixing vehicles.

"Excuse me Dan, wonder if I could call on your skills. My chariot has a wonky wheel, could you have a look at it for me please?"

"By all means Nomass, but my main skill is with waggons. There could be as many as five different woods in a spoked wheel and there's a lot of craftsmanship involved too. I like to keep things simple, but let's go and have a look anyway," Dan said, as they turned their backs on the Romans and walked back together up Watling Street towards the hill.

They were silent, walking side by side, and then, after passing the old fort, Nomass said,

"I wonder if the battle will be tomorrow. I'm getting excited but apprehensive."

"I've got no idea," Dan said, "but you shouldn't be apprehensive, Nomass, you're one of our key warriors . . . . . I'm not sure how these things work. Is the initiative with the Romans to come up to attack us or do you think Boudicca will try to cross the river and try to take them by surprise - might she try a night attack?"

"I think the best thing to do, is to discuss it with Garos," Nomass said, "he seems to be the man in charge and has influence over Boudicca. We can bring it up when we next have a meeting."

"Perhaps these are the things we should have been discussing in the meetings we've been having," Dan suggested.

As they walked back up the hill, there seemed to be more oxen than normal on the slopes of Little Brickhill. The grass was becoming very short and was beginning to get poached with all the oxen treading on the ground. They had not been grazing here very long, but there were a considerable number of oxen. Dan had noticed that all the available tree fodder had also been cut down by tribesmen feeding their animals.

"I think we will have to go further afield to graze the oxen," Dan said, "they seem to be running out of grass here."

"How many oxen do you think we've got here?" Nomass asked Dan.

"I think Scavo and his mates counted over 700 waggons, and even at two oxen per waggon, which is on the low side, that is a lot of oxen. There are also the horses and the pack animals. There must be loads. However, I think it's the least of our worries with this battle looming," Dan said.

## CHAPTER XXXVIII

# Legionaries make Camp

"I only want three cohorts to make camp in sight of the enemy," Legate Suetonius Paulinus said to the assembled senior centurions. "I want the rest of the cohorts to make camp the other side of that rise and behind that wood. That way we will deceive the enemy of our numbers and our time of attack."

Many of the centurions looked tired from the exertions of the day, but Paulinus seemed to be full of vigour and vitality, eager to get the job done.

"Also," Paulinus continued, "let us force march the remaining cohorts early in the morning. They will stay in Towcester over-night tonight. Make them set off first thing, so they arrive tomorrow morning for breakfast. Send a message to them this evening. They can then breakfast, and rest before we attack the rebels at midday. Is that clear?"

"Yes, Sir."

"Right then, organise that for me," Paulinus ordered.

After having breakfast together, Justus and his old mate Flavius took a walk around the new camp as it was being set up. They both wore suitable clothes for their walkabout. Justus put on his full cavalry uniform and Flavius his 'best retired Legionary look.' Flavius had always been a dresser ever since Justus first knew him.

They walked into what would become the legion's fortified camp, minding to keep out of everybody's way. A number of legionaries had already arrived from Towcester and had started preparing the camp for the rest of the Legion, who kept arriving during the day. It was very industrious, a hive of activity, with the legionaries dressed in their camp clothes. They did not look like soldiers at all - more like a bunch of scruffs.

As they were walking around the new camp Flavius said,

"You seem to be a little more troubled than I thought you would be, Justus, what's wrong mate?"

"Well, it's a bit of a long story," Justus began.

"We have a little time on our hands," Flavius responded. Justus began to tell the story of his childhood upbringing and his relationship with his newly found uncle - Paulinus.

"Well, what a story that is, I can see why you're so troubled," Flavius declared. "So Paulinus is your uncle."

"Yes, he is. Please don't tell anyone, Flavius, it would be most embarrassing if people found out. I think Paulinus might hang your guts on that tree, if you did."

"The big concern I have," Justus continued, "is the fact that Paulinus, my uncle, has put my life at risk once already when we did our walkabout though the enemy camp, and is about to do it again. I will be at the front rank of the Legion tomorrow. He is my uncle and he's putting me in all this danger. I don't understand, I am perplexed."

There was a pause while both of them were thinking.

"No, I will keep stumm, your secret is safe with me," Flavius said. "I see what you mean, and I don't have an answer for you Justus, not at this moment in time."

"It is most puzzling for me," Justus mused. "He was so overwhelmed to have found me and gave me this enormous hug. Then he sends me into the jaws of the enemy. I would have thought he would have wanted to protect me and kept me safe. I don't understand."

They continued walking around the developing camp - both baffled!

Justus and Flavius both felt good to be back in the old days, although they were only watching the legionaries digging trenches for the ramparts, digging latrines and pitching those heavy, leather tents. They were taking no chances by constructing a ditch around the complete camp to protect themselves, should the rebels mount a surprise attack.

They also walked past the staging that Paulinus had had erected, from which he was going to address the troops before the battle. He would be standing on a platform 8 feet high and on a slight rise in the ground. It was certainly a stout structure; it had been constructed using two young trees still rooted in the ground where they had grown. The branches had been cut off and two more uprights had been provided to support the platform – although it had been hastily assembled it was a good job for its purpose. Everyone would be able to see their Commanding Officer and hear his address before the battle.

Perhaps the battle would be tomorrow, weather dependent, as Paulinus had mentioned. He was certainly a notable leader, with plenty of dynamic energy and great attention to detail. A leader that both Justus and Flavius had not seen the likes of before.

What a man to have as an uncle, Justus thought to himself.

At the end of the walkabout, Justus and Flavius walked down to the damaged bridge. Flavius still gave no hint that it was him who had caused the damage to the bridge a few days ago. The bridge was being repaired; a century of legionaries were tackling the job very well. The 80 men of the century were very well organised. Some cutting down trees, some transporting the logs while others cut the timbers to size. It was all green timber, but that was all the legionaries could get hold of at this time.

It was phenomenal to watch the men at work, and it would only be a matter of hours before the bridge was fully restored. The whole army could then march across the bridge four abreast and assemble on the far side with ease.

After the walk and chat with Flavius, Justus had to prepare himself for the coming battle. He had already sourced his armour, helmet and shield from a sick legionary who would not be taking part tomorrow. The next thing he felt he needed to do was to recap the route he would use to take the legion up the hill. They would be approaching the valley from a different angle. Although it had been dark and confusing when they were on their 'spying trip', he did not want to get it wrong in daylight, when at the front of the whole legion. And, more importantly, during battle conditions, he would be in the frontline, with the Senior

Centurion, the Primus Pilus directly behind him. He began to get apprehensive about his responsibilities for the big day!

"How do you think the battle will go?" Justus asked Flavius. Even though they were good mates, Justus had always looked up to the elder of the two, for guidance.

"I am not at all sure," Flavius said. "I have never been in such a big battle as this one coming up. The greatest thing in your favour is the training that you and all your colleagues have had. That is the strength of our army; our training, our equipment, our drill and the penalty for failing! Unlike the barbarians on the hill, who are a motley crew, as we saw when we walked through their camp. Did you notice the number of women and children we saw?"

"Holy Zeus yes, thanks, Flavius, for reminding me," Justus said smiling. "They were such an unorganised rabble. There were no guards when we entered the camp or when we left, and we saw very few field defences. Also, how on earth can you fight on the front line, worrying about your family behind."

"You will be fine, Justus, trust me," Flavius reassured him.

Unknown to Justus, Paulinus had already asked Flavius and Dagao to assist with the positioning of the ballista. They both knew the ground conditions the other side of the river and could guide those positioning the bolt-throwing machines. Paulinus did not miss a trick where there was help to be found.

※

That night, Justus was tossing and turning in bed wondering how he would navigate up the valley and into the defile. It all rested on his shoulders, if he got it wrong it would be very difficult to redirect the legion to the right location. Over 5,000 men were dependent on him, and probably the whole outcome of the battle. It was not helping him sleep at all, especially in the early hours, with the night at its darkest. He was hot and sweaty in bed and totally stressed out.

He kept reminding himself what his stepmother had always told him. However much you worry during the night Justus, it will not change a thing in the morning. He did eventually get to sleep and miraculously, in the morning, he had the answer.

## CHAPTER XXXIX

# Tomorrow!

The previous night Dan had been sleeping with his family of two sons, his daughter Anna, Scarr and cousin Cart in a unit that they had formed. They had had a good sing song round their campfire, and had discussed many things about their current situation, about the food stocks and what the family at home would be doing. Others had joined them, possibly because they had no alcohol of their own. Not everyone had a support waggon, full of supplies and drink. Most were aware the battle was imminent, so they all drank rather a lot and slept heavily, under the bivouac they had rigged up between the two waggons.

Breakfast in the morning was late, because most had sore heads. However, when it was finally served up, it was good and wholesome, thanks to Dan's daughter, Anna. She had brought with her two small ponies loaded with food. The two animals were not used to carrying such heavy loads over such distances but the situation required it.

Anna had built up quite a relationship with Boudicca's daughters while she was accompanying them. They were of a similar age and Anna listened intently, when they talked about their Ixworth experience. She was a great listener and knew the girls benefited greatly from talking to her. Anna allowed them to talk about their experience, not interrupting and not giving advice, neither did she mention any of her own experiences, she just listened. Anna spoke to her Dad, Dan,

"I was very pleased to be there for them, Dad," she said, "it was an extremely disturbing experience for them and they both appreciated being able to talk to me. Are we second cousins or something like that, Dad?"

"Oh, that's something I'm never quite sure about," Dan replied, "you will have to ask your mother what relationship you are to them. She knows that sort of thing. You are certainly related in some way, as Boudicca and I are blood relations.

After breakfast, Dan's son Morcant and Scarr went down to the old Roman Fort to see what might be happening, while Dan himself, took his turn to graze the oxen with his daughter Anna. Grazing the oxen had become a chore - not necessary at home, but here with no fences the oxen had to be escorted to stop them straying. The grass in the vicinity of the waggons was quickly becoming short, and they had to drive the oxen further out towards the south-west to get enough grass for them.

The birds were singing, and it was a wonderful day. After exchanging a few family pleasantries about how mum and the family were back home, Dan realised that they had driven the oxen quite a long way from the camp on the hill. The oxen were hungry to find new grass and they had done so, but quite a distance from the camp. The day was turning out to be quite nice, the sun had come out and it was getting warmer - perhaps the warmest day since the previous autumn. There were quite a few others grazing their oxen on the slopes, when Dan noticed how his big brown oxen named Bigg had intermingled with another drove of oxen.

## Initial Dispositions

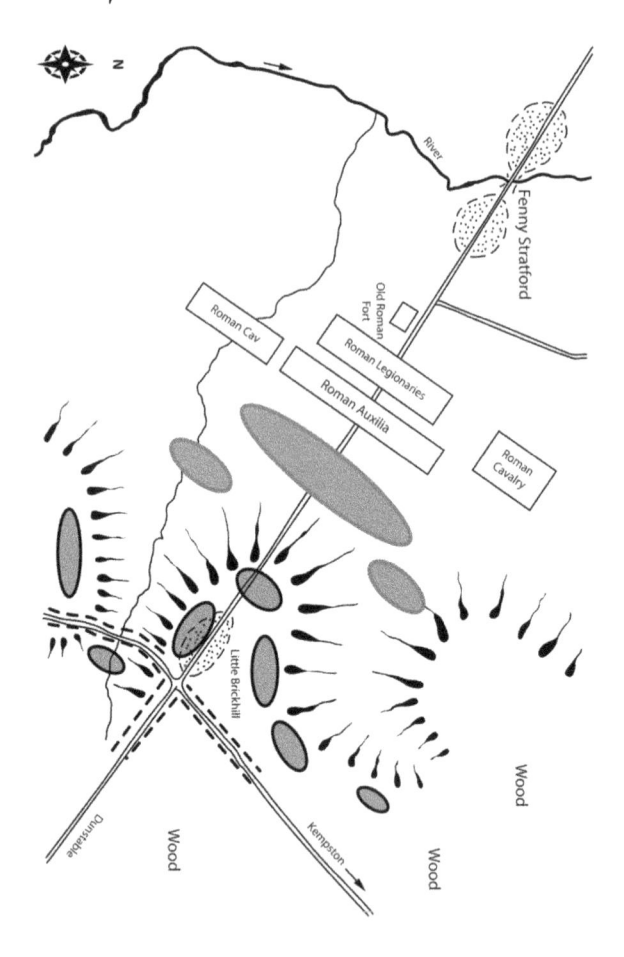

The plan shows the initial positions of troops for the final battle between Boudicca and the Romans.

### Legend

- Boudicca's Chariots and Horsemen
- Boudicca's Warriors on the hill
- - - - Line of parked Waggons

He walked over to usher Bigg back into his own drove and was just about to exchange pleasantries with the owner of the other drove, when there was a shout.

"Oh Wow! Look at that!" a man nearby cried out, exclaimed and pointing in the direction of Fenny Stratford some 2 miles away. All those attending to their oxen, and within hearing distance, looked up to see the glistening reflections coming across the bridge.

"The Romans are coming out to fight!" the man shouted.

Dan jogged round to the far side of the oxen, and shouted to Anna his daughter,

"We need to get back now!" He then waved his arms around, shouting and driving the oxen back the way they had come. Oxen do not move fast - they have one speed - slow. Anna being astute to the situation, was screaming at the oxen and hitting them hard on the rump with her stick.

"We need to get them back to the camp, Dad!" Anna cried out. Dan looked over towards Fenny Stratford trying to work out what the Romans were doing, but it was not easy. Dan's eyes were not that good, and the Romans were a long way off, but he could see they were increasing in numbers this side of the bridge. The numbers of glistening reflections were increasing - the Romans were coming out and over the bridge, in great numbers.

Driving the oxen back to camp was going to take some time. It was like three sides of a triangle, 2 miles between Fenny and Little Brickhill, 2 miles back to their camp and the third side of the triangle, 2 miles from where they were now, to Fenny.

Dan and Anna were panicking, trying to encourage their oxen to move faster, as others around them were doing the same. It was imperative they looked after their oxen! They were their livelihood. Without oxen they could not pull a plough or their waggons - why the hell could they not go any faster?

※

Justus had stayed the night in the Heron Inn, and although he had not slept very well, was up early and shaved for the third time in as many days. Not knowing when Paulinus might pop up, expecting him to look clean and tidy, had encouraged him to shave every day. He also liked to impress Anatolia, Flavius's wife. He put on the borrowed uniform and equipment, checked it all through, and went downstairs to find his friend Flavius. His friend was sitting at a table in the corner, mending one of Anatolia's cooking utensils and waiting for his late breakfast.

They were both well fed by Anatolia, and knowing it was a very big day, chased it down with some good wine. During the whole of breakfast there had been a great deal of activity on the road outside the inn, which the two friends had tried to ignore.

After breakfast, Justus, got up, nodded to his friend, shook his hand in the Roman fashion, buckled on his sword belt and picked up his shield. He then went out to find the Senior Centurion that he was to accompany up the hill to attack the enemy. As Justus left, his friend Flavius had the final word, saying,

"We haven't packed anything, you had better win!"

Justus smiled in response, as he closed the door behind him.

"Justus Rufus Sir," a voice said, as he left the front door

of the Heron Inn. Justus turned round a little shocked, and caught the eye of a young junior officer.

"Yes, that's me," Justus replied.

Sir, you are to follow me," the legionnaire said.

They walked smartly over the bridge. Justus, following the young officer, had only two things on his mind. The first was, thinking back to his training, punch the enemy in the face with the boss of his shield and use his gladius sword to strike him while he is recovering from the shock. The other thing he was thinking about, was the route up the valley. Keep the road on the left - move forward up the slope and away from the road until you reached the stream - follow the stream up the slope. It should be easy, he thought, but there was much at stake.

It seemed like a long walk with the young officer, but Justus soon found himself alongside the Senior Centurion, The Primus Pilus.

"Right, Duplicarius, do you know the way?" he asked in a gruff voice.

"Yes, Sir, I do," Justus answered, with a dry mouth and a slightly intoxicated head. The wine he and Flavius had had with their breakfast was some of the best.

⁂

Dan and Anna were driving their oxen as hard as they could, but the oxen were stubborn critters, and had not had their full feed of grass. Consequently, they were reluctant to go any faster. Thwack! Anna gave Bigg another sharp strike on his rear end.

They were beginning to hear chanting coming from their warriors on the hill to their front right. It was a relief to Dan, knowing that his fellow tribesmen had seen the Romans coming out, and were preparing for battle. A warrior needed time to prepare himself, starting with a good squat to empty his bowels, time to paint his face and spike his hair. One thing he didn't want to happen was to be taken by surprise, and the Romans had not achieved this. The oxen continued to move slowly, despite being hit again, repeatedly, on the rump.

It was then that it happened, a sharp stinging pain on his left forearm. He looked down to see a horsefly five inches above his wrist. He flicked the stick away from his right hand and brought it down hard, squishing the horsefly against his arm.

"Well, that got that bastard!" Dan cried out.

"Are you okay Dad?" Anna asked.

"Damn horse fly bit me!" Dan answered, looking down at his arm and the squished insect's blood. No, it was his own blood that the horsefly had ingested. Damn, it hurt!

"They can be nasty, Dad," Anna said. "I know one of my friends in the village died from a horsefly bite, she was only 15. Don't you remember?" That was all he wanted to know, not only had he been bitten by a horsefly, and it hurt! but he had just been told that his life expectancy might be shortened!

*N.B. Let it be known that the author was bitten by a horsefly not 300 yards from this spot. Horseflies were around – same place 2,000 years ago.*

Dan's thoughts came back to the situation they were in.

"That's the least of our worries, we'd better get these oxen back as soon as possible. Things are going to warm up very soon, I feel," he said, looking down and across at the glinting armour of the Romans, manoeuvring to their positions on the battlefield. Dan was in awe, as the Romans were in regimental blocks, whole groups moving as one, on the slopes below.

Dan, herding his oxen, was getting closer to the Romans now, or perhaps the Romans were coming closer to him – or both. Now that he had semi-recovered from his bite, he collected his thoughts again, and remembered his stick. He jogged back to pick it up. Returning to the beasts he was driving, he took vengeance on them for the situation he was in, and for his arm - it was stinging!

---

Justus was standing on the right-hand end of over 6,000 legionaries. Never before had he been in such company. They had practised drilling with half this number, when he was in the Legion, but this was something special. They were standing there, waiting for orders and things to happen. He took the time to absorb the whole experience. The Legion stood there in complete silence, there was just the rustling of armour and equipment and the occasional clearing of throats. Everyone was quiet, looking up the hill at their adversaries, a long way off, at the top of the hill.

Looking through their own skirmishers to his front, who were partly obscuring his view, Justus could see the route he was to take. The stream he was to follow was over to his front right. The Legion would turn as one, to their right, and he would lead them up the valley, the valley that he believed he could see in front of him. However, he knew that distant views can be deceptive, and he couldn't be certain he would be in exactly the right place to find the valley into the defile Paulinus had mentioned. He knew the defile was there, he had walked it, only the other evening.

Apprehensive yes, frightened no. He was not alone, he knew the discipline of his comrades and was relaxed, calm and collected. He knew he could trust them to take care of each other. God, he felt good, perhaps it was the adrenaline or maybe the wine.

Over to his left, Justus could see the auxiliary troops approaching in a long column, four abreast. They were following their officers, leading out in front, to finish up in front of the Legion. He remembered at the briefing with Paulinus, this was part of his plan. The auxilia were to mask the Legion. There had been some confusion and somehow the Legion had gone out first – would the barbarians see their plan?

Perhaps the tribesmen on the hill would not be confused, as they could see far more of what was happening than the Roman officers at the bottom. Perhaps the Legion would be seen going into the valley and a trap arranged by Boudicca's army in the narrow defile. This was not the way it should happen.

Enough of these thoughts - the barbarians on the hill were disorganised, inexperienced and hopefully were unable to react quicky enough to the Roman army machine and the plan. All would be good, Justus told himself to believe.

꣜

Returning to the oxen and Dan's predicament. He had been slowly climbing the slope, driving his oxen in front of him, and was halfway up the hill. He and Anna had reached a promontory on higher ground than the Romans to his left, but lower than his compatriot warriors on the hill to his right. The tribesmen were chanting, banging their shields and making a tremendous, encouraging roar. They had converted a campfire song into a battle chant with a crescendo. Never in the history of Britain had anyone experienced such a view as this, Dan thought to himself. The Romans down to his front left. The Britons high to his front right. If he stayed here, he could see the whole battle unfold.

"Hey Dad, we've gotta get back," his daughter cried out, as she looked back at Dan. She then returned to the task of driving the oxen and hit Bigg the oxen hard on his rump.

"Yes love, I'm coming." Dan was in two minds. What a spectacle was unfolding in front of him - he might never see anything like this for 1,000 years. He could stay here, but his responsibility lay with his daughter and his oxen. They had to get back to safety.

※

Justus did not have a good view of what was happening. He had a better view than many others, as they were 18 ranks deep, unable to see properly over their comrades to their front. He guessed others were still in the process of being deployed. He did see two ballistae, which having crossed the bridge, were being carried by a dozen men up the road. Every Roman in the army had to cross the bridge, a narrow bridge where four abreast was a maximum. This was perhaps when the Romans were at their weakest, with half the army across the bridge and half the army yet to cross. The rebels should have attacked now, but they were chanting on the hill unaware of the opportunity they had missed.

Justus and his immediate comrades were waiting for the battle to start.

It was the waiting before the battle, that was the worst. This was the moment when there was nothing to do, except watch and wait for the anxiety to take hold of the mind. Will I be injured, or will I die? Has Paulinus made a good plan?

One thing the Romans did know, was that the barbarians would be intoxicated, if there had been any alcohol around. This factor was something they had been taught in their training. It was going to be a momentous day. All those who took part would remember this for the rest of their lives. However, many would not have happy memories of the horrific happenings of the day.

It was then that the trumpets sounded three blasts. All the men of the Legion knew what this meant, and they all steadily moved forward. The auxilia were at the front, leading in one long line towards the hill.

## CHAPTER XXXX

# THE BATTLE

Dan was driving the oxen up the promontory of the hill and looked back over his left shoulder to see the battle unfold. The oxen had slowed, as they were still hungry and did not see any need to move off the grass.

Dan knew this was a unique moment, there would never be such a moment again for many decades, if not centuries. He was present! He was there! He stopped again to look in awe at what was happening below.

The Romans were advancing slowly but surely, towards the hill in Little Brickhill. Dan's fellow tribesmen were chanting on the hill in great crescendos! They were enthusiastic for the battle and had spiked their hair and painted their faces. It was one big party. Everyone was enthusiastically looking forward to the big bash. All his fellow Iceni were singing, and it was a wonderful day for a battle. Especially for the victors. Soon there would be a great clash of arms and people were going to die. What a moment to witness, in one's life!

Then Dan saw the chariots, the chariots of his fellow

Britons. They had come out in a long column from behind the second promontory, which was hiding Little Brickhill beyond. Dan knew there to be perhaps over 600 of them. What an impressive sight the two horse chariots were, advancing in a long line down the road. Dan then saw them turn left, off the road and come towards him. They were keeping some distance away from the front of the Romans, who had already deployed themselves, facing the slopes.

The leading chariot then slowly halted and turned to face the Roman line. Dan believed it could be Boudicca, but she was too far away for him to be sure. Some of the chariots that followed also turned, but others did not, going past his cousin and then stopping and turning. There was some confusion amongst them as to what to do, and how best to display themselves, to impress the Romans. After a while, all the chariots faced the Romans, in a long line. Adversaries ready for battle, facing each other, gesticulating and encouraging their fellows.

Dan thought they should have practised this manoeuvre prior to the battle, as it would have been more impressive. However, it did still look stirring stuff, and he could feel the hairs standing up on the back of his neck with excitement. He could also feel the horsefly bite, that was continuing to sting. Wretched horsefly, it was a little early in the season for horseflies but nonetheless it hurt. Nasty creature!

"Come on Dad, we've gotta get back!" Anna shouted out. This time Dan did take notice and, having taken one last look at the whole picture, turned to catch up with his daughter and their oxen. In doing so, he forgot to take notice of what he was treading in. It was cold and squidgy. It made a real mess on his moccasin, his left one, the moccasin he had mended a few days ago. Yuck, what a mess! He had been totally captivated by the whole scene in front of him, he should have concentrated on where he was going. He quickly wiped off the majority of mess, rubbing his foot on some short, thick grass and then jogged on, to catch up with his daughter.

Dan's oxen were some of the last to come off the grazing slopes. They walked to the road at the top, and urged the oxen through a small gap in the line of parked waggons. Here the ground had been badly poached, and Dan nearly slipped in the mud. Driving the oxen through the gap in the line of waggons, they naturally went on down the road on the left. They seemed to know the way.

It was here that he heard one of the warriors talking loudly to a colleague saying,

"I hope the Romans don't attack us here, we're very thin on the ground in this location."

The big man next to him, with blue and yellow stiped paint over his face, and orange spiked hair replied,

"Yes, I've just come back from having a look at the boys in the centre of our line. They are over 20 ranks deep there, possibly 30." Dan believed they talked loudly for his benefit, knowing he would overhear, and being Boudicca's cousin, had influence. He nearly responded, but decided to keep stumm.

Dan and Anna drove the oxen on further. There were a number of other oxen walking in front of them and he worried there might be a hold up. He was anxious to get back to his own family and waggons, to make sure they were alright.

As they went down the road, the chanting of the

tribesmen to their front left became stronger and louder. The oxen went on in front, following the road, down a slope into the bottom of the valley, across a small shallow ford where everyone took their water from the stream. They then went on, up the other side of the valley.

Dan shouted out to Anna, so that she would hear,

"I'll catch you up Anna, I'm going to have a look to see what's happening." For the second time, Dan's inquisitive nature had got the better of him. In that moment, he was more interested in what he could see, than in his own safety, the safety of his oxen or his family. He knew he was witnessing an event of a lifetime. An experience he wanted to take full advantage of, possibly to the detriment of his loved ones and more importantly, himself.

He looked around for a vantage point, so he could see what was happening. There were many people along both sides of the road, great crowds of them! The oxen, trudging on up the road, had carved a path through the crowd, with their bullish behaviour. There were people standing on top of the waggons each side, women, children, old men. Most of the warriors had gone bravely to the front.

Dan wanted to find a good viewing point. He could not see down the valley to the left, as there were waggons with people standing on them, blocking his view. Then, there on his right, was a waggon with a viewing space on top of it, unoccupied! A lucky break.

Putting his foot on the front nearside axle hub, he grabbed hold of the topside of the waggon and, hoping his messy left foot would not slip, projected himself up. It was a mammoth task for a 53 year old, but adrenaline and motivation got him there. Cocking his leg over the side, and with the help of a couple of young women, he was on top of the waggon, with a much improved view.

"Thank you very much," he said to them, "I didn't realise what a climb that was."

He hoped the waggon owner did not mind, especially as his left moccasin was still very messy and particularly smelly.

## CHAPTER XXXXI

# The Romans Advance

The whole Legion was now moving slowly forward, in one great long line. Justus was on the right-hand end of it and was absorbing the whole experience. He felt good and confident, he knew what he had to do. Although just one soldier, he was an integral part of the best army in the world and knew that this Legion was one of the best the Romans had.

They had moved forward 600 yards or more, when there was a long trumpet sound, and everyone knew that was a signal to stop. 50 yards to his front, Justus could see through the thin lines of their own auxilia and skirmishers, to the enemy. There, facing them, also in a long line, was a number of enemy chariots. They were some distance off, perhaps double bow range, standing there shouting and jeering at the auxilia. Some enemy slingers had dismounted from the chariots and had come forward to sling stones at the roman auxilia troops.

Justus became aware of the Senior Centurion, who had moved into his personal space to get his attention. He spoke gruffly and clearly to Justus saying,

"This is where we move off to the right and up the valley. This is the place, Duplicarius Justus. You know the way, lead on!" Good God! Justus thought to himself, this is where I either do a good job or a bad job. He then turned to the Senior Centurion and nodded, saying,

"Yes, Sir."

The Senior Centurion then spoke quietly to the senior trumpeter of the three standing behind him and issued an instruction. At the same time as the three trumpets blew, he commanded the Legion,

"Face right!" As one, the whole Legion, 5,500 legionaries turned 90 degrees to their right. The crescendo of moving body armour, shields and boots was exhilarating.

Justus was now the leading man of the Legion, and he marched off in the direction he told himself was the right one. Out in front, he could hear the marching ranks of the Legion behind him. He was going past the end auxilia to his left and out onto the open slopes. He knew he had to turn left towards the hill, and he did so. The gruff Senior Centurion was by his side giving him words of encouragement.

"That's good, Duplicarius, give the impression you know where you're going, be decisive."

Justus glanced back to see the Legion. He guessed they must still be 16 men wide, and the ranks should go back a long way - perhaps over 300 ranks. That is a great many trained men. They were moving silently but for the sound of their armour. Part metal armour, part linen, part leather. The ground was soft, their boots making no noise as they trod across the soft grass. Short grass, eaten by the enemy's oxen; horses and mules. They were moving into enemy territory.

## The Battle

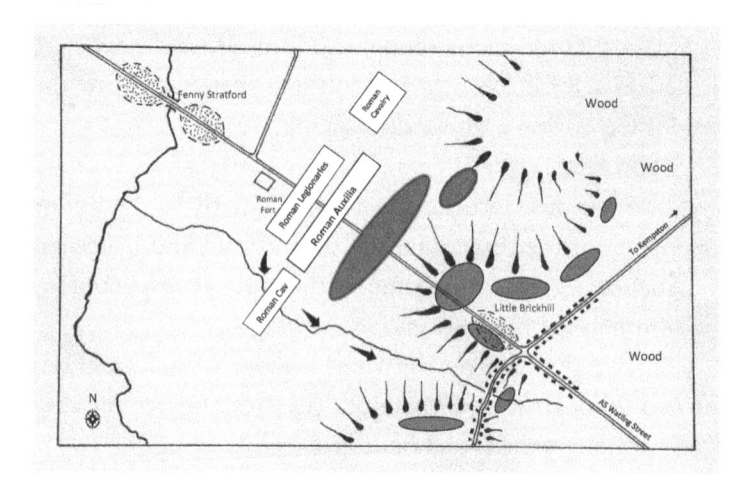

The plan shows the final battle between Boudicca and the Romans.

**Legend**

- ⬤ Boudicca's Chariots and Horsemen
- ⬭ Boudicca's Warriors on the hill
- ➡ Justus's line of Advance
- - - - Line of parked Waggons

Justus could not see the valley he needed to guide the Legion up, but he knew it would be there somewhere. To his front right he could see the stream, there was a line of sparse bushes alongside it – yes, he remembered them, that was the stream. He was relieved to have found it, even though it would have been impossible for him not to. Streams do not disappear.

He became mindful that the uniform he had borrowed from the sick legionary was a little tight around the chest. There was nothing he could do about it now, but he suddenly remembered the superstition of bad luck associated with borrowed equipment. He had to put that out of his mind, and get on with the job.

On reaching the stream, which they approached at an angle, Justus turned slightly left to follow it, as the gentle slope became steeper. His mouth became dry as he looked up to his front left, to see the jeering barbarians on the hill. The Legion marched on. The only enemy in their path were a few nimble young slingers, retreating, as the Legion advanced. There were not many slingers, and consequently the missiles were few and far between. Justus could see them coming through the air, and there would be the occasional clunk as a stone hit a shield or helmet behind him. However, one stone he did not see coming, hit his shield with a thud, making him jump!

Justus then had an idea, so he slowed his pace, dropping back alongside the Senior Centurion - the man in charge. He cranked his head, and looking at the Centurion, made eye contact with him.

"Sir," Justus speaking loudly, began to explain, "the route takes us alongside this stream. The barbarians may well charge us off their hill into our left flank. If we cross to the right hand side of the stream, they will have to cross the stream to get to us."

"That is a good idea, Duplicarius Rufus!" the Centurion shouted above the noise. Justus was taken aback by the Centurion complementing him and calling him by his second name. His senior officer must have been paying attention at the briefing, and perhaps had higher regard for him than he had shown before.

The Centurion bellowed out some orders and within a short time the whole Legion had crossed the stream. Some legionaries slipped in the stream's muddy bottom and others had difficulty in amongst the bushes, but they were all across. They redressed their ranks while being mindful of the occasional enemy sling stone. The Centurion spoke to Justus curtly,

"Carry on, Duplicarius Rufus."

Justus marched on with the Legion behind him. Many cursing muddy boots, but many others appreciating the advantage of being on the right of the stream. The Legion was still marching quietly, which they had been ordered to do. Why advertise your presence to the whole enemy? When marching quietly, only the troops that can actually see you, know you are there. The adversaries behind the front ranks do not! Their vision is obscured by the men to their front and are they are happy to drink and chant!

Tactically, therefore, it makes very good sense to advance quietly and surprise those that cannot see you.

The slope became slightly steeper, the ground under foot was not so soft, the chanting of the enemy grew louder. There must be thousands of them up on the hill, to their front left. Justus was also becoming aware of a similar number the other side of the valley, on their right. Despite the presence of all these enemy rebels, Justus felt exhilarated and confident. He had a competent Senior Centurion one pace behind him, giving him, and every legionary behind him encouragement by just being calm.

As the Legion went on into the ever-narrowing valley with the stream on their left, they came within range of more enemy slingers. Stones rained down on them in increasing numbers, as they marched further up the valley. Young men came out of the barbarian ranks, encouraged by the warriors behind. They used their slings, casting projectiles high in the air from the valley slopes to descend on the Legion. The legionaries held their shields high and interlocked them so that very few missiles did harm. Unfortunately, Justus being on his own in front, was a target from both sides of the valley, and a number of stones came quite close to hitting him. He bravely advanced.

Dang! God Zeus! For half second, Justus wondered what had happened. He thought the sky had fallen in. Then he realised a slingstone had hit the side of his helmet with a tremendous thwack! What a relief, that stone could have done so much damage if it had hit him elsewhere. He dropped back a little to be closer to his colleagues and hopefully not draw so much attention to his minor cowardice.

Then came the point when they were between two prominent hills each side of the valley. Hills that were covered with enemy tribesman cheering and chanting from the heights on each side. They went on into the narrow defile, towards the head of the valley where the sides became steeper. When they reached the place where the enemy were advantageously positioned on each side, they were expecting to be charged from both sides, and they were!

The Centurion had been expecting this moment, and immediately asked the three trumpeters to sound their horns. The blasts went out in a confrontational sound against the roar of the rebels, and immediately the Legion stopped. Eight ranks on the left side of the Legion turned 90 degrees to face the enemy, coming down the hill. On the right flank, eight ranks turned to face the enemy coming down from the other hill.

It was fantastic, Justus thought, to be part of well drilled Legion. All that time spent on the parade ground practising manoeuvres. It had all paid off. Instantly, from having vulnerable flanks, the legion now presented shield, armour, helmet and a seriously dangerous spear called a pilum, ready to face the enemy coming at them on both sides.

The warriors came screaming down the two hills, into the 16 ranks of legionaries - 8 ranks facing out each side. The confident, trained ranks of the Roman army.

## CHAPTER XXXXII

# Clash of Arms

There he was, standing on a waggon, looking down the valley from where he assumed the Romans would be advancing, very shortly. Dan had seen them from his previous position in one long line, facing the tribesmen and warriors on the hill. His fellow tribesmen were chanting loudly, banging their shields and creating quite a racket. It took him a little while to catch his breath having climbed up onto the waggon. He slowly gathered his senses and began to understand what was happening.

He looked down the narrow valley, over many ranks of tribesmen, to see a mass of red shields and glimmering armour advancing up the valley bottom towards him, some 500 paces away and closing. They kept coming, slowly and methodically. It was not long before he could see many young men from his own Iceni tribe with their slings, launching missile after missile at the Romans. They were spread out on the hillsides, so they did not get in each other's way, each needing space to twirl their sling. The stones were being accurately delivered into the centre of the Roman Legion.

He was not sure, but he thought he could see Scarr twirling his sling around his head, 4 to 6 revolutions and release! Everyone but the Romans were shouting and screaming obscenities. The din was tremendous!

Dan tried to judge just how many Romans there were in their serried ranks of over 15 abreast, not faltering as they came up the valley bottom. A fruitless exercise. He saw that they were coming into a trap between opposite hillsides, with a large number of warriors on each hill.

Dan joined in the enthusiastic shouting,

"Come on you treacherous snakes!" he shouted, wondering to himself whether he could have thought of any better words. He envisaged both masses of tribesmen screaming down the slopes from both sides of the valley, trapping the Romans in the bottom. Other warriors in front of him, many ranks deep, were readying themselves to charge down from their position at the head of the valley.

It would soon be all over for the Romans. Dan went with the rhythm of the cheering, as he belatedly looked around for a weapon so he could join in the fight. He grabbed a pair of blacksmith's tongues on the floor of the waggon and as he did so, he saw a blacksmith's hammer, half hidden alongside them. Short, compact and heavy but that would be his weapon. He picked up the hammer and looked again at the progress of the Romans. A short stocky Trinovante man standing on the waggon next to him bellowed,

"Roman rats, come and get it!" Dan thought how stupid it sounded.

There was then a massive noise as the warriors on the right side of the valley began to charge down the hill. Those on the other side of the valley took up the initiative and advanced initially at a trot, and then at a full frenzied run as they gathered excitement. Dan assumed they were buoyed up by adrenaline and intoxicated with alcohol, increasing their bravery and determination.

Then it happened, a trumpet sound was heard above all the other noise of the battle. It came from the leading Romans and all the legionaries turned. Eight ranks on the right turned, as one, 90 degrees to face the foe. Eight ranks on the left turned 90 degrees to face their foe. Dan saw the charging tribesmen half check themselves, as they poured down the hill, but they continued.

Dan pictured in his mind, what was going to happen next. It did. The Legion remained resolute and stationary, a mass of armour and shields facing overconfident frenzied warriors. It was carnage and very sad for the Britons. Professional versus amateur. Trained versus untrained. Prepared versus unprepared. After a short time, those that had not been killed or maimed by the pilum or the gladius wielded by the Roman soldier, became quite sober as they backed away slowly up the incline. Those behind them, further up the slope, seeing what had happened to their friends, turned and retired slowly.

Apart from the screams of the wounded and dying the whole scene went quiet. The tribesmen who had remained on the hill, and the others who had replaced those who had committed themselves to the attack, were quiet. The chanting had stopped. There was chanting beyond the hill over the crest, from people who were unaware of what had happened. Their distant chanting could eerily, still be heard.

There was a trumpet sound and the Legion turned again to face the head of the valley and then continued their advance. A great number of Boudicca's young men had thrown themselves eagerly at the Romans, and had just 'bounced off'.

Dan, still standing on the waggon, was thinking fast. He was going through his options, in the same way as everyone else must have been doing, on the slopes of the valley overlooking the Legion, as it continued up the defile towards Dan. It must only be 80 yards away and advancing relentlessly. Once enthusiastic warriors were turning and trying to get away, while others pushed forward not realising what had happened to those in front.

He saw his chance of escape. On the ground at the front of the waggon was a wooden box which he could use as a step, to get down from the waggon. Without a moment's thought he was down on the ground without injury. That was lucky, Dan told himself, as he had been high up on the waggon. He ran as best a 55 year old could run, along the road in the direction of Little Brickhill. He was running towards his own familiar campsite, Anna, his two sons and his two waggons.

As he ran up the hill between the two lines of waggons, he could hear the screaming and panic behind him. The ranks of tribesmen that had been in front of him must be fighting the Romans coming up the hill. He was getting out of breath - young men and women, were overtaking him in panic, trying to get away.

※

Justus suddenly found himself on the exposed end of the legion. He had been leading it before, but now he was on the flank facing the onslaught of the tribesmen running off the hills. He quickly saw a chance to take a few steps back and be part of the line that faced up the valley. Not all the legionaries were facing out towards the enemy coming down the hillsides. Some, like him, were on the front end of the Legion.

The barbarians came screaming down the two hills from both sides in a thunderous roar. Some were running too fast, and their legs could not catch up with them, and they went flying over themselves, into the ground. Something you did as a child, running down a slope. Both ranks of legionaries, on each side of Justus, chuckled at this, but remained steadfast and ready to face the onslaught of the warriors who had not fallen. Standing steadfast was an important part of their training.

When the enemy came to within a range of about 20 paces, the legionaries took two paces forward and threw their pilums, to great effect! The pilum is a very cleverly designed, heavy spear, with a long thin metal point, that goes straight through an enemy's shield and into the man holding it. Nasty! This checked the second line of the brave enemy barbarians following, and gave the legionaries a moment to draw their swords, the gladius.

The part-time soldiers, the farmers and craftsmen of East Anglia, were no match for the professional, well trained, full-time soldiers of the Roman army. The fight did not last long. Justus, out of breath from the fighting, was relieved to see the 4th and 5th echelons of Barbarians hesitating before they came to fight. They would have to come over their bleeding fellow warriors on the ground, who had fallen in the initial attacks. Some were brave enough, and attempted to charge the bloodied legionaries' swords, but they were not followed by their hesitant comrades.

In other sections of the fighting, the brave barbarian warriors were being pushed hard and squashed from behind by their own fanatical warriors, and were unable to find the space to fight. There was pushing, shoving and squeezing of both groups of adversaries. At the point of connection between Romans and tribesmen, with shields locked together, there were exchanges of eye contact and bad breath as they came together.

The fighting had gone through its climax and the tribesmen were retreating, first from the rear ranks, and then those who then found themselves with no support from behind. The brave ones hung on at the front, hoping the fight would continue, but sensing their rear support retiring, they too, now alone, turned and made off. They felt no need to run, as they instinctively knew the Romans were steadfast and would not run after them.

The legionaries, having been trained for this moment, did not pursue the fleeing tribesmen but remained resolute. They were well aware of feint retreats, where the enemy ran away, drawing them into a trap. Their training at this point, was to redress their ranks. The walking wounded retired or stayed put, while the majority were given the command to resume their earlier direction, and advance up the defile, on their original course.

The barbarians up the valley, were 25 or 30 ranks deep, and were all individuals. They lacked leadership, discipline and were in a mess! All of them were unsure what they should do, except to look after their own skins. Those that stood to fight were few in number, and were not encouraged to do so by those who had already run.

Their next steps were determined for them, by the steadily advancing 5,500 strong, disciplined Legion.

The tribesmen turned and fled, but their route was blocked by their parked waggons, tents, unloaded belongings and the odd latrine. There was panic, as they could not get away and they were crushed against the waggons. Justus and his fellow Romans took full advantage, attacking them in this vulnerable situation and it was recorded in the history books, 40 years later.

*Reader please note - the legionary fighting alongside Justus that day, was Gnaeus Julius Agricola. Later in his life he had a son-in-law named Publius Cornelius Tacitus, who documented what happened on that day, for others to copy, recopy and interpret for the next 1,900 years.*

※

Dan ran on, away from the screaming and sheer panic behind him. He was one of the first to run and thus had a head start on the others. Some of those behind him were being attacked by the Romans and slaughtered. He was slower than most, and was beginning to get caught up in the stream of people running away. Where should he run to? He felt he should tell Boudicca about what was happening, so she could stop the Romans. Where was Anna, his two sons, how could he find Boudicca? Should he save his own skin – the screaming sounded pretty horrendous behind him. He ran!

While he was running, he was thinking. He should stand and fight, if everyone stood and fought, they could win the battle. Where was the hammer - he had dropped it. When? He couldn't just panic and flee, he had to be positive - there were things he could do, and he came to his senses. He would run over to the main body of their army on the hill to his front left. From there, he would be able to see what was happening, and maybe find Boudicca.

He turned off the road, darting between a couple of old waggons and went to his left, and was soon amongst fellow tribesmen who were not running away. Here, they were unaware of the catastrophe unfolding behind them.

Jogging, he found a way through the standing throngs as the ground gently sloped down towards the front edge of the hill. Here it was thick with warriors who had painted faces and spiked hair, chanting and jeering at the Romans at the bottom of the hill. These people were the heart of Boudicca's army – the proper warriors. However, they had never experienced this before, it was a first time for everyone, and they were totally engulfed in the euphoria. Dan pushed his way amidst the crowd of warriors to get to the front.

Dan found his way through the mass of chanting tribesmen, to the front of the hill, overlooking the slopes down to Fenny Stratford. There below him were the army's 660 chariots and Boudicca on her chariot amongst them. They must have been totally unaware of what was happening on their left flank. Down below on the slopes, some younger warriors had dismounted from their chariots and were skirmishing with the enemy using their slings and the occasional javelin against the Romans. Garos had talked about this tactic at Boudicca's meetings. The idea was to encourage the Romans up the hill, where they would then be charged by the mass of warriors at the top. But the

Romans were not advancing, it was just a feint, the real battle was happening on the left flank.

This was total madness Dan thought to himself, as the chariots were not getting stuck in. Perhaps they were being held back by those ballistae and archers who had appeared to have caused some casualties amongst the chariots. The Roman auxilia were staying put alongside their archers. The Britons were losing the battle and were totally unaware. What could he do?

Dan looked over to his left, to where the Romans had advanced up the narrow valley. He could not see over the promontory and down into the narrow valley – the defile - it was a blind spot. The Roman auxilia and cavalry were screening and protecting the rear and flanks of the Legion. From this vantage point, where you expected to see the whole picture, you were unable to! Bother!

It had not been easy for anyone to comprehend what was happening. No-one had a complete picture. Dan himself was confused. Even if you could make out what was happening, who would you tell - who was in charge. Despite all of Boudicca's meetings, they should have made plans and organised it far better.

It was obvious that some tribesmen were aware of what was happening, but could not convey this to others, who were still chanting. Some on the lower slopes at the front and those on the left flank had seen the Roman Legion advance up the valley. Others too, who were skirmishing with the legion's flanks and its rear ranks, had seen what was happening but had done nothing about it. They continued skirmishing with them thinking perhaps they might be winning.

It then dawned on Dan, that the Romans had known this all along. Perhaps they had previously visited the site and understood the topography. They had advanced their main fighting troops, the ones with the red shields, almost unseen by the majority of Boudicca's army on the hill, and now they were reaping their reward. They were getting in behind the rear of her army.

Dan was panicking. Was Garos in charge up here with all these warriors. Someone ought to be in charge, and if Boudicca was down the bottom of the hill on her chariot, then it would be Garos in charge up here. Where was Garos? He must be here somewhere. Dan had to find him, tell him the situation and save the day, before it was too late.

He looked around him for answers and there a short distance away, was Garos. Garos was dressed in all his finery, he had spiked his hair, his thick yellow coloured hair, he had blue and orange streaks on his face and was holding a fine shield in front of his blue tartan cloak. He looked the part. Dan hurriedly pushed his way over to him and touched Garos's shoulder to get his attention. Garos immediately saw the anxiety in Dan's face. They looked into each other's eyes. Dan shook his head, in sadness and utter dismay! He realised it was too late to tell Garos of the situation - the battle was lost. Now the chanting was not so loud, and there was a quietness amongst some of the brave warriors around them. Garos saw the battle result, in Dan's eyes!

Dan walked away.

All Dan knew was that the battle would soon be over, the Romans would be in amongst their waggons and behind the whole army! Killing and maiming all those that got in their way. He walked slowly back through the thick crowds, who were facing the front while he walked on to the rear. He did not want to jog or even walk fast, because now he was looking after his own skin. By running he might well cause panic, and for the moment, he wanted to put as many bodies between him and the Romans as possible. He was being selfish, but he must look after his own skin and if possible, try to find his family.

Garos and the people Dan had left at the front, were unaware of the panic that was unfolding behind them. Boudicca and Nomass in their chariots, and possibly his son Talos, with his sling, were down the front. They would be gesticulating still with the Romans and perhaps thinking the battle was going well. Scavo on that lovely horse of his - his pride and joy. Cart and Anna - where could they be? Anna was getting the oxen safely back. Morcant, where was Morcant? He was becoming a man, a capable young man and father to Dan's grandsons Damos and Thomas. Scarr; he had seen Scarr earlier on the slope. Where were they all, would they be alright?

King Prasutagus's gold that Boudicca had buried in her garden, in amongst the peas. That wonderful gold! What would happen to it if nobody got back to Boudicca's house? His horsefly bite was stinging! Oh, what a mess! What a disaster!

He was walking faster now, getting closer to the road, and as he did so, he could see people running away to his left along the road. Dan now heard the screams and panic of his fellow Britons, fleeing. He could not see anyone he knew amongst them. Nor could he see any Romans. He broke into a jog and jumped over a shield someone had abandoned, he would soon be joining the panicking throng.

It was time to go, Dan. Go back to Norfolk, where he would be with his family, safe and warm in his roundhouse.

# EPILOGUE

I hope you have enjoyed my first novel. This is a work of fiction, although based on written history, archaeology and the many books I have read.

History is an ever evolving subject, depending on what has recently been read, interpreted or found out. This is especially so with the great number of scientific tools and techniques available to us in the recent decades. An example of this, is the fantastic work carried out by Professor Mike Parker Pearson in determining how Stonehenge was moved from the hills of Pembrokeshire to Salisbury plain, by manpower.

Tacitus' account of the activities of Queen Boudicca and her followers and the actions the Romans took to quell her revolt, is the only original source of written information about Boudicca that has ever been found. There was another account put forward a little later, by a Roman called Cassius Dio, who I believe used much of the information provided by Tacitus, but added his own detail. The few words that Tacitus wrote, have been handed down through history by copyists, writing and rewriting the text on new parchment. The original written material had a finite life. Copied out, perhaps every 200 to 300 years by scribes, who we must eternally thank for labouring away, often by candlelight, to copy and recopy handwritten text through the generations. It is highly likely that those copyists will have made mistakes, and that's where my story originated in my mind.

Tacitus was about four years old at the time of the revolt. He learned much of the detail of events from his father-in-law, Gnaeus Julius Agricola, who became the Governor of Britain, in 78 AD. There are records of two major battles during the campaign. However, there were only a few words written that described the location and events of the second. It is believed Gnaeus actually fought in the second battle against Boudicca 1,960 years ago.

For a Roman, Tacitus seems to have been sympathetic towards the ancient Britons and I believe he held them in great regard and possibly believes the Romans were in the wrong (as they were). The Romans were also cruel, very cruel! Look what they did to Jesus Christ - it took him hours to die.

My bibliography is wide ranging, but I am particularly thankful to Peter Connolly, Vanessa Collingridge, Adrian Goldsworthy and The Viatores.

Peter Connelly was a reliable source. He carried out some wonderful experimental, practical archaeology, to find out exactly how artefacts were made and used. He completed some excellent research on the construction of the Roman saddle and how it was used in anger. The experiences I have had that influenced me, when writing this book were:

- Walking the Ridgeway, plus a bit - 118 miles in 6 days. With a warm bed every night.

- A 55mile hike (including 3 peaks) in the Lake District, with a tent on my back and with three good mates. It rained!
- A weekend at Knuston Hall with roman re-enactors. Most enlightening!
- Cycling 380 miles, Penzance to Milton Keynes, with a tent on my bike, over 7 days – twice!

Where did this battle take place? I believe it took place in Little Brickhill, two miles South of Milton Keynes. There are many trees surrounding Little Brickhill today in 2021, that obscure the view from the top of the hill, where the roundabout is, some 250m up from the church. Take a walk down the hill, and there are footpaths and places from where you can view the whole of Milton Keynes, a town of 200,000 people. Many of whom are descended from those who fought on both sides, that day in AD 60.

The other issue to consider, in considering where the location of the battlefield might be, is how far did people walk in those days. Most men would do their courting and marry the woman from the next village if they travelled any distance at all. I have met two women over the course of my life, who had never left the village they were born in. I suggest many people, in years gone by, rarely left the village they lived in. To walk 140 miles into strange lands to fight the Romans, must have been quite an adventure, and most tiring on one's body, feet and footwear, especially if you have never left your village before.

I would suggest to anyone who might be debating where the battle took place, to first ask a good friend to drop them off 140 miles away from home, with some good footwear, provisions for 20 days and a wet tent in a rucksack. Then walk back home! Afterwards, discuss with your friends your experiences on route. This is experimental history/archaeology.

The only piece of information that Tacitus provided to help determine where the final battle took place was:

*"[Paulinus Suetonius] chose a position approached by a narrow defile, shut off at the rear by a forest, having first ensured that there were no enemy soldiers except that at his front, where an open plain extended without any threat of ambush."*

*TACITUS: ANNALS, XIV. 34*

So, this at first glance would suggest that the historian is looking for a position that Paulinus took up, where he waited for Boudicca to attack with her army. However, a copyist only needs to get a couple of words different or in the wrong place and it could be written thus:

*"[Paulinus Suetonius] chose to approach the position by a narrow defile, shut off at the rear by a forest, having first ensured that there were no enemy soldiers except that at his front, where an open plain extended without any threat of ambush."*

*Richard Scholefield, 2021*

This subtle change of words convinced me to think that it was the ancient Britons who waited for the Romans to attack. Not the other way round, as implied by Tacitus. The Romans had to stop the revolt before it had a chance to muster more tribes. Only 3 or 4 tribes joined Boudicca out of a possible 19 living at that time in ancient Briton.

Many more might have joined had they heard of the revolt. Any tribe wishing to join in, did not need to actually meet up with Boudicca, all they had to do was trash their local Roman town, while the Romans were busy dealing with Boudicca. The ancient Britons were happier to use guerrilla tactics to defeat their enemy rather than meet them face to face on the battlefield in open combat. Perhaps that's why Poenius Postumus of Legio II did not come up from Exeter, because he had his own uprising to deal with down in the South West.

It is highly likely that the Romans would have had loved ones in Colchester and St. Albans that they wanted to rescue, and consequently must have been hurrying to crush the rebellion.

Most military historians believe Romans to have been brave and bold and unlikely to hang back. When moving in enemy territory, they would normally make temporary fortifications every night. Generally, this would be the only time when they were not aggressive. If they were cowardly, they may have had to fall on their sword, as, it is reported, Poenius Postumus of Exeter did.

Much is said and written about the religions of the ancient Britons and perhaps I should have emphasised the role that the druids and other superstitions played in the thinking of Boudicca and her followers. I am aware of the respectful attitude Britons had towards hares and the natural world around them but declined to included them in my book. What to include in a book and what to leave out is a debate that every author must deliberate on.

I never had much success with exams, and believe I have mild dyslexia. Many successful people are dyslexic – I suggest checking it using Google. (other search engines are available). It is also sad that many with dyslexia are in prison - something society should sort out.

My slight dyslexia knickers my twists when reading exam questions. My teachers always told me to read the question and answer the question. Many historians when analysing history, jump to conclusions and go along with the popular assumptions, without 'reading the question'.

I have applied logic in my book. Many historians believed the Romans waited patiently for the Britons to arrive. This would mean the Romans would stand on their hill ready for battle and watch the Britons arrive with their waggons, park their waggons, unhitch the oxen, secure the oxen, paint their faces, spike their hair and prepare for battle. All this in front of the Romans! It is highly unlikely that a Roman, a professional soldier, would wait for the hours to roll on by, while the ancient Britons assembled themselves ready for battle. They would get stuck in while the enemy were disorganised.

The historian's assumption, in my view, has to be wrong!

The only gentlemanly battle I know of is Edgehill, the first of the English civil war. I believe the participants discussed where they would fight the battle beforehand.

There is another large clue in the information that has been handed down to us by Tacitus and the all-important copyists. The Duke of Wellington, when asked what happened at the Battle of Waterloo said,

"It's like trying to remember what happened at a ball."

The reason we know what happened at the battle of Waterloo is that we have hundreds of eye-witness' written accounts, and some archaeology.

The other piece of information we have from Tacitus is regarding the ancient Britons. Warriors, women and children, in trying to flee, were trapped by the Romans against their own waggons. For someone to remember this, they must have seen it - that is logical. Therefore, it seems correct to assume that Tacitus's Father-in-Law, Gnaeus Julius Agricola, who was present at the battle, passed this on to Tacitus. If he told his son-in-law, it is highly likely that he must have seen it, (or have spoken to a colleague who fought in the battle who saw it), possibly close up. He may well have been one of the legionaries trapping the ancient Britons against their waggons.

The waggons must have been there stationary for some time, before the battle started. If the ground is the slightest bit wet, it is not sensible to park your waggon on it, instead, you park it on or very near the road. Farmers of today drain their fields with clay pipes or perforated plastic pipes, but in Roman times there was little drainage and flat fields became very boggy. Hence the adoption of 'ridge and furrow' farming, which helps drainage. There is a road at Little Brickhill at right angles to the approach route of the Romans. It is along this road I believe the Britons parked their waggons which were mentioned by Tacitus.

For a Roman to remember the waggons there need only be a small number of them, to trap the Britons running away and consequently be mentioned in the history books. Warriors' memories of battles are very sketchy and localised.

We do not seem to have found any archaeological evidence, in the form of skeletons or weapons or other relevant artefacts, that has revealed the location of the battle site itself anywhere in the country yet. It is a matter of professional analysis and conjecture that has suggested various locations for the battle, over the decades of research on this subject. However, we do have archaeological evidence from Colchester, the once capital of Britain. Also, some excellent archaeological research has taken place in London and St. Albans, the capital of the Catuvellavni Tribe. One day in the future perhaps, we may know where the battle happened, unless some unconcerned developer or unconcerned planner builds over it without realising or having much regard for our history. But ho-hum, we may never know.

In the English Civil War, Essex, one of the commanders of the parliamentarian forces, waited a few days at Little Brickhill for the London Trained Bands to arrive from London, before proceeding to relieve the siege of Gloucester. I believe he, like Boudicca, chose Little Brickhill for the strategic advantage the hill holds for military purposes. The Parliamentarians did the same at Sherington, near Milton Keynes, before going on to fight the battle of Naseby, probably for the same reason - it was on high ground and had military significance.

Some believe Boudicca's battle site was near Coventry and others believe it could well have been, in the Chiltern Hills or somewhere near St. Albans. I believe the battlefield site of Little Brickhill is the logical location, but I could be totally wrong. I have used my many years of experience as an historical war gamer to come to my own conclusions. It is true, however, that most researchers believe it was somewhere close to Watling Street. Nobody really knows, yet!

The other logical place the battle might have taken place, is the escarpment at Dunstable. Before the cutting was made on the A5, North of Dunstable, the slope there was about 1 in 8, *(N.B. work done by The Viatores, Roman Roads in the south-east Midlands)* and it must have been a challenge for transport. The ancient Britons may well have stopped there on top of the escarpment, waiting for the Romans to arrive. A subject for a second book.

Tacitus reports that the number of Britons who were killed at the battle was of the order of 80,000, and that just 400 Romans died. This is a tremendous number of Britons. Based on the numbers present on both sides it would suggest that each Roman killed 8 tribesmen. At the Battle of Towton in the 1461, the bloodiest battle on English soil, historians think 28,000 were slain. In our battle, the victorious Romans wrote the history books, so the figure of 80,000, many believe, is exaggerated. None-the-less there must have been quite an horrific loss of life. I have estimated the number of Britons present at the battle as 60,000. An educated estimate, which is up for discussion and makes the saga of Boudicca interesting!

What written word and legend is there of Boudicca's demise? It is believed, by the Romans who won the battle, she took poison somewhere. Dr. J. L. Scott, keeper of manuscripts at the British Museum, surmised in 1907 that she poisoned herself somewhere near Whittlebury Forest. He had discovered a deed of Edward I, granting land there near 'Dead Queen Moor,' and another relating to 'Dead Queen Furlong'.

Perhaps Boudicca and some of her army went off to join the Silures Tribe in South Wales. A Roman who fails, normally falls on his sword. A Briton who fails, comes back from Dunkirk to fight another day.

What evidence of the location, can be found in place names that are there today? In Little Brickhill there is a farm called 'Battle Hills Farm'. I have been told there is a field on the lower slopes of Little Brickhill called 'Battle Field.' There is a village south-east of Little Brickhill, called 'Battlesden'.

Boudicca, in a similar fashion to Guy Fawkes was accused, after the event, by the politicians (the Romans) of the time, as being the leader of her cause. Politicians like to pick a single person as being the originator of a revolt, as it makes psychological sense to do so. It is easier to justify that it was only one person who initiated the event and not a more widespread uprising. In the case of Boudicca however, it seemed to have set her up as a heroine for all Britons. She might not have been the leader, there could possibly have been someone else, or there might have been a Council of Leaders. It helps the story however, to have one iconic leader - Boudicca.

I have used modern place names throughout the book. Using ancient names for places would add some characterization, but unless you know where these places are, it would make for complicated reading. Also, reading it as many of you will be doing in an eBook format, it is difficult to constantly refer to the glossary. There is a book on 'ancient place names' that the reader could enjoy, should he wish to do so.

I enjoyed writing this book, and hope that you have being encouraged to look further into our history.

There is a museum in Towcester that has a section dedicated to the battle, which I am yet to visit, the moment Covid-19 'lockdown' is over.

**Supply Problems Using Waggons.**

The engraving opposite is from the Illustrated London News and shows in detail a waggon drawn by six oxen during the Zulu wars in South Africa of 1879.

I had many prompts to write this book, and this significant picture was one. It focused my mind on the waggons mentioned by Tacitus in Boudicca's final battle.

If the waggons were there, how did they get there? There must have been similar scenes for her army to travel to the battle site. Noted, that perhaps the roads in Zululand, South Africa, might well be worse than those in Roman times in Britain, but similar situations must have developed when the terrain became rough for Cartimandua and Dan's sons.

The picture shows six oxen and 11 men attempting to move the waggon on dry ground! There may be small boulders in the way and the ground is sloping. What difficulties are there if the ground is wet and undrained? Hollywood films portray wonderful pictures of waggons moving with ease across the American plains. Was it that easy? Might Boudicca's situation have been different, especially when the waggons are full of wine and wet tents?

In my youth, I attempted to move a heavy vehicle up a wet slippery slope with the aid of a number of friends. It was not easily achieved. The vehicle was heavy, and it was difficult to get a good footing on the slippery ground. For those readers wishing to try some experimental archaeology for themselves, could I suggest, they try pushing a heavy motor car on poor wet ground, with the engine turned off, up a slope!

Considering the difficulty of moving heavy waggons, there might well be good reason to suggest that Boudicca's final battle was in the Chilterns, perhaps on the escarpment, just north of Dunstable, or perhaps near St. Albans.

# GLOSSARY

### Auxilia

Auxilia are allied soldiers which supplemented Rome's armies. They did not hold Roman citizenship as legionary troops did, but were a vital part of the army. They are less well trained but still have great skills on the battlefield as light troops.

### Bogs

As all good farmers and engineers know, impervious clay soils need drainage. Therefore, in ancient times many flat areas were boggy. This must have been the case, alongside the Ouzel in Fenny Stratford.

### Boudicca - Spelling of?

Ancient scripts have been copied and copied again throughout history, for which we must be very thankful. Two copyists made mistakes in the spelling of Boudicca on different occasions, but so might others. I have used the spelling with two 'c's and hope no one is offended. How you pronounce Boudicca is up to you.

## Boudicca's Route.

The two largest towns in AD 60 were Colchester, the Roman capital and St. Albans the capital of the Catuvellavni tribe. London was just a small port at the time. I believe there would have been a good road between these two capitals and any heavy goods that needed to be moved between Colchester and London, I believe, would have been moved by boat.

Which route did Boudicca take after destroying Colchester. Some suggest she went straight to St. Albans and then turned south to London. If this was the case, perhaps the final battle between Paulinus and the Iceni might well have been somewhere in north London, and the author has drawn the wrong conclusions.

## Catuvellavni

The spelling of Catuvelauni has differed throughout the book, please be amused by it and not critical.

## Roman Century

Normally, 80 legionaries commanded by a Centurion.

## Character's Names

In choosing the names of my characters for this book I did not want to choose too many names that were unfamiliar. Many of the names I chose for my characters, were taken from records of the historical Kings and Queens of Britain's tribes and also from records of the Romans, as detailed in the many reference books I used in my research for this story. Others were names that are in use today and throughout history e.g. Anna; John; Dan. Only six names are taken from historical records: Legate Suetonius Paulinus, Catus Decionus, Poenius Postumus, Gnaeus Julius Agricola, King Prasutagus and his wife Boudicca.

## **Cohort**

A Legion is normally made up of 10 cohorts. Each cohort normally comprised of 480 men, divided into 6 centuries, of 80 men each. The first cohort of a Legion was larger than the others comprising of 800 men and 120 cavalry.

## **Duplicarius**

A Duplicarius was second in command of 30 cavalrymen, similar to a Sergeant in the army today.

## **Footwear**

It is believed that the Celts and therefore the ancient Britons wore moccasins while the Romans wore boots (sandals – see below). Today, we wear different footwear for different jobs and perhaps the Celts did the same. I can't imagine ploughing a field in moccasins - it doesn't seem practical somehow.

## Front Cover

The front cover was painted by my daughter Anna. The woman in the painting looks a little young to be Boudicca, perhaps she's one of Boudicca's daughters or a mystery figure, the reader can determine her identity for themselves.

## Immunis

The next one up from a legionary in the Roman army, a clerk or technician. An Immunis has the same pay as a normal soldier but no longer did the dirty jobs.

## Ixworth

Ixworth is a small village in Suffolk, north-east of Bury St. Edmunds, and was quite a prominent place in Roman times, being located on the junction of five roads. It may have been the place Boudicca had her meeting with Cactus, but there is no archaeological confirmation of this.

## Legion

5,500 men or legionaries. Divided into 10 cohorts of about 480men each. Sometimes called a Legio.

## Oxen

An oxen is a bull that has been castrated. They were used to plough fields well into the 19th century. Should the reader wish to inquire more about shoeing oxen it is suggested you put the words 'Gordon Lohnas oxen' into a search engine.

**Pilum**

A heavy throwing spear used by the Roman legionaries. Like a javelin, only heavier with a long thin pointed tip that, when thrown at the enemy went through their shield and into the person holding it. Very nasty! Previous theories believed that it went through the enemy shield and then bent making the enemy's shield heavy and useless but recent experiments have shown this to be wrong.

**Place Names**

The author has used modern day place names so that the reader can relate to where events described in the book happened.

**Running Away**.

A unit of men ordered to stand against the enemy in a shield-wall can be difficult to shift, especially if their sergeant who is behind them, is more fearsome than the enemy. However, if they do run away, they will usually break from the rear ranks, as I have experienced myself and talked to fellow wargamers about the subject. I am doubtful if Boudicca had any sergeants.

**Rabbit Holes**

The author spent some of his childhood up on Blows Downs, Dunstable and experienced rabbit holes. Sometimes rabbits dig a hole into a bank horizontally for some distance, and then proceed upwards breaking the surface and the hole beneath is exposed. Grass then grows over this hole, but the hole is still there. They can be dangerous to walkers and cavalrymen like Morinus.

## **Rubies**

The rubies Boudicca wore, probably came from Afghanistan and were traded across Europe to England.

## **Sandals**

Roman soldiers did not wear sandals. They appear to be sandals to us, but the Romans called them boots. Ask a re-enactor and be rebuffed as I was.

## **Sawtry Woods**

Sawtry Woods mentioned in the book is a fictitious place, where cohorts of Legio XIV commanded by Petilius Cerialis were attacked by Garos and his warriors. It is somewhere in the vicinity of Lincolnshire/Norfolk where it is believed cohorts of the Legio XX were attacked and massacred. Sawtry is south of Peterborough on the A1.

## **Slings**

When a young man, the author was introduced to slings by his good friend Jon, who demonstrated that slings are very cheap and very dangerous, as Goliath found out.

**Snails**

Believe it or not, my daughter trained our West Highland Terrier named Barny, to hunt out snails and give them a scrunch. Unfortunately, we had to put poor Barny to sleep - he was allergic to his own saliva and kept chewing his paws. A lovely dog.

**Staging Post.**

There are many names for places to stop and change horses or rest. They could be called, for example: resting stations, posting stations, a coaching station or an Inn. In my investigation, I have read conflicting sources.

**Tinder Fungus**

A fungus that is highly inflammable and has good fire starting properties.

**Transport**

The transport of the day was either by water, waggon or pack horse. It must have been hard work. St. Albans was a significant town in Roman times and must have consumed large quantities of wine, and many other products the Roman world demanded. How did you get it there – oxen? As is the case today, transport must have been big business in the days of the Ancient Britons.

## Turma

30 roman cavalrymen were called a Turma. Also spelt Turmae. Commanded by a Decurion with a Duplicarius (Justus) second in command.

## Walking

The author walked the Ridgeway (an ancient trail through the Chilterns) in 1992 when in his early 40s. It is 85 miles long and he walked an extra 12 miles to get home to Milton Keynes afterwards. It took him 7 days. He was not used to walking and found it very hard. He had a dry comfortable bed every night and was well fed on the route. Our ancient British ancestors following Boudicca, have his total respect. It is therefore his belief that Boudicca's army stopped at Little Brickhill having walked in excess of 110 miles.

Contrary to this, the Romans legionaries were trained to march - it was part of their training and function.

## Wargaming

The author has been a wargamer all his life. The SAS do wargames every day, and that is why they are so good at the real thing. The military play out many war games, it saves lives. It is better to game than to do the real thing. Throwing a double 6 to kill an opponent's model soldier is better than using a real bullet. Camaraderie in the war game fraternity is very strong.

# The Battlefield Site, Today

# BIBLIOGRAPHY

Barker Phil (2016), 'DBMM Army Lists, Book2:500BC to 476 AD, The Classical Period, A Wargames Research Group Limited Publication
Barthorp Michael (1985), 'The Zulu War, A Pictorial History', Guild Publishing
Burke John (1983), 'Roman England', Book Club Associates
Butterworth Alex & Laurence Ray (2005), 'Pompeii The Living City', Orion Books
Collingbridge Vanessa (2006), 'Boudicca', Edbury Press
Connolly Peter (1981), 'Greece and Rome at War', Macdonald Phoebus Ltd
Connolly Peter (1988), 'The Cavalryman, Tiberius Claudius Maximus', Oxford University Press
Connolly Peter (1991), 'The Legionary, Tiberius Claudius Maximus', Oxford University Press
De La Bedoyere 'Gladius Living, Fighting and Dying in the Roman Army, Little Brown
De La Bedoyere 'The Real Lives of Roman Britrain,' Yale University Press
Fields Nic (2011), Boudicca's Rebellion AD 60-61, The Britons rise up against Rome, Osprey Publishing

Goldsworthy Adrian (2016), Pax Romana, War Peace and Conquest in the Roman World' Orion Books

Goldsworthy Adrian (2013), 'The Complete Roman Army', Thames & Hudson

Grant Michael (1974), 'Caesar' Great Lives, Weidenfeld and Nicolson London

Jones Terry & Alan Ereira (2007), 'Barbarains an Alternative Roman History' BBC Books

John Keegan, (1976) 'The Face of Battle' Penguin Books

Laycock Stuart (2008), 'Britannia, The failed State, Tribal conflicts and the end of Roman Britain' History Press

Markham Sir Frank (1973), 'History of Milton Keynes and District, Volume 1 – to 1830, White Crescent Press Ltd

McEvedy Colin (1967), 'The Penguin Atlas of Ancient History', Penguin Books

Ordnance Survey (1983), 'Leighton Buzzard and Stewkley, Sheet SP 82/92, Pathfinder 1071', Ordnance Survey

Ordnance Survey (1992), 'Milton Keynes (South) and Woburn, Pathfinder 1047', Ordnance Survey

Ordnance Survey (2016), 'Roman Britain, OS Historical', Ordnance Survey

O'Sullivan Firmin (1972), 'The Egnation Way', David & Charles

Peddie John (1994), 'The Roman War Machine', Alan Sutton Publishing

Pryor Francis (2004), 'Britain BC', Harper Perennial

Salway Peter (1993), 'A History of Roman Britain', Oxford University Press

Scullard H. H. (1935) 'A History of the Roman World 753 to 146 BC' Methuen & Co Ltd

Simpkins Michael (1984), 'The Roman Army from Caesar to Trojan', Osprey Publishing

Simkins Michael (1990), 'Warriors of Rome, An Illustrated military history of the Roman Legions', Blandford

The Viators (1964), 'Roman Roads in the South Midlands', Victor Gollancz Ltd

Wacher John (1978), 'Roman Britain', Book Club Associates

Wacher John (1981), 'The Coming of Rome', A Paladin Book

War Office (1989), 'Narrative of the Field Operations Connected with the Zulu War of 1879'

Greenhill Books, London and Presidio Press, California

Waite John (2011), 'Boudica's Last Stand, Britain's Revolt Against Rome AD60-61, The History Press

Wiesehofer Josef, 'Ancient Persia from 550 BC to 650 AD', I. B. Tauris

Wise Terence, 'Armies of the Carthaginian Wars 265-146 BC' Osprey Publishing London

Lightning Source UK Ltd.
Milton Keynes UK
UKHW010717180621
385731UK00001B/23

9 781665 589086